DEBORAH J DEAN

WHISPERING NORTH
BOOK ONE

Watchman's Oath

IDEABASKET
•ENGLAND•

For permission requests, write to:
IDEABASKET
Marlowe Innovation Centre
Marlowe Way
Ramsgate, Kent
England
CT12 6FA
www.ideabasket.com

First printed in April 2012.
This edition printed in 2017.

Paperback Edition (cream) ISBN 978-0-9572562-0-0
Paperback Edition (white) ISBN 978-0-9572562-3-1
Kindle Edition ISBN 978-0-9572562-1-7
Digital Edition ISBN 978-0-9572562-2-4

Published by IDEABASKET, www.ideabasket.com
Cover Art and Illustrations by Līga Kļaviņa, www.liigaklavina.deviantart.com
Nissa Art by Pamela Flynn, www.pamelaflynn.com
Copyedit by Deanna Hoak, www.deannahoak.com
Proofread by Robert S Malan, Freeflowedit

Mom

I'll never forget the treasure hunt to the encyclopedias.
Thank you for filling our home with good books.

SPECIAL THANKS TO:

Lawrence, my ever-supportive husband and best friend. You're where my inspiration starts.

Arwen and Briar Rose, darling daughters who spent their youth in chaos while Mommy labored at the keyboard. Thank you, girls, for letting me do what I absolutely had to do—tell my stories.

Emma Borynski, Maryanne Howard, and Pamela Flynn, partners in crime, who understand when I talk hobbits, spaceships, and magic.

Carl W. Thiel, Herb Kauderer, Al Katerinsky, David Salley, Karen Ehrlich, Will McDermott, Jo Danilo, Francina Van Twest—dear friends all, and honest critics. Kathleen Beaton and Daniel McArthur for help with the Gaelic. Dave Mustaine, musician, who unknowingly provided the clay from which villains—and heroes—were herein made. Deanna Hoak, copy editor, for applying her magic polish to this manuscript. Robert S Malan, editor, for a quick and painless proof of the final layout. Līga Kļaviņa, artist, who turned hodgepodge ideas into works of art.

No dedication is complete without an expression of gratitude to my loving Heavenly Father. Any talent I possess is a gift.

CONTENTS

Watchman's
Oath

Outlaws

RONAN TOUCHED LYNET'S ARM. A light touch, yet it conveyed his message. *Be still.* Crawling through the underbrush beside him, so close he could feel her knee graze his hip, his companion held still, waiting. Ronan listened. Hunting required stealth, but his instincts warned of more than deer in the woods this night.

The nocturnal chirp and whir of insects stopped. He heard the faint rustle of a *rift* as it opened. A rift—an unnatural doorway between two physical places—did not happen on its own; someone knew they were here.

Smoke from a newly smothered campfire drifted through the trees. Ronan looked to Lynet. Her slight nod told him she smelled it too and recognized what it meant: close by, their pursuers walked, fresh and rested, from a campsite many leagues away, through the rift to Ronan and Lynet's position in the valley—in a single step.

Up ahead a branch snapped, followed by the distinct sound of fleeing game. In spite of the danger, Ronan felt a burst of frustration; he was hungry, and spooked deer took longer to catch.

This wasn't the first time they'd been ambushed. The closer Ronan and Lynet got to Caeraricin, the more bounty hunters they encountered. With enough paranoia, even passive farmers turned into mercenaries. King Eltanin's soldiers ensured the peasants' fears stayed high with rumors of a *plaga norn*, a plague witch, loose in the land. Eltanin was anxious to keep Ronan out of Caeraricin—not surprising since Ronan intended to bodily remove the usurper from his stolen throne once he got there.

Ronan wanted this fight over with so he could get back to the hunt. Reaching out with his mind, he searched for their enemies' whereabouts. Like his mighty Vökumaðr forebears, Ronan's enhanced senses enabled him to see all life around him, no matter how well hidden. His range did not extend far, but it was enough to give them an advantage.

His inner sight took over, the world erupting into a million strands of color, each with its own quivering tone. Plants, animals, and insects—every living thing within a league's distance—appeared to his mind as unique thrumming strings. Sifting through the tangled life-threads, Ronan differentiated between owls, worms, trees—and men.

Strings of aggressive scarlet spread out from a single point. "Twelve men," Ronan whispered, "up ahead, coming east."

His ability to sense an adversary's intent often spared him and Lynet serious injury, though the sheer number of jumbled life-threads exhausted him. Ronan had learned to live with the temporary weakness, but Lynet hated it. If bounty hunters attacked while he was tired or distracted, she would defend him—and any time Lynet used magic, havoc followed.

He felt Lynet shift her slight weight, poised to run away or swing her sword; whichever command he gave, she would follow. Lynet trusted him. She would not hesitate. He loved her for that, especially in times like these when doubt or pause could cost them their lives.

Another rustle in the air alerted them to a second opening rift. Ronan widened his sweep of the woods. *Mother Earth.* This was no small strike. "More than a score gather behind us." They were short on arrows. Their horses stood half a league away, up on the ridge. Hide spells might work but, without a plan, hiding would only give their enemies time to surround them.

Deep inside Ronan . . . the Hoar Beast, the mighty creature who made up one half of Ronan's soul, sensed the coming danger and stirred. His ancient eyes flicked open.

For months, Ronan and Lynet had resisted using their powers. Outmaneuvering, outthinking their pursuers, they'd avoided releasing the magic that made them the two most hunted fugitives in all of Norðrlönd. Now, so close to their goal, that strategy, however noble, would not save them. Without the Hoar Beast, their enemies would overrun them.

Silently Ronan unbuckled his sword belt, then his leather pouch. "Carry what you can; forget the rest," he told her. Though he did not need it, Ronan welcomed Lynet's help as he pulled off his boots and trappings. Her hands felt warm against his skin, a subtle reminder of why he chose this path. He would defend her, his plague witch, until the day he died.

She did not protest his decision, but Ronan read her thoughts in the thin, tight line of her mouth: *We are stronger together.* She was right, of course. Side by side, their magic could topple nations—but they had made a promise to the Nornir, and to each other, to never willingly use those powers in unison. If they chose to fight with magic, and not the sword, then one of them must run. Whether Lynet liked it or not, it was better for him to unloose the Beast than for her to inadvertently kill everything in the valley.

Ronan rolled his trousers into a ball and stashed them under the brambles. He did that for her, to reassure her he would survive and retrieve them when the fight ended. As he tugged the cotton shirt over his head, Lynet caressed his back—then in a rush slid her arms around his waist and hugged him tight. "I love you," she whispered.

Ronan held still. All that he wanted, would ever want, was right here. He drew her hand to his chest, then to his lips, but love could not protect her once the Beast awoke. She must flee, now.

"Get to the horses. Make a run for it." Ronan's voice sounded harsh and guttural. He hooked his large hand behind her neck and kissed her hard. "I'll find you," he promised. "Now run, as fast as you can."

Lynet picked up the sword belt. "Heal quickly," she said, then pressed a fleeting kiss to his bare shoulder and scrambled out from the thicket. Ronan knew a moment's loss when she raced into the night and did not look back. She had never seen him transform, and in truth, he was glad of it. The Beast came from another age, made of frost, mountain roots, and Nordic wind. Legend said: *When the Hoar Beast roars the wicked lose courage, and in its embrace they abandon hope.*

Ronan felt the Beast's mind ram against his own. His human hands widened. Calluses, earned through years of sword fighting, thickened to become rough paw pads; claws grew by inches to replace fingernails. Ronan's skin itched as coarse white fur spread over his body. A shaggy mane of Ronan's own gray-flecked brown hair grew longer, spreading out across his shoulders and down his neck.

Ronan stood upright and arched his back, preparing for the tear and stretch of organs and sinew. He took several awkward steps as his feet elongated. Ankles and knees cracked as they bulked and sent rope-sized tendons snaking up his thighs to knot around his hips and balance his increasing size. His height shot up; his weight tripled—then tripled again into massive muscle and bone. A cry of pain erupted into a savage roar. He tried to think, to turn his focus on the advancing men and away from Lynet, but the Hoar Beast broke through and Ronan the man was gone.

Lynet ran four paces, three more—before a triumphant cry came from her right, and hands reached out to grab her from both sides. She ducked, then used the sheathed sword as a pike and rammed it up into the face of the first man. Still moving, she swung the sword wide to roundhouse on the second.

"Awake!" she cried. It was a ruse to distract her attackers, for Lynet did not need words. With a thought, she gave a mockery of life to the first man's belt. As it slithered and constricted around his waist, she turned to the second man. His fletching pouch soon twitched and scuttled like a spider across his chest, then sprang to cover his face.

The roar of the Hoar Beast echoed through the valley. From the corner of her eye, Lynet saw a monstrous white creature hurtling toward them. She ran, tripped, but did not slow down. As a man, Ronan would never harm her—but the Beast knew only rage. If she got in its way, the Hoar Beast would tear her apart as easily as it tore into those unfortunate men who shrieked and died in the darkness behind her.

Lynet darted between trees, looking for the quickest way to the ridge where their horses waited. She would make a final dash for DuwaŴyr Mountain. The wise man Cian Druce would take her in, keep her hidden until she figured out what to do next. If Ronan survived the day, he would track her and follow her to the mountain.

Near the top of the hill, Lynet paused to gain her bearings. It was too early in the year for the sun to brighten the midnight sky; even so, the moon's reflection on the eastern sea gave enough silver light to spot the horses.

She shouldered the sword belt and jogged on, whistling between her teeth to alert Lleth. Without the warning, the wolfhound might easily interpret her hurried approach as hostile. She reeked of discord and not a little fear, incentive in itself for the young war hound to attack.

When she reached the ridge, Lleth met her with a passing sniff, then turned his attention back to the fighting far below.

The horses pranced and shied as Lynet gathered their gear. "He scares me, too," she spoke in soothing tones as she stroked her mare's nose. "Let's not wait for the Beast to catch us."

Lynet mounted. Leading Ronan's gelding, she steered them around the rim of the valley and galloped for the other side.

The cries of battle got fainter the farther out of range they rode. Once on the other side of the valley and heading through the northern pass, Lynet slowed their frantic pace. She leaned back in the saddle as the horses slid, knocking rocks and dirt loose while they made their way down a steep dip to level ground.

Her balance still off, Lynet was unprepared for the crackle of magic that streaked past her and plowed into the trees beyond. She jerked sharply on the reins and twisted away—but too late. The exploding wood struck the side of her head and knocked her to the ground.

The horses, already nervous, went mad. Dazed, Lynet could only watch as they reared and stomped their hooves inches from her head. Lleth barked and snapped at the heels of Lynet's wide-eyed mare until it bolted and ran away; Ronan's gelding followed closely behind. The wolfhound returned, gray hackles up, black lips curled tight across bared teeth as he straddled protectively over her.

A second streak of magic shot like an arrow through Lleth's side. The hound yelped and crumpled in a heap on top of her. The sudden thump of deadweight on her belly was far worse than the blow to her head—it meant she was without an ally.

Lynet struggled to get out from under the wolfhound. Her jaw hurt, and she heard an odd ringing sound. She shook her head to clear the fog and felt a trickle of blood leak out of her left ear. *Damn.* She drew her sword, staggering in a circle, searching for her assailant.

"So stubborn," a voice in the shadows drawled. "I clearly have you. Put down the sword before you get hurt."

Carden.

Lynet had never faced the usurper's son alone before.

She scanned the forest until she found him, partially hidden, his long red hair unmistakable even in the dark. On his wide shoulder perched a pair of tiny, dragonfly-winged creatures. Behind him, the rest of the hive swarmed, diving and darting in an insect-like frenzy.

"You brought *puki*." Lynet backed away.

"They won't hurt you." Carden stepped farther into the moonlight. The puki surged past him, spreading out to encircle her. "Unless I tell them to." In his closed fist, he held another spell. She saw its black vaporous tendrils squirming between his fingers, eager to be loose. "I won't let you go, Lynet. I am tired of chasing you. Either you surrender or I'll kill you."

"You wouldn't dare." Lynet tried to sound confident, but with her equilibrium off and puki buzzing around her head, her voice held little certainty. "Your father wants me alive." She hoped it was still true, but she doubted the king's patience would last. Maybe the usurper had given up on capturing her and simply wanted her dead.

"Who's going to tell him?" Carden shrugged. "Put down the sword, Lynet, and I'll let you save the hound."

Lleth. Lynet did not have to look at the brindled-gray mass to know the hound was dead. She felt his spirit lingering nearby. If she acted quickly, maybe she could entice him back before he wandered off to the mystical hunting grounds of Mag Mell.

Carden would take the sword from her either way. She would not fight him with her magic, not after the last fiasco; they both knew that. Lynet tossed the sword aside and dropped next to Lleth. Several of the puki swooped down to land on the lifeless hound.

"Call them off." Lynet swatted at one of the dangerous fairylike creatures. "If they ruin his body, I can't fix it."

"*Thig thugam.*" Carden spoke to the inquisitive puki, and they instantly obeyed, withdrawing to flit and mass around him. His control over the spindly banes filled Lynet with dread. Puki were harbingers of chaos. That Carden managed them at all testified to his growing power.

Lynet ran her hands over Lleth, checking for wounds. Carden's spell had killed him instantly, yet . . . the hound's body showed no mark or sign of injury. "What did you do to him?"

"I stopped his heart—a sharp jolt is all it took. I'd teach you, but then you don't need lessons in killing, do you, Lynet?"

Lynet bristled but did not argue. Carden bred self-doubt; it was his specialty. His silky voice, striking looks, and affable manner all belied the poison in his words—but this time he spoke true, and she had no sharp answer to throw at him. "He is not damaged inside?"

"I said I would let you save the hound." Carden picked up her discarded sword and spun it far into the trees. "*I'm* not the monster, Lynet. Go ahead. He is whole; work your witchcraft before you lose him."

Lynet stroked Lleth's head. Her palms glowed with a soft blue light that seemed to transfer to the hound's coarse fur. She did not need to touch him, but she preferred it. Contact made it feel more like coaxing, rather than the abhorrent manipulation it truly was. With a thought, Lynet gave the individual cells in Lleth's heart new life. She gave life to his red cells and white cells, life to antibodies, bones, and organs; anything shut down she brought back. Without fresh blood pumping through his system, toxins had pooled. Lynet found them and destroyed them.

It was not a proper healing—Lynet did not heal. She merely gave life, or took it. The cells needed to regenerate and repair any damage on their own. She wished she could heal—then she could stop the high-pitched ringing in her left ear and restore her sense of balance.

Beneath her palm, Lynet felt warmth return to Lleth. He sneezed twice and scrambled to his feet. His body was alive—but as she watched him, Lynet's stomach turned. His eyes held no spark of intelligence. Without a spirit, this reanimated creature was a hollow imitation of the wolfhound. With only low-level function, it did not even wag its tail. Eventually, it would die.

Lynet dreaded this part—having no control over whether or not the spirit reentered the body. This was why she did not use her life-gift on humans. Once had been enough to teach her the danger of pitting her will against that of an unbound human soul.

Behind her, Carden whistled low. "Nice work. Now let's go."

"Not yet." Lynet stalled. "He might come back."

"If he does, I'll have to kill him again. Be sensible, Lynet. Come willingly, or I'll knock you out and drag you." He held up his clenched fist to show her the ugly magic seeping between his fingers.

He took her upper arm and pulled her to her feet, then steered her toward a copse of trees; the wolfhound followed blindly behind. Lynet did not resist. In a way, she welcomed an end to the running. If Carden took her to Eltanin—if she could physically see him—she could suck the life out of that backstabbing bastard and put an end to all this madness.

As they entered the grove, Lynet nearly retched from the sickening sweet smell of putrid meat. Thousands of puki flew in a wide circle, maintaining a quivering doorway in time and space. Through the open rift, Lynet saw the inner courtyard of Caeraricin Castle. There would be no extended journey, no chance to escape.

One step through that door and she would be in Eltanin's lair.

Lynet covered her nose. "What is that stench?"

"That is the ripe scent of dead Vökumenn." Carden did not bother to hide his disapproval; most knew what he thought of his father's methods. "Except for Ronan, every last one of them rots in the castle's lower bailey."

Carden watched Lynet's expression turn to horror, and rightly so. The Vökumenn, the god-created Watchmen of Caeraricin, were dead. It seemed impossible. Once released, a Hoar Beast was relentless, inescapable. Yet Carden's father had done it, butchered them all before seizing the Aricin throne.

"How?"

"How do you think he did it?" Carden knew he played with fire. Lynet was dangerous. Still, she would not turn her magic on him; he knew her weakness. Besides, she was smart. She would figure it out. Better to settle this now, before they went any farther.

"I don't understand, Carden. One or two, perhaps, but not all of them dead. The Hoar Beast is mighty, especially with his brothers at his back . . . unless. . . ." Lynet's eyes widened. "They were *men*. He caught them while they were still men." Lynet spun and punched Carden with her fist, a solid punch that caused him to grunt, but not retreat. "*You* did this. Eltanin has no Governance, no ability to control the Vökumaðr. You held them in their human state while he slaughtered them."

Carden let her hit him once more and then grabbed the thick blonde braid at the back of her head. "It wasn't me. Someone did it, but not me. Do not hit me again." He knew she would, but he gave her the chance before he released the spell in his hand. He had held on to the wriggling thing too long; it would hurt like hell, but it wouldn't kill her. The spell slammed into Lynet's breast and instantly knocked her unconscious.

Carden caught her as she fell. "I did warn you," he said dryly, then lowered her to the ground near the vacant-eyed wolfhound. Lynet was a pretty woman, with golden hair and deep blue eyes. Carden might have found her beauty a distraction if she weren't such a pain in the ass.

Now, where was Ronan?

Carden's father expected him to bring Lynet to the castle the moment he caught her, but Carden had other plans. Petty, maybe, but after months of chasing them, he wanted to make sure Ronan knew exactly who had won this battle.

He ordered the puki to watch over Lynet, then headed to the top of the nearest ridge. He climbed nearly a mile to the valley rim before he spotted the Hoar Beast running on all fours across the hilly terrain. The Beast was huge, thirteen feet long, and two thousand pounds of ill intent—headed straight for him. Fresh blood stained its shaggy white coat. Carden hoped some of that blood was the Beast's own.

Carden knew he should be afraid, but adrenaline shot through his veins like a drug. He had won. Victory gave him courage, and he stepped out into the open. Carden had not witnessed the defeat of Ronan's kin, but through an earlier rift he'd glimpsed the skewered, rotting proof of Vökumaðr mortality. For too long he'd danced around Ronan, uncertain of how they might measure up in a fight. Finally, they would learn who was stronger.

Carden did not wait for the Beast to get close. With a stab of his outthrust hand, Carden sent a crackle of lightning straight at the charging Beast. The spell devoured the grass and trees between them, but dissipated into a shower of sparks when it hit the Beast. The acrid smell of singed fur filled Carden's nostrils as the Beast, never slowing down, reached him. Carden was ready, his personal shield solid. Nothing could get through it, nothing—

—except ancient hoarfrost. With one swipe, the Hoar Beast tore down the shield and clawed four long gashes across Carden's chest, from shoulder to hip, tossing him into the air.

Crippling pain knocked the air from his lungs as Carden bounced to the ground several feet away. His vision shrank to tunneled points, and he fought to stay conscious. Disoriented and nearly blind, Carden could smell the crisp scent of winter on the Beast's fur, hear the heavy footsteps as it slowly moved in for the kill.

Desperate, Carden called on the Governing power within him—a token from his long-dead mother. His fingers made the necessary sigil. He felt the magic swell around him like a mighty ocean wave, then splash out to ripple and saturate everything around him. Governance—in a king's hands, it was the power to guide and inspire an entire nation. To Carden, it was a way to bring all nearby sentient life under his control. In his wounded state, the command was simple: *Stay the hell away from me.*

The Beast snarled in protest. It paced and dug up the ground, but it did not come any closer.

Struggling to sit, Carden conjured a flickering tongue of orange and yellow fire in his palm. So uncomplicated a spell, yet it was his best hope, for if frost had an enemy, it was heat.

Carden did not delude himself. Even as his sight returned, his wounds spurted fresh blood onto the ground. Each shudder of pain caused his Governance to slip—and with each slip, the Beast took a growling step closer.

He had one chance. Carden held the flame trapped in his hand, forcing it to grow into a blazing fireball. It blistered him, but he did not let go. Recklessly he fed thread after thread of raw magic into his palm until the blaze became blinding white.

Carden released the Governance that held back his enemy.

The Hoar Beast rushed in, rising up on its massive hindquarters. Its brown-and-gray mane fanned out like the hood of a cobra as it towered over Carden, its roar wild and deafening.

With the last of his strength, Carden hurled the fireball straight into the Beast's open maw.

The flash seared them both, knocking Carden flat while it destroyed the Beast's jaws. Ronan's tawny eyes melted away as his skin bubbled and charred. Thick, white fur caught aflame as he toppled backward, thrashing and bellowing, his massive body a spitting fireball, rolling downhill.

Carden pulled himself up and leaned heavily against a scorched tree. He needed to get to Caeraricin before he collapsed from burns and blood loss and ended up dying out here. Cautiously, he put weight on his flayed hip, and tumbled, screaming in pain. Sheer refusal to die made him try again and again, until he could stand. Cursing with each step, Carden slipped and stumbled his way to the copse where he'd left Lynet, leaving a slick trail of blood on stones and moss as he went.

The moment he came into the grove, Carden knew Lynet was gone. The puki were scattering, flitting off into the trees. The portal grew smaller and smaller as their numbers dispersed. Carden didn't have the strength to call them back. He lurched at the dwindling portal, fell, and crawled through. Behind him the grove disappeared as the portal snapped shut. Carden rolled onto his back on the cold ground of the middle bailey and looked up into the unforgiving face of Eltanin Sihtric.

Gods I Can See

LYNET WOKE TO THE SOFT HUM of insects buzzing in the morning sunlight. Her eyes opened, then crossed as they tried to focus on a tiny puki perched on the bridge of her nose. A multitude of antennae waved like hair around its teeny head. Its huge eyes stared straight into hers. Lynet's first instinct was to whack and swipe the bug from her face. Her second, stronger instinct—the one predisposed for survival—knew annoying a puki was far worse than provoking a wasp or hornet. Wasps grew angry and stung. Puki laughed and killed.

With great care, Lynet brushed the puki from her nose. It giggled and rolled down Lynet's cheek, then shot up to hover and dart in the air above her face. The rapidly beating dragonfly wings tickled as they whipped against Lynet's eyelashes, tangled briefly in her hair, and slapped repeatedly against her forehead. Lynet flinched, but held still until the puki flew off.

She sat up to discover a dozen more jewel-colored puki flitting around her, occasionally landing on her arm or knee. They varied in size from no more than an inch to the length of her hand.

"Go away," Lynet mumbled under her breath as she watched them for any signs of mischief.

"We can't," the tiny voices chorused.

"The *jöfurr* told us to watch you," said an emerald green one.

"So here we are," said another.

A ruby red puki fluttered in front of her, its thin wings making a soft drone. "You are boring to watch."

Lynet heard only one word: *jöfurr.* In an instant, she remembered where she was and why. She scrambled into a crouch, listening for Carden's snigger, certain he would be quick to comment, maybe even attack, once he realized she was awake. The blackguard had actually hit her with that overripe spell. It could have killed her. It seemed Eltanin no longer cared if she lived or died. He was king now, his recent coup accomplished. He didn't need her after all. Mercenaries, and his rotten son, had been enough.

Lynet scanned the thicket. The morning light cast weak shadows, easy to see through. She looked around, then looked again. There was no one here. Except for the dozen or so puki, Lynet was alone.

"Where is Carden?"

"The *jöfurr*?" the ruby red puki asked.

Lynet paused, hating to acknowledge the royal title. "Yes."

"Gone. Back where he came from."

Lynet hoped it spoke the truth but, with puki, who could tell?

She abandoned her defensive posture and stood up straight, a motion that caused her to lose her balance. The injury to her ear was a problem. She needed it healed, but their *lyfja* powder was in Ronan's discarded pouch, back in the valley. She had been careless to leave it behind.

Where was her sword? Carden threw it—

Lynet frowned.

Wait.

This was not the same grove.

Where was she?

Lynet studied the ground. She wasn't as good at this as Ronan, but she figured the crushed grass, dirt in her hair, and paw prints were a good sign Lleth had dragged her here. Did that mean the wolfhound had returned to his body . . . and rescued her?

Even as she posed the question, Lynet knew it was ridiculous. Lleth, no matter how loyal, was no match for the man who wielded dark Nos'kag magic as easily as if he had been born with it.

Still, something must have happened. Carden would not simply leave her behind. He'd hounded her every step since the day she left home. Catching her was his one all-consuming goal. He'd had her dead to rights—the portal wide open, Caeraricin Castle only steps away. Why was she still here?

"Where is Lleth?"

"The fuzzy face?"

"Yes."

"Gone. Back where he came from."

Lynet sighed.

Puki were an enigma, itty-bitty bugs who held the secret to time. They could make you old and decrepit or reverse you to embryo, but they didn't usually bother. They were too busy driving you mad with their chirpy voices and tricky antics. If Carden had instructed these puki to watch over her, she was probably safe. There were no more than a dozen, and she doubted they were eager to rebel against him. Still, she wasn't likely to get a straight answer.

Lynet shielded her eyes from the sun—and felt a rush of panic—*sunlight. It was mid-morning!* How long had she been unconscious? Hours. Hours since the battle in the valley.

Hours . . . and Ronan had not found her.

Her muscles went weak.

She'd known the odds. Known he was grossly outnumbered. Yet she'd let him face their enemies alone because she believed he would defeat them and return to her. They had survived so many battles she'd convinced herself Ronan was indestructible.

He was not.

Lynet had smelled the fetid stink of death through Carden's open portal to the castle. The Vökumenn were all too mortal.

Lynet didn't realize she was running until a branch caught her arm. Frantically, she ripped her shirtsleeve free, took two more unsteady steps, then stood there, trembling in indecision. Ronan had taught her: *Never go back. The Beast will kill you. Wait for me to come to you.*

The battle was surely over. Where was he?

Lynet paced back and forth.

Once.

Twice.

Then took off running toward the valley, a fluttering trail of puki following behind.

Carden paused outside the throne room. Mouthfuls of raw *lyfja* from the king's store had kept him alive, though the process was painful and left hellish scars along his chest. He would have preferred the tender ministrations of the Cú, but no one could find a single court healer in the entire city. It didn't matter; he'd survived.

He'd been stupid to think he was ready to take on the Hoar Beast. At least the scars would remind him to stack the odds next time. Fighting fair was seldom a successful battle plan.

His boot heels clacked on the polished marble floor as he entered the castle's main hall and approached his father's stolen perch.

Carden took note of the hulking Kynneeyn Gorrym leader, Drem, standing to the left of the dais. Drem's men—heavily scarred, disrespectful, and too numerous for Carden's liking—crowded the hall. There were no courtiers. Many of the lords and ladies who had once graced Caeraricin Castle were dead; the rest had fled to their homes, no doubt praying they didn't attract the new king's attention. Servants scuttled out of Carden's way. The stench of rotting Vökumenn filled the air with an ever-present reminder that no help or rescue was forthcoming.

Eltanin Sihtric sat on the high throne, the greatest seat of power in Norðrlönd. His cruel, long-fingered hands curved around the regal emblems on the chair's massive arms. His face was gaunt, his nose sharp, his mouth a thin, humorless line. His white hair hung in straight lines down the length of his back, its color marred by an occasional strand of deepest black that had not yet succumbed to age. It was his eyes, though, which instilled the most fear. They were at once black as night, and red with fire. It seemed the boiling lava of MórNathair seethed within their depths. Carden knew, better than anyone, that his father was not quite human.

Carden knelt before the throne, awaiting the command to rise. He was not surprised when it came quickly.

"How many months has it been?" King Eltanin asked, his voice soft and friendly, although Carden wasn't fooled.

"Nearly five, Your Majesty."

"Five months and here you stand—empty-handed."

"Yes, Sire." Carden knew better than to argue. This wouldn't be pretty. He accepted that.

"Tell me you have killed the Watchman; that at least he is dead."

"His wounds were grave, but he can heal himself, and the woman will bring him back if he dies."

"Ah, yes, the woman. So it is true. She can return the dead to life."

"Yes, Sire." Carden glanced at Drem and saw the pagan chieftain trace a warding symbol on his forehead. Raising the dead was witchcraft outside the realm of natural sorcery, and a concept steeped in superstition.

Eltanin stood. Carden instinctively thrust his right hand out and away from his body. It was a defensive posture, and Eltanin laughed. "Nervous?"

"Cautious," Carden corrected.

"I see. Should I watch my back?"

"No more than in the past, Father."

Again, Eltanin chuckled. "Come, walk with me."

Carden followed half a step behind. He knew punishment was inevitable. However, it would not serve the king to chastise his only son in front of others, at least not yet. His reign was too new, his mercenaries too unpredictable. He needed Carden, and Carden needed the respect of all those in the castle—a respect he would lose if the reprimand took place in public.

They climbed the stone stairs to the highest level of the keep. Eltanin asked about the chase that had cost both time and lives. Carden did not sugarcoat his answers. The questions were a test; he knew his father had spies amongst Carden's own men.

They reached the upper chamber, the king's quarters where generations of Aricin royalty were conceived, born, and eventually died. Eltanin continued through the richly decorated chamber to a small, enclosed room along the southern wall.

"Do you know what this place is?" Eltanin asked as they entered the cloistered room with high stained-glass windows.

The afternoon sun splayed color across the altar, highlighting the carved angels adorning its surface. Carden had never been in the king's private chapel before, though he knew well enough what it represented. "It is a place sacred to the One God."

"Do you believe in the One God?"

"No, Sire. I believe only in the gods I can see."

"Which are?"

"Rán of the Ocean. Balor. And you, Sire."

Eltanin grinned, but not in humor. "Do you mock me?"

"No. I accept that in this world you are now king, and soon you will make yourself a god to these people."

"I will"—Eltanin nodded—"but not yet. First, I need what you failed to bring me." Eltanin slid his hand along the altar. Beneath his fingers the painted winged figures crumbled as black, loathsome creatures erupted from the gilded wood. The sun retreated; the room grew cold. A smell like rotten eggs, or sulfur, burned Carden's nose as the squealing imps performed grotesque acts on each other while they danced and writhed across the surface of the once beautiful altar.

Carden stood his ground and kept his eyes on his father. Though he did not worship the One God, Carden knew no good could come from desecrating this holy place. Gods had a way of making their displeasure known; if not today, then one day soon. Carden hoped to endure his father's judgment, and leave before the taint of this act rubbed onto him.

"Without the witch's power over life and death, I cannot be the god this land needs." Eltanin held out his hand, and several of the creatures clawed up onto it, scrambling along his arm, hanging on like wicked little monkeys with long, jagged teeth. "Do you understand that, Carden?"

"Yes, Sire."

"I do not think you do." Eltanin petted one of the creatures with the back of his finger, then broke its neck and tossed it to the others still dancing on the altar. They hissed and dove at it, fighting amongst themselves for a still-wriggling piece.

Eltanin walked past Carden, his voice a low promise. "But you will."

The hideous creatures squealed in excitement, their ugly little faces all turned in his direction, and Carden realized, too late, he had nowhere to run.

Without a horse, it took Lynet an hour to climb up the valley rim and race down the other side. More than once her feet tripped up, confounded by the ruptured eardrum. Each time she slammed to the ground, the puki laughed, teasing and pulling her hair—and each time, Lynet got a little bit madder.

Once on the valley floor, Lynet headed straight for the stream. Ronan would seek water to bathe his wounds; she would look there first.

She had gone only a few feet when she heard it—the lowing of a wounded animal in the distance. It was pitiful and mulish at the same time, a great voice reduced to a whimper, yet still defiant.

Ronan.

Lynet quickened her pace, then faltered . . . and stopped. No. It wasn't Ronan—that cry belonged to the Hoar Beast. What was she doing? The Beast would kill her. She should be fleeing in the opposite direction.

The sound of shouting up ahead startled her, and Lynet ducked behind a tree. Who was there? Kynneeyn Gorrym out for sport? Lynet bent and drew a knife from her boot. The black-skinned mercenaries often tortured their captives. Already on edge, Lynet's anger flared. Did they have Ronan?

More shouting, followed by the weak roar of the Beast, decided her course. Wishing for Lleth and a decent sword, she stole carefully through the trees. With each cry of the Beast, Lynet grew more incensed. For Lynet, anger in any form was bad. Where a man might break a door, or an ordinary woman spit words she would later regret, Lynet's anger took a different path—her rage, unchecked, called the god of decay from his unholy crypt. She was called *plaga norn* for a reason.

The Beast roared again—this time the sound ended in a gurgle. That cut-short noise tore at Lynet's heart as nothing else could. Before she could call it back, her dreaded magic surged, bathing her in blue light.

A rush of cold wind, and Lynet felt Death walking in step beside her. His gray visage always reminded her of a skeletal puppet master. She should banish him, as she had so many times in the past. Shun him before she did something unspeakable.

Lynet was vaguely aware of the puki leaving. It seemed they did not care for Death's company, though why, she could not guess; puki often sent creatures into his waiting arms. Yet, for all their devilry, Lynet knew *she* was

Death's champion; she who could take the life from an entire army with a single thought. He was her constant companion, standing ever in the background, eager to receive the fruits of her unguarded emotions.

In her youth, those emotions had presented Death with quite a feast: lazy sheep, wriggling fish in the stream, a tree that scratched her face, all the insects and flowers in an entire meadow the day a bee stung her. Even her favorite horse, when it shied and stepped on her foot, dropped dead the instant Lynet's toe broke. Before she understood how to give them life again, many had died. But even the life-gift was a curse. Lynet could not heal, could not reverse age. Most importantly, she could not force a soul to return to its body. Not even when the soul was a close friend.

Reeling from that early lesson, Lynet had made a vow never to use her magic on humans again. She had renewed that vow when she fell in love with Ronan. Through his tuition and the adoption of his moral code, Lynet finally gained full control of her powers. Sometimes she cheated Death, like when he'd tried to claim Lleth. Sometimes she took a life. Always she maintained control. Always she made a choice. Once she had even killed Carden—sucked the life from him—only to give it back within seconds. It had hurt him terribly, but he'd lived—and now he knew her bluff. She would not kill him with magic, though his father did not warrant the same restraint.

As she drew near, Lynet heard the repeated *woof* of a large dog and the tortured cry of the once-mighty Beast.

Something inside her broke.

Her principled vow meant nothing if she could not save the man she loved. For, when Ronan died, he would stay dead. He'd made her promise she would not bring his body back to life. When his death came, his soul, both sides of it, would leave and not return.

Lynet's entire body blazed with a cold unburning fire; a blue flame that pooled in darker hues in the palms of her hands. If Ronan died, then Death could take them all.

Lynet burst through the trees.

The sight that greeted her was so foreign and unexpected that she stopped in her tracks. The Hoar Beast, nearly devoid of fur, its face flat instead of muzzled, hung suspended like a giant pink pig inside a magical Sphere that hovered ten feet above the ground. Below the Sphere stood a middle-aged man shouting commands to a young woman who was wresting with Lleth, her feet digging and sliding in the dirt as she held him back.

There were so many things wrong with the scene before her that all thought of revenge ebbed away. Lynet felt her gray companion fade away, back to his crypt, as it became clear she would not use her dread magic after all. She hardly cared. Her head was spinning with more important questions.

17

Who *were* these people, and what were they doing? Why hadn't Ronan returned to his human form? How much pain could he endure, caught as he was, halfway between man and Beast? Why didn't Lleth bite the girl, instead of allowing her to hang from his neck like an ill-disciplined child? Maybe the hound hadn't returned to his body after all.

Too many things to sort through at once. Lynet decided to resolve the easy one first and hopefully gain herself an ally.

"Lleth!" she called to the wolfhound, and felt relief when he shrugged off the young woman and came running. His eyes keen, Lleth wagged his tail as he sniffed her for information, then stood at her side.

The young woman picked herself up and brushed off long robes of purple, blue, and russet silk. A wizard. Only a wizard would wear something so inappropriate out in the cold forest air. The girl smiled wide and strode without hesitation or caution up to Lynet. Either she was powerful and therefore unafraid of attack, or she was too inexperienced to know better.

"Thank you," the girl said. "He was tiring me out."

"He could have killed you." Lynet returned her knife to her boot.

"Why would he? We are here to help." The girl shrugged and scratched Lleth's ear. "The hound was getting underfoot, and Scartozzar needs room while he works."

Lynet's eyes narrowed. *Scartozzar.* Ronan had warned her about him. The wizard was a thief and a liar. They had added a full day to their journey in order to avoid the caves of Aros where the ridiculously named *"scar-toes-are"* and his apprentice lived.

"Tell him to stop . . . or I'll stop him," Lynet warned.

"Don't be daft. The Beast is dying. Scartozzar is trying to calm it so the Watchman can gain custody of his body and heal himself. But it isn't easy. The Beast is blind and in pain; it is fighting any call to calm. I think it believes that if it relaxes it will die—not that it isn't dying already."

Dying.

Lynet shoved past the girl to where Scartozzar stood conjuring, his hands twirling as he muttered under his breath.

"Stay back," he ordered.

Lynet did not obey. "What are you doing? He needs a healer, not a sorcerer."

Scartozzar did not even glance her way. "He needs to heal himself."

Lynet watched in silence as the wizard ripped a bit of raw *lyfja* from the leaf in his hand, wrapped it in a magic bubble, then sent it through the Sphere. It rose to the Beast's mangled face and then whooshed straight up his nose. Ronan roared in agony.

"You're force-feeding him."

"He is too stupid to eat it on his own. Without it, he'd already be dead."

Another tiny bubble zipped through the Sphere and shot up Ronan's nose. Again the Beast roared. Without Death's goad to confound her, Lynet recognized that roar for what it was: angry, yes; full of pain, yes—but a good pain. It heralded the mending of a broken body.

"How can I help?" Lynet asked.

"Stay out of my way," Scartozzar snapped.

"I am the object of his Oath." Lynet did not back down.

"Talk to him, then; tell him to stop this lunacy and change into a man."

Lynet pursed her lips as she stepped under the suspended Sphere. Much as she distrusted Scartozzar, the wizard was right; Ronan needed to heal himself, and the only way he could do that was as a man.

"Ronan!" she called to him. "Ronan, I am here. You saved me. Now you must save yourself."

Lleth came to stand beside her, his head slipping under her arm to nuzzle her side. He whined; then he lifted his nose to the sky, and the whine became a low, mournful howl.

The Beast answered. His roar elongated and joined with Lleth's until the two sang in eerie unison. Lynet watched and listened, wishing she could communicate with the Beast as easily as Lleth.

An idea sparked, and Lynet spun to face the wizard. "Can you give me Lleth's voice?"

"You think howling like a mindless animal will help him?"

"Yes—I mean no, not a mindless animal. Me, my thoughts and words in Lleth's voice."

"The spell you seek takes hours to conjure," Scartozzar said. "Far easier to give the dog understanding of your words. He is intelligent; it would take little more than a nudge to complete his understanding."

"Do it."

Scartozzar stuffed the *lyfja* leaf inside his sleeve and pulled a vial from one of the many pockets in his robe. He studied it, then gave it a quick shake. "An unfinished spell I can piggyback to serve our cause. Stand away from the hound. You don't want any of it to splash on you."

Lynet did not ask why. She knew enough of wizard spells to know they seldom did anyone any good.

Scartozzar chanted over the vial, pulled the stopper, and dumped the magic onto Lleth's head. The wolfhound growled and snapped, but did not leave his place beneath the Beast.

"Go ahead; talk to him."

"Lleth? Can you understand me?" Although Lynet had hoped the magic would work, it still surprised her when Lleth's head jerked up and he turned around to face her. His reaction, however, was not expected. His lip curled, and his hackles rose as he took slow steps toward her.

"Lleth, it's me. The wizard has enchanted you."

Lleth growled low in his throat and immediately lunged after Scartozzar.

The wizard clapped his hands twice, and Lleth jerked away, shaking his head like a dazed puppy. He walked in several small circles, whining, then seemed to come back to himself, and returned to his position beneath Ronan.

"What did you do?" Lynet asked. "Did you stop it? It worked."

"Yes, and he didn't like it. Find some other way." Above them, the Beast shuddered, its arms hanging limp. "And you'd best hurry. The Watchman loses his battle."

Lynet felt weak. The constant shift between hope and despair had taken its toll. She didn't know what to do. Should she punch the wizard in the head and let the Beast out of the Sphere? Should she do nothing, stand still while the gods took Ronan back, knowing it was forever?

Should she . . . sing?

The thrill of the *Kærásti Fórnsöngr* swelled in her throat the moment she considered it. To sing the Song of Sacrifice to the Hoar Beast was the grossest of crimes. She knew it was wrong, and she didn't care. She would do whatever it took to save him. Lynet opened her mouth and damned them both. The tender music of lovers filled the air. The haunting tune, if shared, formed a bond of spirit no force on Earth could break.

"Are you mad?" Scartozzar and his apprentice cried out in protest.

Lynet ignored them and kept singing.

The Hoar Beast reacted to her voice, its body jerking in spasms, its roar garbled and choked. Lynet did not stop singing. If this was the only way to save him, then so be it; they would deal with the consequences.

The Beast shook and shrank. The last of the grizzly white hair fell away; the massive muscles retreated into the telltale contours of a seasoned soldier. The transformation happened quickly, and Ronan dropped to his bare knees inside the Sphere, his eyes still missing from his face, his hand reaching out blindly toward her.

Scartozzar lowered the Sphere to the ground, where it dissolved.

"Stop," Ronan begged, his voice weak. "You cannot sing to me."

Lynet rushed to him, throwing her arms around his naked body. "I've stopped. You did not sing along; we are safe. Please heal yourself."

Ronan collapsed in her arms, his body burned and trembling. Lynet had been strong and brave, but now her strength failed. She wept over him, watching as he fought a battle she could not join.

God-appointed defenders of Caeraricin, each Vökumaðr shared his existence, his life space, with a Beast, and in return, the gods gave them the power to heal; but Lynet had never seen him this badly injured before. Was it possible to recover from such grave wounds?

Charred skin peeled away, leaving black chalky smudges on her hands and clothes as she held him. Ronan groaned and twisted as new tissue grew beneath the old, and fine, dark hair sprouted on his legs, groin, and belly. His face—his mangled and sightless face—worried her most. He was a warrior, a soldier—how would he cope without his sight? She would gladly be his eyes, but for him it would never be enough.

His hand searched for hers. Lynet grabbed it tight. "I'm here."

Ronan returned her grip—held it . . . then released a long, untroubled sigh. . . . His head fell back. His body went lax, and still.

"No!" Lynet cried and hugged him with all her might, desperate to keep his spirit inside him. "No, Ronan, don't leave."

Scartozzar knelt beside them, touched Ronan's forehead, muttered something under his breath, then stood and backed away.

Lynet felt light-headed. How could she obey Ronan's wishes? How could she let his body die, knowing she could save him?

"Let him go," Scartozzar said behind her.

"Stay away," Lynet hissed. "He is not even cold."

"Your grief makes you careless, woman. He is not cold because he is not dead. The Vökumaðr may be strong, but he is too weak to heal and stay conscious. I am surprised he lasted as long as he did. Now, let him go and I will transport him to the sea caves where he may recover in peace."

Lynet let go as Ronan's limp body floated up from the ground and hung sagging in the air. She did not protest. She was too numb.

"We should hurry." Scartozzar's apprentice looked nervously at the trees behind them. "Whoever did this will be back."

Nornir Meddling

RONAN FELT LIKE A NEWBORN CUB, with eyes sealed and undeveloped. Without his sight, his other senses filled in the gaps, giving him an idea of his surroundings. He heard the waves outside the caves and smelled the salty sea air. They'd brought him to Aros, an unnatural ring of caverns jutting out into the eastern sea. Carved out of shale and reinforced with primitive cement, the caves were all that remained of an ancient settlement. Few ever came here anymore, its treasures and secrets plundered long ago. Ronan found it curious that Scartozzar had made it his home of late. What did the wizard expect to find here?

Ronan shifted uncomfortably on the bed. Hard and crude beneath his back, at least it kept him off the damp ground. He heard Lleth panting at the entrance to the room, and though he trusted the hound to alert him of danger, Ronan could not relax. He tracked often, mentally following Scartozzar and his apprentice as they moved around the caves. He would know if they left, or contacted Eltanin.

Lynet slept in a chair near his bedside; her golden thread shone clear and bright in his mind. The lingering tone of the *Kærásti Fórnsöngr* floated in the air around her. Always there, the song was lovely, colorful, and toxic to the touch—like living with a poisonous butterfly.

The *Kærásti Fórnsöngr* came often enough to the people of Norðrlönd. The song ensured strong magic survived. When like recognized like, lovers could share their powers. It required a literal sacrifice because one, or both, could lose more magic than they gained in the process.

As far as anyone remembered, the Vökumenn were unaffected by the *Kærásti Fórnsöngr*. It would go against the laws of nature for Vökumenn to share their gifts with humans. They were a race created by the gods for a specific purpose. No others were granted their exceedingly long life and healing power.

Ronan had assumed the song would never come to him.

He rubbed a callused hand over his face and head. His hair and beard were growing back; he had two working ears and a nose again, as well as human teeth and jaw. Everything was as it should be, except for his eyes. He'd never had to regrow eyes before. Like every other aspect of being Vökumaðr, it was not pleasant. His upper and lower eyelids had fused together, shielding his newly formed eyeballs. The insides itched and burned as fibrous strands of tissue attached themselves to his nervous system and brain.

He supposed he should be grateful. The Beast could take massive amounts of damage and barely feel it. Not until the frenzy passed, and the man awoke, was there an awareness of just how close to death he had been. Without his advanced healing ability, Ronan would have died years ago—the first time he returned to find his body broken, blood flowing from multiple wounds, his leg crushed, his spleen punctured.

Healing was a necessary part of a Watchman's life.

It would go faster if he focused, but Ronan had too much on his mind. They were only a couple of days' ride from Caeraricin. Ronan was an outlaw, the high price on his head his reward for refusing to kill Lynet. Once word of their whereabouts spread, bounty hunters would be out en masse, willing to share in the riches if it meant less danger to themselves. Eltanin would send more men. Carden would be back. The sooner they moved on, the better.

Their original plan, to join Ronan's father and retake the throne, was pointless now. Scartozzar's description of the takeover had spared no detail. Ronan's father, his uncles, and kin were dead. At first, Ronan had not believed it, but he trusted Lynet. She had smelled the stink of decay through the puki portal; moreover, she believed Carden's account of Eltanin's doings.

So much carnage. The queen and Prince Maxwell, dead. Numerous courtiers slaughtered or missing. There were rumors Prince Edan survived, but no one knew for sure.

Ronan stretched, keeping limber the freshly healed skin of his chest and back. He would need both strength and mobility in the days ahead. With or without his kin, Ronan intended to sneak into Caeraricin. If Prince Edan lived, Ronan would rescue him, and together they would deal with Eltanin.

Lynet would insist on going with him, of course, but alone Ronan had a better chance at stealth. Still, he was loath to leave her here at Aros. In spite of Scartozzar's help, Ronan did not trust him. How ironic that after deliberately skirting this place, they'd ended up here anyhow, indebted to the wizard they'd meant to avoid. The Nornir had to have their laugh, didn't they? Goddesses of fate, the three hags twisted the paths of destiny, weaving patterns too complicated to unwind, all for their own sadistic pleasure. Ronan had known their meddling all his life.

A fissure of light, like a curtain rising, prompted him to sit up and grin, as first one eye, then the other broke its lidded seal. He glanced around through half-opened slits, confirming his impression of the room, then settled his gaze on Lynet. She looked ragged and tired, her cheeks sunburned, her braid undone. Golden curls clung to her neck and lay curved around one breast, stuck to the sweat-dampened linen of her shirt. She was a right mess, and the most beautiful thing he had ever seen. Gently he stroked her cheek, and those blue eyes he loved fluttered open. A sleepy smile spread across her face as she left the chair to sit on the bed beside him.

"You can see?" she asked, kissing his face until she appeared satisfied she'd covered it all.

"I can see." He smiled. "I will be your protector for a while longer."

She slid her arms around him and nuzzled close. "How are you feeling?"

"I'm starving," he answered honestly. Healing required fuel, and he hadn't eaten a decent meal in days, no thanks to the now dead men who'd interrupted his hunt.

"Me too." She traced her fingers along his bristled chin and dropped yet another kiss onto his face. "But we survived. *Again.*"

"Again," he agreed, enjoying the feel of her pressed against him. "And I gave Carden a lesson in hoarfrost he is not likely to forget."

"You shouldn't be so cocky. He nearly killed you."

Ronan took a handful of her golden hair and drew her face to his, whispering against her cheek, "You shouldn't use such provocative language. You sang, Lynet. Do you know what it did to me—what it took to keep silent? We can never. . . ."

"I know." She kissed him one last time, then drew back. "I'll tell Scartozzar you are almost healed. He asked to be told right away."

Ronan let her go, her hair slipping like water through his fingers as she left the bed. "Don't trust him, Lynet."

She walked to the doorway and pushed aside the threadbare tapestry. "Not an inch."

Carden stood, stone faced, on a hill overlooking the wide, bustling city that was Caeraricin. Caeraricin was the seat of the high king and the central government of Norðrlönd. Of the Six Kingdoms, it alone enjoyed the blessing of the gods. Carden wondered how long that blessing would last with his father on the throne.

The cold north wind blew through the scattered trees at the top of the hill. Carden did not feel it. He was cold inside already. Fury screamed at the edge of his mind, screams he ignored. To acknowledge them would be to acknowledge the violation he had endured.

His father's temperament had changed. Where once he'd been coolly tolerant of Carden's rebellious nature, Eltanin now demanded complete obedience. Carden knew he was no match for his father, knew his own future depended on his usefulness. He would either find Lynet and bring her here, ensuring a place at his father's side, or . . . well, there really was no acceptable alternative, was there?

Eltanin had offered Carden one final chance to snatch Lynet away and claim the victory before he summoned his demons and went after her himself.

Carden needed a plan, a good one. One that didn't involve limping home half-dead. He'd lost face this time; it couldn't happen again. He'd made a mistake underestimating the Hoar Beast. No—correct that—his mistake was thinking he could succeed without killing Ronan.

Carden turned away from the city and headed to where he'd left his horse.

The problem was he respected Ronan—had ever since they were young men posturing around the castle. Carden admired the way Ronan stood up to Prince Edan. Carden hated Edan.

As the three men grew older and Carden embraced Nos'kag magic, Ronan had stood firm against him, though the two never came to blows. Carden knew it was his own cowardice that kept them from facing off. He felt confident in his mastery of dark magic, but the Hoar Beast was the monster of childhood nightmares.

Today, Carden's father had changed that little misconception. Carden now knew the difference between a child's nightmare—and true horror. He would not endure that again. If securing Lynet for his father meant killing Ronan, then so be it. If it meant killing everyone in his path, he could live with that, too.

The image of soft, violet eyes flashed across Carden's memory. He'd left Ronan in Nor'Uaithne Valley, not far from the sea caves at Aros. If Ronan retreated to the caves to heal, then Scartozzar would be one of those in Carden's path. No love lost there, but where Scartozzar was—so was Neira.

The sun broke away from the horizon and inched up the sky. It was morning. The waves rumbled, the sound deep and rhythmic. Seagulls squawked and flew among the craggy rocks. Ronan could understand why ancient peoples had settled here; the caves allowed a man to belong to both the earth and sea, without having to make a choice.

He'd spent the night tracking down his and Lynet's horses, and gathering what he could find of their scattered supplies. Now outside the sea caves, Ronan prepared for the last leg of his journey. He rubbed salve into a sore on the mare's withers. He would be resaddling her shortly, and with luck, the salve would keep the mare comfortable on the hard ride ahead. Lynet's mare had suffered the least damage in their wild flight from the Beast. His gelding was nearly lame.

He'd just put the remainder of the ointment in his bag when he heard Lynet's footsteps in the sand. Ronan did not look forward to this parting.

Lynet clutched a silk shawl around her shoulders. The flashy wizard's purple did not suit her, though he liked the way the fluttering fabric clung to her body. She didn't meet his eyes, but combed the mare's brown mane with her fingers. "You intend to go without me?"

"Yes. You would not be safe."

"You realize that is ridiculous. I have not been *safe* since the day I first left my home to come with you."

"This is different." Ronan tossed a blanket over the horse's back. "If my kin are dead, there will be no safety within the castle walls. Without good men to lead them, any remaining soldiers will be riotous and violent. There could be legions of Kynneeyn Gorrym despoiling the city. Nowhere would you be safe. Even as the Beast, I could not keep you from harm once we reached the city. I am one Watchman—only one."

"I can take care of myself."

"You aren't skilled enough with a sword for the numbers we would face."

"I don't need a sword."

Ronan lifted the saddle from the sand and swung it up onto the blanket. "And do you think with so many coming at you at once you would be able to discern those who deserved to die from those who were frightened and merely following the orders of their king? Would you kill them all because you did not know the difference?"

"If I make a mistake, I can fix it."

Ronan turned then, not surprised, but disappointed in her reply. "No you can't, Lynet. You made a choice not to use your power on humans. Will you throw it all to the wind? All our training, all your resolve, all the tears and sleepless nights as you struggled to control the killing. Does your promise to me, and the Nornir, mean nothing?"

Her lips trembled, but her eyes were without tears, and her words, when they came, did not answer his question. "You cannot go alone."

"I have ways of hiding. I will slip in, rescue who I can, and slip out." He dropped a kiss onto those trembling lips. "I will not wage war on Eltanin by myself. I am in no hurry to die, *ástin mín*. Have faith in my judgment."

"So, I am to stay here?"

"Yes."

"Alone with a wizard we do not trust?"

"Not alone." Ronan turned back to the mare. "I'm leaving Lleth."

Lynet poked him in the rib. "Not funny."

Ronan grinned and tightened the saddle girth. "He is good company, a fair fighter, and trustworthy." Behind him, Lynet slid her hands up under his tunic while he laced a leather bag onto the saddle. His stomach clenched at her icy touch. She was a snowbird who followed the sun to steal its warmth.

"Do you trust Neira?" she asked.

"No. Neira is Scartozzar's apprentice and Carden's . . . well, who knows what she is to Carden; their alliance is nearly as old as she is." Ronan doubted even Scartozzar knew of all the times Neira had snuck off with Eltanin's son. Ronan knew. He was a Watchman. It was his task to uncover secrets and see through lies. "I do not trust her, not completely. Still, they are all we have. Scartozzar, though snappish and arrogant, is no fool. He knows what you are capable of. He will behave."

Ronan finished with the saddle and turned to face her. Gently he drew her hands from under his tunic and kissed them. "Trust me. I won't be gone long. I will be back for you."

"Because you have no choice," Lynet said. "Because I am some prophetic prize you swore to protect." Ronan recognized the pout as more than childish protest; she was afraid.

Ronan lifted her chin, weighing his words carefully.

"Yes, the Watchman's Oath binds me to you. This—" He placed her hand firmly against his chest, so she could feel the faithful beating of his heart. "This binds me more surely than any pledge or magic. I will come back for you, Lynet, because I have no life without you."

Ronan dipped his head and kissed her. A slow, tender, open-mouthed kiss that hinted at what he longed to do. He cupped her cheek with his callused hand and held her as his tongue pushed past her teeth. Even after months of kissing her, Ronan still thrilled at the answering touch of her tongue. He was Vökumaðr, part animal, and still she welcomed him, wanted him. He slid his mouth over her face and throat, chafing her skin with the brush of his unshaven whiskers. He loved her, would make her his wife if he could . . . but he could not. Stolen kisses were all they would ever have. To give in to the heat of lovemaking would release the song. And if they sang the *Kærásti Fórnsöngr*, the world as they knew it would end.

Slowly, he pulled away.

She mouthed the words, "Heal quickly."

Ronan nodded, then swung up into the saddle. With a click of his tongue, he headed for Caeraricin Castle.

As he entered the forest shadows, Ronan looked over his shoulder for one final glimpse. He could see her outline, standing near the shore.

She waved.

An odd sensation filled his heart, one so strong he almost left his quest and raced back to her. Almost.

Ronan nudged the mare and continued his journey north, unable to shake the feeling he had looked on his beloved for the last time.

Scartozzar

H E HATED BEING RUSHED. Haste never produced anything of worth, especially not magic. A spell needed time to grow up, to gain loyalty and character. Well, maybe a common spell could be rushed—Fire or Salt—but certainly not any of the useful or more powerful ones. Those took weeks to mature. Scartozzar did not have weeks. The attack would come within the hour.

In the three days since Ronan had left for Caeraricin, everything had gone wrong. Ronan was dead, caught in Eltanin's trap. Lynet, heartbroken and threatening to destroy all of Caeraricin, had become dangerous—too dangerous to remain unbound. Now Eltanin's forces were on their way here.

"Neira!" Scartozzar shouted as he sped down the cold, damp passageway. The curly-haired wizard was a skilled magician, but he understood his limits. Every drop of magic he possessed he'd stolen from someone else; none of it was his by birth. Those few who did know—mainly the women he'd robbed—wanted him dead. Perhaps today they would get their wish.

Scartozzar paused near a bend in the corridor where the wall seemed especially wet and nasty. He listened for his apprentice, but with the tide coming in, the rumble of waves made it impossible to hear. With an impatient whisk of his hand, Scartozzar brushed aside the illusion protecting his personal chambers and strode through a doorway that seconds earlier had appeared as a solid wall of slimy, mold-blackened shale.

To survive, he needed to finish the Sphere out in the main cavern, then hide all evidence of it—and the ungodly woman caught inside it—before Eltanin's forces arrived. Then Scartozzar could do what he did best: lie.

On a table near the wall lay his latest experiments, bowls and jars filled with glowing, palm-sized orbs of magic. Inside the orbs, defense and protection spells aged, gaining strength and potency. Scartozzar snatched several of them up and shoved them into the hidden pockets of his robes.

None of them were finished and ready for battle, but they would have to do. Fortunately, he had a few tricks he could fall back on. Simple, effective magic he had polished over the years.

"Neira!" he shouted. Where was she? Running with the Vökumaðr's hound again? The girl's thrill-seeking would bring her to grief this time.

Another incoming wave thrummed against the wall. Scartozzar frowned as the percussion vibrated his body, causing him to take an awkward step back. Was that the tide . . . or a challenge to the cavern shield? He abandoned the remaining orbs and hurried to an ironwood chest near his bed. Kneeling in front of it, Scartozzar pushed open the heavy lid. Shoving aside wax-coated jars of sulfur and quicklime, Scartozzar dug to the bottom of the chest. Reverently he drew out a thin, lightweight box, the length of a man's forearm. The wood was black with age. As he handled it, delicate inlays of yellowed antler splintered and fell away. One corner of the fragile lid was broken off and missing. Through the hole, Scartozzar saw rotting cloth, and the cold glimmer of an untarnished blade.

This the usurper must not get. Snatching a coverlet from the nearby chair, Scartozzar hurried from the room, wrapping the box as he went. When he reached the main cavern, he called again for his apprentice.

"NEIRA!" His voice hit a pitch that dared her to ignore him.

The girl materialized so quickly from the shadows that Scartozzar collided with the wolfhound running at her side. Beneath the cover of her silk hood, Neira's cheeks flushed pink and she gasped for breath. She nodded toward the front of the cavern. "They are here."

Scartozzar was stunned. The warning had barely sounded. How could they be here already—time porters! Blasted time-altering puki. The Kynneeyn Gorrym were not alone. Carden was with them.

Scartozzar's jaw set. It didn't matter. The usurper's son was proud, and pride made men careless; Scartozzar could use that to his advantage. In any case, Carden was not invincible, at least not yet.

"Take this." Scartozzar pressed the wrapped bundle into Neira's arms. "Go out the western passage. Run into the foothills and hide. Use every spell you know to avoid capture. Take the wolfhound. Do not come back here, and do not presume to help me. I can take care of myself. If I do not join you by nightfall, make your way north to the Annars. Give them that. They will keep it safe until I return."

Neira began to argue. "Carden will not—"

Scartozzar caught her silk-clad shoulder, his voice dropping to a tone more serious than any he had ever used with her before. "Men change, Neira. Carden ceased being an ally long ago. Listen to me. You must flee. You know what will happen if Eltanin gains both the dagger and Lynet."

Neira glanced at the spell Sphere in the center of the cavern.

"I will not let Eltanin take Lynet," Scartozzar said grimly, "no matter the cost. You can do no less keeping Dwynai, the *stealing dagger,* out of his hands."

"I will not fail," Neira promised as she gripped the bundle. A deep boom echoed through the caves as the challenge to the shield became an open attack. The wolfhound jerked, his body anxious, ears alert, tail stiff behind him. "Easy, boy." Neira patted his neck. "This battle is not for you." With a crook of her finger, she summoned a cloak from a nearby peg, then hurried down the tunnel leading to the Kyleglen foothills. Lleth ran at her side. Where the tunnel curved, Scartozzar saw her pause and look back.

Their eyes met.

She was a clever girl, good at magic, good at wriggling out of tight spots. Scartozzar had no time for regrets. She would survive; he did not doubt it.

As soon as Neira was out of sight, Scartozzar turned to the Sphere. Nearly six feet in diameter, it represented the most sophisticated piece of magic he had ever attempted. Its eerie light reflected off the walls and shallow pools of the cavern. Inside, ribbons of effervescent magic continued to separate from the outer shell and wrap like a transparent mummy's cloth around the woman suspended in its center. Lynet's body was tense, her eyes closed in a fitful sleep. As Scartozzar watched, her hands clenched into fists as if she knew what he was up to, and she would resist him if she could.

It was foolish to tempt the Nornir like this, but if the gods could make mistakes, why couldn't he? For this was certainly a mistake on both their parts. Inside that bubble breathed something that should not exist: an emotion-driven mortal with the power of death and life, not only in her hands or womb like a normal woman, but in her mind. With a thought, Lynet could lay waste to an entire village, a country, perhaps even the world—and with a thought, reanimate it all into life. Who could blame Scartozzar for wanting to tap into it—to skim a single layer off the surface of that almighty power?

Eltanin wanted it. If stealing Lynet's magic was possible, it was better it came to Scartozzar than to that throne-grabbing foreigner. Of course, Scartozzar would need the newly discovered Dwynai to complete the process; simple enough, so long as Neira kept the dagger safe.

Scartozzar had never resorted to using magic to steal magic before.

He'd always gotten it the easy way, by wooing a woman until she heard the *Kærásti Fórnsöngr* and willingly shared her riches with him. He'd left behind many broken hearts over the years, each new lover gifting him a generous share of her abilities, which he in no way reciprocated.

The natural laws of Norðrlönd could not help him this time, though. Lynet's heart belonged to the Vökumaðr. Not that Scartozzar wanted a lover's portion of Lynet's hellish power, anyhow. It was too volatile, too wrong. Someday she would lose control. When that day came, Scartozzar hoped to be powerful enough to survive the aftermath.

He had a plan—one he hadn't been entirely honest about. No one, not even Neira, knew the extent of it.

When the Sphere was ready, Scartozzar would change Lynet's appearance and send her to the Outside world, to the house where he grew up. There she would be safe from Eltanin. Scartozzar had already woven a memory spell into the sparkling ribbons surrounding her. Lynet would remember none of this—not the lies he had used to get her into the Sphere, nor the pain of losing Ronan. Time on the Outside flew at an alarming pace; lifetimes came and went in the space of a few Norðrlönd years. If the hags of fate were smart, Lynet would live out her life in blissful ignorance and pass on to the grave without Eltanin ever finding her.

But not before Scartozzar took his fill. As soon as he could, he planned to slip across the Divide, taking Dwynai with him. One small stab of the stealing dagger would transfer Lynet's magic to Scartozzar. He would hold the dagger for no more than a moment, absorbing only what he dared. Lynet would wake from a troubled dream to find she'd cut herself, and not know how.

Another tremendous blow struck the cavern, followed by the ominous sound of shale cracking and splintering overhead. Scartozzar's ringed fingers fashioned a sigil in the air. He wrapped his mind around his emotions, squeezing them tighter and tighter until they had no choice but to ignite into flame. With a flick of his wrist, he aimed the hot searing spell at the ceiling, fusing the cracks that stretched and spidered out across the cavern roof.

Scartozzar sensed the battle raging outside. Damaged, clinging to life, the cavern shield struggled to withstand the heavy barrage. There was no time to conjure a new one, but perhaps Scartozzar could give the dying shield strength. He chanted the first verse of a Renewal spell even as the walls quaked. It was too little too late. The shield dissolved. The wall fell.

Rock and sand blasted the wizard, knocking him down, pelting, choking him with dust. In the center of the room, the cosseted Sphere swirled unmolested, the sleeping woman untouched by the world around her.

Shadow fell across the rubble. A towering figure stood outlined by the sun. His long red hair blew wildly in the sea breeze. With a subtle gesture, the intruder sent a flash of light into the dark places of the cavern—searching.

Scartozzar guessed his intent. Eltanin's son would exploit any weakness, but Neira was safely out of reach.

Carden brushed a puki from his shoulder and entered the sanctuary. A tight, mocking sneer curved his lips. "The puki tell me you're hiding something"—Carden's attention turned to Lynet—"and so you are." He tested the glowing outer shell with his fingertips, jerking back, stung, as white sparks flew. Carden snorted. "What is this?" He circled the Sphere, looking for a way inside.

Scartozzar stood, but did not answer.

Through settling dust and broken wall, Scartozzar saw a dozen mercenaries streaming across the sand toward the caverns. Behind them, where the tangled forest edged the shore, trees toppled, their ancient trunks uprooted, as some unseen terror ripped them from the ground in a wide path of destruction. The earth shuddered beneath the weight of slow, mammoth footsteps. Nos'kag magic, like a black smoke, crept down from the forest and spread across the sand. Fear filled Scartozzar's heart. He knew of only one man with power enough to summon a dreaded demon of Ogluidh.

Eltanin himself had come.

Against that depraved wizard and his foul demon, Scartozzar was flatly outmatched. With the Vökumaðr's aid, Scartozzar might have stood a chance, but Ronan was dead. There would be no heroic rescue.

Scartozzar had two choices. He could grovel and feed Eltanin lies, or fight and try to last long enough to send Lynet to the nonmagic Outside world. His survival instinct was strong, and lying might gain him a few weeks of life, but Scartozzar wanted more. If Lynet stayed here, Eltanin would take her awful magic. Scartozzar did not need a vision to predict who would be the first to die when Eltanin tested his new power.

There was no choice, not really. Scartozzar would do whatever it took to send Lynet across the Divide.

Black lightning crackled the air.

Scartozzar spun as a dark spell streaked past, shattering more of the wall behind him. Shards flew, slicing into his side and arm. Blood spread across his finely embroidered sleeve and dripped down his fingertips.

Across the cavern, Carden's face contorted with anger. "You actually turned your back to me? Do you think me so little threat?" Carden's fist snapped open, releasing another spell.

Scartozzar smashed a protection orb onto the ground. A wall of magic splashed up to shield him, but it was not enough. The force of Carden's spell broke through the shield and plowed into Scartozzar's chest. He landed several feet away, gasping for breath.

Slowly, Scartozzar got to his feet, blood flowing freely now. His casting fingers felt oddly numb. He might very well die this day, but he would be damned if it would be at the hands of this overweening upstart. Forcing his tingling fingers to obey, Scartozzar began the first mutterings of an attack spell.

He hated being rushed.

Betrayed

EIRA RAN. LLETH KEPT PACE AT HER SIDE. Often the wolfhound paused, or trotted back the way they came, his keen nose testing the wind. Neira kept running, knowing he would catch up. The hound was spoiling for a fight—so was she. Scartozzar was wrong to send her away. She should be there, beside him, as she had countless times before. He had been her mentor, her guardian, since she was nine years old. She'd spent over half her life in service to him. How could he doubt her skill or her loyalty?

At the crest of the first hill, Neira turned and looked down on the sea caves below. Kynneeyn Gorrym overran the broken caverns. Through the split walls, she saw the flash and shadow of opposing magics as they clashed. Borne on the frigid ocean wind, the sounds of battle swooped up the side of the foothills, clear and chilling to her ears.

A monster, twenty feet tall, horned and cloven hoofed, joined the fray. Nos'kag magic oozed from it like a black fog, rolling along the ground, saturating all with dread and fear. Three Kynneeyn Gorrym warriors faltered as the fog surrounded them. Two broke off and ran. The demon scooped up the deserters and pushed them twisting and screaming into his mouth.

Where was Eltanin? Neira glanced around her, afraid of seeing the molten-eyed wizard.

A shocked cry rent the air—a familiar cry.

White light exploded out of the caves. Like a thousand needles, it shot in all directions, piercing the sky, the land, the water.

Neira shrank to the earth. Her arm swept the air as she raised a shield over herself and the hound. The white needles showered down, bouncing riotously off the surface of the shield, burning holes and fissures into the dirt and foliage around them. Neira held onto Lleth, overwhelmed by the finality of that stunned cry.

What should she do? *What should she do?* Grief and fear caught as dry sobs in her chest. *Nothing.* She could do nothing.

The ground shook. Neira watched in horror as a giant form rose up from the depths of the ocean—Rán, the grave goddess of the sea. Her body appeared as a wide green wave, her arms white foam, her hair and headdress a ruby-colored coral. She looked down on the scene before her and with a circling of her arms crashed against the ancient caverns, destroying, reclaiming, wiping out all trace of human settlement, until only eroded stone and sand remained. Neira covered her face in despair. Did even the gods obey Eltanin's command?

Rán slid into the ocean. The sea calmed. Silence. No birds, no wind. Then from the ruins arose the black demon. Rocks and sand rolled from its wide back as it staggered to its feet.

Ronan tried to lift his head, but the filthy strap at the back of his neck held tight. He was naked, lying face down, his cheek flat against the stone floor. Dried blood caked his nose and matted the whiskers around his mouth. His strength returned, but he did not doubt his tormentors meant to resume their games before he fully healed. How many days had passed since he tried to kill Eltanin? Three, four? He knew only that he was never conscious long enough to escape.

His Vökumaðr body kept him alive—but it could not clear the haze in his mind that blocked his connection to the Hoar Beast. Each time he awoke, Ronan called to the Beast, grasping for the rage that defined the Vökumaðr.

There was no answer.

Was this how his father had died, his uncles, his kin? Trapped in human form, unable to commune with their animal halves. Controlled by some force outside themselves.

Someone controlled Ronan now. He listened to the Governance, tried to see past the haze to the mind that held him. There was only fog, a thick smoke that hid the identity of his master.

In their youth, Ronan and Prince Edan had spent long hours training in the use of the Hoar Beast. They practiced the Summons until Edan could call forth the Beast in full battle rage, and send it safely back again. It hadn't been easy, and several times the only thing standing between the prince and certain death was King Urien, who would enter the Beast's mind and send it back to the astral plane where it slept.

Ronan always knew exactly who was in control. But not this time. Something was in the way, blocking both his communication with the Beast and his ability to see the mind of the person who held him bound.

Only a member of the Royal House had the power to control the Vökumenn. Of all the vile counterfeits Eltanin knew, there was no spell to mimic that innate gift.

Who had betrayed the Watchmen?

Ronan heard the jingle of Boadhagh's keys in the hall and the footsteps of at least three men—along with the taunting *clunk, clunk, clunk* of a club as it rapped against the stone wall.

Boadhagh. Ronan had little respect for the beefy jail keeper. Vökumenn settled disputes and meted out punishments on the battlefield; to them, the king's prisons were unnecessary. Ronan's father, Jarl Bernhard, believed imprisonment did no good as a punishment; the offender seldom learned anything other than how to hone his skills. In contrast, the jarl's "lessons" instilled in criminals a lifelong fear of wrongdoing—if they survived them.

Boadhagh had resented the jarl's interference in what he considered his rightful jurisdiction. Ronan was sure he now paid the price for his father's trespasses.

Torture and abuse suited the jailer. Boadhagh had fashioned himself a club with crude spikes of iron protruding out on all sides so it resembled a warrior's mace. More than once, Ronan had felt those spikes rip into his flesh, felt his bones crack under the force of Boadhagh's blows.

Clunk, clunk.

Reflex took over and Ronan yanked on the crisscrossed tangle of ropes and chains. It was futile—still he pulled. His muscles strained, newly healed skin stretched and split. Without the Beast, he had only a man's strength. Frustration welled inside him until it burst out as the roar of a cornered animal, echoing off the walls of his cell.

He heard hesitation in the footsteps outside the door and took what satisfaction he could, though he knew it would not stop what was coming.

The key turned in the cell door.

They always asked questions: Drem, the Kynneeyn Gorrym chieftain; and Mathkr, the heathen pig good King Urien threw from his halls last summer. They asked Ronan about the *forspá*, about Lynet and the dagger called Dwynai. Once they had even asked about Prince Maxwell, which made no sense. The prince had died in the takeover. Ronan recalled few details of the exchanges, since Drem allowed Boadhagh to beat Ronan almost senseless before the interrogations began.

"Still alive? Amazing," Mathkr said as they crowded into the cell. "If you cut off his arm, Boadhagh, will he grow a new one?"

Boadhagh rapped the club on the stone floor beside Ronan's face. "Only one way to find out."

Ronan did not flinch. He could not call the Beast, but he could control his body and his ability to heal. Ronan looked inward, focusing his mind and body on survival. He had to.

Lynet waited for him.

As the first blow broke his shoulder, Ronan saw Lynet's sweet face. He remembered her standing on the shore at Aros, her golden hair floating in the wind, her deep blue eyes following him as he slipped . . . farther . . . and farther . . . away.

Neira ran headlong through the trees. Lleth hurtled alongside, often disappearing into the distance, then waiting for her to catch up. Neira hardly noticed, more concerned with the demon chasing behind.

On she ran. Her silk hood bunched around her neck. Her damp, chestnut hair stuck to her face. She clutched at the stitch in her side as she darted between trees and ducked under low-hanging branches. The pounding of her heart matched her steps—erratic, noisy, each beat echoing the same frantic message: *Scartozzar is dead. Scartozzar is dead.*

The home they'd shared for the last year was gone. Nothing remained except for stray bodies of Kynneeyn Gorrym caught in shallow, muddy pools, their black skin dotted with sand . . . and the deep imprint of the demon's footsteps as he turned toward the foothills.

Scartozzar should have let her stay with him.

She could have helped, could have reasoned with Carden. Together they could have defended the caverns. Now, Scartozzar was gone, leaving her to protect the dagger on her own.

Neira tightened her hold on the precious bundle, tears streaking her face. She was angry with both of them: Scartozzar for his lack of faith in her, and Carden for failing when she needed him.

And now, this overwhelming responsibility, to keep the dagger out of Eltanin's hands, fell to her.

Eltanin. The most powerful wizard Norðrlönd had known in a thousand years. Through his treachery, the kingdom was in upheaval, the Vökumenn defeated, the royal family murdered.

Now he had Lynet. Why else would the demon chase after them? Eltanin wanted—needed—the dagger to complete his plans.

Neira checked the sky overhead. She'd been running for close on two hours. The sun edged the horizon, but it was not yet summer. She could not depend on it to light her way throughout the night. Not that she could keep running. DuwaŴyr Mountain, the sacred dwelling place of the Annars and home of the wise man Cian Druce, was several days away over hilly terrain. She needed more than speed; she needed some kind of strategy.

Limping, her breathing ragged, Neira halted and dropped another spell onto the ground behind her. Their footsteps vanished. A mile behind, two sets of prints—one belonging to a girl, one to a large dog—crisscrossed her trail, then raced off in another direction. Praying the ruse would buy her time to rest, Neira stumbled to a pile of moldering leaves at the base of a gnarled beech tree and collapsed onto them.

Lleth rooted and scratched at the ground, circled the area and then plunked down, panting, beside her. Neira reached out and halfheartedly scratched his ear, her eyes closing in exhaustion. Her mouth was so dry. She knew a spell for drawing water from the air. If she rested a bit, perhaps she'd have the strength to conjure it. When she woke up, she could—

Her eyes snapped open. Did she dare fall asleep? The spells she left behind might fool Eltanin for a while, but he would soon figure out her intent and use Carden's nasty, time-twisting puki to leap ahead and overtake her.

Neira swayed as she stood up and extended her left hand away from her body. Better to face the enemy rested than to let Eltanin catch her too tired to put up a fight.

Clearing her mind, Neira sorted through her memories until she found one of Scartozzar conjuring a Warn spell. As the scene unfolded, she slowed it down to catch each inflection of his voice, every nuance of the sigil. Neira had a unique gift—the ability to recall her past exactly as it had happened. At times like this, when she needed to work a spell she hadn't used in a while, the talent was a useful ally. When it replayed the loss of a loved one to the last excruciating detail, it was no less than a curse.

Neira copied the motions from memory and uttered the words to bring a Warn spell to life. She didn't have time to nurture it to full grown; an infant spell would have to do.

From deep inside her came the miracle of *spellbirth*, that amazing moment when a spell gained cognizance and life. Neira opened her hand and released the spell. Hovering in the air above her, it shimmered, taking on the camouflage color and shape of the leafy canopy overhead. The spell was young and inexperienced, but happy to serve as lookout. Grateful for the magic's cooperation, Neira wrapped her cloak tight and burrowed under the rotting leaves. Beneath her, she clutched the bundled dagger. At her back, the wolfhound lay watching the path behind them.

A Life Forgotten

T HE WOMAN OPENED HER EYES. Sunlight filled the small bedroom. She'd expected . . . something else. What? Flashes of light. Falling rock. The sound of the sea. That made no sense. Probably a dream. With a drowsy smile she rolled over and reached for—

Who? No one was there.

She glanced around the room, her eyes alighting on familiar objects, books, and furniture. Everything untouched and in its normal place. Except . . . what was that small squarish shape on the wall? Her mind provided an answer. *Light switch*. She frowned. Light switch? What was a light switch? What did it do?

She left the bed. Cautiously, she flipped the lever on the wall. The lights in the room came on. Again, her mind provided the word: *electricity*. How could she know this—and not know it—at the same time? She turned and caught a glimpse of her reflection in the vanity mirror. A pale, black-haired woman stared back at her. The neck of her ill-fitting nightgown slid low over a bony shoulder.

Who is that?

Her stomach turned cold. With unsteady fingers, she touched her cheek and lips. Her skin was abnormally pale, almost translucent. Her hair was black, darker than the deepest pitch on a sailor's mop. Her eyes had no distinguishable color—no blue, no brown, just dark. Dead. She looked dead. Panicked, she ran her hands over the curves of her body. No injuries. No holes. She seemed fit enough.

Her mind rebelled. That ghastly person in the mirror was not her. She was . . . *who*? What was her name? Her back hit the door as she stumbled away from the mirror. This was her room, but what was her name? Why couldn't she remember her name? She fumbled with the knob and yanked open the door. Her fingers trailed along the faded wallpaper as she fled down a familiar hall. She recognized the three paintings in the corridor, eerie portrayals of a gray stone fortress. Her bare feet remembered the wear in the rose-patterned carpet and knew to step over the frayed tear near the window. She knew this house. She knew where the stairs led, knew which way to go to find the kitchen, the bathrooms, and the front door. How could she know the house and not know herself?

She raced down the stairs, faltering on the last few. Her stomach felt sick. Now where? *Voices.* She heard cheerful voices coming from the kitchen and hurried toward them. The smell of baking bread and fragrant flowers met her as she entered. A kind-faced woman sat at the wooden table. The woman was chubby and middle-aged, her faded ginger hair pulled into a loose knot at the back of her head. She had the thick arms of a person who worked hard for a living, and she was using that strength to twist and braid green vines into a wreath.

Beside her darted a funny little boy, less than three feet tall, and yet as perfectly proportioned as any slender, gangly youth. His almond-shaped eyes took up half of his face, leaving just enough room for a tiny, sharply pointed nose and laughing mouth. His hair was fine and wispy, and danced around his face as he moved—which he did constantly. His ears extended out into thin, delicate points with tufts of hair at the tips. Even his skin was peculiar, rough and red like a pecan shell. She knew him; knew he shouldn't be here, knew she must protect him from those who would not understand. Yet, she also knew she'd never set eyes on him before in her life.

"You're awake!" the boy said happily. He danced over to take her hand. The air around him seemed to move and ripple.

Fig. His name was Fig . . . and the woman was Trilla . . . no . . . that wasn't right. Maple, her name was Maple. How did she know this? "I'm afraid," she whispered. "Maple, what's happened to me? Who am I?"

Maple set aside the half-finished wreath. "You're Lynet, child," the woman said gently. "It's all right. You are safe now. The danger is past."

Lynet. At last, something felt right. She was Lynet. Relieved, she gripped Fig's hand and waited for the nightmare to end now that she knew her name.

A strand of unnaturally black hair slid over her bare shoulder.

She waited.

Nothing changed.

No flood of memory, no waking up from a bad dream.

Lynet caught the strand of hair and showed it to Maple. "Why don't I recognize this?" She trembled. "Why do I know you and Fig? How can I know you and not know myself?"

Maple's brow furrowed. "Sit down. Tell me what you do remember." The matriarch turned to Fig. "Go get Alder. Tell him Lynet is awake."

The boy giggled and moved so fast, Lynet barely caught a glimpse of him going through the door.

Maple pulled out a chair. "Sit, dear. What do you remember?"

"I don't remember anything until I see it." Lynet sat at the wooden table. "Then I know what it is automatically." She pointed to the refrigerator. "That thing is a fridge. The name just came to me. What it does I don't know. Wait—you preserve food in it." Lynet looked at Maple. "What is wrong with me?"

"I'm not sure. . . ." Maple hesitated, then continued. "You were in an accident. Do you remember what happened?"

"Accident?" Lynet shook her head. "What accident?" The jumbled images of her dream flashed behind her eyes. *Clouds of dust and broken shale. Shouting. Bright, piercing light. The thunder of the sea.* "What kind of accident? Was it near water? Was anyone hurt?"

The lines around Maple's mouth grew tight. "Do you know why you're here with us?"

"No," Lynet said flatly, tiring of the endless questions, both from Maple and from her own troubled brain.

"You were with our foster son, Scar," Maple said finally. She seemed to have made a decision, and her tone grew more confident, although Lynet had no idea whether she told the truth or not. "After the accident, he sent you here to recover. You've been asleep for several days."

"Days?" Lynet asked in alarm. "Why days? Was I hurt?"

"You didn't appear to be," Maple mused, "but obviously something isn't right. You were unconscious, peaceful. We thought it best to let your body sort itself out; apparently it needs more time." Maple smiled and picked up the vine wreath. "Don't worry. We live in a quiet neighborhood, and Devil's Gate has been closed for centuries. You're safe. No one knows you're here."

"No one knows? Why not? What about my family?" Lynet sank back, her hands on her forehead. Her head pounded so hard she thought it might burst. "Do I even *have* a family?" she asked. "Where do I come from? Where is Scar? When can I talk to him?"

Maple's hands grew still. "Scar didn't come with you, though we expected him. In fact, we hoped you could tell us what happened to him."

Maple's tone—the concern in her voice—troubled Lynet more than anything she had seen or heard since she woke up. Whatever ruined Lynet's memories had done something equally awful to Scar, and now he was missing. Did they blame her?

Was she to blame?

A burly, brown-haired man strode into the kitchen. As it had before, Lynet's mind provided a name: *Alder Macarthur. These are the Macarthurs.*

Alder's arms were big, his eyes the color of chestnuts. His body stood thick and tall, like the trunk of a large tree. "What's the boy done this time?" Alder's voice rumbled through the room like far-off thunder. "Fig says the girl's memories are scrambled. What did Scar do? Put his own in there?"

Maple got to her feet. "Now Alder, it's too soon to make any assumptions. She's barely awake. We know nothing for certain. Perhaps Scar told her about us. There's no reason to think—"

"There's *every* reason to think," Alder interrupted. "You know what that boy's capable of. Playing with the mind is magic of the darkest sort." He shot a glance at Lynet, then turned his thunder to Maple. "How bad is it?"

Maple sighed. "She doesn't know who she is."

Alder's face went the deep red of autumn leaves. "Mother Earth! How will she protect herself? How will we protect ourselves from her? We can't do this. Where are the confounded Vökumenn?"

"Protect me from what?" Lynet stood. "Am I in danger?"

"Of course not. Alder is overly excited, that's all. You are perfectly safe." Maple came around the table to her husband. Her voice lowered. "Laburnum House has protected us for years; it will safeguard Lynet as well. The Vökumenn will come. Whatever Scar did will sort itself out. In the meantime, it's best if we don't talk about *certain things*."

The storm sputtered. Lynet watched as Alder's face lost its ripe red color. The room seemed to sigh as he let out a breath and nodded to his wife. Maple stroked his arm and smiled at Lynet. "You have questions. I don't know if we can answer them all, but we'll try. Now, however, is not the time. Why don't you go upstairs and lie down? I'll call you when dinner is ready. You can meet the rest of the family. When all of us are together, we will talk."

Lynet intended to hold out for answers—but swift movement outside the window caught her attention. She hurried out onto the porch and watched as a shiny red *vehicle* rolled down the street and out of sight.

Alder joined her. "Automobile," he said with obvious dislike.

Lynet was curious about the automobile, but it was just one of many wild concepts flooding her mind. She stepped down off the porch, rubbing her bare arms in the chilly spring air. She should put on sensible clothes, and she would, soon enough. Lynet walked across the lawn. *Garage. Fire hydrant.* Again, an inexplicable spark of recognition provided Lynet with the name and rough, often confusing, meaning of each new thing she saw. Her heart leapt at the swift flow of discovery. *Telephone lines. Satellite dish.* She laughed. There was so much to see, to know, to understand. Her name was Lynet. She was as ugly as the dead, with no recollection of her past—and right now, she didn't care. Nothing—no worry, no fear—rivaled her wonder at this strange, amazing world.

A Life Surrendered

YNET CANNOT STAY WITH US," Alder said. It was evening. Maple sat at the kitchen table, bracing for an argument. Across from her sat Alder's apple-cheeked sister, Jól, and her husband, Treddian. Maple knew they looked to Alder for direction. If Maple disagreed, it would be an uphill battle—but how could she not? For the first time in years, she was afraid. The decision made this night, whichever way it went, would change everything.

"We can't protect her," Alder continued. "Already Ysbail drives me mad with her mental taps. One loose thought and the Red Wicche will bring Eltanin's men down on us."

The others nodded in agreement.

"Ysbail is getting bolder," Jól admitted.

"She nearly caught me off guard this afternoon when I left the house," Treddian said. "She has become quite insistent in her attempts to peek inside my head."

"She seeks Lynet. If we turn the girl out, then the Red Wicche will find her," Maple said. "We've become complacent over the years; it will do us good to guard our thoughts. Ysbail hasn't searched this place for ages; she has no interest in us."

"She would if she knew *you* lived here," Jól pointed out.

"She doesn't," Maple said. "I am of no concern to her anymore. Lynet, however—"

"Lynet," Alder cut her off, "holds the powers of the Sòlasach. Do any of you know what that means? We haven't strength among us to contain it."

"Scartozzar exaggerates," Treddian said. "Suthainn magic is a myth. The Sòlasach left Norðrlönd eons ago and took their dreaded magic with them."

"What if it *is* true?" Jól asked. "Can Lynet control it? Does she even remember how? Her memories are all mixed up. It does seem dangerous."

"It would be more dangerous to abandon her," Maple said, her tone every bit as serious as Alder's. "We must assume Scartozzar is right, and Lynet holds the keys to life and death. In her present state, she may not know she has them. We cannot be faint-hearted. She needs our help."

"Help with what?" Jól asked. "She certainly doesn't need protection, does she? The girl can kill anyone."

Maple looked steadfastly at her husband; he was the one she needed to convince. "Lynet doesn't remember who she is or where she is from," Maple said. "If she doesn't remember Norðrlönd, then I think it is safe to assume she doesn't know she has magic. In fact, that might be a good thing. The less she knows, the easier it will be to protect her from divination. Ysbail searches for someone with great inner strength and power. Right now, Lynet appears to Ysbail as a naïve, non-magic Outsider. The Red Wicche will flit over her without notice."

"Lynet can't possibly stay naïve, not while she lives in this house." Treddian flung his arms wide to include all of them as well as the ever changing building they lived in.

"She can if we stop using magic ourselves; if we hide it from her and let Lynet think we are a normal Outsider family."

"Impossible. What about Fig? She's already seen him. Miss Moat and her young roam all over the place. Not to mention Laburnum House itself. You think Lynet won't notice the first time a window moves or a room grows an extra door?"

Maple sighed. "No, I suppose there are certain things we can't hide. Nevertheless, I think it is a mistake to turn Lynet away. Scartozzar entrusted her into our care. Evil men will use her magic against us, against the whole world, unless we stop them."

Alder pounded his fist on the table, rattling the cups and saucers. "Where are the damned Vökumenn? They are the guardians. This should not be our problem."

"And yet, it is," Maple said softly. "A problem we cannot ignore." She covered his fist with her palm and did the only thing she could do: leave the decision to her husband, and trust him to make the right choice.

Neira liked to dream. In her dreams, she was brave and daring. She was brave now. Eltanin closed in, but she wasn't afraid. She stood boldly, waiting for him to come. At her feet lay a pile of glowing orbs. She was ready.

"You cannot fight, child," a musical voice cautioned. "You must surrender."

Neira turned. "Surrender? Eltanin does not take prisoners. He will kill me."

"No, little one. He needs you."

Neira looked around. "Show yourself," she demanded. "Who are you?"

A tall, white-haired woman stepped from the shadows. Her eyes were as colorless as crystal, but her body glowed with the light of the stars.

Neira did not know if the Seer was part of her dream, or if this was a vision inside a dream. "Systir Isleen." Neira dipped her head in a quick bow. "I'm on my way to your mountain. Scartozzar sent me. I have something to give you."

The Annarian Seer shook her head. "Not yet. Today, you must go with Eltanin." She lifted a delicate white hand. "Do not speak. Time is short. Listen."

Neira prayed this was a dream. Isleen did not understand. Neira had the dagger; if she surrendered, Eltanin would take it.

"One prophecy, one forspá, does not determine the whole, Gwyneira. There are many pieces to the puzzle, and everyone has their own part to play, including you."

Neira shook her head. She was already playing her part by bringing the dagger to Isleen for safekeeping.

"Two tasks I give you," the Seer continued. "The last of the Vökumenn is condemned to die. Without him, a true king will never sit the throne. You will find him in chains in Caeraricin."

Ronan? Neira felt giddy with relief. Ronan was alive, but that meant . . . Scartozzar's vision was wrong—again. "Yes. I'll get Ronan out. Together we—"

"No," said Isleen. "You must remain at the castle. Only you can turn the heartstone to flesh. That is your second task. Norðrlönd will never be free so long as the heartstone is bound. Release it. If you fail, all is lost."

The Seer retreated into the shadows, her voice no more than the whisper of the wind. "Aid unsought you will be . . . for the proud . . . never ask. . . ."

Neira woke with a start. The Warn spell squealed like mad overhead, "Danger! Danger! Danger!"

Lleth stood a few feet away watching the trees, his body tense, his tail straight and stiff. A low growl rumbled in his throat. Neira scrambled to her feet and conjured a shield. Her left hand shot out away from her side, ready.

Nos'kag magic seeped through the trees, fouling all it touched. She backed away, but the shadow surrounded her; climbed up her body like a choking vine, seeking a way past the shield. Neira grew weak, her mind confused as a chilling dread filled her breast. She stumbled and brushed at the shadow, fighting to maintain control of her senses. She called a second shield, inside the first, and wrapped it tight around her. She could beat this. She was resourceful and absurdly lucky; she just needed time to think.

The ground beneath her shuddered. Something huge approached. An unimaginable evil.

Slowly her left hand drooped. The will to conjure faded, along with her strength. In some corner of her mind, Neira recognized the woe and hopelessness that accompanied creatures of Ogluidh. This perverted fear, draining her will and rendering her limp, was the tool of demons.

Eltanin had found her.

Neira heard the groan of dying trees as the creature rammed its way through the woods. The Warn spell continued to shrill. Its voice rattled Neira's nerves, but she couldn't think how to make it stop.

The steps came closer.

Thud.

Thud.

The demon would kill her. Eltanin would take the dagger.

"You must go with Eltanin." The message from her dream echoed in the air around her. *"Surrender."*

Never. Neira shook her head to rid herself of the Seer's unwelcome speech. She refused to surrender to Eltanin. And refused to defend her choice to a crazy voice inside her head. Angry, Neira pushed her left hand away from her side as she gasped out the words of an Attack spell.

Thud.

Thud.

Lleth's hackles rose. His long teeth glistened, his body quivering, but not with fear. A demon's magic could not fool the dogs of Norðrlönd; they saw through the thickest of spells. Neira wished she had Lleth's instinct and strength of will. The closer the demon came, the harder it was to draw breath. If she did not control her fear, she would be prostrate on the ground, leaving Lleth alone to—

Die.

If she stood against Eltanin, the wolfhound would die.

If she surrendered, let herself be captured, Eltanin would take the dagger, and still Lleth would die.

Thud.

"Lle—" Her voice cracked and she tried again. "Lleth. Come here."

The hound came, bumping into her, knocking her back several steps. Neira caught her balance, but not before the half-formed Attack spell squeezed rebelliously through her fingers and escaped. *Damn.* Raw magic was dangerous.

Appalled that the spell mutinied now when she was already in so much trouble, Neira snatched the wayward magic from the air. Mimicking one of Carden's favorite tricks, she conjured anew. The magical energy fought, but the new spell consumed the old as Neira transformed a nearby fallen branch into a thin coil of rope, which she used to fasten the bundled dagger around Lleth's neck. "Take this to Cian Druce," she told him. "He will give it to the Annars, and they will keep it from Eltanin."

Thud.

The dog whined and sidestepped around her. Lleth was a royal war hound, bred for battle. He *wanted* to fight.

"Please." Neira held his wiry face, hoping that traces of Scartozzar's Translate spell still clung to him, and that he would understand the importance of the errand she now transferred to him. "Take the dagger to the Druce. I'll be all right. Take the dagger to Cian Druce."

Thud.

Neira stood and pushed against Lleth's hindquarters. "Go. You must go." The wolfhound gave an unhappy bark, circled twice, then disappeared into the trees, heading toward DuwaŴyr Mountain.

Neira had no strength left to conjure a decoy to cover his tracks.

Thud.

Lleth needed time to escape, to get the dagger away from here. She had to keep Eltanin's attention on her and not the hound. With the Warn spell still shrieking in her ears, Neira turned to face her enemy.

The demon broke through the trees in front of her. A black mountain of fat, muscle, and claws, it opened its mouth and the howling cries of a thousand damned souls filled the air.

Neira shook in terror. She could not run. She could not speak. Her knees buckled and she sprawled onto the ground. Nos'kag magic engulfed her, turning the blood in her veins to ice, pouring into her mouth, filling her stomach, churning and bubbling until she heaved and vomited.

Thud.

The next step would be on top of her.

The Outside World

ARE THOSE FRIES READY YET, JOEY? The lady at table six is threatening to come back here and cook them herself." Lynet shoved her order pad into her white cotton apron pocket, grabbed two glasses and filled them with fizzing soda.

"Don't make him mad," a waitress with short, white, spiky, red-tipped hair warned her. "He'll send them up raw."

"He wouldn't dare," Lynet grumbled, but not loud enough for Joey to hear. Some days she wondered why she bothered to work at this seedy little diner. She didn't need to. In fact, Maple told her at least once a week to quit her job, which truth told, was probably why she stayed. She loved the Macarthurs, but they didn't understand. She needed to keep moving, keep busy, or she'd go crazy.

Lynet glanced at her watch. "Eibby, can you cover for me? I have to make a phone call."

"Sure. Just don't get sidetracked. You did that to me Saturday and it wasn't fun."

"Two minutes, I promise." Lynet handed Eibby the drinks. "These are for table two."

"Wait. You are *not* going to see another crackpot doctor, are you?" Eibby sighed. "Lynet, there is nothing wrong with you. So, you forgot a few things, no big deal. People suppress bad memories all the time. Let it go. If you forgot, it was for a reason; don't fight it. Your brain doesn't want to remember. You should respect that."

"I need to know, Eibby. Don't harass me. I get enough at home. Waiting is not helping. Besides, hypnosis could be the trigger to jog my memory."

"So could bungee jumping." Eibby offered. "Come with me on Saturday. Nothing like the fear of death to make your entire life pass before your eyes."

"Ah, no." Lynet didn't bother to argue.

"I've got tickets to the Sabres game next month against Pittsburgh. If you come with me Saturday, I'll take you to the game."

"You'll take me to the hockey game either way," Lynet called over her shoulder as she went out the back door.

Lynet stood outside in the alleyway and let the cool autumn breeze blow away some of the stink in her hair and on her clothes. It was the thing she hated most about working here. Every night, she went home reeking of the deep fryer. The job wasn't completely awful, though. She liked working with Eibby. They'd become fast friends. Lynet swore, without the overly dramatic Theatre major from the University of Buffalo to run around with, she would have gone mad these last months.

Lynet punched out the doctor's number on her phone.

Busy.

Maple had promised Lynet her memories would return—well, they hadn't. Days had evaporated into weeks, and then months, and here she was, still no closer to understanding why her life read like a cheap murder mystery. At least she knew who she wasn't; the ideas, the memories in her head were not hers at all. According to Maple, they belonged to a foster boy who had grown up and moved away—Scar, the man who'd sent her here after the 'accident', then disappeared.

It was strange, though—not just the memory sharing—but Scar himself. Maple had shown her pictures of him—he was not the red-haired man she'd expected. Of course, Lynet didn't know if the face she remembered was even real. Perhaps the handsome redhead was from a dream or, more likely, her desperate imagination.

Eibby thought the guy was Lynet's ex-boyfriend, the one who'd messed up her head. Lynet wasn't so sure. He was gorgeous. Why would he date someone who looked like she'd fallen off a meat wagon?

Lynet hit the redial button.

Still busy.

As crazy as her ideas usually were, Eibby Laux was Lynet's lifeline to normality. Buffalo was her hometown, and she knew all the best places to hang out. In the months since they'd met, Lynet had been to three different art galleries, choked on Widow Maker hot sauce at A Taste of Buffalo, and worked her way through an entire basket of Anchor Bar Buffalo wings. She'd visited the Botanical Gardens, been elbowed and doused with beer at more than one concert at Thursday at the Square, and melted in the heat watching Eibby perform at Shakespeare in the Park.

Then there was the Barony of the Rhydderich Hael, a local branch of the Society for Creative Anachronism. Of course, Eibby belonged to it. They were just like her—passionate and a little nutty. A Middle Ages reenactment group who liked to dress up in long gowns and armor, play lutes, and fight with remarkably-loud-when-struck rattan swords and foam maces.

As far as Lynet was concerned, Eibby was the perfect friend: funny, open, and nonjudgmental. She didn't care about Lynet's super-private home life, which was a good thing, since Laburnum House was impossible to explain.

Lynet tried the number again and got through. "Hello? Is this Doctor Hind's office? Um . . . I have a problem."

"Go. GO. Nooooo!" Lynet screamed at the hockey players on the ice as a scramble near the goal ended with the Pittsburgh Penguins gaining the puck.

Eibby laughed and offered Lynet more nachos. "Here, give your voice a rest before you lose it entirely."

Lynet scooped jalapeño cheese with a handful of tortilla chips, keeping her eyes on the hockey game. They had fantastic seats, at the top of the glass behind the goalie. It was perfect for seeing all the gory detail any time a player got shoved face first against the clear barrier. Lynet couldn't explain why the violent sport thrilled her, but it did. She loved the fast pace, the chase, the stretch of muscle and the crisp *crack* every time a player whacked the puck.

A couple of players got into a fight, gloves came off, and Lynet shouted with the crowd as her favorite forward entered the penalty box. "This stinks." Lynet checked the game clock, and used the lull to grab a drink. She and Eibby were rummaging at their feet looking for root beer when the crowd roared. Lynet looked up to see the Sabres charging for the goal, Penguins scrambling to keep up. She jumped to her feet cheering as the puck shot toward the net.

At the last minute, the goalie smacked the puck away, clipping it at an odd angle. The puck flipped up into the air, cleared the glass wall, and spun straight for Lynet. She threw her arms up to cover her face—

There was a flash of blue. A distinct '*ting*' as the puck ricocheted off her arm, and bounced back toward the ice.

"Oh my gosh! Are you all right?" Eibby threw her arms around Lynet, catching her as she swayed. "Did it hit you? Are you bleeding?"

Lynet felt like jelly. Her nerves tingled as if her entire body was one big jolted funny bone. *What happened?* She should be flat on her backside with a bruise the size of a fist. Instead, she was fine; more than fine; nothing broken; no blood. The puck was back in play—and every inch of her prickled and stung like waking from a deep sleep.

"Did you see that?" she asked Eibby. "The flash of blue?"

"Blue? You mean like little blue birdies singing cuckoo over your head?"

"No, there was a blue spark. Eibby, the puck never even hit me."

"Yeah, well, here comes Security. You better not mention any blue flash, or they'll drug test you."

Lynet looked overhead to see her pale face on the JumboTron as Security and ushers converged on their row of seats. Two big men in white shirts and black badges insisted Lynet come with them to the First Aid Office to be checked over. Lynet was glad to leave the spotlight.

A short time later, she sat on a chair, glass of water in her hands, while a handsome male nurse shone a small light, first in one eye, then the other.

"You look pale," he said with a smile.

"Well, it *was* frightening." Lynet didn't bother to say she tended toward deathly white as a skin tone every single day.

He examined her forehead and bunched her sweater up to check her arm. "I don't see a bruise on you. You sure you're the one who got hit?"

Lynet looked at Eibby, then at the nurse. She didn't want to be here. The tingle was fading; she needed to escape and find someplace quiet where she could figure this out before the feeling left completely. "Honestly, my eyes were closed and I ducked. It probably hit the chair."

"Sounds like you were lucky. A rogue puck can break a nose or pop out teeth. You don't even need stitches. The bad news is"—he rolled his chair over to the desk and picked up a small stack of stapled pages—"you still have to fill out a bunch of legal forms."

Lynet made a sour face.

The nurse chuckled. "My name's Jack. What's yours?"

"Lynet."

"Well, Lynet—that's a pretty name, by the way—if you would be so kind as to fill this out, and maybe mention I was especially helpful," he ended with a wide, friendly smile and wink.

Eibby mouthed a *"he's cute"* behind Jack's back.

"Sure, give it here." Lynet took the pen and waiver form and filled in her name and address.

"Our standard procedure is to insist you go to the nearest emergency room to be sure you're okay," Jack said.

"I won't need to," Lynet said. "I'm fine. Really."

"I don't know. Your color hasn't come back yet."

"Lynet is a walking Halloween advertisement," Eibby drawled. "That pallid white never goes away."

Lynet stood up and handed the form to Jack. "I'm fine. Here, I've signed and dated this. Fill in what you want. Can we go?"

Jack seemed to consider. "You don't look very healthy. I would prefer it if you stayed for at least twenty minutes of observation time. The game is over anyhow. Think of it as waiting for the parking lot to empty so you don't have to battle traffic."

Lynet flopped down on the chair. The tingle was gone completely now, along with any hope of trying to understand it. Her life was one tease after another, always the same: a moment of crystal clarity—too fleeting to grab hold of—followed by the silence of an empty brain.

Eibby sat down beside her and leaned in close. "Cheer up. He has to be better than that weird hypnosis doctor you tried last month. If you quit pouting, maybe he'll ask you out."

"Alder!" Treddian rushed into the house. "Alder. It's happening, just like you said it would."

Alder met Treddian at the bottom of the staircase. "You've been to Devil's Gate?"

Treddian nodded, out of breath. "It's glowing like embers in a fire, the surrounding ground and trees are all scorched. Is it going to open? I thought the Sòlasach closed the Gate forever."

Alder slowly sat down on the stairs. "Nothing is forever."

He knew the Fomorii, the demons of Ogluidh, had not been idle these long centuries. In their dark places, they still festered and plotted. Still, he had hoped for a few more hundred years of peace.

"They sense Lynet," Alder said. "They feel her magic and recognize its evil. We all feel it. The more she remembers, the worse it will get. The Fomorii will find a way to slip through the Gate. Sooner or later they will come for her."

"But why?" Treddian asked.

"Because, to them, Lynet is a goddess; the literal embodiment of destruction. In their eternal war against the Outside world, she is their best hope for victory."

The Watchman

THE CELL DOOR CREAKED OPEN. Ronan opened his eyes. Battle-honed reflexes demanded he call a shield, but Ronan knew if he did, the newly added copper collar around his neck would tighten. The restraint was sentient. If it sensed magic, the collar would shrink and suffocate him until he lost consciousness. He lay still, waiting for the intruder to move into his line of sight. The cell was dark, but he did not need much light to see.

A soft rustle of silk brushed against his naked skin, and Ronan felt the warmth of human breath. "I'm going to unchain you," the whisperer spoke close to his ear. Too close. The rush of air distorted the words and sent an involuntary shiver up his back.

What new torment was this?

Perhaps Boadhagh was bored. It had been three nights since the jail keeper last swung his club. Had the novelty of beating and crushing Ronan's bones, only to watch them straighten and heal again, lost its luster? Even Drem no longer came to stare. Although Mathkr still took perverted pleasure in the way Ronan's skin sealed itself when a bone punctured through. He had even brought Loptr, Prince Edan's ne'er-do-well cousin, with him once, but the weasel hadn't had the stomach for it, and Mathkr had more fun questioning the young lord's manhood than breaking Ronan's bones.

After weeks of torture, were they ready for something different?

Ronan did not call the Beast—the Beast could not answer—but that did not mean Ronan was unarmed. He was Vökumaðr. If this unwanted visitor freed his hands, then the visitor would die.

Ronan heard the scrape of a key inside a lock, then felt the chains binding his right leg loosen and drop away. The straps at his hips were next. Ronan moved slowly, not wishing to startle his assailant. He flexed his thigh, and winced as unclamped nerve endings ached deep in the muscle.

The rustle of silk moved to the other side.

Silk. The incongruity of that finally registered. He sniffed the air—a *woman*. Why was there a woman in his cell in the middle of the night? He could not use tracking to identify her. The copper collar did not distinguish between racial and traditional magic. It would choke him either way.

Ronan closed his eyes and let years of training tell him what his magic could not. Her movements were determined, her fingers deft as she released his other leg. She did not hesitate; each action seemed calculated and planned. Her grunts gave an indication of her strength. The sound of her footsteps told him her weight. Her breasts felt full and high against his ribs as she struggled to untie the straps. She was young, with newly developed curves and lingering, childhood fat. Though she was strong enough to free him, she did not have the muscles of a serving wench. Her scent, too, was different—clean and tasting of cinnamon.

Ronan had lived his entire life in this castle. He knew most of the servants and all of the soldiers. He tried to recall the women who served in the keep. None of them fit this description. Who, then? A noblewoman? A sorceress? A whore from the city?

"Mother Earth," the girl cursed softly as one of the filthy leather straps snapped free, sending her back on her heels, "that hurt!"

Ronan's eyes opened in surprise. *Neira?* Immediately, his guardian instincts took over. If Boadhagh caught her helping him, the jailer wouldn't just kill her. Ronan pulled his legs up under him and tried to break free. "What are you doing here?"

"Shhh!" Neira hissed. "Boadhagh sleeps just down the hall. We drugged him, but I don't know if he drank it all."

"We? Is Scartozzar with you? Where is Lynet? You didn't bring her here, did you? Where is she?"

"I'm alone." Neira yanked again at his bonds.

Although relieved Lynet played no part in this attempted rescue, Ronan was not satisfied. Why was Neira here alone? What was Scartozzar planning?

She knelt by his head, and Ronan saw the young girl clearly. She looked exhausted. Dark circles smudged her eyes. The lines on her face were reminiscent of dazed boy soldiers who, sticky with gore and still clutching their weapon, somehow survived that first awful battle. Her neck was stained green beneath a telltale copper collar—she was a prisoner as well. How had that happened? He wanted answers, but first he wanted freedom.

The shackles on his left arm fell away. Savagely, Ronan tore at the strap holding down his head. Rising to his feet, he ripped free of the final ropes, stretching the muscles along his spine and across his shoulders. He was stiff and his body ached from lying so long on the stone floor, but his tolerance for pain was high. Swinging his arms up over his head, he brought them down in a swift, controlled motion. Satisfied he could wield a weapon, Ronan picked up a length of chain and headed for the door.

When Neira rushed to stop him, Ronan snarled and the girl shrank back, startled. He was grateful for her help, but if she thought they could escape without a fight, she was naïve.

"Stay near," he told her. "I'll protect you."

Neira did not argue, although Ronan felt her unease. She had no doubt expected him to docilely follow her directions. Not the best plan. The girl was a magic maker. War was Ronan's domain.

Ronan eased open the cell door and looked out into the narrow hall. The way was clear. Ronan knew the layout of the prison cells tucked between the soldier's quarters and the king's stable. The original underground dungeon had caved in centuries ago. A jail in the lower city now housed the looters and murderers of Caeraricin. This small stone prison was a repository for *special threats* to the kingdom. Ronan was the sole prisoner.

They crept along, hugging the wall until the hall opened up into a guarded entrance. A small rickety table and two chairs blocked their path to the door. On one of the chairs sat Boadhagh, his torso sprawled face-forward across the table, his beefy arms hanging over the sides as he slept. At his feet lay the club, rotted pieces of Ronan's flesh still clinging to the wood and rusty spikes.

Silently, Ronan motioned Neira to go on ahead. Boadhagh must die. It was not just a strategy for escape. The jailer took a macabre pleasure in beating the helpless. He was like a sick dog, and Ronan intended to put him down before he hurt anyone else.

Neira pointed to the club and mouthed, "You should take that. I don't have a weapon. We might need it."

Ronan paused. Boadhagh's instrument of torture repulsed him. Perhaps it was foolish, but he would rather use his bare hands than have anything more to do with that hated club.

He regretted his hesitation when Neira impatiently tried to lift the heavy club herself. "Leave it," he whispered sharply, then regretted that, too, as she flinched and lost her grip on the club. Ronan lunged to grab it—too late. The club landed with a solid *thunk* on Boadhagh's booted foot.

The jail keeper howled in pain, kicking over the chair as he scrambled to stand, clumsily pulling a knife from his belt. The club rolled twice and stopped, the sharp spikes caught at an angle between the legs of the table. Ronan whipped the chain in the air, but not before Boadhagh grabbed a fistful of Neira's hair and stuck the knife under her chin.

"Get back!" Boadhagh's tongue slavered around his words. "I'll slice her open." His hands shook; already Ronan saw a thin line of blood on Neira's neck where Boadhagh's knife sawed back and forth. In his drugged state, the man was dangerous. The longer Boadhagh remained armed, the more likely it was that Neira would die.

Ronan swung again and brought the chain down onto the edge of the table, noisily flipping it over. Boadhagh stumbled in surprise, dragging Neira along with him. "I said get back!" he shouted, but Ronan was unmoved. He had used the tumbling table as a distraction; in his hand he now held Boadhagh's spiked club.

"If you let her go, I'll be quick," Ronan promised as he circled to the right, away from the door, giving Neira a chance to escape should Boadhagh release her. Fear oozed from the jail keeper, stirring the growing rage in Ronan's belly. It was a good thing Ronan could not call the Hoar Beast. No one in the lower bailey—Neira included—would survive if Ronan loosed the wrathful creature now.

Neira shifted her weight and leaned to one side. Stupid girl. There was nothing worse than a novice in battle. Even drugged, Boadhagh was strong; he would slit her throat if she tried to break away.

The girl made a quick motion, forcing Ronan's hand. He sprang at Boadhagh—then jerked back coughing as a cloud of cinnamon spice filled his mouth and nostrils.

"Ahhh!" Boadhagh released Neira to clutch at his eyes, swinging the knife blindly with the other hand.

Neira dropped to the floor.

It was all the room Ronan needed. With a mighty swing, he brought the club down onto Boadhagh's head. The jailer's skull cracked with the dull sound of bone and iron being driven into spongy tissue. Boadhagh crumpled into a heap, one leg twitching violently even after he was dead.

Ronan pulled Neira to her feet. "Well done," he admitted, still spitting cinnamon from his mouth, annoyed with himself for underestimating her. He knew her teachers.

"I work in the kitchen." Neira wiped her cinnamon-dusted hands on her robes. "You use what you have." She pointed to Boadhagh's trousers with the toe of her boot. "Maybe you could use those?"

Ronan did not argue. He welcomed clothing, no matter how bug-ridden it might be. Stripping the dead man of his trousers, Ronan rolled him over to hide the partially broken face and growing pool of blood. Neira had said nothing when specks of blood and brain sprayed along her arm, but Ronan knew she was shaken. Her face was pale, and he saw her trembling even through yards of wizard robe.

Ronan cinched the baggy trousers around his waist and tied the belt until he was satisfied they would not be a hindrance. He picked up Boadhagh's knife and the length of chain, then nodded for Neira to follow. The club he left on the floor. Its purpose served, Ronan would not touch it again.

They stepped out of the prison and into the night air. Ronan's pupils enlarged, his senses alert to movement and sounds in the dark. To that part of his mind controlled by the Beast, the world became an ordered hierarchy of prey, from rats and falcons, to dogs, horses, and cunning man.

Ronan felt the copper collar's confusion. This was not magic. It was a type of instinct. The Vökumaðr walked a fine line between warrior and creature. If the collar chose to choke him for being what he was—both animal and human—his bid for freedom was over.

He waited.

The collar remained cold and still, granting free rein to those parts of him not tied to magic.

Ronan slid his fingers along the hammered edges of the copper ring, feeling for a way to remove it. Next time the collar might panic and choke him to death. He needed to rid himself of it.

"I've already tried," Neira warned. "If you so much as scratch it, Eltanin will know, and he will come."

Ronan let go of the collar. Eltanin would not lure or trick him into another hopeless battle. He was free. He would stay free.

Ronan turned and sprinted toward the western wall. Neira trailed behind. They kept to the shadows, skirting the greater part of the castle grounds— but there was one place they could not avoid. Ronan's steps slowed as they reached the main gate of the lower bailey.

Fifteen tall spikes stood in the center of the courtyard. Moonlight gave an unearthly glow to the skewered human forms.

Neira touched his arm and Ronan flinched. "Don't look," she said. "The crows have left nothing you would recognize."

She was wrong.

Ronan knew his kin.

Hrolleif's long gray hair fell over an eyeless skull. His sons, Enar and Bodolf, dangled shrunken and brittle, to his left and right. Gilby had lost his arms in the battle. Ronan saw the fresh bone and gristle that had started to grow before they silenced the jokester's laughter. Bjame's large carcass had separated and fallen to the ground. His head, still stuck to the end of the pike, was the only vestige of a once-mighty man. Sijur, Gaute, Birger, Cullen, and Duer—the faces of his uncles and cousins seemed to hover in front of the sagging jaws and hollow sockets. Ronan felt a whisper of the Beast as he saw what they had done to the women, sweet Aife and fighting Hekja. Arild, the jarl's brother and closest friend, would have fought like a lion at the jarl's back to protect them. Kynneeyn Gorrym had left little of him to display.

Ronan stepped from the shadows and walked to the empty post that waited for him. Next to it hung the greatest Vökumaðr Ronan had ever known: Jarl Bernhard, his father.

Tears stung his eyes. Caught halfway between man and Beast, the jarl was deformed and viciously mutilated.

"You almost made it." Ronan reached up, intending to hold his father's feet. "If we had been together—"

"Don't touch!" Neira stopped him. "He is bait."

Ronan sniffed the air. The sweet smell of rotting meat had permeated the castle for weeks—a potent reminder of Eltanin's strength and total dominion over Caeraricin. All that remained was the musk of an animal as it returned to the earth and the faint scent of hoarfrost. It was enough to mask the trap.

"Eltanin holds their souls hostage, to ensure you will not escape."

Ronan grabbed Neira's neck, horrified by her words. "You lie!"

"The spell on the jarl waits for your touch," Neira rasped. "Volcanic fire will engulf this courtyard. If you touch him, we will die."

Ronan released her and stared hard at the ghostly faces of his uncles and kin. The hovering shapes were more than Ronan's memories—they were all still here. Trapped.

"If you sacrifice yourself, then your kin will go free. No spell can hold a spirit freed by fire." Neira rubbed her throat.

"How do you know this?" Ronan demanded. Was this escape nothing more than an elaborate ruse? Neira had once followed Carden like a devoted puppy; did she now serve Eltanin?

Behind them, they heard the scuff of hurried footsteps.

Neira shrank into the shadows, blending almost as easily as Ronan did. Which of her tutors had taught her that trick? Scartozzar was a lying, two-faced thief; hiding no doubt served him well. Still, there was no greater deceiver than Carden Sihtric.

Ronan joined her in the darkness as two of the night watch came down the stone steps along the wall and into the courtyard. They spoke quietly and reached the bottom of the stairs before the Watchman emerged from the shadows in front of them. Startled, one drew his sword; the other took a scrambled step backward.

Ronan knew them by name. Men he'd trained himself. There was no time to gain their allegiance, no time to tell if they would sound an alarm or offer their swords to help him. The slip of a knife between the ribs, a twist of the chain around a fragile neck, and they were dead. Ronan shoved his regret into the deepest corner of his mind. He would face those men again, maybe even today, in the halls of Mag Mell. He could only hope they understood—he trusted no one.

Commotion sounded in the distance.

Ronan looked again at his father hanging in the courtyard. Eltanin had won. He would see the end of the Vökumaðr race. Ronan would trade his life for the souls of his kin . . . but not today. Today, he would return to Lynet and keep his Oath.

Ronan grabbed Neira's arm and dragged her along behind him. He did not know whose side the girl was on; he would keep her close until he'd searched her heart and figured it out. "We'll drop down through the gallery on top of the castle wall. There is a sally port, one way only, used by my kin in times of war. Stay beside me. If we keep to the alleyways, perhaps we can get through the city to the front gates without further detection."

Neira dug in her heels. "I can't go. I have to stay."

Ronan was not surprised. She'd played her part; now the little schemer wanted to slink back to Eltanin. His fingers dug into her arm. He kept walking, pushing her ahead of him. "You'll come with me to Aros."

"There's nothing left there."

Ronan stopped. "What do you mean 'nothing left'? Where is Lynet?"

"I don't know." Neira tried to yank free of his hold, but Ronan did not let go. "Eltanin and his demon attacked us. Rán destroyed the sea caves. Scartozzar was killed."

"Where is Lynet?" Ronan asked again. The girl's fear had become an acrid stench in his mouth and nose.

"I don't know . . . and neither does Eltanin."

Ronan let go of Neira's arm, though his sustained growl warned her not to run. *"Where is Lynet?"*

Path of Visions

NEIRA HELD STILL. Instinct told her any motion would incite the predator. Ronan would be on her in an instant, unable to stop himself. If Eltanin had not seized the throne, Ronan Loðungr would have become jarl, the supreme commander of the Caeraricin army. He was his father's son—a man of deep moral convictions—and a Beast beyond all nightmares. Here, outside the laws and protocol of the world they used to know, Neira did not dare test him.

"When you didn't come back, Scartozzar made plans to alter Lynet's appearance and hide her on the Outside." Neira's voice shook. "If Eltanin does not have her, perhaps Scartozzar succeeded before they killed him."

"You are sure Scartozzar is dead?"

Neira faltered, gutted by the harshness of the question, and by her absolute certainty of the answer. She had seen the devastation at Aros, but more than that, Neira knew Scartozzar. If he still lived, he would have come to help her by now. He had seen her through every stage of adolescence, and taught her all manner of magic, including the mysteries of *spellbirth*, that single spark of intelligence that gave magic a mind of its own. He was her mentor, her teacher, her friend. Scartozzar would never willingly abandon her like this.

"He is dead." Neira held no hope.

"Where did he send Lynet?" Ronan's impatience vibrated the very air.

"His childhood home. I spent a summer there, but I could not tell you how to find it. The Outside world is vast, Ronan—bigger than you can imagine. Time passes swiftly there. Lynet may already be old and gray. You won't recognize her, and you will get lost."

"I will find her," Ronan corrected. "Let's go."

Neira did not move. She was terrified of him, but she dared not obey. "I have to stay. I have no choice. Isleen charged me with a task. I cannot leave until it is finished."

"Isleen." Ronan spoke the Seer's name with such emotion Neira felt her own heart wrench. The *forspá* had changed more than one life the day Isleen came down from her mountain.

Legend said the Vökumaðr could read a man's heart. Neira knew Ronan read hers now, looking into her soul as he searched for truth. His eyes, those yellow flames that inspired both fear and loyalty, seemed haunted and uncertain as he studied her.

When his words came again, they were low, gentle. "For your own sake, girl, come with me. Isleen is not always right. Once you start down the path of visions, there is no turning back. If you follow her counsel, it will change you forever." He lifted his hand, but did not touch her. "Come with me."

She wanted to, desperately. As frightened as she was of the monster Ronan could become, Neira feared Eltanin more. The dark wizard probed her mind, took delight in hurting her. Neira did not doubt that if she stayed she would end up deranged, mindless or worse. Still, the Seer was right about one thing: Eltanin wanted her alive. He never pushed hard enough to break her, not like he pushed the princess. Neira's face grew grim. So long as there was a chance to stop Eltanin, she would continue to look for the heartstone. Caeraricin would not be the only kingdom to suffer if Eltanin stayed in power. "I can't come with you."

Ronan nodded, then cupped her face with his hand. Neira felt hope swell within her. Like many, Neira believed in the Vökumaðr's ability to bolster a coward's heart. She had witnessed its effect more than once, as the jarl's gift transformed dispirited rabble into a fighting force. She felt that energy now as it restored her courage.

"Will you return with an army? The people will rally to you."

Ronan's hand fell away.

"King Urien is still alive," Neira continued quickly. "The princess is mad, Ronan. I've heard her screams in the middle of the day. I think Eltanin will kill her soon."

The Watchman stepped into the shadows. Neira could not see his expression, but she felt his cold anger at the mention of the royal family. He would not return. The last Vökumaðr was abandoning Caeraricin.

A cry went up behind them.

Neira whirled around.

"The prisoner has escaped! To the west wa—" Boadhagh's knife streaked through the air and sank deep into the soldier's left eye.

Neira turned to Ronan—but the Vökumaðr was gone.

She was alone again.

Hitching up her blood-splattered robes, Neira raced toward the middle bailey, making for the kitchens and safety.

The alarm issued from all corners of the castle now. "The king is murdered. The Watchman has killed King Urien!"

Neira reeled in shock. The king was dead? Now?

Understanding hit her with such force it sucked the air from her lungs. Ronan's escape had been too easy. What a fool she'd been to think her plot to drug Boadhagh had gone unnoticed.

Eltanin had purged the castle of all who opposed him, but he could not kill everyone in the country who remained loyal to House Aricin. Now, the Aricin king was dead and Eltanin could blame it on Ronan. It would give the people someone to hate, someone to vent their futile anger on. The peasants were superstitious. Many feared the Vökumenn. Eventually they would accept Eltanin's slaughter of the Watchmen.

Neira felt sick. Had Isleen seen *this* in her vision?

Her mind reeled. Whom did Isleen serve? Did Eltanin rule the Annars in the same way he controlled the goddess Rán? Was no one left to oppose him?

Trembling, Neira slipped into the kitchen and leaned against the wall. She couldn't worry about that now. She had her own skin to save. If Eltanin suspected her hand in this, he would soon send guards to her door. Better to be in bed feigning sleep than out here skulking in the shadows.

Neira hurried up the stairs to the servants' quarters, praying all the while she'd made the right choice in staying behind.

Lynet slipped quietly down the stairs. She'd learned the creaks and groans of the floorboards over the last year, so she was reasonably sure she wouldn't wake anyone this time. Fig was a light sleeper. She swore the boy had some sort of *snoop radar*. If she was up to something, he had to be a part of it.

At least she didn't have to worry about Alder finding out. He was gone again. He spent many nights away from home. Maple said it was for work, though Lynet doubted it.

Nothing was ever that simple.

She paused on the second floor and stepped carefully over one of Miss Moat's brood. Dust bunnies were inherently lazy. They liked to flop down in the middle of a good munch and fall asleep, not rousing until the next piece of fuzz or fluff caught their attention.

There were no lights on at the end of the hall. Auntie Jól was heavily pregnant and often took late-night walks to ease her discomfort, but it looked like she and Treddian were asleep.

It was because of Jól's late-night excursions that Lynet was up tonight. More than once Lynet had seen Jól walking out to the lilac bushes in the northwest corner of the garden. The woman spent hours there, hidden among the branches. What was a pregnant lady doing in the middle of the night in a lilac grove?

Not that odd behavior was unusual in this metamorphic house. Lynet had lived here long enough to know that whatever else he might be, Fig was not the product of a medical condition, and flowers in New York did not grow year-round simply because an old woman wished it so.

It was *magic.*

Yet, as obvious as it was to her, for some reason the rest of the world did not believe in magic. Even Eibby, who was undoubtedly the most open-minded person Lynet knew, thought the idea of magic in Buffalo was nuts. The day Lynet asked her boss about magic, Aliysha's answer had been full of voodoo and wives' tales—nothing Lynet could use to explain her home life. When Lynet mentioned *everyday magic*, like the kind that helped with the dusting or seasoned a meal, Aliysha had questioned her about substance abuse. Lynet had quickly dropped the subject.

It was frustrating. She knew magic was real. She'd experienced it herself months ago at the hockey game. At least that's what she thought it was.

Lynet peered down at the gently snoring dust bunny, its features defined by fibers, fine dust, and pollens. Without dust bunnies, she would have to get down on her hands and knees to clean the cobwebs and dirt from the endless hollows and nooks of Laburnum House. Magic was amazing. Why would anyone want to deny it existed?

Lynet gave the bunny a gentle pat, then made her way to the ground floor and out the west door. Armed with a warm sweater, tall boots, and a flashlight, she felt prepared for anything—although she'd rather not use the flashlight in case anyone from the house saw her. Lynet and Maple hadn't argued in ages. Lynet wanted it to stay that way. They'd called a truce. Maple didn't mind her making friends, so long as she didn't invite them over. Moreover, since Lynet had given up going to every shrink, shaman, or charlatan she could find, the Macarthurs had finally relaxed and embraced her as one of the family. Lynet had grown to love them, especially Fig.

Of course, the Macarthurs remained secretive about their magic, never actually admitting they used it. Lynet supposed they wanted to blend in. Still, she occasionally caught Treddian calling the remote to his hand from across the room, or Auntie Jól levitating a heavy laundry basket up from the basement so she didn't have to carry it.

Lynet had experimented with magic—quietly, on her own—since the Macarthurs still overreacted anytime she raised the subject. She'd tried making a book move. Tried to force a red traffic light to turn green. She had even tried making a flower grow. Nothing. Nothing ever happened. No tingling sensation. No blue flash. Lynet simply didn't understand magic. She had no idea how it worked, and no one offered to teach her. She always ended up feeling embarrassed and stupid.

Out on the porch, Lynet waited for her eyes to adjust to the dark. The moon shone from behind silver clouds, giving a soft glow to the stone birdbath and the pebbled footpath that led to the lilacs. She hurried down the path, glancing back often to the upper windows of Laburnum House.

Thick and tangled, the little grove looked as though it had been there a long time. She fingered the juicy lilac petals and drank in the scent. They smelled so good. She poked around, but couldn't see any gaps in the middle. It appeared an impenetrable wall of branches and leaves; still, she knew there was a way in. If a large, pregnant Jól could slip through, surely someone as spindly as Lynet would fit.

A rustle of leaves.

Lynet spun around. "Who's there?"

No answer. The breeze fluttered. It felt cold, colder than it should, especially in early summer. Lynet rubbed gooseflesh on her forearms through her sweater. Muttering she was too old to believe in the bogeyman, Lynet turned again to the wall of branches. What was so special about these lilacs? She glanced up at the house—still dark, no lights on. Lynet decided to take a chance. She held her hand over the flashlight and flicked it on. The light made odd patterns between her fingers and gave the lilac bushes a rather sinister look. She put the flashlight right up against the branches and wiggled it between the thick leaves, hoping to see through to the center so she could figure out how to get in.

The light didn't penetrate far. Frustrated, Lynet pushed the flashlight in farther, clear up to her elbow.

The flashlight went out.

Lynet snatched her arm back.

The flashlight glowed brightly again.

Leave.

Lynet blinked. Had she just heard a voice in her head? She turned the whole way around.

You are not safe here.

"Who's there?" Lynet whispered.

The leaves rustled behind her. She whirled around and pointed the beam of light toward the sound, but there was only shadow—a shadow that moved. Lynet watched in horrid fascination as the shadow drew itself in and took the shape of a tall, winged figure.

71

The wraith comes for you.

The figure floated toward her. The air grew colder still.

Run.

Lynet threw the flashlight at the advancing shadow and raced for the house. She gasped as the awful cold caught up to her. Darkness, like great flapping wings, wrapped around her from behind, lifting her off the ground. The house shrank away as the wraith took flight, dragging her up with it, her legs dangling useless in the air. Lynet tried to scream, but no sound came out. Helplessly, she struggled against an enemy with no tangible form.

Bright green light lit up the entire garden. Alder stood at the edge of the privet. "Ho, stop!" his voice boomed.

The black aberration froze, as if held in place. Lynet hung defenseless in the air. Alder grew in size, until he was taller than the house, his face large and angry in front of her. "Be gone with you!" he ordered. "This ground is sacred to the Mother. Your presence here is forbidden."

The wraith shrieked and released Lynet, letting her drop. Alder broke her fall with the edge of his huge hand; still she landed hard enough on the ground for her legs to buckle beneath her. The shadow shot straight up into the sky and vanished.

Alder walked across the grass to where Lynet lay bruised and shivering. With each step, he grew smaller and smaller until he was his normal height and size again.

"Not safe out here anymore," he said gruffly as he helped her to her feet. "I won't ask what you were doing. Your business. But the garden is no longer safe at night."

The Oath

"YOU CANNOT MEAN YOU WANT HER FOR YOURSELF." Cian shook his balding head. A short man, with bright eyes and a mind as keen as a dagger, Cian Druce bore the respect of king and peasant alike. "Ronan, you know what is at stake. I sent you to protect Lynet because of the *forspá*. I certainly did not mean for you to fall in love with her. You know that is impossible."

Ronan continued to sharpen his sword. He did not look up or trust himself to speak. He'd been staying with Cian, at the base of DuwaŴyr Mountain, for the past month, ever since Neira rescued him, though he hadn't come here straightaway.

Once beyond the knapped flint walls of Caeraricin, clear of any outside control, Ronan called to the Beast. The collar's crude magic could not hold it. With a roar of defiance, the Beast's massive strength ripped away the collar and gave Ronan his freedom. Human again, Ronan hurried on to Aros.

The main cavern was gone, the inner chambers claimed by the sea, the devastation complete. What force could wipe away all trace—had Rán herself done this? There was nothing left to track: no remains, no lingering signature of either Carden or Scartozzar. If Scartozzar was dead, then his body must be lost in the sea. Few would mourn; many wished the rogue wizard dead. As for Carden Sihtric, it would take more than a cave-in to finish off that pugnacious bastard—but where was he?

What Ronan sensed of Lynet felt odd. She was alive, but something had changed. A shift in the Divide confirmed Neira's story; Lynet had crossed over to the Outside world.

From Aros, Ronan traveled north to the Annarian temple. There he gained help from the Annars—no easy feat—but, in the end, they gave him both a way to cross the Divide, and a spell embedded in an Annarian crystal, which ensured Ronan would never again be subject to Carden's Governance.

At last, he entered the cluttered hut of Cian Druce. A familiar face greeted him there—Lleth. Their reunion was the high point of Ronan's stay.

"You do remember the *forspá*?" Cian asked.

Ronan grunted. How could he forget the prophetic words that had so transformed his life? Isleen was like a hornet's nest. The nest hummed and brooded and you knew it was there—but you were wise, and you avoided all contact, hoping it would leave you alone. Nevertheless, every now and then a storm shook the nest, and the hornets streamed out.

As the Annarian advisor to Caeraricin, Isleen's counsel commanded grave respect in King Urien's court. The day she had come swooping down from her mountain to declare the will of the gods played in Ronan's memory like a bad dream. How did the confounded verses go again?

Old lines dying, time quick changes
Evil doth break through
To heal the breach, a riddle solved
In this the king must choose

Ancient imprints on the girl
Upon the isles far
Powers of the four winds bought
A dying race restored

Redemption paid by allies true
Weapons of the gods
Pathways opened, flesh and stone
By magic false—all lost

Every scholar in the kingdom had argued their interpretation until Cian Druce arrived, coaxed out of the mountains by a plea from King Urien himself. Cian had studied and pondered the verses for days.

It seemed the border between Norðrlönd and the Outside world was on the brink of collapse. Time, the plaything of puki, teetered too far out of balance—days too short on one side, too long on the other. Carelessness and treachery riddled the barrier with holes and weakened its very fabric. Each time an Outsider learned the truth about Norðrlönd, the veil between their two worlds grew thinner. The *forspá* told of a final breach, a Great Rift torn in the Aragaidheal Divide.

According to Cian, there was only one way to repair the damage.

The rightful high king (they assumed it meant Edan, as his father was aged and already married) would set it all aright—by marrying the girl from the outer islands. He would sing the *Kærásti Fórnsöngr*, take her ancient magic, and use it to close the Rift.

Personally, Ronan thought it meant Lynet would somehow kill all the puki at once, and stop the displacement of time forever. But his interpretation didn't matter. In fact, no one's did.

The *forspá* was an unending riddle. Everyone who heard it recalled it differently. The only constant was the contention it caused. It especially infuriated the prince. Riddles drove Edan crazy. He was practical, levelheaded—and he hated magic with a passion. And no wonder. Ronan knew no one worse at magic than Prince Edan. Even something as commonplace as conjuring fire failed spectacularly in Edan's hands. The last line of the prophecy, about magic ruining it all no matter his efforts, was the final straw. Had it not been impossible to enforce, Edan would have outlawed magic altogether.

The only part Edan had agreed to was Cian's plan to fetch the woman. If such a girl existed—one with power over life and death—then Edan would bring her under his protection. Better that than let her run free where those hostile to the crown might find her and use her magic against them. Since there was but one way to bind her powers to his house and make them inaccessible to all others, Edan would make her his queen.

When the king suggested Edan's use of magic might improve once he married, Edan had said quite seriously he could rule a kingdom without magic. He was not foolish enough to fight a *forspá*, and he would accept responsibility for the girl as he did everything he was destined to bear. Still, Edan Aricin had faith in only two things: his sword arm, and the knowledge that Ronan watched his back.

How their lives had changed.

Ronan exhaled heavily. He'd been raised in the stone halls of Caeraricin Castle. All his life he'd known that at Prince Edan's coming-of-age, he would swear his allegiance by taking upon him the Watchman's Oath. Ronan would become the prince's bodyguard and surest protection for the rest of their lives. When Edan finally sat the throne, Ronan would replace his father as jarl and take control of his country's army. None of that would happen now.

"I probably won't be back in time for the big ceremony," Ronan told Edan as they stood on the battlement overlooking the sea. Neither one of them relished the upcoming display of pomp and pageantry. Ronan was glad for an excuse to be somewhere else.

In a few short weeks, the prince turned thirty and officially attained ruling age. Amidst lavish spectacle, Edan Aricin would be crowned heir apparent in the presence of the entire court and assume responsibility for much of Caeraricin's administration. Kings and queens from the Six Kingdoms would attend, each prepared to swear allegiance to the next high king of Norðrlönd. On that day, Ronan would kneel before Edan and take the sacred Watchman's Oath.

"There can't be a ceremony without the Watchman's Oath," Edan said, as if that settled it, and they were off the hook.

A brisk wind whipped up around them. Edan gathered his dark hair into a high royal tail, wrapping a quarter of its length with the wide piece of rawhide he kept tucked in his leather vest. In their youth, the windy eastern battlement had served as a retreat from armory chores and Carden's foul moods. Now it was a practical place for a man to gather his thoughts without the constant wheedling of advisors and courtiers.

"We can finish the oath-making once you get back," Edan continued. "We'll tack it on to the end of the brúðmessa, and have the whole thing, marriage and coronation, over and done with in one afternoon—."

"That will not do," Cian interrupted, as the old man bustled out to join them.

"Why not?" Edan asked.

"The Oath must not be wasted on you."

Cian's words were met with stunned confusion.

"What are you talking about?"

Edan scowled. "Wasted on me?"

Cian tried to unroll a scroll he carried, but the wind nearly tore it from his hands. "See this—" His long gray beard flapped wildly against his face, catching on his pointy nose, making further speech impossible to understand.

"Perhaps we should step inside," Ronan suggested.

Cian led the way into an alcove. As soon as they were sheltered, he reopened the scroll and tapped on a cluster of small islands marked on the map.

"There. The Isle of Nairn. I've made some inquiries—don't ask, it wasn't pleasant—to help you in your search, Ronan. There are four settlements in the center of the island. You will find the woman in one of them. It is a difficult journey to Nairn, and the enemies of the king already hunt for her. She is surrounded by divining mist. Either she or her family protects her, a situation that cannot last. Ysbail is gifted when it comes to probing the minds of others; she will find the woman soon enough.

"Unless you are sworn to her, Ronan, the Beast will not naturally protect her. You will need all your skill, and the Oath's golden shield, to find her before the others do."

Ronan shook his head. "No. No, this is wrong. I've spent my life growing into this role. I've put up with Edan's annoying habits since I was sixteen, convincing myself he was worth the sacrifice. I cannot consecrate my life to anyone else. Besides, the woman will have no ability to control the Hoar Beast. In berserkr form, I would kill her rather than save her."

"Well, that would solve the problem of keeping her magic out of the hands of the enemy," Edan said, ever ready to dismiss magic as a solution to anything.

Cian frowned. "Those are too close to the words Eltanin uses to poison your father's ears. Remember the forspá, Edan. You will need her." Cian turned to Ronan. "When you take your leave, King Urien will command you to kill the woman if she resists. This you cannot do. She is the key; somehow, she is the key. You must take the Oath so you can disobey even a direct order from the king. You cannot harm the object of your Oath."

"The Beast does not obey the Oath."

"The Beast obeys you."

"No." Ronan shook his head. "I do not control the Hoar Beast. We tolerate each other at best."

"You would control it if you accepted the berserkr *madness." Cian rolled up the map and stuffed it into a cloth sack. "Bevyn waits below with the horses. I've told him you travel light." Cian handed Ronan the sack. "Well, what are you waiting for? The prince will hear your Oath, and I will be your witness. There is no time to spare. Make haste! Make haste!"*

Edan protested. "But the Oath Ring—"

"He can swear on his own Vökumaðr heart," Cian said. "It will be ávarðr Guði, accepted by the gods as more binding than any ceremonial ring."

Ronan knelt, astounded at how fast Cian had wrested their own fate from their hands. "Ek segi þat Æsi Vökumaðr eiðr." He stumbled over words he had rehearsed since childhood, faltering as he swore to guard and protect a faceless woman two hundred leagues away. A golden shield appeared, hanging suspended in the air above him, forged from the magic in his lethbeithíoch *body.*

As the Oath ended, the shield glowed brightly. Then, instead of enveloping Edan with an outline of golden light—a mark visible only to Ronan to aid his efforts to track and protect—the shield sped out over the ocean, flying south toward the island of Nairn and an unknown girl.

Cian interrupted Ronan's thoughts. "She is not for you, Ronan."

"Lynet will decide for herself." Ronan looked up from the sword. "You cannot control her. She has a will of iron."

"The woman is a gift from the Sòlasach. You have heard the *forspá.* Prince Edan will need her powers if he is to restore order and save us. If she sings for him, and gives him her mighty magic, he will be able to—"

"Edan betrayed my father, exterminated my family—my entire race! He is not worthy of any power," Ronan shot back.

"You do not know that." Cian lifted his hand to stifle any protest. "Yes, I have heard of the horrors done at Caeraricin, but Edan does not sit on his father's throne. Is that not enough to make you doubt? If Edan were responsible, even in part, for confining the Watchmen to their human form while Eltanin's forces slaughtered them, don't you think he would now rule in his father's stead? You know as well as I that he was prepared to assume control of the kingdom. Why is Eltanin on the throne? Do you think Edan simply stood aside and let him take it?"

Ronan had no answer. Jarl Bernhard was dead, his spirit mercilessly trapped inside his own decaying body. Someone had made that possible. Some noble had done the unthinkable and, in their moment of greatest need, prevented the Vökumenn from assuming their Beastly form. Who, if not Edan? For all his power, Eltanin did not have Governance, and Carden had been many leagues away, hot on their trail in Sharsis. King Urien was old and weak; he could no longer hold Ronan's father, let alone control fourteen of the strongest minds in Caeraricin.

Ronan knew Edan was to blame. He had felt his *eiðbróðir*, his childhood brother, in the castle. It was because of Edan that Ronan stormed the throne room. Fearing for Edan's life, Ronan had attacked the guards, transforming into the mighty Hoar Beast, coming to the aid of his prince. But someone had sent the Hoar Beast back to the astral plane, and Ronan, the man, had been overpowered. Somebody had betrayed him. Who else, if not Edan? No one but the prince, who had trained for years, had that kind of control.

"I have heard news from the north," Cian continued. "They say Prince Edan was in the mountains during the attack on the Vökumenn. They also say Ysbail captured him and keeps him locked in her fortress."

"I felt him at Caeraricin. He was alive. He was there."

"Then he was a prisoner, as you first thought."

Ronan did not speak, his mouth set in a grim line. It was useless to quarrel. Cian was wrong, and no amount of arguing would convince him.

Cian went on, his voice quieter now. "Ronan, I have only the good of Caeraricin in my heart. What have you in yours? What do you think will happen if Lynet sings and the two of you combine your powers? Can Lynet be trusted to use your Vökumaðr skills for good? Will the Hoar Beast understand why everything dies, why enemies simply fall to the earth without a single strike of his mighty claws?"

Ronan pushed away from the table and strode to the door. "You do not need to lecture me. I know the danger."

"And the stakes?" Cian insisted. "The Aragaidheal Divide is breaking down. If it collapses, Norðrlönd will be irreversibly sucked into the Outside world. Our lives are not the only ones at risk."

Ronan knew what the fall of the Divide meant. Norðrlönd would reappear in the middle of the Norwegian Sea, and once more block passage of the warm ocean currents. All the land to the north and east of its large land mass would freeze and ice over, plunging Europe—perhaps the whole Northern Hemisphere—into a new ice age. Worse still, the Northlanders' longevity and way of life would pass into myth as Norðrlönd raced forward in time to catch up, its peoples and creatures aging in an instant, their buildings and bridges crumbling to dust. The reindeer-like Senteer, the Grót craftsmen, the Great Worms—all irrevocably lost. The old gods would fade, crushed under the might of Christianity. *Spellbirth*, the miracle that gave reason and sentience to magic, would die, its spark extinguished forever.

Lynet was the key. Cian believed she could mend the rift in the Divide before it was too late—but she could not do it alone. The *forspá* dictated she and Edan would repair the rift together. But the prince was a traitor and Lynet's heart belonged to Ronan; so long as she loved him, she could not sing the *Kærásti Fórnsöngr* with any other man.

The prophecy had fallen apart.

"I leave in the morning," Ronan said. Tomorrow he would cross into the Outside world. He and Cian had argued for the last time.

Shackles

"HAND ME THE CHICKEN," Margaret demanded.

Colm hesitated, unwilling to push the sizzling meat off the iron skewer and into her waiting hands. "It's hot. You'll get burned."

"Rather that than have the fiend take off my head." Margaret's words silenced any protest from the rest of the kitchen servants. She wrapped a kitchen rag around her hand. "Now give it here."

Defeated, Colm lowered the meat. The old woman snatched the chicken from the skewer and immediately stuffed stewed fruit into the sizzling cavity.

Every day, Margaret took the king of Caeraricin his meals. Her grandmother had assigned her the task when she was a young maid, and Margaret had done it faithfully all her life. When Eltanin usurped the throne, Margaret girded up her aprons and told the kitchen *sgalags* she would continue to serve the meals. "Someday, a true king will sit the throne again. We must be ready." Age had diminished her size. Her spine stooped and her fingers shook, but Margaret took pride in her duties and expected the rest of her staff, free or enslaved, to do the same.

Neira turned back to the table. Colm knew arguing with Margaret did no good. What was he on about? He'd better not cause trouble today. She drew a bread knife from the wooden block and sawed a round loaf into three even wedges, resisting the urge to imagine the bread as Eltanin's heart. Perhaps she should imagine Isleen's heart instead. It was, after all, the Seer's fault Neira was here, a *sgalag* in a collar, scrambling to please the so-called king.

A king who liked to blast her mind with questions: *Where is the dagger? Did Scartozzar find it? Where is the woman?*

She supposed a common servant would have no defense against his onslaught, but guarding her thoughts was the first mental activity Neira's mother had ever taught her. Her family kept many secrets. She'd learned to hide them all, long before she came to live with Scartozzar. More than that, she'd studied under one of the strongest, guarded minds in Caeraricin—Eltanin's red-haired son.

As far as Neira could tell, her resistance amused Eltanin. She was sure he could crush her mind if he pushed. But then he would never get his answers—and he desperately wanted to know the whereabouts of Lynet and the dagger Dwynai.

Neira placed the bread on the heaped dinner tray and brushed crumbs from her robes.

Wilda shooed her aside and plunked a thick chunk of pungent cheese on the tray. "It's ready."

"Not quite." Colm rushed to add a mug of sweet-spiced Llanerc mead. His arthritic fingers trembled and Neira held her breath, praying he would not spill it. They were late enough already.

Margaret inspected the fare. A smile wrinkled her face as she pulled a tiny silver spoon from her apron pocket and slid it into the small bowl of salt on the tray. "Fit for a king," she said, with an approving nod.

Neira gripped the edges of the tray. They needed to hurry. She gave a heave to lift it up, but Colm shouldered her aside and took it from her.

"The tray is too heavy for you today," he said, his thin arms wobbling under its weight. "And do not bother to argue. I will not be moved."

Neira sighed. Colm was a good man, but past his prime, and there were days when his insistence on doing tasks he was no longer fit for caused them all grief. Still, she could not deny her relief at escaping a visit to Eltanin's austere throne room.

Eltanin had made Neira a part of his personal household. Keeping her underfoot meant he could assault her mind whenever he chose. He could easily threaten to kill any of the others in front of her to gain cooperation, but she supposed he enjoyed hurting her too much to make it quick. And he did hurt her. Entering the mind was a delicate business; few had the finesse to penetrate without inflicting damage. Eltanin, though determined, was clumsy. The damaged princess was proof of that. Only by erecting the barriers taught by both her mother and Carden had Neira held on to her sanity.

"I will take the tray up for Margaret," Colm said firmly. "You stay here, out of sight. You're not healed from the last time." He nodded to the black-and-blue welts on Neira's throat.

Neira lifted a hand to the copper collar, as if to hide it from their gaze.

"I wish I could pry that evil thing off you," Colm said gently, and Neira felt a pang of regret for her uncharitable thoughts. Colm was a kind soul, even if he inevitably caused them extra work.

"It's all right. I'm used to it." She smiled, wishing he would leave it be. The collar was more magic than metal. The one time she had tried to remove it, the hated thing screamed for Eltanin.

It was hard for the others to understand; they did not wear collars. Then again, none of them knew the higher spells. Eltanin was no fool. Common magic was necessary for the upkeep of the castle. However, anyone with the ability to conjure a rival spell was either dead, sworn to Eltanin, or wore a copper ring—and as far as she knew, Neira was the only one.

Colm snorted as if to say she didn't fool him, then hefted the tray in his skinny arms and left the kitchen, following Margaret.

Neira watched them go with a sense of unease. Two of the grooms were missing, and no one had seen George, the master tailor, in a fortnight.

She adjusted the collar, trying in vain to lessen the drag of the invisible chains hanging from it. None of her friends knew why the ugly bruises did not heal, and she was reluctant to tell them. What good would it do? There was no physical way to remove the silent, unseen shackles that bound her waist, wrists, and ankles.

With each move, Neira felt the chains jostle and bang—but, created by magic, they were impossible to see or grab hold of. Her hands, her clothing, passed right through them as if they didn't exist. Late at night, while she slept, they bit icy cold into her skin. Alive and cognizant, the chains seldom interfered with her chores, but became troublesome and contrary any time she sought rest or pleasure. Eltanin had attached the chains to the collar the morning after Ronan escaped. The usurper was wrong if he thought they were worse than the collar itself.

Forged by evil, the copper ring around her throat had but one purpose— to prevent Neira's use of magic. Throughout the day and night, it waited. If Neira's fingers moved too fast, if her lips formed the slightest chant, if it even suspected her of conjuring—the collar squeezed until she fainted. It heeded neither reason nor plea. It cared not if it made a mistake. If it distrusted her, it silenced her.

Since the day of her capture, Eltanin had starved Neira of magic. She could think of no worse enervation for a gifted wizard's apprentice than to be stripped of the use of her powers.

Neira cleaned crumbs from the bread knife and put it away. She was not the only one to suffer at Eltanin's hand. All were in danger here. She would make no complaint that might stir her friends to rebellion. Anger, no matter how righteous, was a death sentence. She had done enough, dragging them into her plot to drug Boadhagh and save the Watchman.

"They'll be fine," said Wilda, wiping up the table. "Margaret knows how to handle people. She won't let Colm make a mess of things."

Neira wasn't so sure, but she could not let concern for Colm distract her from her plans. Once she finished grinding enough wheat into flour for tomorrow's loaves, Neira intended to continue her search. So long as Eltanin gave her freedom of movement, she would continue to use it to spy on him and learn the secret of the heartstone.

Colm placed the unwieldy tray on the worn buffet table in the throne room. He knew what Neira and the other younger servants thought of him, and he accepted their criticism, but he wasn't going to stop doing his share of the work. With so many dead, it fell to him and a few other men to make up the difference so the women were not overtaxed.

Colm removed the plate covers and arranged the silver and napkins neatly, as befitted a king.

When all was to Margaret's satisfaction, they turned and headed quietly for the door. The new king did not like servants standing over him. He preferred to eat alone. They would return later to collect the dishes and remove the tray.

"Wait." A cold voice slid across the room. "One of you will stay behind. Choose between yourselves—I care not which."

The indifferent way King Eltanin bade them 'choose' set Colm's stomach into knots. For a dizzying moment, he let his fear run free. He thought of his wife and grown son and felt a fierce urge to embrace them. His belly puffed up and down in silent laughter as he imagined telling them how fantastically close to death he had been—and how he escaped.

Behind him, Colm heard the swish of wizard robes. The idyllic vision faded. He was not important, not like Margaret. Many good men would have died the first few days of King Eltanin's rule had she not been there to talk some sense into them. Many more would have met a gruesome end in the weeks that followed.

"Go on," he told her with a confident nod to the door. "I'll be along later. I'm sure it's just some little thing the king needs sorting out."

Margaret's eyes swam with emotion as she squeezed his hand; her knotted fingers felt fragile against his own. "I will tell Jonna you love her," she said.

Colm lifted his chin and nodded.

He watched her shuffle from the room. His hands were wet with sweat, and his heartbeat fluttered like an old bird's. Colm straightened his brown tunic, pausing to appreciate the cheerful embroidery Jonna had stitched along the hem. Maybe it would be all right. Just because a couple of servants had disappeared did not mean he was next. Tears stung his old eyes. He brushed them away, trying not to feel ashamed of his fear. He was a man. He would face this. With a deep breath, he turned toward the evil that had so thoroughly defiled his beloved homeland.

Ronan stood on the deck of the Icelandic shipping freighter *Ís Hafmeyjan*, the Ice Mermaid, and watched the horizon. They would make port in Newfoundland this evening. He would be glad to stand on land again.

He had spent the last five months searching for Lynet in England, Wales, Ireland, and Iceland. Neira was right: the Outside world was larger than he'd expected. Even with his enhanced Vökumaðr skills, the sheer volume of people on this side of the Divide overwhelmed him; the first time he tracked, it nearly knocked him unconscious.

Cian was right, too. Without the Watchman's Oath, Ronan would have had no hope of finding Lynet. With it, he was able to skim over millions of life-threads and focus solely on that one golden shimmer far away in the distance. It wasn't much—more a sensation of being *pulled* than anything he actually saw—but it gave him a direction. Always west.

Following that faint tug, Ronan and Lleth traveled from London to Caerphilly, then across the Celtic Sea to Ireland. They got as far as Cork— before the Outsider cash he'd brought with him ran out. Neither Ronan nor Cian had realized how long it would take to find Lynet. Luckily, Ronan was strong and able-bodied. There was always steady work for a man willing to put his back into it.

He shoveled and hammered his way across Ireland, doing odd jobs, until he reached the coast. There he signed on to a fishing boat headed for the Faroe Islands. Ronan found Faroese similar to his Vökumaðr mother tongue, and learned the nuances by listening to the fishermen. Joining them meant going north, but it seemed the quickest way to earn the cash he needed. Lleth surprised Ronan by adapting to life on a ship and making friends with the crew, especially the skipper, who allowed Lleth to come aboard during the shorter runs. At other times, Ronan left the wolfhound to run free in the peatlands. Lleth always came back covered in mud and as frisky as a pup.

Ronan spent the winter hauling cod and haddock from the sea and, while on land, learned to drive a truck. Finally, when spring came and he'd made enough money, he and Lleth headed west again, landing in Iceland.

The pull of Lynet's golden thread pointed across the Atlantic, and Ronan had no choice but to sign on as a fisherman again in hopes of getting ashore in Canada without too much trouble. The sailors warned him that North America was not as welcoming as they were.

Ronan was prepared to do whatever it took, including reading the hearts of crooked men who always seemed in a position to offer aid for a price. Aid he may very well need since, the closer they got to Newfoundland, the more he felt a *pull* to the south. Ronan had hoped to avoid the United States; he did not relish the challenge of sneaking across its heavily guarded borders.

Alder leaned against one of the ancient gnarled yews on the east side of the garden on his way back from Devil's Gate. He was tired and winded. Winter was a season for slumber, a time to draw in sap and wait out the cold. The magic of the earth waned whenever snow covered the land. Laburnum House itself slowed and grew sleepy during those long, dark months. Alder would have liked to have had a good, sound winter nap himself. But the demons of Ogluidh knew the land's weakness.

It had taken all of Alder's considerable strength to keep the trees around the Gate awake and alert during the bitter cold months. He'd succeeded to an extent. No Fomorii had crossed over the abyss, although several shadow wraiths had slipped through.

Alder had planted a barrier of Norðrlönd yew, and fast growing poplars around the Gate last year. Now that spring was thawing the ground, he'd added rows of succulent lupine and other longer lived perennials to increase the Earth magic guarding the knoll.

He flexed his hands and grumbled; he was stiff and sore—his stomach growled—and he was hungry. Alder picked up the empty seed bag he'd been carrying and headed once more toward the warm, welcoming lights of home. He had done all he could. They'd survived their second winter with Lynet living under their roof. The Mother must provide her own defenses now. Alder needed rest. If an attack came, someone else would have to protect them; he had nothing left.

Isleen

THE SEER WALKED DOWN THE WOODED PATH leading to Cian Druce's cottage at the foot of DuwaŴyr Mountain. A long, luxurious cloak and hood covered her brightness. Unlike the rest of the Annars, who were lovely and pleasant to behold, the Seer's beauty was dazzling. So bright, it was said, she could blind the unworthy.

Isleen's hair was as white as the Northland snow, her eyes as crystalline as winter ice. Her tall, graceful body shone with a pale luster, sprinkling a momentary glitter onto everything around her. Without the cloak to hide beneath, she would alert humans, creatures, and insects alike of her approach.

Beside her walked two tall Annarian *arreyder*: Halvor and his brother Arneot. Sentinels, they kept watch over the mountain and especially the Sisterhood. Today, when Isleen set off down the path to Cian's hut, the brothers quietly, and without need for explanation, fell into step beside her. They talked in low voices as they walked, occasionally pointing out a concealed animal or bird to her. Although the brothers each carried a sword and bow, the Annars had no natural enemies. They counted the creatures and trees of the forest as their friends. Other races, no matter how fierce or troublesome, were dealt with as necessary, but never feared.

Their step was nimble and light. Annars were used to walking. Destined to live each moment in the here and now, they could not move outside of time. Neither puki nor time portal affected them. Although they fashioned stoppieces for others, the Annars would never see the Outside world themselves, for they could not cross the temporal currents of the Aragaidheal Divide.

Isleen's mind was troubled, yet she found comfort in the cheerfulness of her escort. Of the several *arreyder* on the mountain, Isleen knew Arneot and Halvor chose to accompany her because they appreciated Cian's endless curiosity. If needed, the brothers would gladly protect the old man, although more for their own pleasure than for any benefit to Cian or mankind. From their point of view, Cian Druce and the problems of the moment were fleeting. A thousand years from now, they would still be young and living on their mountain, and the concerns of today would be forgotten history. This they accepted without sadness or regret; it simply was.

Few gained entrance to their sacred mountain. The Annars were a private race, with limited patience for the devotions and greed of men. Many of them, however, considered Cian the wisest of all humans. Though harsh to pilgrims and treasure seekers, the Annars valued Cian's sincerity. Consequently, they had bestowed on him a rare privilege: to live in their shadow, unmolested, as neighbor and friend.

The trail took a distinct turn, and Isleen stopped. What if her vision had already come to pass? Arneot went on ahead, but Halvor paused, his expression curious. He offered his hand. "Come. We will not allow anything to spoil the day. If there is trouble, Arneot and I shall face it."

Isleen took his hand as he led her confidently around the bend and into the clearing. All was peaceful and calm. Birds sang in the trees overhead. Isleen realized her companions knew from the start there was nothing to fear; the whisper of the forest assured all was well long before they arrived.

Her pride stung, Isleen went to Cian's door and knocked. She knew it was ridiculous to envy Halvor's affinity with the forest. The *arreyder* were special, even among their own people. Still, it irked her to be reminded of her lack of magic. The Sisterhood had a mighty gift: the ability to see into the future—but all gifts come with a price. They had no other power. No traditional magic, no tinkering with the physical world. They were completely dependent upon others for their comfort and safety. For her, it was worse. The prophetic gift she had enjoyed for hundreds of years was now flawed and diminished.

Isleen knocked again, then warily opened the door. "Master Druce?"

The wizard's hut was a monument to clutter. Books, drawings, notes and maps were stacked in lopsided piles on every available surface. Inkwells, telescopes, and globes served as paperweights. One table buckled under a pile of instruments for measuring the stars and weather. On the floor near her feet sat a curious-looking compass with madly twirling spindles, apparently converted to a doorstop. The most remarkable object in the room, however, was an enormous flying contraption that hung suspended from the ceiling. Its wings and tail swayed and turned at the slightest breeze.

Isleen did not know if it was safe to walk beneath it, so she stayed where she was. "Master Druce?" she called again.

He isn't here; you can snoop.

Oooh, so many things to touch. Pick something up.

Hush. I've no need of your nonsense. Isleen pushed aside the annoying voices in her head. Remnants of a curdled spell, the twin tongues were a constant reminder of how far she'd stooped in her effort to understand mortals. For a time, she had even lived among humans. What had it brought her? Appreciation of their troubles? Compassion for their short, tedious lives? Hardly. Betrayed by her human lover and attacked by a superstitious mob, Isleen's reward was the irritating babble of a foiled spell's split personality. Nos'kag magic often developed a voice of its own—but it was rare indeed for the voice to stay after the spell was gone.

Isleen scanned the hut, but saw no other entrance or exit. She considered sending Halvor to look for the wise man outside when—Cian stepped, quite literally, out of the bookshelf! His nose was pressed to the pages of a floppy, oversized leather book. So intent was he on the text, that he didn't seem to notice her until she cleared her throat.

"Systir Isleen!" Cian bowed low, then straightened with a delighted laugh. "What a surprise—come in, come in. What brings you down from your mountain? I hope nothing is amiss, though I am glad of the company, whatever the reason. Take off your cloak and have a seat—oh wait!" He hurried to his desk, rooted through the drawers, then turned back around with a pair of large, black glasses balancing on his pointy nose.

Isleen peered at him with amused interest.

"They are called *sunglasses*," he said, answering her unspoken question. "A student of mine brought them from the Outside. Ingenious, aren't they? Handy too. Make yourself at home. I'm so pleased you're here."

Isleen doubted his good humor would last once she told him the reason for her visit. She removed her cloak. Instantly, light filled the room, sparkles of glittery dust catching on everything as she passed. Isleen took the seat he offered. She had learned long ago not to tower over humans when delivering bad news. They seemed to equate height with threat. She was here to gather information; it was best to reinforce the illusion of camaraderie.

"I have seen a vision," she said in a voice that, to Cian's ears—indeed to all human ears—would sound like the solemn knell of a bell.

His expression changed, and Isleen sighed. The same look, the same worry and apprehension, always accompanied the announcement *I have seen a vision.* Honestly, what did they expect? She was a Seer. Giving humans knowledge of the future was never positive or in their favor. She would be glad when the Aricin line fell and her role as advisor ended.

Liar.

You enjoy playing goddess.

Isleen ignored the voices, as she often did, consigning them to the drone of background noise.

Cian frowned. "As it's brought you the whole way down here, I gather it was not a very nice vision."

"No, it was not," Isleen said. "I saw this hut destroyed, and the trees in the grove devoured by magic. I do not know who or what caused the destruction, but it was gruesome to behold."

"I see." Cian's lips pursed. "I don't suppose you saw me alive and standing off to the side somewhere in this vision of yours?" he asked, and she knew he did not expect more than the slight shake of her head. "Well"—the old wizard's nose crinkled under the weight of the sunglasses—"what, dear lady, do you suggest we do about it?"

Kleng squatted uncomfortably inside the underground cavern, listening to the pitiful screams of the man he held in his clawed fist. Like most demons, Kleng liked to play with his food. He tore off an arm, then a foot. The screaming stopped. Kleng shook the man, eager to hear more, but the body was limp and unresponsive.

He shifted his massive weight from one cloven hoof to the other, looking around the cavern as he waited for the screams to resume. For all its size, the room felt cramped and confining to him. Minutes passed. Impatient, Kleng held the unconscious man up by his leg and bent the bone until he heard a crisp, fresh snap. The screams started up again.

With a satisfied laugh, Kleng lifted what was left of the squirming body high overhead and drew patterns of squirting blood on the cavern floor. The cries for mercy grew weak. Kleng gave an interested sniff, then opened his mouth and dropped the man onto his big, spongy tongue. Slowly he chewed, savoring the unique salty taste of human fear and suffering.

Humans.

Kleng hated them.

Most especially, he hated being subject to the galling, inconvenient whims of one. Kleng smacked his black lips and imagined the masticated remains in his mouth were those of the master wizard. How delicious *that* would be. Eltanin was long and thin; Kleng would use him to pick his teeth before biting and crunching.

Blood and drool ran down Kleng's chin at the mere thought of eating his tormentor. Humans were good for only one thing—food. His starving demon gullet could consume an entire village with ease. If allowed free rein, Kleng could happily feed on thousands, maybe more.

But he had no freedom, no choice. The molten-eyed sorcerer was strong—too strong—and no matter how many times Kleng swore he would not come when summoned, he could not refuse Eltanin's call.

He scraped his teeth with a shiny black claw, deliberately dragging out the last swallow. He knew Eltanin grew impatient. Kleng wished his fiendish specialty—the ability to embody fear—worked on the wizard, but the foul conjurer was well protected.

Kleng gave a thick belch and asked in a voice layered with shrieking, hellish howls, "What does my master require?"

The wizard stood securely inside a circle of salt and ash on the cavern floor. Salt and ash was a powerful combination—one Kleng could not sweep away. Summoning demons from Ogluidh required skill. Newly called, Kleng and his brethren were too vengeful for Eltanin to control with any reliability. The circle protected the wizard while he worked his magic, forcing the demon into servitude. The time and labor necessary to exact such control was not wasted on brief meetings such as this one. For these, Eltanin simply threw fresh meat. Kleng preferred short visits.

"You know what I require, Kleng," Eltanin said with deceptive softness. "Have you found it?"

Kleng shifted on his haunches and glared down at the infinitesimal man. He wanted nothing more than to reach out and squeeze the wizard between his fingers until he heard the satisfying pop of exploding organs.

"None of my kind knows where the Great Rift is. It does not exist."

Eltanin did not answer; instead, he flicked his wrist and sent a scalding blast of White purifying magic deep into Kleng's fat belly.

Kleng cried out. His many-voiced howl echoed off the cavern walls. His arms stretched above his head, scraping the roof, as his breath and body fouled the air. The wizard's ability to control both White and Nos'kag magic made him dangerous; too dangerous for Kleng to challenge.

"It exists," Eltanin said coldly. He lowered his hand and ended the demon's misery. "Go back to your abyss, Kleng. When I call you again, you will not come alone. I desire to speak with Balor. Bring him to me—or the next time you enter here, I will end your life."

Eltanin uttered the enchantment to dismiss him. In response, a spinning smudge appeared on the wall behind Kleng. It increased in size, twisting the rock. Trails, like melting sludge, spread out like a pinwheel as the wizard opened the gate between Norðrlönd and Ogluidh.

Kleng's ears rang with the absurdity of Eltanin's words.

"You are mad," he said as the hole gaped behind him. "I cannot bring Lord Balor. Do you think a pathetic human can summon the god of the Fomorii? He will plague me for eternity if I dare to deliver such a message."

Kleng tried to laugh, but the abyss engulfed him. The doorway closed with a swift sucking sound as it dumped him onto the flat, barren expanse that led to Balor's realm.

"I'm not sure what to do," Isleen said, in answer to Cian's question. "That is why I am here. Perhaps if you tell me what you are working on—what avenues you pursue, or what enemies you have made—I can better understand the vision." It was important she understood. Not for Cian's sake, of course, but for her own. If death came to DuwaŴyr Mountain, Isleen intended to be prepared.

She could read his mind. Lift the veil and peek inside his busy brain. But Cian's thoughts were such a chaotic mishmash of half-finished ideas and unrealized plans, it was easier to ask.

"Well, like any man who has lived long, I do have enemies," Cian admitted. "Most are as old as I am, though, and would not waste their limited energy on a quarrel."

"What of Eltanin?" Isleen asked.

"Apart from snatching Maxwell out of his grasp—they all think he's dead, you know—I can't say as I've gotten in Eltanin's way. I doubt the new king considers me much of a threat."

Isleen shot to her feet, astonished. "The bloodline is not broken?"

If Cian spoke true, then the situation was not as desperate as she first believed. Her insight into the fate of the Aricin family had stopped abruptly the day Eltanin took the high throne. Isleen had assumed them all as good as dead. Which had left her aggrieved because, as much as she protested, Isleen found it deeply gratifying to have an entire country hanging on her every word. If Maxwell lived—he would come to her for advice.

"No, no. The bloodline endures. I daresay I believe Edan is alive as well."

Isleen's face grew sour. "If that ungrateful Watchman had done as I intended, the kingdom would be safe right now. I do not know why I bother. None of my efforts ever produces the desired results. I have done more to aid humankind than any Seer before me, from living among you, to orchestrating heroic events. Never—well, maybe not never, but certainly not very often—have my plans been realized."

"We humans are a stubborn lot," Cian said. "I don't imagine your efforts were appreciated, either. We tend to get a little prickly if we think some outside power is in charge."

"But it is for your own good!" Isleen said in exasperation.

"From your perspective," Cian pointed out. "From ours, it seems an awful lot like meddling."

"The gods gave the Sisterhood their visions to help humankind, to help the high king rule and bring order to the Six Kingdoms."

"That was a long time ago." Cian shrugged. "Have you considered that maybe you were born to this responsibility with—if I may be so bold—lesser abilities because it is time for change? Perhaps the gods believe, as I do, the age of intervention, if not passed, is near its end."

Isleen decided she would be quite happy to see this hut and Cian Druce obliterated by whatever was coming. *Lesser abilities.* She used to be whole, her visions clear and accurate. Before she left her chair to walk among the humans, Isleen had been the brightest star on the mountain. But all that changed when she fell in love.

It was her darkest secret. No one knew or suspected the truth, not even her far-sighted sisters. They assumed the gods clouded her visions to test the high king and his descendants. It galled her to think that mere humans thought she had been born with *lesser abilities.* One day the world would learn exactly what had happened—when she hung her ex-lover from the Náströndu Gates as a warning to all who would dare toy with her affections. For now, Isleen consoled herself with the knowledge that the villain suffered. It was less than the faithless mortal deserved for stealing so much of her precious magic, and giving back nothing in return.

"You speak of change as if it were a good thing." Isleen's tone was cool, but civil. "We elected this life. The gods gave us a choice when they separated Norðrlönd from the rest of the world. We gained long life and control of magic in exchange for a promise—a promise to remember the Old Ways. If we reject or abandon the laws they gave us, Norðrlönd will fade and rot just like the Outside world."

Cian sighed. "You cannot hold back the change. It has already begun. If Edan is alive—and let us continue to assume he is—the true heir to the Caeraricin throne will not recognize your authority. Edan Aricin is a man who despises magic, believes it makes men weak. If Eltanin is cast down and Edan crowned high king, there will be no peace between you. You will continue to act as you see fit, and so will Edan."

As annoyed as she was, Isleen did not doubt Cian's words. She had met Prince Edan, not long ago. His father had still been king, and consequently, the prince held little interest for her, though she remembered well his ice blue eyes and open hostility.

Isleen gathered up her cloak. She hadn't the patience for much more. "Have you any other pursuits I should know about before I take my leave?"

"There *is* something. I've been searching for the Great Rift. It's all theory and guesswork, of course, but I've pinpointed two places where I think it might be located. As the Seer who voiced the *forspá*, perhaps you have a better idea of where—"

Isleen interrupted. "You and your kind are the ones who interpret the crisis as a *Great Rift*. Those were not my words."

"But surely—" Cian said.

Isleen lifted a hand. "I imagine there are countless holes in the fragile fabric of the Divide. Too many for any *one place* to be more of a threat than the others. All I know is the day will come when the Divide will come crashing down and expose our world. Norðrlönd will reappear, and the great wheel of time that grinds away at the Outside will reduce us to powder. The warm, nurturing waters that flow through our lands will turn from their course, and the great cold will come again."

She neglected to add that, when the destruction ended, only the Annars would remain. A few thousand years older maybe, but they would survive. Denied passage to the Outside world for so long, there were those of her people who regarded the impending collapse of the Divide as an opportunity, and not a disaster at all.

"Well, we can't have that," Cian said. "I've never been to the Outside world, you know, but from what I've heard it isn't the sort of place you'd want to spend your final moments."

Cian picked up the book he'd been studying when Isleen first arrived. "One last thing. I've been trying to figure out how useful Lynet's magic will be." He riffled through the pages. "Suthainn magic is astonishing, yes, but also quite limited." He found the entry. "See, here, Buwlch of Lannderfold details the four capabilities—well, supposed capabilities—of Suthainn magic. It has been, after all, a millennium since the Sòlasach lived here, so this could be a wild exaggeration, and probably is. Even so, I do not see how Lynet's magic can help anyone. What is the girl supposed to *do* to the Rift?"

Isleen sighed. "Again, you ask questions I have no answers for. The gods hide her from me. I would not know her if she walked through that door. The Suthainn magic she possesses is far reaching, and yes—frightening. I shudder to think what Eltanin would do with such power. However, you must understand two things. First, we do not know which of the four powers Lynet possesses. There are rumors she controls Life and Death, but who knows—perhaps she has them all.

"Secondly, a *forspá* is not a vision. I did not *see* anything. I was merely a channel, a worthy vessel for the gods to use to speak out their commands. While I have studied the verses and formed opinions of my own, I am—as are you, Master Druce—only guessing."

She caught Cian's disappointment, and could not hide her smile. The *forspá* caused such an entertaining stir. Even she could not have predicted the way each person heard and remembered it differently. It was fascinating to watch the key players run in circles, each of them convinced they understood the meaning and significance of their particular part.

Cian looked uneasy, so Isleen injected some warmth into her smile. She laid a slender hand on his arm. "Do not despair. I believe that, as the time draws near, these mysteries will open to me in vision. Then, my friend, if the gods are kind, we will gain answers to our questions."

Confident, aren't we?

What if there are no more visions?

Isleen smiled and pulled on her cloak. That was simple enough. If the day ever came when her visions stopped—she'd invent one.

Tiny

WITH THE WORST of the Kynneeyn Gorrym gone, Mathkr to the north and Drem to the Caeraricin border to meet with the barons who'd sworn allegiance to Eltanin, Loptr had crawled back out of the shadows. *So, where was he?*

Neira didn't want the weasel to catch her out here alone. Loptr liked to sneak up unawares, and bait her with thinly veiled sexual threats. Many of the castle slaves shared Neira's contempt for the wiry, dark-haired duke, but Eltanin favored the traitor so, even though they grumbled, no one dared do anything about him.

Neira glanced around once more, then climbed up onto the parapet on the seaward wall of the castle. Shading her eyes against the slanting sunlight, Neira tried to catch a glimpse of the white stone shrine on the island about three or more leagues from shore.

GoðaBlót, a dark splotch on the gleaming history of Caeraricin, a place where ancient kings had made human sacrifices to appease the unquiet sea. After a while, the people of Caeraricin had accepted that the sea could not be pacified, and that they would run out of people to sacrifice long before Rán ran out of storms.

She squinted but couldn't see any more than the tiny island's stark silhouette. The shrine, originally built as a shelter for the altar, now housed the last of the Aricin bloodline—Princess Audun.

Neira liked the princess. Maxwell and the courtiers had spoiled Audun, but she had treated her servants well. Likewise, she had always been nice to Neira and the other apprentices of Ddewin Tower. It made Neira furious to think of Eltanin tearing Audun's mind to shreds, then dumping her on that cold, wet island to die.

Of course, out there, away from the confines of the castle, perhaps Audun would escape. From what Neira understood, there were no guards on the island, only Audun and a couple of nursemaids. Once a day, a boat rowed out to take them food—and no doubt check if the princess still lived.

Neira looked down at the high tide crashing against the rocks below. The waves left trails of white froth on the mossy stone. She glanced back out to the island. As nice as an escape sounded, it was unlikely. Wilda had seen the princess the day they moved her. She said Audun seemed barely aware of her surroundings. Mostly, the princess had wept and babbled, and eaten only what her maids spoon-fed her.

A gust of wind carried cold sea spray up the side of the stronghold, dampening Neira's hair and robes. She jumped down from the wall. The tattered silk of her apprentice robes did little to keep out the chill. She knew she should ask Margaret for material to make warmer ones, especially now that she couldn't work any warming magic, but this filmy covering represented the last tie to her old way of life. Neira was loath to give it up.

Was it possible to save Audun? Neira had helped Ronan escape and, even though it had all gone pear-shaped, the Vökumaðr remained free, not rotting in the courtyard with the rest of his kin. Perhaps Neira could do the same for the ill-starred princess.

How, though? First, she needed to get out of the castle and find a boat. It would not be easy. The castle walls were a literal extension of the stony eastern peninsula. Protected on three sides by jutting rock and deafening waves, the cliffs formed a natural foundation from which ancient masons had built the original castle. There were only two ways out: one was the front gate, which opened on the streets of the city, a place currently forbidden to her; the other was a well-guarded postern on the south side of the castle, which led to the seashore. It was a small gate, only big enough for one person to go through at a time. Originally intended for use during a siege, it was also a quick way for kitchen servants to bring in fresh fish or seaweed for meals. Even though Neira served in the kitchen, Eltanin had given strict orders that she could not pass. It was impossible for her to leave unobserved.

Unless—

Neira considered Ddewin Tower.

Standing over forty feet higher than the rest of the castle, the bluish gray ragstone tower was once home to the wisest wizards in all of Norðrlönd. The outside walls were made of shallow ashlar blocks, the face smooth and polished to prevent assailants from climbing up—though vines had taken hold over the years, winding their way along the southern curve, giving squirrels access to the lower windows. Connected to the main castle by way of a plain, unremarkable door, the tower's upper nine levels were guarded by increasingly intricate magic. Only the ground floor, which housed the library, remained accessible to everyone.

Neira had lived in that tower in her youth, back when she and Scartozzar enjoyed the good graces of King Urien. Then, it was a busy, unruly home to the many sorcerers and rivaling novices who served Caeraricin. It was quieter now, as only a few minor apprentices had survived the coup. They had all come streaming out through that plain, unremarkable door, uttering their incantations and preparing for battle—the Kynneeyn Gorrym had picked them off one by one.

Scartozzar would have laughed himself sick at the stupidity of it. For all their bookish knowledge, court wizards were grossly unprepared for war, specializing instead in backbiting, philosophy, and affairs of state. Scartozzar had left the court for that very reason—to learn more about siege defenses and, if possible, unearth the composition of Greek Fire.

He'd told her once that Vökumenn made the country weak. Everyone, from King Urien to the lowliest pig herder, depended on the Vökumenn for security. Eltanin had obviously agreed, since he removed the Watchmen first, before taking the castle.

Neira tilted her head back, looking up to the top of the tower, looking specifically for the window, third from the left, which faced GoðaBlót.

Did that bare, plain looking room, where she'd often snuck into as a child, still hold its secrets? There was no way of knowing, of course, without going inside and triggering the lock. Every wizard who'd ever lived in that tower changed it to some degree, put his or her stamp on it, altering the layout. Neira doubted even Eltanin knew all of the secret passages—or of the hidden tunnel leading into Nótt Forest—or the number of times she and Carden had raced down that tunnel, laughing on their way to freedom.

Unconsciously, Neira fiddled with the set of charms dangling on her belt. Life used to be one joyous adventure after another.

Carden's eyes crinkled in amusement.

"If I give these to you, Tiny, you have to promise to treat them with the respect they deserve."

Neira nodded fiercely, tickled that he still called her Tiny, his pet name for her since she was nine. Now, she was a grown-up twelve. Carden was in his mid-twenties, and she loved him with all the tender yearnings of her young heart.

Carden handed her a carefully carved seashell encaging a tiny white pearl.

"This represents the treasures revealed by the low tide. Respect Rán, and she will bless you with riches." He tweaked her nose. "And stay off the shore when the tide comes in. I won't always be here to rescue you."

She took the shell as if it were made of the purest gold, clutching it in both hands.

"I will," she promised.

"This. . . ." Carden paused, weighing a misshapen black stone in his palm.

His voice grew serious as he seemed to consider the wisdom of giving it to her. Neira held her breath, waiting. "Well, you know what this is. Keep it as a remembrance of our secret, and of my gratitude."

Solemnly, reverently, she took the stone, knowing how precious it was to him.

"This third one is special." He grinned. "I got it for you the last time I crossed the Divide. It symbolizes adventure."

Carden held up a foreign coin with an eagle stamped in the silver. "There is nothing more adventurous than being in a strange country, far from home, and not knowing the currency." He laughed and handed her the coin. "So study well before you travel. Oh, and bring me something when you do"—he winked—"or else I'll think you grew up and stopped loving me."

Then he bent down and sent her into a fit of giggles by kissing her soft cheek and whispering, "Don't ever stop loving me."

Neira smiled. Her thumb smoothed over the fourth charm, a ring she'd brought back for him from her own first grand adventure—she'd lacked the courage to give it to him.

Neira felt herself blushing and she raised her face to the breeze to cool it. Had she the courage now? She was a woman, not the wide-eyed little girl he knew. She'd changed so much in fact that Carden had walked right past her—not even recognizing her—the last time she saw him.

Scartozzar had been in perilous negotiations with both the king and Eltanin, and had ordered her to remain in the background, unnoticed. Neira obeyed, but regretted it. She was not the only one who'd changed. Age had strengthened Carden, giving him an air of grace, nobility, and power that took her breath. He'd stormed down the hall, scarcely glancing at her as she stood in the shadows, her hood low over her face, trembling like a rabbit.

Sounds, like screams, from somewhere deep beneath the castle, jolted her from her thoughts. Neira pressed flat against the wall, out of eyesight of the back garden door. *Stupid. Stupid.* Silly daydreams only made her vulnerable: dreams of Carden, or of rescuing the princess. As much as Neira wanted to help Audun, she needed to stay focused on the heartstone. It was her sole reason for being here.

It seemed a simple enough riddle: *turn the heartstone to flesh.* The heart made of stone was surely Eltanin's. Neira had to soften him, to turn him from his association with demons and Nos'kag magic. Of course, as soon as Eltanin became vulnerable, she intended to drive a knife through that newly softened heart. Had Isleen seen *that* in her troublesome vision?

Not for the first time, Neira questioned the Seer's allegiance. Something wasn't right about this whole thing. Still, she had to try. If a way existed to defeat Eltanin, Neira would find it.

Each night, while the castle slept, Neira slipped into the library, looking for a spell or secret to use against the usurper. Mainly, she studied the small number of firsthand accounts describing Nos'kag magic. There must be a weakness in it, especially when wielded by a human. Nos'kag magic was not natural to man—no mortal had ever been born with it. The only way to gain its dark power was to defeat a demon and take his magic from him. This was why there were so few records.

The danger did not end there. All the books and scrolls Neira had read were unanimous in one regard: once Nos'kag magic was inside of you, *it was impossible to get it out.* You could learn to control it, to use it alongside White magic, but you would never be rid of it . . . and you could never trust it. A distressing thought, since the two men Neira cared for most had both embraced Nos'kag magic like a lover.

Her studies taught her several useful things: the preparation necessary to summon a Fomorii; how to protect herself from the initial onslaught; even how to escape, should one have her in its clutches. But how to control or dismiss the creature was still a mystery—and what was the sense in summoning a monster if you could not control it or send it back when you were through? Neira was beginning to think the secret was exactly that, a secret, not written, but passed down orally from master to apprentice. She supposed, if it had been recorded somewhere, Eltanin would have destroyed or concealed it by now.

Not that Neira intended to summon a demon. But, if Eltanin set one against her, she would gladly send it back to the abyss if she knew how.

Neira heard a shuffle and inched around the corner, expecting to see Loptr up to no good. It was Margaret, heading for the thin patch of garden inside the enclosure, where they grew leeks and herbs for the various meals prepared each day. Neira watched, deciding whether or not to reveal herself.

The old woman set a wooden tote on the ground and searched her discolored apron for a small trowel. The tote was one of Margaret's own designs, neatly organized into sections, each compartment able to hold a different herb or root.

"I saw you up on the parapet," Margaret called. "No use hiding; I know you're here. I suspect others do, too."

Neira sighed heavily and stepped out of the shadows. What she wouldn't give for a sprinkle of Vökumaðr Hide magic. "I wanted to see GoðaBlót— in case I could swim to it."

"The currents in that direction are strong." Margaret clucked her tongue. "That is why it makes such a good prison. And why do you look for more trouble? Haven't you enough of it here in the kitchens?"

"I'm not looking for trouble. I'm curious."

"You're foolish. What would you do if the wind suddenly stopped while you balanced up there peering out and you dropped like a stone?" The old woman held up a hand. "And don't tell me you'd fly. I've heard that before; haven't ever seen it done."

"It's no more dangerous than you allowing Colm to help with the king's meals. With so many to feed, you could assign Colm any task to keep him busy and out of the way. You must be careful, Margaret. Eltanin is using us as pawns in—"

Margaret's expression went oddly blank.

Neira did not trust that look. "Where is Colm?" she asked. "Did he come back last night?"

Margaret shook her head. "Not yet. We're all busy. The king has guests coming in from Llanerc tomorrow, you know. There are extra chores to be done. You're just trying to get out of them by messing about out here."

"And you're trying to hide something from me," Neira said. "If you do not tell me, I'll worm it out of Wilda. What do you know?"

Margaret put down her trowel and let out a heavy, tired sigh. "Colm is missing—vanished like the others."

Neira nearly exploded with frustration. "We have to stop this. We have to find out where they are going, what is happening to them—before any more of us disappear."

"No. We cannot stop it." Margaret grabbed Neira's arm. "We cannot stop Eltanin. You know that. Our efforts would only bring suffering on every servant in this castle. Look what happened the last time you decided to interfere. The Watchman killed King Urien."

"He did not!" Neira gasped and tried to pull away.

"So you say." Margaret did not let go. "We helped you drug Boadhagh, and what did we get? Six people died that night, including the king. What do you plan now? Would you sacrifice us all for one fleeting moment of righteous anger?" Margaret pressed on. "You think you are invincible, that you are immune to his evil because he needs you for something. But what if that changes? What if you push him too far? How will all your learning help any of us if you are dead?"

The old woman might as well have slapped her, Neira was so shocked. Not once had she considered that Margaret and the others might need her, might look to her for wisdom and worldly skill. Unlike common servants, Neira had traveled far as Scartozzar's apprentice, even to the Outside world. Her friends must think she knew things that could make their lives easier, if she would only share.

Was she holding back? Neira seldom stepped in when she saw the others laboring with tedious chores, although she thought often enough—to herself—that there were easier ways to get the job done. She was just so wrapped up in her own problems, and Isleen's task, that she hadn't given the others much time or thought.

Neira blew out a deep breath. Another unwelcome responsibility. Her shoulders were not so broad she could carry the weight of everyone. Still, she was her mother's daughter. If nothing else, she would soldier on.

"You're right." She patted Margaret's hand. "We can't fight Eltanin. It's better if we just stay out of his way."

Margaret seemed satisfied. "Come," the old woman coaxed. "Help me gather the herbs for Wilda's beef-and-turnip stew. She plans to simmer it through the night so we can all have the best bits before the guards gorge themselves on it tomorrow."

Neira pulled up her hood and dutifully did as Margaret asked. None of them understood. She had an obligation to her family and, through Isleen, to the people of Norðrlönd. For good or ill, she was committed to seeing this through. She might make mistakes, but wasn't it better to fail than to give up without trying? Colm was missing. He must be somewhere in the castle, probably the lower caverns. Did no one think to look there? Were they all so afraid of Eltanin they preferred to do nothing?

Solving the heartstone riddle came first, of course, but Neira would not abandon Colm. If no one else would step up and search for him, then she must do so. As soon as the castle was dark, she would go find him.

Scent on the Wind

ONAN STOOD AT THE END of Briar Lea Road on the outskirts of Buffalo, New York. *Lynet was here.* Nearby, so close he recognized her scent on the wind. Ronan drank it in, aching with hunger, starving—but not for food.

He was Vökumaðr, and she was the object of his Oath.

Her golden thread sang a steady note in his mind. She was happy, healthy. He could not wait to wrap her in his arms. She would be angry with him for taking so long to get here, for trusting Scartozzar, for leaving her behind. He would deal with her displeasure, so long as he could kiss her and hold her.

Lleth nosed the grass, lifted a leg and marked his territory.

Ronan grinned. Perhaps it was time he did the same. Clicking his tongue at the wolfhound, Ronan headed down the quiet suburban street.

He pinpointed the house—three-storied, painted yellow and green, with a multitude of porches, nooks, and dormers. Clouds of lace shielded the windows from nosy neighbors. Red roses climbed along the eastern wall. Hummingbirds, extinct in Norðrlönd, flitted through patches of pink and purple flowers. Ronan paused to watch, fascinated by their strange ability to fly both forward and backward.

Like most Northlander homes, there were no fences, just a low row of hedge along the front. The lot was deep, two acres at least. Laden fruit trees lined the back where a trellis arch covered a path leading deeper into the woods. Lilacs filled one entire corner of the garden.

The Mother surely blessed this ground. Tall, aging yew trees shaded the house on three sides. Ronan doubted the folks who lived along this road noticed the way the gnarled trunks leaned in around the house. Or how their many-fingered branches stretched and tangled together as they protected the inhabitants from any passing divination. This house was a sanctuary. A place where history lay thick and the land remembered how it was before the gods separated Norðrlönd and its people from the Outside world. No wonder Cian had been unable to locate Lynet from the other side of the Divide. The Earth magic here was strong, the vegetation lush. It brought a shiver to his skin, and Ronan called a shield tight around him, then realized he had probably just given away his position. If wizards hid in that house, they now knew he was out here.

In the weeks you were held prisoner, years may have gone by on the Outside. Who knows how long it has been for Lynet, or what kind of life she has fashioned for herself?

The echo of Cian's warning brought him up short. By Ronan's reckoning, at least two years had passed on the Outside since they parted on the beach at Aros. A long time for a woman to wait.

Ronan growled in frustration. Perhaps he should hang back and observe before charging in to reclaim her. He picked up a stick and threw it for Lleth to chase, then walked casually past the house, resisting the urge to break down that wreath-guarded door and cry out her name until she answered.

Lleth returned with the stick, and Ronan threw it again, farther this time. While the hound played, Ronan scanned the nearby trees and houses, looking for a place to settle in and watch—

The thrill of an illicit song stopped him in his tracks. Around him, the air swelled with music so sweet and rich it hurt to hear it. The *Kærásti Fórnsöngr*. He hadn't felt its taunt since the day he'd left Lynet to go face Eltanin.

Ronan turned as the front door of the yellow-and-green house opened. His chest expanded; his heart pounded an eager thud against his ribs. No matter the seasons or distance between them, no matter the cruel workings of the Nornir—Ronan's reaction to Lynet never dimmed. He loved her, and though the gods cursed that love, he felt only fierce joy at seeing her again.

Ronan called to Lleth and they started back. His spirits high, he rubbed the wolfhound's head, laughing as the dog ran in playful circles around him.

He'd found Lynet. His world was right again.

Out of the corner of her eye, Lynet noticed a stranger and his dog roughhousing as they walked from the wooded park at the far end of the street. A vague sense of familiarity came over her. The setting sun cast long shadows on the road that extended nearly to the driveway, giving the impression she was connected to them by a thin river of shade. Lynet stared hard. The man's laughter and clear whistle were pleasant to her ears, and she enjoyed watching the way he moved. His shoulders were broad and masculine, and he walked like he feared nothing in this world.

No matter how familiar he seemed, there was no chance she actually knew him. Accepting that, Lynet resumed carrying an armload of books to her car—a cheery sunflower-yellow Neon that Alder had bought her not long after she arrived in Buffalo. She was easing the door open with her knee when a mass of brindled gray slammed into her, knocking books into the air and pitching her flat onto her back on the damp grass.

Up close, the wolfhound was enormous. His paws straddled each side of her head; his tail swept back and forth. Lynet turned her face away but could not escape the dog's wet tongue. It flicked over her, washing her cheeks and chin with all the exuberance of someone who has rediscovered a long-lost friend. Lynet laughed, bewildered and amused by the dog's obvious excitement. She tried to sit up, but he stepped around and over her, continuing to lick her forehead, her arms, her hair. His bark a deep woof, the hound called to his master to come see what he had found.

The stranger caught up, and pulled the hound off her.

"Stöðva. Stöðva sik," the man repeated firmly, speaking in a language Lynet did not understand, but the dog obviously could, for the sky overhead became visible again.

Grateful, Lynet looked up into the man's face. "Thank y—" she started, but the words died on her lips.

She could not breathe.

Her heart held still, squeezed by some fierce emotion that just as suddenly released in wild, pounding, unreasonable joy. Bright tears caught on her lashes as hope flowed to some vital, hollow place inside her.

Frightened by what was happening, Lynet scrambled to her feet. Keeping her head down, she brushed herself off, not daring to look at him while she tried desperately to rein in her crazy emotions.

"He's glad to see you." The man's voice was full of humor as he restrained the dog with a leash and moved to stand between them.

"Apparently," Lynet said, keeping her eyes on the animal pacing and whining behind his master's blockade. "He's beautiful—so energetic and happy. What's his name?"

There was an awkward pause, and Lynet felt the air between them change from comfortable warmth to trembling uncertainty.

"Llethbhràthair," the man said, and the dog woofed in answer. "I call him Lleth. Although, I think he would answer to anything you wished to call him. He seems quite taken with you." The stranger gave a hesitant smile, his teeth white against the uneven shadow of his close-cropped beard.

Lynet's emotions ran rampant. She wanted to cry, squeal, laugh, and dance all at once. She took a step closer to him. The delicious scent of male sweat and worn leather filled her senses. Without conscious thought, her breathing changed cadence to match the steady rise and fall of his chest. Her insides fluttered as she watched his muscles strain against the seams of his jacket while he held back the wolfhound. His eyes, the topaz-yellow of a cat, did not waver as he watched her, though his mouth held a hint of amusement as he waited for her to finish her appraisal—waited, it seemed, for something more.

"Umm, do you live around here?" Lynet tore her eyes away and busied herself with picking up her scattered books. "I'm Lynet, by the way; Lynet Macarthur. I'm afraid I don't know everyone who lives up and down the street." Her words were clumsy, even as small talk, since she was pretty sure she would have noticed *him* living nearby. The reaction she was having was hard to ignore.

"I'm not a neighbor. Not yet, anyway." He gave a curt command to the dog, then knelt to help her with her books. "My name is Ronan." He indicated the houses nearby. "I'm apartment hunting and heard one might be available around here." His fingertips grazed intimately over her palm as he took the stack of books out of her hands. "Where do you want these?"

Lynet curled her fingers to keep from chasing after that sensuous touch. Good grief, what was wrong with her? She acted like she'd never seen a gorgeous man before. "In the car. I'm on my way to the library."

He put the books on the passenger seat and stood back.

The silence was disconcerting. Could he hear the rapid beating of her heart? "There's an apartment at the top of that blue-gray building over there," she blurted out. "I think it's vacant. I haven't seen a light on in weeks. I hear it's small. People who move in don't usually stay long."

"Thank you. I'll take a look."

He didn't seem in a hurry to leave, but Lynet couldn't think of anything else to say. She was wary of strangers. The Macarthurs had become militant about where and when any of them left the property. The shadow wraiths grew bolder with each attempt on the house. Lynet needed to get to the library and return by nightfall. Alder insisted everyone be inside Laburnum House before dark. At least one member of the household kept watch every night, and Alder had garnered the help of a rather large pair of stripy cats. They looked harmless during the day but, at night, the pair grew horns and gained about a hundred pounds.

In the year since the first attack, Lynet had learned of Laburnum House's role as a sanctuary for all those seeking refuge from the creatures that crossed over from the abyss through a passage called the Devil's Gate.

In modern times, the Gate had been dormant—but some evil now stirred.

Alder believed Lynet was the cause, so he was especially harsh on her, demanding to know her whereabouts at all times. Lynet had learned not to argue, as it made no difference.

"I, um, better go; the library closes early on Wednesdays." Lynet put her hand on the car door, but didn't get in. What was wrong with her? She knew better . . . and yet, something held her still, something good and delicious and right. Baffled, Lynet shook her head and forced herself to get in the car, then on impulse, called out the window. "Maybe I'll see you when you move in. Even bring a plate of cookies to say welcome to the neighborhood."

Ronan's smile widened. His canine teeth were a hint longer than she had expected, and gave his expression a disarming edge. "I like sweets," he said, his voice a low, throaty rumble. Then, with a click of his tongue, he and his dog headed for the blue-gray building across the street.

He stopped suddenly and turned back. "Do you sing, Lynet?" he asked.

She was surprised by such a funny question, but didn't see any harm in answering. "No. I'm likely to split your ears if I sing. I'm that bad at it. Why?"

"Curious." Ronan shrugged, then walked off, leaving Lynet feeling confused and oddly empty.

Ronan stood on the rusted iron stairs attached to the outside of the blue-gray building, where he'd just rented a small apartment. The building was once a barbershop with the barber living upstairs, his business below. Currently, a local trucking company used the bottom floor as storage. The place was old and unkempt, the railing on the stairs loose, but Ronan didn't need a rail for balance, and he didn't anticipate having visitors. The rent was unreasonable for so small a space, but Ronan would have agreed to any amount. The main living area had a window directly overlooking the street below. From there, Ronan could watch the yellow-and-green house unhindered.

Even though the owner had left twenty minutes ago, Ronan still stood outside, his jacket collar turned up against the evening breeze, his thoughts so disjointed he could barely hold onto them. He felt out of his element, uncertain of his next move.

Lynet did not remember him.

He'd searched her face, her heart, looking for a twinkle of laughter or a sense of playfulness—but found nothing.

Of all the problems he and Cian had anticipated, this was not one of them. Why didn't she remember him? What else had she forgotten? Norðrlönd, the *forspá,* her ruinous magic—how little it would take to destroy both this world and Norðrlönd with the careless use of something she could not control.

Lynet didn't remember him.

He found that hardest to accept. How could she not know *him?* She loved him, had burrowed deep in the protection of his arms every night for months as they fled Carden's men. How could she forget that?

What if she never remembered him?

He slammed his fist against the railing. Lleth jerked, sniffing the air for danger. Ronan gave the hound an apologetic pat, and tried to ease the tension in his own body. What had Scartozzar done to her? No memories of him or Lleth. An incomplete Hide spell—Scartozzar had messed that up bad. Lynet was caught between images. Stripped of all color, she didn't look like herself, nor did she look like any disguise. That actually worked in Ronan's favor. He doubted anyone from Norðrlönd would recognize her, which meant he had a better chance of keeping her safe.

Ronan ran a callused hand through his shaggy brown hair. He had expected to find Lynet, argue with her, revel in her forgiving kisses, and then return to Norðrlönd before Eltanin's scouts caught up with them. Ronan knew the scouts were out there but, without the advantage of tracking and the Vökumaðr Oath, they would be searching blind. Until, of course, Ysbail found her; then Eltanin would send everything he had.

Ronan wasn't sure what to do.

Stopping and settling down was not in his plans. It was too dangerous. If Lynet didn't know how to keep her magic bound, and Eltanin's men attacked, it could all be over in an instant. But what else could Ronan do? Kidnap her? She didn't know him. What if she saw *him* as the threat? He could just as easily be the catalyst as Eltanin or his soldiers.

It was Nairn all over again. As before, Ronan needed to gain Lynet's confidence and trust. Hopefully, it would go a little smoother this time. Ronan knew exactly what wound her up and made her dig in her heels like a stubborn goat. If he was careful, he could reteach her—help her remember the things she already knew. It wouldn't be easy, and time was not on his side. He would have to live a double life, fit in, and act like an Outsider—all the while keeping constant watch for the attack that would surely come.

Ronan walked down the rickety wrought iron steps. Staying here meant finding another job.

For now, he would keep his identity a secret from Lynet and whoever else lived in that house. He would befriend her until she trusted him enough to listen to the truth, or until her memories returned. Then, together, they would figure out where to go from there.

Wolf in the Sanctuary

ET GO YOU STUPID . . . OUCH." The ladder teetered back—then
shot forward—bumping against the bookshelf as Neira wrested a
heavy, dust-covered scroll from the very back of the top shelf. She
yanked and wiggled it out from under a stack of ancient parchments.
Several dislodged sheets fluttered to the floor.

Neira could not believe the scroll was still here. She'd hidden it ages ago.
Of course, power-hungry apprentices seldom studied Animal magic. If you
weren't born with the racial magic of a particular animal, then it did no good
to study how to use it—which is why hiding something in this section of the
library was ingenious. No one ever came here.

Neira climbed down the ladder, juggling the scroll. Thankfully, Aod had
been around earlier to relight the torches, so she wasn't stumbling about in
the dark. Still she tried to be as quiet as possible. It was late, and she did not
want anyone to catch her in the library. If Eltanin found out about her
nighttime activities, he would restrict her further. Until she discovered a way
to defeat him, she must take every precaution. This library was the only viable
source of lore available to her.

She was halfway down the ladder when the unexpected smudge of
fingerprints caught her eye. Years' worth of dust covered every shelf—but
not this one. Someone had been here recently.

Neira read the book titles behind the fingerprints: *Vacuity of Pig Bones or
Flight of the Bumblebee*; *Varg i Véum (Origin of the Phrase "Wolf in the
Sanctuary")*; *Vökumenn of the Æsir*; *Varieties of Sprites, Fairies, and Puki*;
Venomous Creatures and Antidotes; *Vooga Chambers for Dwigdíg Beetles*. What
was so interesting about these titles? She tucked the scroll under one arm and
leaned over the edge of the ladder to get a better look—when a sound from
the doorway startled her.

Neira nearly lost her balance.

She hugged the ladder, wishing she knew a spell for invisibility, wishing she wasn't wearing a collar that would stop her even if she did.

The footsteps came closer, heading straight for her, then abruptly stopped one row over. Neira heard rummaging as books and parchments were shoved aside. Something heavy dropped with a bang and Neira held her breath, afraid they'd heard her gasp.

The room went quiet.

Neira was wondering if she could squeeze herself up onto one of the shelves when the footsteps hurried out of the room. She frowned. Who *was* that? They certainly weren't studying. She scrambled down the ladder and hurried to see if she could get a glimpse. It had better not be any of the kitchen help. Neira had endangered them enough already. She didn't need anybody following her. She could do this herself.

Neira snuck around the corner in time to see Paldro, one of the surviving apprentices, eating as he walked, a small leather sack clutched in his hand.

So, she was not the only one who used this out-of-the-way section of the library as a hiding place. It looked like the portly boy found it a convenient spot to hoard extra food. He was probably the one who'd disturbed the dust on the bookshelf.

Neira went to a study table and cleared a space amidst the disarray of books and parchments. In times past, the youngest apprentices were assigned the weekly task of tidying the library, making sure all the items were returned to their proper place and nothing left out of order. In recent years, haughty apprentices had flatly refused such menial labor. The library was a mess. Seldom used, this section was neater than the rest, but even it had become cluttered and disorganized. She supposed the first time Eltanin needed to look something up, the few sorcerers who remained in this tower would be sorry they hadn't treated the library with more care.

Neira spread out the scroll and placed books at either end to keep the map flat, then lit a candle and bent over the faded drawing. Pleasant memories filled her head as she located favorite parts of the castle. The map was minutely detailed, having been updated each time the castle was enlarged—both through normal construction and by decades of meddlesome wizards who added their own form of architecture to Ddewin Tower.

As far as Neira was concerned, it was a treasure map. She'd discovered it years ago as a child and used it often to gain access to places she had no business being.

Tonight was no different.

Ignoring the urge to examine the always-fascinating Ddewin Tower, Neira applied herself to the task of finding a way into the ancient dungeons. She already knew many of the inked-in arrows and squiggles indicating the kitchen, stables, and paths to the seashore—all places a young apprentice might sneak off to, to clear her study-weary head. However, she had paid no attention to the subterranean caverns back then. To her delight, she found those sections similarly detailed. The faded markings outlined ancient prison cells, guardrooms, and weapon chambers. A tall, spidery script warned that the caverns had collapsed and the dungeon was no longer accessible.

There had been three separate cave-ins over the years. The first, and worst, had taken place eight hundred years ago. One had only to go to what remained of the old postern in the east curtain wall to see the descending stairwell blocked by rock and rubble for a glimpse of the devastation. The most recent cave-in, no more than a hundred years previous, had completely closed off the underground tunnel to the sea.

Yet someone was getting in and out. How?

Neira checked the king's chambers first, since that seemed the most likely place for a secret entrance. She found several hidden tunnels snaking through the castle and grounds. Too bad she wasn't privy to Eltanin's quarters; she'd have access to everything. One of the passages on the map clearly led down to the lower caverns. It, too, bore the spidery script labeling it *inaccessible*.

Neira didn't believe it but, true or not, she had no intention of going anywhere near the viper's nest. There had to be another way down there.

She branched out from the king's rooms, searching the map for another entrance. There were countless scribbles to decipher, each in a different hand and often written generations apart. The dim light of the flickering candle didn't help. Neira swore the self-important wizards deliberately overwrote their predecessors, obscuring the details, ensuring the map stayed unfathomable and misleading.

An hour passed, and the candle burned lower. Finally, she discovered a hidden hallway not far from the room she shared with Wilda, which excited her for a moment, but it went only as far as the storage cellars. Disheartened, Neira was wondering how in heaven's name she was going to sneak inside Eltanin's chambers—when a tiny star inside a circle caught her attention. It seemed to be a delineation of some sort, and she searched the scroll to find the matching symbol.

At last—the passageway. She traced it to Ddewin Tower. Here, somewhere on the ground floor, was a door leading to a tunnel that opened into the caverns below. It looked as if both the king and the residents of Ddewin Tower had once had an escape route to the sea.

So . . . where was the door?

Neira continued to study the map, concentrating on the tower. She was amused at the number of errors she found. The walls indicated on the map were seldom a true representation of the walls and passageways she knew actually existed. Evidently, some wizards preferred to keep their secrets to themselves. Herself included. After all, the passageway into the Nótt Forest was not on the map. She had used the exit numerous times as a child. Not once had she felt inclined to tell her master, much less put it on a map for all to see. No, some things were better left to the studious seeker.

Neira inched around the table, turning her head sideways to read several lines of minuscule print written along the very edge. She choked back a squeal of triumph as she found the words to open the door. They were common-enough phrases, and she hoped she could get away with saying them herself, and not have to trick Wilda into doing it for her.

She heard a noise, like the brush of cloth on stone, and Neira froze, still bent awkwardly over the parchment.

Was it Paldro again?

She waited, listening intently, wondering if she dared move. Minutes passed; the sound did not come again. Slowly, she straightened and rubbed the small of her back. She was tired. Her mind was playing tricks, exaggerating the normal creaks and groans of the castle.

Neira glanced at the window. Night was turning gray. She had maybe an hour before sunup and her kitchen duties. If she wanted to try this, she needed to hurry. Rolling up the map, Neira buried it beneath the books and scrolls on the table. She'd find a new hiding place for it as soon as she got back. Taking the candle with her, she sped out of the room, determined to find the secret door to the caverns below.

Ronan massaged the bridge of his nose, working his way up to the tight frown in his brow. His father had had a scowl that could halt the hearts of his enemies. At the rate he was going, Ronan would wear that same look in his elder years. He supposed that wasn't a bad thing, although he didn't particularly care to cultivate it. For all his skill and experience in battle, Ronan preferred peace to war—all Vökumenn did.

Whenever Ronan thought of his father, the image of fifteen spikes in a dark courtyard swam before his eyes. One day he would return to Caeraricin and free his kin, but not yet. They were dead. Lynet was alive. For now, his responsibility was to her.

Ronan rested his shaggy head on the car seat while he waited. He needed more sleep. No, what he needed was more time. Sometimes he swore he heard minutes whizz past him, sniggering his name. He wanted to reach out and seize a fistful, and make them work for him for a change—but he did not have that power. Summoning was a gift given to nobles, not their servants.

A door opened on the north side of the yellow-and-green house, and he watched Maple Macarthur come out into the morning air. She turned and looked in his direction, but did not acknowledge his presence. Ronan always kept his back to the sun, and knew he was sufficiently camouflaged by a patchwork of sunshine and shadow. The woman would have to come to the front of the lawn and stare into the pitted Malibu across the street to be sure he was in there.

Maple hobbled to the lilac bushes in the northwest corner. Setting down her basket, she pulled a pair of clippers from her apron pocket. With strong hands, she cut and gathered the branches and put them in her basket. Her upswept, loosely curled hair was mostly gray, but Ronan saw glimmers of ginger when she stood in the sunlight. Plump and feisty, the matriarch had taken a liking to him, inviting him into the garden, showing him her carefully tended vegetables.

There was something curious about Maple Macarthur. He couldn't quite pinpoint it, but Ronan was confident it would come to him. That wasn't all he felt confident about. His plan to gain Lynet's respect and trust was working. The Macarthurs had accepted him as a neighbor and friend. He'd even joined them for dinner several times over the last two months. If he didn't know better, he might think the Nornir had decided to give him some peace and quiet for a change.

Ronan picked up a pair of dirty work gloves and inspected them for wear. He'd gotten a job working in the town of Depew, at the tungsten factory. The owners were good men, brave enough to occasionally hire down-and-outs to give them a second chance. The work was hard and the pay low, but Ronan enjoyed physical labor; it kept him limber. The men he worked with were decent enough, even if some had criminal records. Most were trying to pull their lives together. Ronan admired that.

He supposed he'd made friends there, too. The guys included him in their daily game of telling tall tales during lunch. Ronan enjoyed the camaraderie. He missed his uncles' yarns as they boasted of outrageous battle feats. Though not as colorful, his coworkers could tell good stories, too. Three of them were only boys by his reckoning. Still, Ronan wasn't so old he couldn't remember what it was like to be their age, with nowhere to direct all that manic energy. Without his father's discipline and guidance, Ronan was sure he'd have turned out just like them, stranded between youth and adulthood, not knowing how to get what he wanted out of life.

Ronan pushed the gloves into his jacket pocket and grumbled when he heard the snap of several stitches. It was a good jacket, but it was old. He'd found it in a charity shop, shortly after crossing the Aragaidheal Divide. He didn't know who the previous owner was, or how it came to be in the cramped shop a couple of blocks from the High Street in Canterbury, England. He'd simply stepped in out of the rain and discovered a curious-smelling place full of donated, secondhand items. The dark leather coat thrown in a heap by the far wall was destined for the bin. According to the clerk, it was too old and damaged to sell. That made the price right as far as Ronan was concerned.

It took a while to get the hide soft again. By the time it was finished, Ronan had crossed the British Isles and was heading for the Faeroes. Still, it had been worth it. He'd patched the delicate lining and sewn a secret place in one of the pockets for the Annarian crystal; a few more stitches fixed the torn left cuff. It fit him well across the wide measure of his shoulders, although the sleeves were a bit long. He didn't mind. It kept the wind and rain out, and he could enjoy the familiar feel of leather. Autumn was on the way. The air was chilly, the dew fresh and sparkling in the sun. He would need the coat if they stayed for the winter.

Ronan was assessing the damage to the pocket lining when a noise from the front porch told him it was time.

He turned to watch as Lynet swung open the sage green front door of Laburnum House. She danced out onto the painted floorboards in her bare feet, spinning on her toes. Her hair, like a stream of unnaturally black ink, swirled around her shoulders. She wrapped her hands around the painted porch rail and with an expression of absolute devotion, leaned out over the railing and lifted her chin to the sky.

It was silly to be so besotted, and he laughed at himself for it, but this morning ritual was all he had; a poignant echo of their life together, before Scartozzar had stripped her memories. He remembered stoking the morning campfire, watching Lynet stretch toward the sky to bask in the early rays of dawn. Even in the rain she did this. Always looking upward, seeking out any break in the clouds that would afford her a glimpse of the sun. It was a habit from her youth, a remnant of the religion handed down by her father. A spiritual man, Aengus had taught his daughter to revere the sun goddess, Álfröðull, and fear the wolf who chased her across the sky.

Ronan doubted Lynet understood why she did it, now, with her memories gone, but apparently some inner part of her still found comfort in the ritual, as she never missed a day.

She checked her watch, gasped in disbelief, and raced into the house. Ronan smiled and shook his head. The whole concept of time was lost on Lynet. Oh, he understood the confusion well enough; it was not easy living here when their internal clocks were set to a different pace. But, where he had been able to adapt, Lynet had not. Forever rushing to catch up, she remained bewildered by the swiftly turning days and nights.

Ronan studied the house while he waited. He had been watching it for two months now, and he swore the thing ebbed and grew with the pull of the moon. Each morning seemed to bring some new and unexpected intricacy that he had somehow overlooked.

Lynet rushed out the door. The hem of her skirt twirled around her knees as she hurried to place her things in the car, then dashed to the giant stoneware pots near the hedge to pick some fresh flowers. Ronan frowned as she left the passenger door wide open, her back to the road the entire time. What was she doing?

It made Ronan's warfaring instincts bristle. What an easy target she had become. It was not safe, especially with wraiths nearby. Ronan had spotted them several times on his nightly prowl. What frustrated him most was the fact Lynet used to know better. Under Ronan's watchful eye, she had learned to pay strict attention to her surroundings, to know instinctively when danger approached, and—most importantly—how to avoid situations where she would be forced to protect herself with magic.

All that was forgotten now.

Lynet backed her little Neon out onto the road, and Ronan waited, knowing she would stop to talk to him, knowing that behind those beautiful dark eyes there would still be no hint of recognition. Oh, she knew who he *pretended* to be, an unskilled laborer who lived next door, but the true man— the Vökumaðr, the Oathmaker—was gone.

Lynet pulled up beside him and rolled down her window, her wide smile becoming a lopsided squint as the rising sun shone straight into her eyes.

"Beautiful morning, isn't it?" Lynet laughed.

"Very." Ronan nodded. "Lots of sun. It will dry the dew and take the chill out of the air."

"Well, I for one loved the cold air last night. Summer lasted too long this year. I don't like the heat." Her cheeks flushed with pleasure—a flush that deepened as she continued to meet his gaze. The moment lingered, as it often had of late, and Lynet retreated first, looking down and away.

Ronan noted the wild flutter of pulse at her throat. It gave him hope. He'd been careful, moving slowly, letting her set the pace of their relationship. Finally, she was warming to him in the way he wanted.

"Oh, wait. Maple told me to ask you over to dinner tonight. I know it's short notice, but she's baking a special dessert and wished to invite you."

"Of course," Ronan said. Lynet was his only reason for being here. He would take any offering, with both hands.

"Great. We'll see you tonight." She waved and drove off down the street.

Ronan gave her a head start, a little one. Lynet enjoyed driving that car of hers faster than was wise, and could lose him the closer they got to Lancaster. Not that he couldn't find her if she did. Ronan had tracked her halfway across the globe; he could do so again. Still, he liked keeping her in sight until she was safely at work. He had placed a Ward spell on the diner. If any Northlanders stepped foot in it, the spell would alert him. He could be at Lynet's side in less than eight minutes. Something he'd proved twice already when Maple met Lynet for lunch.

They weaved in and out of traffic, he being careful to keep a measured distance. Lynet was unaware Ronan followed her, and he wanted it to stay that way. As far as she knew, he simply drove in the same direction each morning on his way to the factory. It took skill for him to blend in, especially during other times of the day, or on weekends. The salt-corroded Malibu was an easy-to-spot eyesore. Western New York winters were harsh. The chemicals used to keep the roads clear of ice ate through car metal like it was tissue paper. Fortunately, that meant rusty cars could be bought on the cheap.

Up ahead, Lynet pulled into the diner parking lot and was soon inside.

Ronan rubbed his hand down over the whiskers on his face and throat. Between the constant watch, and the swift passage of time on the Outside, he felt exhausted. He continued down the street and headed for the tungsten factory. No chance of rest. He had work, dinner with his *ástmær*, and then his usual prowl of the town to make sure no one knew they were there. He'd made friends with the two *cornioggath*, the Norðrlönd tabbies Alder had enlisted to the cause. The cats weren't too keen on Lleth, though the hound paid little attention to them. After living with the Hoar Beast all his life, the wolfhound was not impressed, not even when they grew horns and became the size of panthers.

"Did you see Ronan this morning?" Eibby straightened the coloring books and sorted the crayons the waitresses passed out to the kids who accompanied their parents to the diner. It was the mid-morning lull between breakfast and lunch, the only real time to chat.

"Yes, and he's coming over for dinner tonight. Maple is making one of her spicy pies. She especially wanted him to come."

"Why does Maple let him in the house and not me?" Eibby shook her head. "Your family is too weird, Lynet. Seriously, you should run away and join the circus."

"I'm sorry," Lynet apologized for what felt like the billionth time.

"Not your fault you have stinky relatives." Eibby shrugged. "So, what are you wearing tonight?"

"Does it matter?"

"Yes, because you're going to obsess. I know you. Just don't try to color your hair again. It doesn't work, and it makes Fig crazy."

Lynet agreed. Fig always got mad at her fruitless attempts to change herself. He loved her exactly as she was, and didn't seem to care that she looked like she'd spent her entire life locked in a crypt. Good thing, too, since there wasn't a tanning cream or hair bleach in any department store or beauty salon in all of Western New York that worked. She knew. She'd tried them all—even cosmetic contact lenses. On her unnaturally dark eyes, the blue appeared flat and lifeless. Lynet had worn the silly things for less than a week before tossing them in the trash. Fig had hated those contacts. They'd creeped Eibby out, too, which wasn't easy, as she had a high tolerance for anything offbeat and strange.

Lynet finished bussing her tables and picked up some discarded trash on the floor. She didn't want to admit she was obsessive, but what else could you call it? She hated the way she looked. Deathly white skin and extraordinarily black hair might be popular with the local Goths, but even they sidestepped when she passed by. Her skin was too translucent, her hair more like a void than a color. It was as if someone had stripped the pigmentation from her completely and left only a ghostly black-and-white drawing, like the illustrations in old fairytale books.

"Wear the yellow dress," Eibby said, as she handed Lynet napkins to fill an empty dispenser. "You look good in it, and it helps you feel confident."

Lynet smiled. She might hate her appearance, but Ronan didn't seem to mind. "He does like yellow."

"We should double date sometime. You and Ronan, me and Jack." Eibby had started dating the handsome male nurse not long after the incident at the hockey game. Luckily, it hadn't changed their friendship.

"Yeah, well, if Ronan ever makes a move, you'll be the first to know."

Grizarbr

RONAN SAT AT THE TABLE in the break room, repairing the lining of his jacket pocket. He'd borrowed a needle and thread from the office secretary. The sooner he mended it, the easier it would be. He'd learned in his youth to fix damaged gear quickly, else he would regret it later. He finished the final knot and snapped the thread with his teeth just as Jim and Karl came in and plopped down at the table.

Karl opened a can of soda. "So, what do you think Tony saw?"

"Deer in the woods," Jim said. "What else could it be? He reads too many freaky comic books."

"Or he was high."

"What's that, then?" Ronan asked, not wanting to seem disinterested.

"Tony claims he saw centaurs in Niagara Falls last night."

"He took a picture on his phone," Karl added, "but you can't see anything. Just a bunch of trees near an old school on Lewiston Road."

"Centaurs?" Ronan asked. "Half-man, half-horse—here in New York?"

Karl nodded. "Yeah. Like I said, he's on drugs."

Anything mythical was a red waving flag to Ronan. If Tony's tale was more than the simple blurring of drugs and imagination . . . then Senteer had crossed to this side of the Divide. Strong stags with the upper bodies of men, Senteer could easily be mistaken for mythical centaurs. Their appearance on the Outside meant Eltanin knew Lynet was here.

"I'm heading out for some air." Ronan stood. "I'll be safe outside, right? No Cyclops or anything strange going to get me?"

Jim laughed. "Yeah, you're safe, big guy."

Ronan stepped outside. He'd relaxed his guard these last few weeks, settling into a comfortable routine of work during the day and evenings spent watching over Lynet and Laburnum House. While he grew lax, Eltanin had moved in. So much for the Nornir giving him a rest.

Ronan scanned the trees in the deserted lot next to the factory. Senteer were trouble. Nimble assassins, they were rarely spotted. Still, sending Senteer to a populated area was taking an enormous risk. Had Eltanin's lust for power made him blind to consequences? Even common thieves obeyed the first law: *Norðrlönd must remain hidden.* Each time an Outsider discovered their secret, it punched another hole in the fragile fabric of the Aragaidheal Divide.

Ronan felt the Beast within him stir. He was Vökumaðr, his kind created by the Æsir for one purpose—to protect Norðrlönd. Eltanin must be stopped, before his greed destroyed the Divide completely.

Dinner was over, the table littered with empty serving dishes and the remains of pot roast, carrot-and-rutabaga mash, and a few thick slices of crusty bread. Bowls, baskets, and vases of Maple's flowers and sprigs filled any available space. Petals fell onto the tablecloth and fluttered down to the floor, where Lleth kept things clean and tidy.

No one seemed eager for the evening to end.

Ronan studied the Macarthurs as they bustled around the dining room: Alder tuned his fiddle. Treddian and his wife argued over whose turn it was to change the squalling baby—no small thing, as Jól had a voice like the rattle of tree branches in a storm. Fig danced around them all, twirling and spinning, not waiting for the music to begin.

The boy was out of place here. Too unusual to be human, too large to be a sprite. Ronan had a few theories about where Fig got his exotic features, although the idea was preposterous even to him. Still, odd unions happened, and there was no denying the boy's unique genetic makeup. Whatever his heredity, Fig was hardier than he looked, and unbelievably quick. He would be in front of you one minute, then, before you blinked, off somewhere else. Ronan knew of only one race of creatures that nimble. Puki seldom came to this side of the Divide but, when they did, it meant trouble.

Trouble, however, would have to wait until nightfall. Ronan relaxed back in his chair. Layers of happy chatter and bursts of song washed over him. For a man born to war, the noise of merrymaking was like cool water to a parched throat. The day had been full; the evening promised more of the same as he prowled the night looking for Senteer—but, for right now, he welcomed this small measure of peace.

Ronan closed his eyes. He liked this little Northlander family, almost trusted them. He would take them into his confidence, if not for the fact they were somehow connected to Scartozzar. It was better if the Macarthurs believed him to be simply the Outsider neighbor who lived down the street.

Jól started a song and Alder boomed in, his deep bass rumbling the dishes on the table. Ronan chuckled. His eyes still closed, the Watchman willed his troubled mind to rest. A moment or two could do no harm.

Lynet glanced up and faltered, her conversation with Fig forgotten, her whole world narrowing to that one spot, that one face at the other end of the table. A warm tingle swept up from her belly and filled her breast. Ronan exuded maleness like a scent. She couldn't be near him without feeling . . . feminine. When he touched her, she ached to touch him back. When he whispered, she wished to press her mouth to his. His physical presence seemed to fill the room and tug at all the parts of her that made her a woman.

There were times when Lynet was afraid to be alone with him. Afraid of her own reaction to him. She supposed it was a good thing Fig or one of the others was always around. Especially right now. She could easily stroke her fingers down his whiskered throat and sniff that hollow spot below his ear.

Lleth got up and nuzzled Ronan's arm until the dozing man lazily scratched the wolfhound's head. Lleth's tail swished and thumped against the table. The hound was devoted to him. Lynet watched Ronan's hand moving slow and sleepy against Lleth's head, and her insides fluttered.

She was falling in love.

It was foolish, really. And hopelessly one sided. No matter how kind he was to her, he wasn't likely to fall for her in the same way. What man wanted to be saddled with a woman who had no past, who might wake up tomorrow having forgotten him completely?

As if he'd heard her, Ronan's eyes opened, those tawny flames looking at her from behind lowered lashes. She could almost feel his gaze sliding over her face, her skin, her parted lips. Heat flushed across her cheeks and she tore her eyes away, certain he'd read every wicked thought in her head.

Ronan took in every alluring signal—her racing pulse, the flush on her cheeks, the way she tried to ignore him and pretend he hadn't just caught her eyeing him with an expression of desire so strong he nearly left his chair. One word from her and he would scoop her into his arms and take her out under the stars—

Ronan closed his mind to the image of her warm and responsive beneath him. Yes, when he first came to the Outside, he'd intended to find Lynet and continue the relationship they'd started in the wild. But lately, another thought filled his dreams. He could not leave his father and his kin trapped; nor could he turn his back on the people of Norðrlönd. Soon he would return to Caeraricin and face Eltanin. How could he willfully begin a life with Lynet, knowing there was little chance he would survive?

Ronan reached for his glass. How the Nornir must laugh at him. So many twists of fate destroying any hope of a normal life for he and Lynet: Eltanin's treachery. Prince Edan and the *forspá*. Even the dreaded *Kærásti Fórnsöngr,* something that for all others signified joy, for them meant only ruin.

"Pie!" Fig shouted, and Ronan welcomed the diversion as Maple brought out a steaming, rich-smelling dessert.

Maple cut and dished out the pie. The hard crust pebbled, bits of it rolling off onto the tablecloth. The scent of the herb used to make the crust wafted to him. Wrapped in his thoughts, it took Ronan a moment to realize the significance of that scent.

Grizarbr.

Instantly, Ronan stood, reaching for his weapon, only to remember it wasn't there; he didn't wear a sword in his guise as an Outsider. He made a half-circle, taking note of everyone in the room, the position of their hands, their stance, which foot held their weight, the focus of their eyes.

Alder continued to play his fiddle. Fig bounced beside Maple, anxious for the first piece of pie. Jól burped the baby. No one seemed to notice Ronan's alarm. Slowly, he relaxed his posture. Were the hags of fate playing a game? Was this all innocent—Maple serving him grizarbr—or did the matriarch know more about him and his errand than she let on?

To most, the grizarbr leaf was a pungent, aromatic spice. But to the Vökumaðr it was much more. Like catnip to a tomcat, the grizarbr leaf aroused him, knocking down walls of self-restraint and freeing him of all inhibition. Some said the gods fashioned the drug to appease the Watchmen, to give them brief periods of intense pleasure, enough to keep them contented with the hard life they were destined to live.

Maple handed him a big double helping.

Ronan stared into her heart and saw no malice. Although there was . . . something . . . so vague and fleeting, he wondered if he'd imagined it. Either way, it was not hostile.

Ronan took the plate.

I Remember

RONAN GRIPPED THE PORCH RAIL overlooking Maple's garden and marveled at his own stupidity. The evening breeze was cool. He gulped it in, hoping to clear his head. It helped, though it could not ease the fire ignited in his belly by the grizarbr. He was aroused, his thoughts, laced with sultry images of Lynet hot and panting beneath him.

The screen door opened and closed behind him.

He did not turn. He did not need to. He could smell her. His senses were so raw it was dangerous to be anywhere near her.

Lynet came and stood beside him, her long hair blowing in the breeze. Several inky black strands flicked across his arm and tangled tantalizingly around his wrist. Carefully, Ronan unwound them, liking the feel of her hair between his fingers. He resisted the urge to grab a handful and bring it to his nose. His palm opened and he released the strands back into the breeze.

"Some unseen power rules this corner of the world." Lynet sounded thoughtful, and Ronan was grateful for the distraction of words. "Maple's vegetables and vines reach for the sun, no matter the season; well, not in the dead of winter but, once the snow is gone, it doesn't matter how little sun there is, or how thick the frost; that woman can grow anything. It's like magic." Lynet looked up at him. "Do you believe in magic, Ronan?"

Magic had ruled Ronan's life in one form or another since the day he was born. Royal magic bound him to the high king in the same way Vökumaðr magic controlled his senses. The madness ruling him right now, however, had nothing to do with magic, and everything to do with being a man. Unleashed by the grizarbr, the notes of the *Kærásti Fórnsöngr* filled his head with impossible promise.

Ronan turned to face the house. He could see Jól at the sink, one hand clutching a dishcloth, the other, her squirming son, Eburos. Relying on the maternal scene to keep him grounded, Ronan answered.

"Yes, I do believe in magic. How can you live in the world and not believe? But I am not convinced it is Maple's will alone working its magic in this place." He glanced at Lynet and tried to keep the conversation light. "I have read, however, that talking to plants helps them grow. Do you think Maple talks to her vegetables?"

Lynet's eyes grew wide with laughter. "She does. Well, she sings more than talks. She has a gorgeous voice. If I were a plant, I would grow thick and lush merely to please her."

Her laughter washed over him, bathing his senses, and Ronan wondered if he dared continue to speak. The way he felt, his voice was likely to turn into a growl before long.

Lynet didn't remember it, of course, but Norðrlönd wives often sang fertility songs while they planted their fields. Maple seemed happy with Alder. Until a woman gave her whole heart to a man, she could not sing, at least not anything anyone would want to hear. If Maple loved Alder, then Lynet's description of her voice was probably true.

"Do *you* sing to the plants?" Ronan had asked Lynet once before if she could sing. Had her answer changed now that he was a part of her life again?

"Oh my, no!" Lynet shook her head. "I have the worst voice you've ever heard. If I went out in the middle of all that green and opened my mouth, the ground itself would shrivel and die, not just the plants."

The words she chose startled him, momentarily cooling his desire. Lynet had no idea that, with a single thought, she could make that very thing happen—the ground shrivel and everything living in it die.

He'd not thought of it before but, in a way, her memory loss was a blessing, with much of her previous heartache forgotten. She wasn't haunted by the faces of those she'd accidentally killed. Or burdened with the weight of an unwanted, horrific power. Maybe, just this once, the Nornir played fair. Maybe Lynet's memory loss was a good thing. She no longer recognized the *Kærásti Fórnsöngr*. Perhaps they were safe. So long as she didn't fall in love with him again, there was no danger of her singing the forbidden song.

Ronan's moment of charity toward the Nornir passed.

No, those hags never played fair. It may be an answer of sorts, but it also amounted to his own personal hell. He wanted her. He knew he could make her love him again. Knew she would respond if he pushed her; if he touched her body in the ways she liked; if he opened his heart and showed her his strength, his purpose.

Yet, to what gain? Did he want them locked again in that same wretched stalemate, forced to abstain from lovemaking for fear the song would burst from them, giving the Hoar Beast power over the god of death?

He was in no shape to make a decision now.

"I won't ask you to prove it, then" Ronan said, finally. "I'm in Maple's good graces. I'd like to keep it that way."

Lynet laughed and said something meant to tease him but, as he watched her soft mouth move, his thoughts scattered and made conversation impossible to follow. She leaned close, and the heat of her body melted his resolve. He wanted to ravish her right here on the porch.

The outside light flipped on, and Fig Macarthur came marching outside to join them. In his hand, he waved a box of what looked suspiciously like hair color. He shook the box accusingly at Lynet. "You promised!"

The boy's shrill tone was a shock to Ronan's drugged system, and he nearly grabbed Fig to stop the prattle, only just stopping himself. Ronan stood absolutely still, his body rock hard with tension.

Fig shouted and kept the box out of reach as Lynet grabbed for it. The ruckus drew Lleth out onto the porch, the huge hound weaving between them, banging Ronan with his long tail.

It was too much. Ronan knocked Lleth aside with his leg, plucked the box from Fig's grasp, and handed it to Lynet. "Now go!"

"Thank you." Lynet snatched the box and turned to flee into the house.

"Wait." Ronan caught her arm. "Not you." He made a pointed jerk with his head to Fig. *"Now."* The boy blew a raspberry and disappeared, presumably back inside, although Ronan did not actually see him leave.

Lynet stood silent, her face covered by a curtain of inky black hair, the troublesome box hidden in the folds of her yellow dress. She did not look at him, and Ronan knew she would dart the second he released her.

Lleth's ears perked up and he trotted down the steps and out into the dark. As quickly as the interruption came, it was gone, and they were alone again.

Anger cleared his head. Ronan could not allow the grizarbr to snare him again. With the possibility of Senteer nearby, he needed to be fully alert. In fact, so did Lynet, and the Macarthurs. It was time to tell them all the truth.

With callused fingers, he raised Lynet's chin, surprised to find her eyes swimming with unshed tears, her jaw thrust out as if defying him to make fun of her. The expression confused him.

"What is wrong, *ástmær?*"

She tried to turn away, but he held her there, waiting.

"I'm sorry I upset Fig," Lynet burst out, "but I hate how I look. I know I should be satisfied I'm whole and healthy. I shouldn't try to change myself, to be somebody I'm not, and yes, it's stupid and vain, but—" She grabbed a lock of her hair and showed it to him. "Look at it, Ronan. It's like a black hole sucking the very life from the air. It's blacker than anything in nature. Even a black widow has a reflection on its back—this gives no light." She dropped the lock in disgust and made a soft hiccupping sound.

Ronan pulled her into his arms, hiding his chuckle. The whole world was upside down and conspiring against them—and his witch was worried about the color of her hair. There was so little he could do about the world, but this, this worry he could fix.

Ronan kissed her hair, feather light, then drawing on powers known only to the Vökumaðr, quietly called a Restore spell to life. It would dissolve Scartozzar's magic and restore Lynet's physical appearance. It could do nothing for her memories, but it would make her look like herself again. Lynet's sniffles masked his whisper as he commanded the spell and then dropped it onto her bowed head.

Lynet drew in a sharp breath and pulled away from him.

"Did you do something?" She shivered, rubbing her palms up and down her arms as if trying to stop a tickle. "*Déjà vu.* I've felt this before. Bubbling, swirling"—her excitement grew—"like a liquid, wrapping around me." Her eyes widened. "What is it?"

Ronan paused, unsure of where to start. There was so much to explain. Somehow, he did not think the announcement 'I placed a spell on you' was the best way to begin.

Lynet closed her eyes and tried to recapture the feeling—no, the *memory*. This was from her past; it was too strong to be otherwise.

She stood inside a translucent sphere, made of swirling liquid light.

Curious, she reached out to touch it, but it tingled as if alive, and she snatched her hand back, afraid. Long, bubbling vapors of light separated from the outer edge to wrap around her, covering her from head to foot. It felt like cool watery ripples washing over her skin, scrubbing, stripping away some outward part of her. The sensation was pleasant, almost tickled.

The ripples dissolved, and more of them pulled away from the outer shell—but, these were different.

Purposefully, they clung to her eyes and head. The cleansing, stripping feeling increased. Her heart fluttered in panic. Something good was being taken away, something she did not want to lose.

Lynet resisted, her hands forming fists at her side, but the liquid ribbons wrapped tighter, suffocating her with an effervescent film. An unbelievable sadness filled her heart. Something precious and dear was being washed from her mind and memory. The ache of it grew until a sob burst from her lips.

Lynet retreated from the memory, trying to open her eyes. She had not wanted the stripping then; she did not want to feel it now—but the vision held fast, refusing to release her, rushing the images forward in time.

Bright flashes of light, and rumbling destruction surrounded her. She heard voices raised in battle. Heard the desperate chanting of a man close by. Lynet felt fear creep through her veins like ice as a monstrous black evil loomed up in front of her.

With a sharp shake of her head, Lynet forced her eyes open, surprised to find she'd been crying. "I remember," she rasped. "Not much, only a few seconds, but I remember."

Had no one thought to use magic on her, to stir her memories? Ronan was astonished. He had assumed the Macarthurs tried everything; they'd had two years to figure it out . . . but perhaps they didn't know of her powers. Perhaps they didn't realize how dangerous she was.

"I remembered," Lynet said again, her whole face transformed with wonder and excitement.

"Was it a good memory?" Ronan touched her cheek, happy for her discovery, encouraged by it. If she could remember a second, she could remember more. Perhaps not all, but enough to give her control of her magic. Because, no matter his belief that her memory loss was a blessing, that it relieved the burden she carried and eliminated the danger of the Kærásti Fórnsöngr, in truth, it was only a matter of time before Lynet's ignorance killed them all.

"No. It was awful. Full of loss and sorrow and, at the end, terrible fear."

Had she witnessed the destruction of the sea caves? He wanted to question her, to solve the mystery of those last moments before her world changed to this one, but he knew he must tread carefully.

"Are you afraid now?"

"No. . . ." Lynet said slowly, as if realizing it for the first time. "No. I am not afraid. *You* are here, and I know in my heart you will protect me."

"Yes, I will." Ronan gave a slight bow of his head, satisfied with her answer. In another place and time, he would have laid his hand flat against his chest and, in the soft language of the north, renewed his Oath. She trusted him, and soon she would trust him enough to follow him through the Aragaidheal Divide, to home.

Lynet shivered and hugged her arms close about her. Exhaustion smudged the translucent skin beneath her eyes. Ronan knew the potent mix of memories, coupled with the Restore spell, would soon cause fatigue and probably more tears. He'd missed his chance to explain.

He whispered, "Perhaps you should rest. You look tired."

Lynet nodded, her smile faint. "I don't know why I'm getting so emotional. It was just a few seconds, nothing earthshattering. Sorry."

"You are a woman." Ronan brushed his thumb over her cheek. "Emotions are a natural part of you, *ástin mín*. Your tears do not trouble me."

She swayed, and Ronan steadied her. She needed to rest while the spell ran its course. "Get some sleep. I will see you tomorrow, early. We have much to talk about."

Lynet squeezed his hand, then went inside.

Ronan stood, watching her go, knowing that the next time he saw her there would likely be more tears, and possibly shouting. She would not be happy that he had been lying to her.

"You shouldn't have done that."

The voice behind him caught Ronan completely by surprise. Muttering a curse at his own carelessness, Ronan turned to face his accuser.

Passageways and Secrets

SHOULDN'T HAVE DONE WHAT?" Ronan asked with forced calm as Maple came up the porch steps, Lleth trotting beside her. The matriarch carried an armful of freshly cut flowers, their petals closed into tight buds for the night.

"Removed that spell from Lynet," Maple scolded. A lock of graying hair fell forward onto her brow. She brushed it back with garden-stained fingers and looked Ronan square in the face. "It was placed there for a reason."

Ronan casually removed his empty hand from the pocket where he kept the Annarian crystal hidden. The crystal had been made for him at great cost and for a specific purpose. A single use was all the magic it contained, but with it, Ronan stood to gain equal ground with his enemy. This, however, was not the enemy.

"I'm sure I have no idea what you're talking about." He smiled amiably.

"Zerker, you can't hide from me. I can smell you."

The smile faded.

The word *zerker* was a less than complimentary term for Vökumaðr, used only by the elite. *Mother Earth, he was a fool!* How could he not have known? Yes, he'd sensed something unusual about Maple, but not this. His instincts were worthless here, on the Outside, where every natural skill and spell took twice the effort. Never would he have had such poor judgment in the Northlands, or failed to recognize her.

His mind rebelled against the enormity of Maple's revelation. Not only was she clever, this pretending Maple Macarthur was also one of the few people with the power to control the Vökumaðr. A noble from one of the royal houses; a queen or princess. How powerful was she? *Who* was she? Dare he pit his will against hers? Under a queen's Governance, Ronan could find himself helpless. Unlike the Aricins—whom he had loved and trusted—Maple was a stranger.

Ronan felt the Beast stir, eager to challenge Maple's command, and rip her apart if she failed, even as Ronan's back bent in a short, respectful bow. "How long have you known, my lady?"

Maple waved her hand. "No, no, we'll not have any of that here. I am what you see, nothing more. You can relax, Zerker. I have no desire other than to help you."

He nodded in acquiescence, not trusting her words, but hoping all the same that she meant them. It was his gift to read the hearts of men, to recognize a lie, but the magic surrounding Maple was thick, and he could not rely on his skill to tell him for sure.

"I've known *what* you were since you first set foot on my street," Maple continued; "knew you were coming long before that." She sat on the bench under the porch light. "Someone had to come eventually; couldn't leave the girl here forever. Prince Edan will need her soon now, I expect."

Ronan was dumbfounded. *She didn't know.* Maple thought the *forspá* was still intact, thought Edan and Lynet would marry and heal the Divide. Maple didn't know the Aricin dynasty was in pieces, the Divide weaker than it had ever been before—knew nothing of Eltanin's treason.

Was it to Ronan's advantage to tell Maple the truth?

Ronan was a Watchman of Caeraricin, a god-appointed guardian. It was his duty, his purpose, to serve and sacrifice for his king. But he would not give Lynet to Edan. That falsehearted prince could rot, for all Ronan cared. He owed the traitor nothing. Ronan's father hung trapped inside his own decaying corpse because of Edan's betrayal.

"Lynet does not need the spell's protection any longer." Ronan chose to sidestep the subject of Edan until he learned more about Maple's intentions. "I am taking her home. Besides, the spell was never supposed to leave her like that. I know the Hide spell. Only the first half of it took, removing all trace of color. The second half, the disguise, never happened."

Maple peeled leaves from the flower stems, preparing them for one of the endless vases, pots, and terracotta containers. "When will you leave, then? She knows nothing of Norðrlönd. It would be ill-advised to run off before she understands the danger."

Ronan tapped a leaf off the porch with the side of his shoe. "Soon." He looked out across the moonlight gardens. "I have things to take care of, to ensure we travel unhindered, and you will need time to prepare Lynet, to help her, as you say, understand." He glanced at Maple. "It will not be easy for her to leave you. You're the only family she knows."

"Why is that?" Maple found a ladybug in one of the flowers and, with a scoot, sent it flying off. "Why can't she remember her family? Scartozzar sent a message before she arrived, telling us enough to prepare, but he never said anything about memory loss. Although, I've come to believe it is the reason why he gave her some of his own memories, to fill in the gaps, and so she would feel comfortable with us while she waited. Of course, we thought she was only supposed to be here for a short while, for safekeeping. Something went wrong. . . ." Her voice trailed off.

Ronan's bearded lips pressed tight as her words confirmed what he'd come to suspect himself—not only was the Hide spell corrupted, but Scartozzar had deliberately ruined Lynet's mind as well. What else? What other mischief did she carry inside her, brought on by Scartozzar's treachery? Ronan had been an idiot to trust him.

"Have you heard from Scartozzar recently?" Ronan asked, unsure which answer he preferred. It would be a relief to know for certain the wizard was dead, as Neira believed. At the same time, Ronan would be glad of the chance to rip Scartozzar apart if the bastard still lived.

"We have not heard a word, not since before Lynet arrived," Maple said. "That was not part of the plan, either—but we cannot risk a message. I have my reasons for staying hidden, Zerker." She nodded to the gnarled yew trees standing guard around the property. "Scartozzar knows this."

"Scartozzar disappeared when Lynet did," Ronan said, deciding to make the situation clear. "No one across the Divide knows what has become of him; many have marked him a traitor."

"Scartozzar a traitor?" Maple jumped to her feet, petals and leaves scattering. Her whole body shook. "I'll Mind Burn anyone who says such a thing. He is no traitor. Never. All the work he did here on the Outside, his experiments, the risks he took—they were all for his king. Don't you dare draw breath in my sight if you're accusing him of something different!"

Ronan raised his hands to her, palms out. Maple could summon the Beast, could order Ronan to do anything, and if her will was stronger than his, Ronan would be powerless to refuse. Until he knew her intent, he would placate her, whatever it took.

"I tell you only what has come to pass, my lady. I took no part in the rumors, although I do not trust him. Scartozzar had more purloined magic inside him than any other living wizard—both light and dark powers, in amounts that should not be mixed. Where his true loyalties lie, no one knows for sure. And now he's gone, either into hiding, or he's dead, a victim of whatever destroyed the sea caves at Aros."

Maple sat down slowly, as if she'd aged a great deal in that moment. "He can't be dead. He's too clever. Prince Edan will set things right. He'll make sure everyone knows my boy is not a traitor."

"Edan has no power," Ronan said. "Eltanin Sihtric sits on the Caeraricin high throne."

"I'll need all the correct ingredients," Neira said aloud, as she meandered up and down the hall where she thought the secret passageway was hidden. "Eggs, milk, and a big blob of butter." Pretending to make a list, she ticked the items one by one.

"What else? Oh, I know, *hlýðið, á orð.*"

Emotion and expression were essential for *spellbirth*. However, once it was alive and guarding, a Lock spell did not care how many breaths, minutes, or hours it took between words. All it required was the Open command in the correct sequence and with the expected pronunciation.

"*mín, opna.*"

Taking her time, Neira repeated the phrases in a staccato pattern, hoping to keep the hated collar ignorant of her intent. She wasn't exactly *performing* magic, just interacting with it; still, it was a risk, but if it worked, perhaps she could use the same strategy again on another spell. At least here in the library, if it went wrong, the only danger was a careless apprentice trampling on her head while she lay sprawled unconscious in the middle of the hall.

"*leyndarmál, dyr, þitt, and flour, of course.*" A soft click sounded along the corridor as a section of wall the size of a small door swung open.

"And that should do it. Instant cake."

Neira snatched up her candle, glanced around, then slipped through the door and pulled it shut. The passageway stank of damp and mold, and Neira twisted her hood around to cover her nose. Her dim candle flame gave off enough light to see the moss-covered stairs and wet, dripping walls, but little else. She went slowly. Every time she slipped and grabbed the wall for support, Neira cringed. Who knew what lived down here. Spiders, snakes . . . or worse.

It took less than ten minutes to get to the end of the tunnel. There appeared to be a secret door here, too. She pushed against the stone, relieved when the rock swung out into a vast, empty cavern. A brisk wind blew into the tunnel, and Neira shielded her wildly flickering candle. It smelled of the ocean. Could that be right? Had Eltanin reopened the outlet to the sea?

Neira shoved loose rocks into the doorjamb to keep the door from sealing behind her. She did not know the opening phrases for this end and didn't want to get trapped down here. Once the door was secure, she went in search of better light. Fresh faggots lined the wall; another sign of recent use. Neira lit a torch, then snuffed out the candle. She waited briefly for it to cool, then dropped the warm wax and dish into her pocket for the return trip.

Sputtering torch in hand, Neira ventured farther into the cavern. It was huge. She could not imagine how the castle stayed erect with this massive opening beneath it. There had to be more than rock holding it up. She glanced around, but could not see any pillars or supporting foundation. How odd. Unless—she fingered the collar around her neck—unless the beams and trusses were like the chains. Invisible. Untouchable. That would certainly make them resistant to sabotage. Unlike her chains, however, the foundation must be fashioned from White magic, as Nos'kag could not be trusted.

Neira's mouth twisted. How easily she got sidetracked. The mystery of the castle foundation was not on her list for tonight.

She lifted the torch high, looking for signs of Colm or any of the other missing servants. The flickering light revealed a platform of stone overhead, extending out into the center of the cavern. The cavern had two, maybe even three, levels; each one defined by a jagged overhang. The bottom, where she stood, was a shore for the quietly lapping seawater. The walls wore deep lines of erosion. The ground was dry, though, and had been for some time. Proof that magic held back the high tide.

The breeze grew stronger. Neira pulled her hood low and peered into the shadows near the water's edge. She could make out several rowboats turned belly up on the shale floor: black boats, with dotted patterns on the side—the same pattern worn by the scarred Kynneeyn Gorrym.

Shock took Neira's breath—is *this* how the mercenaries entered the castle, undetected, the day Eltanin took control? Had they rowed in with the tide, then slipped up the secret passage through the king's chambers?

Where was the king's passageway? It could be anywhere along these walls—and it could open at any moment—exposing her and her ill-planned plot to save her friends. Neira had thought the cavern unused, but it was obviously a frequently accessed port of entry. There must be a third way down here. She couldn't imagine Eltanin allowing his private quarters to be invaded by hordes of mercenaries, no matter how useful.

That wasn't the only danger. Anciently, spells guarded this secret inlet, preventing any invasion. What watched the entrance now? What magics did Eltanin have in place to catch anyone sneaking about?

Neira looked behind her.

The torch she held revealed her as an easy target but, other than lighting all the torches in the cavern, or stumbling around in the dark, she had few options. Besides, she would not be here long.

Her eyes skimmed the darkness, looking for a trap or sentinel. Not for the first time, Neira wished for the night vision of the Cú. Keen-eyed dogmen, Norðrlönd's healers could not be fooled by shadows—and their canine sense of smell probably helped as well.

A ripple in the water splashed near her shoe, and Neira turned back to the sea. The passageway was open—but how? The tunnel to the sea had collapsed nearly eight hundred years ago, rocking the foundations of both cliff and castle. It would have taken a tremendous amount of effort to reopen it without bringing down the entire eastern wall. Demons did not have that kind of finesse. They were all about destruction and chaos. It would have taken the Kynneeyn Gorrym years—generations of labor—to do it by hand. So, when was it opened, and by whom? The work must have been phenomenal. Who among them had—

Carden.

Only Carden had that kind of unmatched power. Neira could almost see him down here, hammering away at the tons of rock, his fierce will holding up the outer walls as he worked—his aggressive magic made for such a task.

Neira took a shocked step backward. *Had he known?*

As he carefully reopened this centuries-closed passage, had Carden known what his father planned? Had he agreed to smuggle murdering mercenaries into the heart of Caeraricin?

Carden hated Prince Edan and wished all kinds of pain and ruin on his head. But what of the others? What of the queen, and the servants, cut down as they stood protecting the young princess? What of Maxwell and Torin as they defended the west gate? What of all the novice apprentices who met their end, weeping over the bodies of their fallen masters? Dead, so many dead. Carden had not been here to see it. But, if this work was indeed his, then . . . he was responsible.

Staring at the reflection of the torch in the lapping water, Neira felt her childhood dreams topple like sandcastles wiped by the tide.

For as long as she'd known him, Neira had loved Carden Sihtric. As a fresh-faced apprentice newly called to Caeraricin, she had watched in awe as Carden battled on the training floor. Crushing his opponents, he took on wizards and apprentices alike. His magic was brilliant, his will unbending. He took her under his wing, and the warring factions in Ddewin Tower treated her well, out of fear of him.

Oh, she knew he had faults. Proud. Manipulative. She could not count the lies she'd caught him in. Yet he always treated her with kindness. More than that, Carden saw in her what Scartozzar did not—a spirit who longed to soar. Tied down by her duties and responsibilities, Neira yearned for adventure, and the right to choose her own path. As no one else did, Carden understood her heart.

Neira absently fingered the black, misshapen charm on her belt. Had it all been an act? Or the distorted, rose-tinted dreams of adolescence?

Men change, Neira.

Scartozzar had warned her. Was this tunnel evidence of those changes in Carden, brought on by his use of Nos'kag magic? Changes the books in the library said could not be undone.

No. There had to be some other explanation. Carden would not do this.

Neira had taken comfort in the knowledge that Carden was absent from Caeraricin during the slaughter. It seemed proof he was not a part of his father's plan. But what if Carden had merely done his bit months before?

Neira turned away. Scartozzar was right: she didn't know Carden anymore, hadn't been privy to his thoughts or ambitions in years. Where he was—and what kind of man he had become—she dared not guess.

Neira left the water's edge and crossed the sandy floor to the crumbling shale steps. On the second level, she found evidence of the Kynneeyn Gorrym: pieces of leather, a dull knife, and hastily doused fires. They must have stayed hidden in the cavern until Eltanin called for them.

This second level sloped sharply. She continued up above the watermark until she came to a row of prison cells. Nearby was a room with the rotting remnants of ancient beds and chairs, no doubt housing for the guards.

A third chamber, partially blocked behind a pile of fallen rock, appeared to be the weapons storage she'd seen on the map. The door was torn off, the broken hinges rusted into dangerous deterrents; ones she was happy to avoid.

With the Cú outlawed—all six of the city's healers gathered up and carted off on Eltanin's orders—there had been an unsettling rise in the number of accidental deaths. No one knew where the blue dogmen were, or if they were even still alive. It was one of Eltanin's more ridiculous ideas. How did he hope to survive an attack? With *lyfja* alone? Did he think his position so secure, no one would dare strike out at him?

Neira moved the torch, still peering into the room. Three distinct shapes were carved into the far wall—niches for weapons or treasure. Her curiosity piqued, she wished she had some *lyfja* herself, so she could chance getting closer—but the tiny store she kept hidden in her belt had been taken from her the day of her capture. Still, she could see well enough. Two of the empty niches looked like they used to house weapons, long and thin. The other was large and roundish, for a shield, perhaps? Whatever their use, the kings of Aricin once considered the items important enough to hide away in the bowels of the castle. Where were the items now? Probably in the king's personal chambers high in the keep—a place she wasn't ever likely to see.

No matter how interesting, this was not getting her any closer to Colm or the other missing servants. So far, she'd found no sign of them anywhere.

To the south were eight stone steps. Unlike the ones she'd just come up, where the crumbling shale formed a natural stepped incline, these had been deliberately cut.

Neira went to the stairs and placed her foot on the first chiseled step—then hesitated. An uneasy feeling swept over her.

For the first time, she sincerely wondered if she should stop, leave this place and not come back.

Neira believed in inspiration, impressions outside her own mind that gave warning or encouragement. It was an Outsider idea; one she did not share with her kinsmen. To her own people, Norðrlönd was ruled by temperamental, warring gods who had little interest in mortals. Neira knew the gods existed—she saw Rán often enough—but she did not pray to them. For her, faith in a loving, benevolent god, a father figure, held more appeal. So she often tried to listen for inspiration—and right now, she felt quite strongly she should not go up those stairs. Something evil waited there.

Neira sighed. Colm obviously wasn't here. Maybe she—

A noise echoed in the cavern below.

Startled, Neira spun around. The chains at her back swung out, throwing her off balance. She swept her arms in wide circles to keep from falling, but lost control of the torch as it flipped out of her hand and clattered to the floor. The flames spit and hissed, throwing a gigantic, distorted shadow of her across the ceiling of the cavern. Another wild flicker and the flame went out, leaving her in utter darkness.

Instinctively, Neira's fingers traced a quick pattern in the air as she called a protective shield.

The copper collar jerked tight.

Aghast, Neira stopped in mid-conjure—but it was too late—the collar was awake. Now it would choke her, squeeze until she passed out, leaving her sprawled on the cavern floor at the mercy of whoever, or whatever, was down below. Desperately, Neira clawed at her throat, trying to keep the hated thing from strangling her. She pleaded with it, begged, but once animated, the collar did not care about excuses.

Neira's limbs tingled. Her skin grew cold, her mind drowsy. She sank to the ground, marveling at the lack of pain when she struck the hard rock . . . odd . . . her sense of smell still worked . . . she wished it didn't . . . as the acrid smoke, from the smothered torch, seeped into her nostrils.

Senteer

RONAN CROUCHED IN THE QUIET ALLEYWAY. Vandals had shot out two of the nearby streetlamps, leaving the Niagara neighborhood in shadow. Not a problem. The darkness worked in Ronan's favor, as he did not need artificial light to find his quarry. He peered through the ramshackle fence separating the abandoned Wentworth Boarding School from the low-rent apartments behind him.

Once a school for orphans and destitute children in the 1800s, the building was converted to a day academy for privileged boys following the First World War. The school retained its prestigious status for many years, right up until the night two of the little boys disappeared. The academy closed shortly after. The cold, stone structure was boarded up, the grounds left to seed with thistle and knotweed.

Lleth shifted impatiently and pawed at the ground.

"Come on, then." Ronan was anxious to learn the truth of his coworker's story claiming he'd seen centaurs here.

Quietly, they crept toward the rear of the school.

Around them, normal Outsider activities took place. An elderly couple talked as they swung peacefully on their front porch. A mother quarreled with a teenage son as he stormed out of the house. A car pulled into the parking lot on the opposite side of the apartments, horn honking.

These were facts Ronan noted and remained aware of, even as he focused on the school. From his inquiries, he'd learned that the neighborhood was generally quiet—apart from domestic violence and minimal drug dealing. The one thing folks hadn't mentioned was *magic*.

Pockets of magic were rare on this side of the Divide. On his travels, Ronan had found only two other places where magic pooled, and for good reason. When the Æsir first created Norðrlönd as a haven for their followers, they stripped the Outside world of as much magic as they could—siphoning power away from unbelievers and infusing it into every living organism in Norðrlönd. The bits of magic that remained on the Outside dug in deep, hiding, unnoticed. Some of it had gathered here, near the school—making it a logical place for scouts from Caeraricin to meet and regroup.

Ronan found a spot near the old carriage house where he could view the back of the building. Moonlight reflected off the slanted windshield of a sports car parked unexpectedly at the rear entrance. The double doors of the school, usually locked with a knot of rusted chain, were now swung wide, the chain trailing onto the ground. Figures moved just inside the darkened doorway. Ronan could hear them arguing, their voices tense and gaining volume. Something was afoot.

Ronan rested his hand on the hilt of his hunting knife, a curved, thirteen-inch blade good for close-range fighting. The Shadow spell he wore hid him from most, but Ronan knew that if there were trouble, it would be skill, not magic, keeping him alive.

Raknfeld stepped warily past Stian's tense flank. None yet questioned his position as leader of the herd, but he knew the challenge would soon come. Ever since Eltanin first transformed Raknfeld's sturdy four-legged body into full human form, his kin had been nervous around him. Once a proud and mighty stag, Raknfeld knew his diminished presence no longer inspired the same level of confidence. To show weakness now would invite Stian to make his move to replace him.

"I know it reeks of industry," Raknfeld snapped, his sharp tone giving no indication of his concern. "If you are so eager to go home, then I suggest you hasten to find the witch. We cannot return to Norðrlönd with empty hands."

Half human, half Nordic reindeer, Stian paraded around Raknfeld, his hind legs dancing sideways in the enclosed space. "We've scoured the island and this whole upper region. She is not here."

"We *think* she is not here," corrected Gitta, the only doe allowed in this elite inner pentad. "Niagara is vast, with many people. It is hard to be sure."

"You can tell that to the king," said Raknfeld. "Tell him you have been bested by a bunch of pathetic, two-legged Outsiders."

Raknfeld heard the intake of breath and knew his insult would be particularly offensive to Maoltuile, the eldest of the council. Raknfeld hoped it was enough to incite the old bull to sound the challenge. Maoltuile he could defeat without effort—he wouldn't even have to kill him. A swift victory would stave off any further dissent and give Raknfeld time to accomplish his task.

Even the part the council didn't know about.

He stepped through the school's double doors and out into the moonlight. Whoever challenged him risked exposure, another factor in his favor. Raknfeld stretched his neck, missing the ripple of muscle that used to contract and twitch his hindquarters.

It was not easy living as a human—but it did provide a necessary disguise. It allowed him to move among the people of Western New York unchallenged, as one of them. He fit in well, his russet hair combed away from his face, his dress shirt tucked neatly in his pants. In his true state, a thick layer of white hair protected Raknfeld's arms and chest. He'd needed no other covering.

It was different as a man.

Raknfeld had never worn clothes before; and while they were less restrictive than he'd expected, he absolutely hated the shoes. Noisy and clumsy, they separated him from his intrinsic bond with the earth. He removed them every chance he got.

"I sent scouts to the towns in the south. They continue the search there tonight." Raknfeld stopped near the parked BMW. "When we finish with the city, we will move east. Eltanin is sure the witch is here somewhere."

"I will go no further into Buffalo," Gitta protested, as she pranced boldly out of the school. Her large cloven hooves made no sound on the stone drive as she followed Raknfeld into the courtyard. Gitta's haunches were tan, the flip of her tail ivory. A velvet mane grew across her chest and along her proud human back, spreading into a fine down to cover her stomach and strong forearms. She looked steadfastly into Raknfeld's eyes and voiced the challenge the others dared not.

"I will not go."

Signaling a firm command to Lleth, Ronan slid deeper into the shadows. The hound and the reindeer-like creatures were natural enemies. Lleth was never happy with Senteer around, but it was too soon for a fight.

Ronan needed answers.

How many were there? What type of arrows did they carry? Three, possibly four Senteer he could take unaided. More than that required a force he wasn't willing to let loose on this undeserving community.

Ronan felt the Beast's interest grow as he readied himself for battle. Senteer were no ordinary opponents. The unscrupulous often hired them as kidnappers or assassins. Their powerful legs and heightened senses helped the Senteer to blend in, strike, and retreat with extraordinary stealth. Skilled archers, their mode of killing was as silent as their footfall.

The Beast saw them as fodder.

As he had his whole life, Ronan relied on his strength as a god-appointed guardian to navigate the delicate triggers that determined which side of him came into play. As eager as the Beast was to tear through the Senteer, the man was the best choice here. Ronan eased his knife from its sheath and balanced his weight, poised and ready to spring.

"You will do what I tell you to do!" Raknfeld whipped a Grót blade from his pants pocket. The edge gleamed as he held it ready to strike. His outrage that the awaited challenge came from Gitta—a doe—was evident as he came toward her, herding her. She was a fool. He would end this now and leave her broken and bleeding carcass as a warning to the others.

They'd gone no more than a few feet when his russet head jerked up in alarm. Peering into the shadowed recess of the school, Raknfeld gave a sharp command. "Enough! The *jöfurr* comes."

Their lack of concern told him that the others had already heard the approaching footsteps, but did not care if the *jöfurr* caught them in dispute. Raknfeld cursed. Their rebellion was ill timed. Eltanin had sent him here on more than one errand. He needed his herd's cooperation if any of them were to survive this.

Raknfeld slid the closed blade back into his pocket, deliberately relaxing his muscles, and taming his angry expression. The *jöfurr* must not suspect he had any plan other than to aid and bring him home.

Through the age-worn stone of the school, Ronan felt him. Without seeing him, without hearing his voice, Ronan recognized the familiar, obdurate life-thread that was Carden Sihtric.

Ronan was stunned.

He'd scouted this building for nearly an hour. How could he miss someone as blatant as Carden? Ronan reached out, searching. It was dangerous, but he had to know. Trusting Lleth to warn him of attack, Ronan closed his eyes and sought his enemy.

There.

Ronan saw the shields—layers and layers of them wrapped around Carden. *Who* was he hiding from? Ysbail? Eltanin's *wicche* hammered on Ronan's brain daily, but why would she need to find Carden—and why would he hide from her?

They were questions Ronan had no time to sort through. The game was up. No more hiding in plain sight. He must grab Lynet and leave this place. Tonight. Before Carden found them and attacked.

The rumble of a motorcycle coming down the street became more than background noise. Something about the *tick tick tick* of the motor sparked Ronan's memory. Karl rode a motorcycle with that exact signature.

Damn. Ronan had not anticipated this. Karl, too, it seemed, wanted to check out Tony's story about centaurs. Curiosity would get the boy killed.

Ronan scanned his surroundings. Toys littered the grass of the house behind him. The older couple still spoke in soft tones on the porch across the street. If the fight spilled out of the school courtyard, people could get hurt. The *tick tick* of the motor grew closer and slowed down. Any minute, Karl would drive around the corner and end up with a Senteer arrow in his chest.

There was only one thing to do—face them head-on, and hope Karl had the sense to stay out of any fight that wasn't his. Ronan sprang toward the Senteer, Lleth charging beside him.

The female turned, startled, her white tail flicking up in alarm as she pulled a dagger from her belt. A large male trotted out through the wide doors. On his back was a quiver; in his hands, already loaded, a tightly strung bow. Ronan knew from experience that either poison or flesh-eating acid clung to the arrow's barbed tip.

Lleth lunged at the female. Ronan dove to the ground as an arrow whizzed over his head. He rolled, slicing tendons in the stag's hind legs, before leaping to his feet. The rear end of the Senteer dropped, unable to support his weight.

"Vökumaðr!" the man with them shouted. "Call the others!"

Ronan saw movement in the dark doorway. How many *others* were there—and did they include Carden?

The motorcycle came around the corner, pulled into the alleyway, and skidded to a halt.

Time for a change of plans.

Ronan didn't pause. Ordering Lleth to run, he jumped onto the back of the motorcycle, nearly knocking Karl off.

"Let's go! Out of here, now."

Lleth abandoned his fight and took off in a zigzag pattern. The female, bleeding, but not incapacitated, threw her knife after him, then reached for her wounded companion's bow.

"What are you doing?" Karl demanded, as he swung a fist at Ronan, in the same moment an arrow flew past his head, and shattered against the side of the apartment building. Ronan shielded his face as a spray of splintered wood and toxin flew in all directions. Instinctively, he lifted the end of his coat and used it to protect Karl from a second arrow. It caught in the hem of the leather, missing the boy's face by mere inches.

"Go, now!" Ronan yelled in Karl's ear.

Karl twisted the bike handles, gassed the engine, and sped out onto the road. Two more arrows flew. One dug into the middle of Ronan's back. He grunted in pain, but did not fall. The light chainmail he wore beneath his clothes stopped the point from digging into his flesh.

They rode on for four blocks. By the time they reached the main drag, Ronan knew the Senteer did not follow. Senteer could outrun a horse, and probably a motorcycle in light traffic. If they were in pursuit, they would have caught up by now and the battle begun in earnest.

"We're safe," Ronan said. "You can let me off here."

Karl pulled over and flicked off the motor. "What the hell was that about? What *were* those things?"

Although unfelt, Ronan knew that another thread in the fragile fabric of the Aragaidheal Divide had just snapped.

"Some crazy drunks with a bow and arrow." Ronan got off the bike and sheathed his knife. He watched for Lleth, and was satisfied when he recognized a familiar gray shape in the distance. It would take the hound a few minutes to catch up.

"Bullshit." Karl swung off the bike. "Tony was right. They were centaurs—four legs and all."

"It was a drunk and his friends, nothing more." Ronan yanked the arrows from his coat and sniffed the tips. Poison. He broke off the shafts and tossed them away, but kept the arrowheads.

"That's not what I saw." Karl paced back and forth in front of his bike, looking like he wanted to hit somebody.

Ronan picked up a discarded coffee cup and wrapped the poisoned points inside, before shoving it in his pocket. They might prove useful in future.

"Do you think I'm stupid?" Karl grabbed Ronan by the arm. "I saw them with my own—"

Ronan seized Karl by the front of his jacket and slammed him up against the security grille of a shop window. "You saw a couple of drunks. If you value your life, go home and forget tonight, Karl. I can't protect you if you come back here on your own."

Ronan stared hard at the young man, trying to push home his message, but he saw only bold-faced rebellion in those hazel eyes. Ronan recognized the look. He saw it often enough in young soldiers. Too much bravado and not enough common sense.

He released Karl and headed back toward the parking ramp where he'd left the car. Karl followed him. Ronan wasn't surprised.

"So, what were you doing with a bunch of drunks in the middle of the night, clear up here in Niagara Falls?" Karl asked.

Ronan didn't answer, just kept walking.

"I'll tell you what I think," Karl continued. "I think you're smuggling drugs across the Canadian border. And those centaur things are holograms to keep people away from the boarded-up crack house you're using for a drop point." Karl easily kept pace with Ronan's long strides. "So, should I call the cops and report you?"

"Do whatever you want," Ronan said.

"I want to go back and see what technology you're using. Where'd the arrows come from? Motion-sensitive activators?"

Ronan stopped at the ramp entrance. "If you go back there, you will be dead before you get two feet onto the property. Nobody will find your body, and you will have wasted your life for nothing."

"Are you threatening me?"

"I never threaten. I don't have to."

Lleth trotted up, panting, and Ronan knelt to check the wolfhound for wounds. Blood stained his coat, and he had a small gash on his shoulder, but other than that, Lleth seemed unharmed. If poisoned, the hound would already be dead. Satisfied it could wait until they were home, Ronan motioned for Lleth to jump the barrier, then pushed through the turnstile and entered the parking ramp.

Karl followed, falling into step beside him, stone-faced and quiet.

Ronan mulled his choices. Karl was a decent kid. Ronan knew he had a juvenile criminal record, but he'd managed to stay out of trouble the last couple of years, and he worked hard at the tungsten factory. Ronan also knew if he didn't give Karl an explanation he could accept, the boy would go looking for answers. Ronan couldn't let that happen.

The Senteer had recognized him. By now, Carden knew Ronan was here. Even so, Buffalo and Niagara Falls were both heavily populated cities. It would take time for Carden to find Lynet—unless Karl gave him the clues he needed to narrow his search. If Karl walked into that lair, Carden would scan his mind, and that would lead them straight to Depew. From there it was only a few miles to Town Line and Lynet.

Either Ronan convinced Karl to leave it alone, or he stopped him. Ronan didn't relish killing the boy, but he wouldn't allow Karl to endanger Lynet, or the Outside world, if Lynet panicked and blasted death to the four corners.

Ronan stood at a crossroads.

If Carden rushed to attack before Lynet learned how to control her thoughts, she could kill everything in sight—including Ronan—and no one could stop her. Yet, if Ronan took the life of an innocent youth, if he started down that slippery slope of justifying cold-blooded murder, where would it lead him? Ronan was the last of his kind. His actions would define the Vökumaðr in the hearts and memories of the people of Norðrlönd forever.

Ronan opened the car and waited for Lleth to jump in the backseat, then turned to Karl. "Look. I know you're curious. But it isn't worth your life. Go home. If you're still alive tomorrow, I'll tell you what I know. Just not here. Too many ears."

Karl held his gaze for a drawn-out moment, and Ronan feared he would have to kill the boy after all. Finally, Karl said, "Sure. I'll see you at work."

Ronan got in his car and pulled out, but did not go far. He parked and walked to a place where he could watch, sincerely hoping the boy would make the right choice.

In the distance, Karl stood by his motorcycle. He picked up the arrow shaft Ronan had discarded earlier and twirled it between his fingers, all the while staring in the direction of the old school. Finally, he got on his bike and headed south to Buffalo.

Ronan was relieved, though he doubted the boy would live for long. Once Karl realized Ronan was not coming back to work, ever, he would probably head straight for the Senteer. By then Ronan would be long gone and unable to help him.

Ronan rubbed his face. He was tired. Carden was once more on their trail, and Eltanin had traded Kynneeyn Gorrym for Senteer.

He looked at the horizon. In a couple of hours, it would be morning.

It was time he and Lynet disappeared.

Butterfly

L YNET HURRIED TO GET A GLIMPSE *of the red-haired man, who seemed so full of purpose, striding down the street. He paused, then stepped into a dark alley. Lynet ran to catch up. Out of breath, she came around the corner, only to discover that the alley was really a green, mossy meadow. Dew clung in great drops to the grass, and her ankles got wet as she followed him.*

The man turned briefly, saw her, but said nothing, simply continued on his way.

The pathway dipped, and Lynet slipped on the wet grass, tumbling down the side of a hill—down, down into a beautiful valley. She got to her feet, surprised to see the red-haired man standing in front of her.

He reached out his hand.

Lynet hesitated, unsure she should take it. Now that she saw him clearly, the intense look in his eyes scared her.

He shrugged one broad shoulder, then raised his arms. Immediately, a swarm of brightly colored bugs filled the air around him, darting and diving. He winked, said something she couldn't understand and the bugs grew, blossoming into fat flying piglets.

Lynet laughed in delight. The red-haired man laughed as well. She liked the sound; it made him less intimidating.

From out of nowhere, a dark gray storm cloud took shape behind him, but the red-haired man didn't seem to notice, too intent on amusing Lynet.

Lynet pointed, shouting, trying to get him to turn around and see, but he didn't seem to hear her, and Lynet watched, helpless, as the ominous thundercloud grew.

It spread closer, enveloping several of the piglets. They squealed and squirmed. Then, like popcorn under heat, their insides erupted, turning them inside out— changing them into black, grotesque creatures with long, pointy teeth.

They attacked the red-haired man. Lynet tried to run away, but her legs wouldn't move. More of the piglets transformed. They dropped to the ground and scrambled along the grass toward her. Lynet felt like she waded through treacle. The creatures overtook her, clawing and pulling her hair.

Out of nowhere, Lleth arrived. Biting at the black sprites, his jaws crunched and tossed them aside, one after another. Lynet thought she might escape, but then a huge, ugly monster took shape in front of her. Black and fat, with horns on its head and cloven hooves. She screamed—

Lynet jumped up, the covers flying, her pillow spinning to the floor. Her heart pounded so hard it sounded like drums in her head.

A dream—only a dream.

She sank back in relief and covered her face with her arm. No, not a dream; a full-fledged nightmare. Her whole body shivered as she tried to shake off the last dregs, wondering if she would ever be able to fall back asleep, or if she should just get up and start her day.

Something light flaked off her forearm and dropped onto her cheek.

Cautiously, Lynet opened her eyes. Tiny flakes, like scales, caught in her lashes. Lynet brushed them away, only to find more of the scales falling from her fingertips, making it worse.

Alarmed, she sat up and held out her peeling arms. She looked like she was shedding! Was she still dreaming? In growing panic, Lynet grabbed a handful of sheet and rubbed it briskly over her arm. The scales came off easily, spilling onto her covers and nightgown.

Lynet did not see the mess—her eyes were fixed on the unexpected color on her arm. She rubbed again, revealing more of the warm, cream-colored skin beneath. Lynet leapt from the bed to stand before the mirror—calling wildly for Maple to come see.

Her whole body was in color!

Lynet ran her hands through her hair, then grabbed a brush and began combing away flat, black flakes. The strands changed before her eyes, black whisking away to reveal soft, golden blonde curls.

Maple bustled into the room, out of breath. "What's wrong?"

"Is this real?" Lynet asked, her sea-blue eyes welling with joy. "Am I dreaming, or is this really happening to me?"

Maple's face crinkled into a dozen wrinkles. "Real enough. Looks like whatever made you sick has finally run its course."

Lynet had never considered herself sick but, if Maple wanted to call it an illness, that was fine. Everything was fine—more than fine. She kissed the old woman's cheek, broke away, and whirled about with all the glee of a child on holiday. Black and white flecks floated through the room, laying a fine dust on her polished dresser.

"Let's get you bathed and see what we've got under all of that." Maple shooed her out. "Off you go to wash. I'll tidy your room."

Lynet danced down the hall to the bathroom, sidestepping a group of dust bunnies hopping toward her room. They came from all parts of the house, answering Maple's call to clean. Lynet sang as she turned on the faucets and poured loads of bubble bath into the water. Let Treddian tease her about her off-key voice; nothing could dampen her spirits now.

A short while later, Lynet stood at the breakfast table, turning this way and that so the family could get a good look. The hem of her dress swirled merrily around her cream-colored calves. Her hair, like warm honey, wrapped and unwrapped around her waist in golden waves. The flush on her face was a rosy pink, not its usual ash gray.

"You're beautiful, Lynet." Fig took her hands, and she spun him around until his tiny feet lifted off the ground and flew in the air behind him. "Like a butterfly just out of the cocoon."

"Not that you weren't lovely enough before," Alder grumbled, "but I suppose we'll be chasing men off with brooms, now."

Auntie Jól agreed. "You'll be the apple of many a young man's eye."

Only one pair of male eyes mattered, and Lynet released Fig in mid twirl. His agile body did a double backflip, and he ended nimbly on his toes. Fig never landed any other way.

"I'll be back!" Lynet laughed, and raced out the door.

Maple watched from the window as the girl ran across the lawn. Jól came up beside her. "When will you tell Lynet the truth?" Jól asked. "It isn't right to leave it so late. She should have time to understand and deal with all this."

"When she gets home from work," Maple said, as she brushed her hands on her apron, and turned away from the window. "Let her have this final day in the Outside world."

"The Watchman won't like you waiting."

"He came to see me this morning before dawn. I sent him on an errand. By the time he returns this evening, I will have told Lynet all she needs to know. Timing is everything. Until the Watchman is ready to take responsibility for her, it is best not to say too much."

Neira groaned as she pushed up from the cold stone floor and yanked the hated collar down away from her windpipe. She was cold and stiff, and confused. Something sharp pricked her ribs, and she twisted around to find a shard, pointed at both ends, caught in her robes. Neira muttered as she worked the piece of shale out of the silk. Lovely, another hole to mend—

Confusion cleared in an instant as she realized, first, she could *see* the tear in her robes. It was morning. Second, she was still in the cavern beneath the castle. She wasn't dead or discovered, at least not yet. Neira got to her feet and looked around. High overhead, cracks in the eastern wall let in streams of sunlight, like pale blue ribbons, which illuminated the cave, revealing the many recesses and nooks previously hidden by shadow.

Lastly, she remembered the footsteps down below, her panic, and failed attempt to conjure a shield.

Whose footsteps had she heard? Neira picked up the cold torch and held it like a club. Cautiously, she crept to the edge of the overhang.

Below her, the cavern opened up. Water gently lapped the crescent shoreline. More sunlight came in with the sea, bouncing its way through the crooked tunnel. No sign of anyone. The door to the library still stood partially open, rocks wedged tight, exactly as she'd left it. Was it possible she'd heard a rat or some other nocturnal sound and only thought it was a footstep? Had she brought this all on herself?

Now she was mad. Neira knew better than to let fear confound her. Some might insist a good dose of fear was necessary, even healthy. Neira disagreed. Fear was the enemy. Always. She was a girl in a man's world. She'd spent her young life pushing through fear to ensure she stood equal to the wizards and apprentices of Ddewin Tower. She wasn't going to let a roosting bat or falling pebble stop her now.

Neira strode back to the eight carved steps. Again, she felt the subtle warning of the night before. There was a trap here somewhere; she would bet her life on it. She knelt down, grabbed a handful of sand and shale and threw it onto the stairs. Instantly, she felt the prickle of something malevolent.

Definitely a trap.

She picked up another handful and tossed it, watching, listening. She spotted the trigger. The third step up, and by the looks of it, it was waning. Each time the trap sprung, it would lose a bit of its strength.

What kind of trap was it?

Neira placed her foot on the first step. Nothing. She moved to the second. There, she could sense it now—a Fear spell. She couldn't tell exactly what kind of Fear spell, not unless she stood inside it, but it did explain why she'd overreacted to the noise last night. Even in daylight, it made her skin tingle.

Neira continued to toss stones and fragmented seashells onto the step until they formed a small pile of rubble. She hadn't felt a reaction the last few throws, so the magic was probably spent. She tossed two more handfuls for good measure. Still nothing.

Confident her trick had worked and the spell was harmless, Neira gripped the torch and headed up the stairs, eager to gain the top.

She was halfway over the trap when the air stirred.

Something moved in front of her—something tangible, living.

The spell may have faded, but it was not dead. Neira felt its anger at being provoked. A thick vapor gathered. Spidery fingers formed in the mist, and before she could run . . . they grabbed her.

In horror, Neira felt her limbs freeze, felt terror build in her chest until her heart beat so wildly she thought it would burst. She could not fight it, nor stop the rising panic. All feeling left her hands, and Neira watched helplessly as her makeshift weapon clattered useless to the ground.

The worst was yet to come.

Monsters and demons formed in the mist. From childhood creatures under the bed, to fiends she'd actually fought, they all took shape and stepped, tangible, from the vapor.

Neira closed her eyes. Too scared to speak aloud, she repeated the truth in her head: *It's only an illusion.*

She heard the creatures circling. Heard best the wheezed breathing of the *uvættr*. Nearly seven feet tall, the monster was all arms and legs, with decaying skin and the promise of disease. Four years ago, one surprised her and Scartozzar in the foothills near the wastelands.

Too late, Neira understood the nature of the spell. It read her fear and, in an instant, the memory of that day became real.

Neira's eyes flew open. She was in the foothills. Dry, hot wind blew sand and the foul breath of the *uvættr* across her face. Exactly as it happened before, the monster swiped its filthy claws at her, ripping open her arm. Neira cried out, clutching her forearm. Blood streamed down to coat her fingertips as she struggled to keep casting, to remain coherent and on her feet, even as the *uvættr* sickness coursed through her body. She turned to Scartozzar for help, but he wasn't there. She spun around, looking for him, but the surrounding foothills came in and out of focus, like the background in a dream—

Was she still in the cavern?

Neira fought to wake from the illusion even as she ran, stumbled and fell. Nothing seemed to work. She didn't know how to make it stop. If she died in the illusion, would her body die in the cavern? There was no trigger, no doorway she could see, just sand and sagebrush and the distant ruins of Auðn. She scrambled backward up the crumbling hillside as the *uvættr* lunged after, intent on finishing the kill.

In the cavern, Neira forced her lips to move. With desperate effort, she pushed enough air out through her teeth to whisper, "Scartozzar struck you down. I saw you die."

The wheezing and the wind grew silent.

Neira broke from the illusion and truly opened her eyes. She was in the cavern beneath the castle. The mist was gone. The spell done.

Neira nearly collapsed with relief. Sweat had formed on her upper lip, and she wiped it away with trembling fingers. How stupid could she be? The greatest wizard of their age had conjured that spell. Even near death, Eltanin's magic was potent.

Footsteps sounded behind her—lots of them.

Neira's heart sank. She was so close, only a few steps away, and now it was finished. Eltanin would punish her, and she hadn't even reached the top. Neira turned, expecting to see Kynneeyn Gorrym running up to grab her.

She saw no one.

Where were the footsteps coming from?

Shuffling and voices sounded overhead. Neira looked up at the top of the stairs. The sounds grew as someone was dragged, protesting and sobbing, to the very edge of the ledge, just out of sight.

Was it Colm? Was he still alive?

A cry of pain echoed around the cavern, and Neira gasped—a woman's voice. Margaret? Wilda?

Neira leapt forward, intent on helping her friends—but her legs refused to obey, and she fell, slamming her elbows and chin against the hard stone. Pain exploded behind her eyes. Her tongue grew numb on one side and she tasted the iron of blood in her mouth.

Overhead, the woman pleaded. *"We guarded the truth. All these years we kept it secret. How could you know?"*

Neira reeled—she recognized the thick accent of her people; more than that, she knew that voice. "Mother?"

Of all the nightmares she'd had as a child, only one followed Neira to adulthood—her family destroyed because of her carelessness. Neira had worked hard to lose her accent, to blend in with the people of Caeraricin. Scartozzar had tutored her repeatedly on her language, her posture, exorcizing all trace of privilege in her manner. It would take so little to turn her into a pawn if anyone discovered her identity.

The woman groaned as if struck or kicked.

Neira was furious . . . and then frustrated. No. No. No. Mother was not here. It was a trick. The Fear spell was still alive—still attacking. She struggled to stand, cursing the seized muscles in her legs. She grabbed her ankle and tried to lift her foot—to step up and off the trapped stair. But her mother's cries of pain were like fuel, feeding her fear. Even though Neira knew the voice wasn't real, the spell was stronger than she was, and no amount of reasoning would release her. Helpless tears slid down her cheeks.

"Please, not our daughter. All our hopes lie with her. Release her. Take me instead. Take me!" Her mother's voice hit a pitch that begged Neira to run, to crawl, to do whatever it took—even if it meant cutting off her own useless feet—anything to get free and save her.

"How could you know?" The repeated question sounded so hopeless it nearly broke Neira's heart.

Then she heard it, the cold taunt of her mother's tormentor.

"How do you think I found out?" Carden's tone was hard, mocking. *"Gwyneira told me. Your precious daughter betrayed you all."*

There was a moment of silence.

Neira felt the spell poised, anticipating her reaction. Waiting for that swell of triumph when its victim went mad with grief.

Neira coughed—short, awkward sounds that sputtered, erupting into a spate of tearful laughter. The spell had got it wrong. An error so blatant the magic lost all hold over her. She had kept her secret, even from Carden, and he had never called her Gwyneira a day in his life.

Black vapor again took shape—but it was too late. Neira was free. She stepped up onto the next stair.

"Fool." Neira drew her hand through the vanquished vapor, watching the spell die and dissipate. "What assumption did you make? That, because I doubt him, I would think the worst?" She snorted. "Silly spell, you have no idea what Carden's *worst* really is."

Neira ran up the stairs.

"Now, let's see what you guarded so well."

Siren's Song

RONAN JERKED THE LACES ON HIS BOOT, his movements stiff and fuming. He'd left Niagara Falls last night and gone straight to the Macarthurs. There, in the predawn hours, he'd told them about the Senteer and his decision to flee with Lynet. While Ronan outlined his plan, Maple said she'd known all along Carden was in Buffalo.

Ronan stomped his boot down and grabbed his bath towel from the sofa where he'd thrown it. He was more than angry; he was dumbstruck by his own stupidity. He'd actually allowed the Macarthurs to convince him that they were harmless.

Making the sigil, Maple Macarthur drew herself up to her full height. "Why did you let them see you, Zerker? We were safe here, hidden. Now you must make it right. If the Senteer know of this sanctuary, you will kill them all. Do not let even one return to Eltanin with news of us or this place."

Her Governance slammed into Ronan with the subtlety of a sledgehammer. He did not resist. If he pitted his will against hers, she might unexpectedly raise the Beast.

"Once Laburnum House is secure," Maple continued, "you may take Lynet across the Divide. You will protect her and deliver her to Prince Edan. Swear to me now, Watchman, you will take your own life, rather than fail me."

Ronan rubbed the towel through his still-damp hair and across his bare chest. Her threat had taken him by surprise. Like all Vökumenn, Ronan belonged to the high king. He was bound to House Aricin, obedient to any of that bloodline. Unfortunately, over the centuries, the magic that governed the Vökumenn had passed through marriage and birth to all six of the ruling houses. Many nobles now held the power of Governance, though few had the inner strength to control it.

Maple's will was unquestioned, her threat real. Yet so unnecessary.

Ronan was a guardian. Created by the Æsir to defend Norðrlönd and its people. The Macarthurs were Northlanders; therefore, they were his responsibility. If his actions put them at risk, then he would fix it. As for Lynet, Ronan had been her protector since the moment he first set out for Lunedalr. The Oath he'd made could not be undone, not in this life. Until he died, Ronan would be the wall between Lynet and anything that tried to get too close. He did not need a member of the nobility to remind him of it.

He whip-snapped the towel in frustration and hung it up.

He would find the Senteer and determine what they knew. And, much though it pained him, he would silence Karl. Perhaps Ronan could tie the boy up and leave him somewhere in the factory, where the guys would eventually discover him . . . but not for a couple of days. Not until Ronan and Lynet had escaped to the wilds of Norðrlönd.

Ronan looked for his shirt, then remembered he'd left it to dry, draped over the balcony. He stepped out into the sunshine.

Maple hadn't included Carden in her command, but he was the surest way to locate the Senteer. Finding him would be difficult, but not impossible. Ronan had gotten a good look at the shields around Carden last night. He would focus on those, but keep his distance. Ronan did not intend to give that smug bastard even a whiff of Lynet.

It would be best if they simply ran.

Maple's interference put everyone in jeopardy. Ronan could not refuse her outright, but he did have his Oath. If Maple's Governance endangered Lynet, Ronan would obey the higher law. Again, Cian's insistence that Ronan swear the Vökumaðr Oath to an unknown woman many leagues away was proving invaluable.

The front door swung open across the street, and Ronan looked down, surprised to see Lynet. What time was it? He checked his watch, then listened to see if it was ticking. That couldn't be the right time. The woman never left the house this early.

She did not pause, but hurried down the porch stairs and out across the wet morning grass. The rising sun reflected off her skin and hair, until she glowed as bright and golden as a mythical flaming bird.

The sudden onslaught of the *Kærásti Fórnsöngr* nearly brought Ronan to his knees. *Gods above, what had he done?*

The Restore spell. Vökumaðr magic to banish a disguise and return a body, in an instant, to the natural shape and pigments of birth. He'd used the spell on Lynet last night. The corrupted Hide spell would have slowed it down, but the transformation finished just the same.

Laughing and barefoot, Lynet picked her way gingerly across the road, waving up at him, her happiness tangible even at a distance.

Stunned, Ronan stepped back into his apartment. What had he been thinking? That spell, even half-done, had been a protection not only to her, but to him as well, keeping the *Kærásti Fórnsöngr* at bay. His mind spun with the enormity of his folly.

He heard her on the stairs, her small fist rapping impatiently on the door. The pie—he should never have eaten the blasted grizarbr pie!

Lleth woofed. Noise bombarded Ronan's ears—barking, knocking, the swell of the *Kærásti Fórnsöngr*. He had no choice but to unlatch the door.

Lynet burst into the room. "Look at me! I'm human!"

She was breathtaking, warm, happy, and inches from him. How he longed to catch her up in his arms and hold her tight against his chest.

Lleth pushed between them, wagging his long tail, and Ronan used the momentary gap to hold Lynet at arm's length.

"You are beautiful, *ástmær*." He twirled her around as if in a dance, scrambling for words and conversation. "This color suits you. Fig was wrong to complain about the dye."

"It wasn't the hair color," Lynet protested. "I never used it, and it's not only my hair. My skin. My eyes. Everything has changed." She took his callused hand and laid it against her cheek. "Look at me, Ronan. All of me."

She didn't need to ask. Ronan had never stopped looking at her. He saw her face in his waking dreams. She said everything had changed but, to his fierce Vökumaðr heart, nothing had changed. He was as in love with her now as he had ever been.

She whispered, asking for what he dared not give. "Please."

His fingers cupped her face; her skin felt soft, like velvet petals on a wild rose. He had only to tighten his hold, to draw her into the circle of his waiting arms. He stroked her lower lip with his thumb. She was too willing. In the past, it had taken both of them, acting together, to keep their passion under control. This time it all fell to him.

Ronan felt her desire, hot and blatant. If he gave in, there would be no turning back. No stopping until he had consumed every inch of her, the *Kærásti Fórnsöngr* complete, their powers joined for all time.

Her fingers stroked his ribs, and his stomach muscles tightened in response. Her palm came to rest over his heart. It beat strong and quick, unspoken proof of his rising passion. She pursed her lips and gently blew, stirring the dark hairs on his chest.

He whispered her name, and she answered, her nose sliding feather-light against his skin until she found his hard male nipple. A flick of her tongue and he was undone. Like a unicorn trapped by a virgin's kiss, he could not move. *Would* not move. He wanted her to continue, wanted her to lick and kiss and never stop.

All around him, Ronan heard the *Kærásti Fórnsöngr*. It came from her, from him, from the earth, the sky. It was a prayer. It was a siren's song. A music he could not ignore, repeating what he already knew: she was his equal in every way, a woman worthy of his Vökumaðr heritage.

He pulled her into his arms. His callused hands rubbed her back, her hips, crushing her against him.

Lynet sighed.

He followed the sound, his open mouth finding hers, his tongue taking, plunging in and out between her lips, warning her of what would come. Blood rushed to his loins. He would finish this now. No more suffering, no more waiting. She belonged to him. The Nornir would have to live with their mistake. Ronan was tired of living it for them.

As if in answer, the voices of all his mighty ancestors shouted with one accord: *You are Vökumaðr. Your life is not your own. The Oath is all.*

Ronan pushed the kiss deeper, blocking out their cries—but he could not escape the truth. If he took her as his heart and might demanded—the song would burst through. They would sing the *Kærásti Fórnsöngr*, Lynet's terrible magic would pass to him, and the rage of the Hoar Beast would pass to her. Together, they would become the death of *everything*.

With a roar of frustration, Ronan tore his mouth from hers. His eyes bore into Lynet's as they stood there gasping.

"We cannot do this," he said, his voice hoarse with longing. Hands stretched wide, Ronan took a physical step away from her. He could barely think. His loins screamed for him to be a man, not a servant of the Fates.

Ronan watched helplessly as embarrassment stained Lynet's cheeks. Her once-bright eyes clouded with confusion, her disappointment an open book for him to read. She had hoped her transformation would please him. How could he tell her that that transformation was their doom?

Lleth whined, disturbed by the abrupt change in the air. Ronan pushed him away and told him to go lie down. When Ronan looked back, Lynet was gone, the apartment door open, the rippling edge of her dress the only thing he saw as she fled.

Ronan threw back his head and cursed at the sky. He could lead armies to war without fear, yet, in this arena, he had no skill. They were at the mercy of gods—who had no mercy.

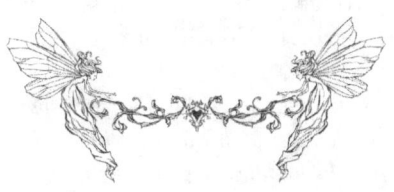

Son of Kings

CARDEN SIHTRIC STOOD LOOKING OUT his apartment window. It was a common-enough stance. He was always looking out—out on the world he meant to conquer. Today that world seemed pretty skank. No different from normal, he supposed, but today he actually noticed it. Sure, the Outside world had its perks, but there were days when he missed the clear Nordic skies and the fierce swell of magic.

The unexpected appearance of Raknfeld and his herd signaled an end to Carden's holiday. He'd experienced the sweet taste of autonomy in this normal life he'd set up for himself. Part of him didn't want to give it up. He turned the metal crank to open the top window, and let in some air.

On the other hand, the arrival of the Senteer did bring his goals back into focus. While here, Carden had lowered his sights and accepted mediocrity in place of greatness. He'd succeeded at everything he bothered to try, but it did not change the fact he'd settled, taken his eye off the mark. While this fistful of Buffalo gave him pleasure, it was not enough. It would never be enough. Not while he was here, and the kingdom he hungered to rip from his father's grasp lay across the Aragaidheal Divide.

Carden leaned his forehead against the window, his long red hair sticking to the glass. What a hellish time it had been, this climb to independence.

He had arrived on the Outside wounded and bleeding, with most of his memory gone. The first two weeks were wasted in Saint Joseph's Hospital, where the barbarians on this side of the Divide actually used a needle and thread to sew a man together, as if repairing a coat or pair of trousers.

Once discharged, Carden had spent the next couple of months on the streets. He slept in cardboard boxes, ate whatever he could steal, all the time trying to figure out who he was, where he was.

Flashes of memory would come to him like open war frontal attacks, throwing people and places at him in a chaotic stream. Most of it made no sense—wild, outlandish images that seemed to have no foothold in reality. He feared he was going mad—right up until the night the rat died.

Carden smiled.

He'd been sleeping rough under an overpass down on the waterfront. It was early summer, the weather cold and rainy.

Carden wrapped himself in sheets of discarded newspaper, trying to stay warm. The running ink added to the layer of dirt on his thin, stolen coat. Shivering, nursing a black eye and cracked ribs, he huddled, reliving the humiliation of trying to get a job earlier in the day.

The place with the Help Wanted sign had been one of those filthy, elbow-room-only cigarette shops on the West Side. He might be losing his mind, but Carden was sure he could count higher than the cretins hanging around that place. Of course, his saying so probably influenced the owner's decision to throw him out, and set those same cretins onto him with a baseball bat.

In the hours since, Carden's anger had built, and his stomach growled. A colossal headache pounded against the inside of his skull. His breathing was shallow and uneven as he tried to avoid the pain that caught at his ribs every time he inhaled.

Up to that miserable bundle of hate and anger scrambled a rat. A big black rat. Sniffing, scratching, it looked for a place to burrow in and get warm.

Carden's lip curled. He pulled back his booted foot, poised to kick in the rat's face. "Burn in hell, you filthy—" The rat made a startled squeak—then promptly burst into flame and keeled over dead.

Wet, cold, barely able to feel his fingers, Carden pushed the shredding pieces of newspaper from his face. He stared at the rat for nearly an hour, unmoving, searching through the crazy memories in his head. Wondering, for the first time, if perhaps there was some thread of truth to them after all.

Slowly, plagued by doubt, Carden gathered up what was left of the newspaper from around his shoulders and rolled it into a ball of paper mush. Casting his eyes around to ensure he was alone, Carden focused his anger and hate on the center of that sopping wet mass. The newspaper erupted into flame; the blaze spilled onto the mud and grass, catching on his coat. Carden rolled on the ground to put it out, crying in pain and laughing aloud. The thrill of creating fire released a new spate of memories.

This time he did not dismiss them as nonsense.

Carden pushed back from the window. He'd kept to himself after that, hiding, thinking, sorting through the pictures and stories in his head, stitching them together. The more he worked at it, the more he remembered: his childhood by the lake; the call to the castle at the age of eight; a year spent on the Outside learning the hazards of democracy; and fiery glimpses of an awkward adolescence.

Seeing little of his father, Carden had been the equivalent of a slave in his youth. A *sgalag* in the upper chambers of Ddewin Tower, where King Urien's advisors and their wretched apprentices lived and acted out their petty rivalries. Always at the call of some arrogant wizard or another, Carden watched enviously as the princeling Edan Aricin and his Beast learned the art of war in the training fields far below.

How he hated them.

Of course, not all his youthful memories were bad. Some even bordered on the sublime—like that heady moment when he first challenged his brutal father. Carden wore a scar beside his left eye for his efforts that day—but, at the age of fifteen, he stopped being his father's whipping boy. Eltanin took notice of him after that, deciding it was time to teach his son how to control all that fledgling power.

Carden put on his suit jacket.

He'd spent weeks under that overpass, relearning the lessons his father had taught him about the birth and timing of spells. It was difficult, learning to use his powers here in the city. Not so much because of his jumbled memory, but because of the environment.

When the old gods first stripped magic from the Outside, it created a hunger in the soil, the rocks, the minerals and sand. Anything made from those substances—the pavement, buildings, metals—shared that hunger. Nearly everything around him absorbed and swallowed magic. Consequently, it took more control to conjure and cast.

In one area, however, Carden's magic found little resistance.

His mother had been a princess of the House of Lann in the Western Kingdom. Through her, Carden enjoyed a magic his father, who was not of noble birth, did not possess—Governance.

Through her, he was truly a son of kings—born to reign, lead, and when necessary . . . force.

On the Outside, Carden easily persuaded people to believe anything he wanted them to. Many obeyed without question, although humans had too deep a survival instinct to drop dead at his bidding. Still, even the strong-willed could be swayed to some degree.

From a broken bum homeless on the streets—to a successful local attorney, Carden had created a comfortable life for himself through lies, persuasion, and raw, awakening power.

Carden picked up his briefcase and thoughtfully fingered his car keys. Soon he would go home and face his father, whom he hadn't seen since they'd battled Scartozzar in the caves of Aros. So much had happened since then; so many triumphs to hide. It would not be easy. Father, after all, prided himself on his ability to probe minds.

Carden grinned. Since that day, so many years ago, when he had returned from PenyCefn so crippled and broken he'd needed a little girl to take care of him, Carden had been keeping secrets from his father.

This time would be no different.

Lynet stayed in her room for over an hour. She would be late for work, but she didn't care. She was too embarrassed to leave her bed. Every time she thought she was ready to get up, her mind led her back to that horrifying moment when Ronan rejected her, and she burned with shame all over again.

Lynet pulled a pillow over her face. She honestly hadn't meant to throw herself at him. All she'd wanted was for him to see her like this, and think she was pretty. Everything had happened so fast: the brush of his beard, the warmth of his bare chest, the thrill as his mouth took hers—in that moment the universe changed.

Her universe.

Not his.

Not even this amazing transformation in her appearance could change the blunt fact—Ronan did not want her. He'd kissed her for all of ten seconds before deciding he'd had enough.

Lynet pushed away the pillow.

"I'm so stupid," she said to the ceiling, then sat up. A lock of golden hair fell thick and springy across her arm. Lynet rubbed the curl between her fingers. The texture differed significantly from the straight, fine strands of yesterday. It was certainly harder to get a brush through.

None of this was commonplace. Humans did not molt, or change appearance overnight. Maple called it a sickness, but Lynet wasn't fooled. It was magic. Someone had *done* this to her.

Not that she was unhappy; she loved it. All the same, she didn't like the idea of people using magic on her willy-nilly, without her consent. In fact, the more she thought about it, the angrier she got. Who had done this to her? Ronan? No, he thought her color came from a box. It must have been Maple or Alder, but then why the surprised act this morning when she showed them her new look? More importantly, why had they waited two freaking years, when they obviously could have changed her long before this?

Lynet slid from the bed and opened her dresser drawer.

She wasn't going to wait around for the next whim of magic to hit her. She needed to understand how it worked, and how to protect herself.

She took a small rock from the drawer. Lynet had seen Maple pull salt from a rock not long after she first arrived at Laburnum House. Unfortunately, as soon as Maple realized Lynet was watching her, the matriarch stopped, and from then on bought her salt at the supermarket.

Lynet weighed the rock in her palm. It was an ordinary rock; one she'd dug up from the garden. She'd tried a couple of times to draw salt particles from its molecular structure, focusing her mind on vibrating the salt out— but nothing happened. Nothing ever happened.

She wondered if emotion made any difference, because she was a boiling kettle of resentment and embarrassment right now. Lynet tossed the rock from one hand to the other, back and forth, letting her feelings escalate, until she wanted to chuck the rock and break something.

Of course, the rock stayed the same—no salt, no heat, nothing.

Infuriated, Lynet yanked open the drawer and shoved the rock under her neatly folded clothes. What was wrong with her? Why couldn't she do it? She slammed the drawer, glanced up into the mirror—and froze.

The eyes staring back at her didn't merely *look* blue . . . they *glowed* blue.

"Eibby. Eibby! Look at my eyes. What do you see?" Lynet yanked off her sweater and dumped it and her handbag on the diner counter.

Eibby turned around, two drinks in her hands—and promptly dropped them. "Lynet? What have you done?"

Customers looked up curious about the drama, and Joey called from the kitchen, "That better not be the burgers I just put up."

"Spilt drinks," Lynet hollered back, and grabbed the mop from the cupboard. "I'm so sorry, Eibby, I didn't think it would scare you. Although, I have to say I'm pretty freaked out about it myself."

"Freaked out?" Eibby used wads of napkins to pick up the broken glass and dump it in the bin. "You look gorgeous! Lynet, your hair, your makeup; you look like a supermodel."

Lynet stopped mopping. Eibby meant her new coloring, not her eyes. She dug in her handbag and pulled out a mini mirror, then slumped against the counter. Her eyes weren't glowing anymore.

"Seriously, you win." Eibby pulled a necklace out from under her blouse and dangled it. "I was going to show you this cool black swan necklace Jack gave me—it'd been in the hospital's lost and found for like two years—and wait for you to be impressed but, it's no contest, your new look trumps all."

Lynet wasn't really listening. The blue glow had happened twice now. That meant it wasn't a fluke and she could do it again—later, as soon as her shift was over, she would try. Lynet pulled her hair up into a knot and wiggled two straws through to hold it in place. For now, she needed to get busy; she was seriously late. She'd be lucky if Aliysha didn't fire her.

"You know, you remind me of that Waterhouse painting." Eibby came back from delivering a pair of new drinks to the customers at table three. "It's called *Lamia*. I have a copy of it in my bag. There are legends about this woman, very beautiful, who lures men to their deaths, because she's really a snake who likes to eat gorgeous men; oh, and her own children."

"I remind you of a snake?" Lynet drawled.

"Who eats children," Joey added from the back.

Eibby grabbed her backpack and pulled out a tatty green sketchbook. She never went anywhere without her sketchbook. In it, Eibby recorded translations, headstone rubbings, sketches of made-up creatures, unusual words, histories of old abbeys, and all kinds of Wiccan weirdness. It was a travel-size encyclopedia of anything and everything bizarre.

"Here. See?" Eibby showed her the picture she'd torn from a book and glued to the page. "She's actually quite lovely until you notice the shed snakeskin still wrapped around her waist."

"I did not shed my skin," Lynet lied. Eibby had a knack for figuring stuff out, but Lynet was fairly sure the whole skin-shedding story on the very day she had, in fact, shed hers, was a coincidence.

"So, did you show Ronan your new look yet? What does he think? I bet he loves it." Eibby rattled on as she flipped the book closed, shoved it in her bag, then turned to greet some new customers. "Welcome. Would you like the breakfast or the lunch menu?"

Lynet plucked her order pad from the box under the counter and went to the chalkboard to sign herself in. The last thing she wanted to do was talk about Ronan. She was still stinging from his rejection.

"Lynet?" Aliysha said in surprise, as she came out through the swinging kitchen doors carrying plates of hot food. "I thought you weren't coming in this afternoon. Weren't you supposed to go to Traffic Court today?"

Crap. How could she forget? First, the molting, then Ronan, then the glowing eyes. Court was the farthest thing from her mind. Like a pinball, Lynet ricocheted around the room: grabbing her handbag, dropping off her order pad, snatching a mint, erasing her name from the chalkboard. "Oh my gosh, am I really *that* late?" Lynet gaped at her watch and was already thinking up excuses to tell the judge by the time she got to the door.

"If they throw you in jail, call me." Eibby yelled after her. "I'll set up a fund for bail. Drive carefully!"

Lynet broke every traffic law between the diner and the courthouse, and still she arrived too late. Not only had the judge automatically found her guilty because she failed to show, but he'd set a maximum fine, not to mention the points on her license.

It took forever to get through the process. The line at the first desk was agonizingly slow. Then she banged her knee on the doorjamb as she went from one official-looking counter to the next trying to get her papers stamped, recorded, paid for, and over with.

Finally, the only thing left to do was pay the clerk an indecent amount of money, and she could escape this evil place and forget it even existed. Lynet raced upstairs to the teller window, only to find a 'CLOSED' sign taped to the glass, and no one in sight to take her money.

It was the final straw. Her eyes welled up as she sat down miserably at the top of the marble steps. She hadn't cried earlier when Ronan rejected her. She hadn't cried when she banged her knee and gave herself a huge bruise; she hadn't even cried when the nasty court official handed her the judgment. But right here, right now, Lynet was at her limit. The whole rotten day seemed out to get her. She wanted to rant at the sky and cry her eyes out all at the same time.

A door opened and closed behind her. Lynet heard the steady tread of someone walking down the hall toward her and the stairs. Embarrassed, she brushed away the tears from her cheek.

A pause in the footsteps made her look around.

Standing a few feet away, looking down at her was . . . the red-haired man from her dreams. He wore an expensive-looking suit and carried a sleek leather briefcase. His long red hair was pulled into a tight ponytail at the base of his neck. His eyes were fierce, intelligent, his bottom lip full and mocking. Everything about him spoke of power, authority, and unrestrained arrogance.

Lynet lost her ability to speak, and possibly the ability to breathe.

Without warning, a violent pain stabbed behind Lynet's eyes, and with it came a memory so sharp and clear it caused her entire body to tremble.

Flashes of light and dark exploded around her. Pieces of the cavern roof caved in. Dust and powdered shale rose up in clouds to smother the damp sea air. A male voice, thick with pain and out of her line of sight, chanted words unintelligible in the din.

Amidst the chaos, a huge, monstrous figure loomed up in front of her, horned, black and terrifying. Its drooling mouth opened wide as if it meant to eat her.

The sphere, which protected her, shattered in a spectacular flash of white light.
From out of nowhere, the red-haired man slammed into her from the side. His arms wrapped tight around her as they tumbled through a swirling narrow tunnel. . . .

Lynet gasped. The red-haired man was real. Did that mean the destroyed cavern was real as well?

"Do you need help?" the man asked. His silken voice slid across her mind; it felt nice, soothing. He stretched out his hand.

"Um . . . I'm not sure." Lynet smiled uncertainly and watched herself put her hand in his, allowing him to pull her to her feet.

He did not step back, but stayed there, tall and solid, filling her vision.

"Do . . . you know me?" Lynet asked. The words sounded ridiculous spoken aloud, and Lynet felt herself blushing.

"Should I?"

Lynet sighed in disappointment. So, he was merely another jumbled piece of information Scartozzar had put in her head, and not part of her past at all. "Sorry. For a minute there you seemed familiar."

"No need to apologize. You seem familiar to me, too. Maybe we've met before. Do you come to court often?"

Lynet wrinkled her nose. "This is my first time." She gave the papers in her hand a little wave.

"Perhaps somewhere pleasant, then. The Albright-Knox? No? Burchfield Penney Art Center?"

While she'd been to both galleries, Lynet knew this was the first time she'd seen him in real life. "Probably my imagination."

"We've met now." He smiled. "I'm Carden."

"Lynet."

"Well, Lynet, you look distressed. Tell me what's wrong." His smile widened. "I have some influence around here; perhaps I can help."

The Gift

R ONAN STOOD OUTSIDE the law offices on Delaware Avenue in Buffalo, puzzled. For some unexplained reason, Carden Sihtric had been living in the city for the last two years, the same amount of time as Lynet. And that made no sense. Both of them were here, so why hadn't Carden snatched Lynet from the Macarthurs and taken her to his father? Even in a city the size of Buffalo, surely he would have found her by now. Especially with the help of the Senteer. Yet, crazy as it seemed, everything pointed to Carden postponing the chase in order to experiment with life on the Outside.

Why? Carden Sihtric never wasted effort on something unless there was a substantial payoff. What did he have to gain in this country so far from home? Why give up an entire kingdom in favor of one unexceptional city and its suburbs? Carden held more power in Caeraricin than anyone, other than his father. So what kept him here?

Ronan squinted up at the tall, impressive building. Carden's gall amazed him. The man had manipulated his way into a position of power within the community, playing god with people's lives in a courtroom. He'd even convinced them to pay him for his trouble.

Ronan was considering his next move when he heard a familiar *tick tick tick* as a motorcycle pulled up to the curb next to him.

"You didn't show up at work." Karl turned off the bike and unstrapped his black and red helmet.

"What? So you followed me?" Ronan asked.

"Trust me; I'm not that into you." Karl pointed to the law office. "I have an appointment upstairs. What are you doing here? Did you and your drug buddies get busted after I left last night?"

It was as good an excuse as any, so Ronan took it. "Cops raided the place. Someone identified me. I came to see if this firm can keep me out of jail."

"They're good. I see Henry Miller. There are a couple other big time lawyers in the office too, although I've never met them." Karl opened the door. "You coming in?"

"In a minute. I have to make a call." Ronan watched Karl go through the heavy double doors and into the office, then looked around, waiting, fully expecting to hear the Nornir cackling in glee.

When would those hags grow tired of messing with his life?

Carden need only scan Karl's mind to discover Ronan's whereabouts and, by association, Lynet. Even if Carden no longer cared, he would tell the Senteer, and they would grab her. Then again, was Carden likely to notice some punk kid coming in to see his lawyer? The courts were full of rebellious youth—"Mother Earth!" Ronan cursed so loudly people on the street sidestepped him in alarm.

Why would the Nornir bother with Karl when another, even better, twist of fate lay open to them? Carden pretended to be a lawyer. Lynet was due at the courthouse today for her speeding ticket. There was a chance, however slim or unlikely, of them being in the building at the same time. Chance didn't really come into it though, did it? The Fates would make the impossible happen if it suited them.

He pulled out his phone and called Lynet.

No answer. She'd probably turned hers off while in the courthouse. The building wasn't far from here; he'd better go meet up with her.

Dense traffic slowed him down, and Ronan had plenty of time to curse the Fates, repeatedly, before he arrived at the courthouse—to find the offices already closed. He called the diner, and the Macarthurs. No one had seen Lynet since she left for court.

Where was she?

For a Watchman of Caeraricin, there was only one way to know for sure.

Ronan went back to his car, got in, and locked the door. People hurried past him, most with their heads down, talking on the phone or texting. He did not sense any danger but, in crowds this large he could easily miss the signs. He raked a straggle of hair from his forehead. Tracking was never easy; it would be doubly hard in the middle of downtown. He blew out a breath and steeled himself for the onslaught.

It was quick in coming. No sooner had he called on the Vökumaðr tracking skill than his perception of the world changed.

Thousands upon thousands of life-threads thrummed. He heard the tired complaining of till clerks, and the frustration of impatient shoppers. Mothers with small children, restless businessmen heading home from work, insecure teenagers vying for peer approval—it all clamored at a pitch that would drive him mad if he held on too long.

Ronan filtered through the noise—searching for the single, sweet note that was Lynet. If she was still on the Outside he would find her but, if Carden had captured Lynet, and taken her to Norðrlönd, there would be emptiness in place of the golden thread.

Determined to find her before that happened, Ronan pushed aside everything that wasn't Lynet: the rants of people, the frantic scrambling of insects, the complex ethos of dogs and cats. As he did so, a familiar note quivered and grew steadily clearer. Although too far away to see clearly, the golden glimmer of her life-thread told him which direction to go.

Ronan released the tracking and started up the car. She was close: south and west. He estimated five or six miles, no more.

He drove through crowded streets, pulling over occasionally to track. Finally, a flash of sunflower-yellow caught his eye. It was Lynet's Neon, complete with one of Maple's pink posy garlands hanging from the rearview mirror, parked at the Chinese Palace restaurant.

Ronan made a U-turn and pulled up directly behind her car, blocking it in, then switched off the engine and jumped out.

He felt Lynet clearly now—and she was not alone.

Ronan's senses sharpened. Like a predator moving in for the kill, he sprinted up the front steps of the restaurant—then abruptly stopped just outside the entrance. What exactly did he plan to do? He and Carden avoided each other for good reason. If Ronan went into that restaurant prepared for battle, people would die and the building would fall.

The glass doors opened. A quiet-talking, self-absorbed couple came out into the warm summer air. Ronan's anger flared as he watched Lynet smile up at Carden. *Smiling?* Of course . . . she didn't remember Carden. In an instant, all doubt swept from Ronan's mind—consequences did not matter. Reaching for the Annarian crystal hidden in his jacket pocket, he closed the gap between them.

Carden glanced up, and Ronan saw those keen, flashing eyes narrow. Carden leaned close to Lynet, and whispered into her hair. At the same time, his right hand flicked out, away from his side as his fingers made a sign and motion in the air—he was obviously not above using magic in the open.

Ronan felt the Beast roar with rage, ready for battle, hungry for it.

The setting sun glared on the glass doors as a small family came out of the restaurant behind them. Too many people would get hurt if Ronan attacked Carden—and that red-haired bastard knew it. Ronan fingered the Annarian crystal. For it to work, it needed blood. Relatively easy to get in a fight, but not here, not like this.

Lynet pulled away from her companion, turned, and finally saw him. "Ronan. What are you doing here?"

Yanked from primed battle posture, Ronan struggled to keep his voice from growling. "Looking for you. I wanted to apologize for this morning; maybe make it up to you."

Lynet's cheeks flamed. "It . . . was my fault. I shouldn't have bothered you." She glanced at Carden, then Ronan. The look of confusion on her face, as if she didn't know which man to focus on, tore at Ronan's heart. The Fates had gone too far this time. Did they think to pluck her from him? To give her dread magic to Carden instead? The Hoar Beast prowled on the edge of Ronan's consciousness, waiting for the moment to burst through and swipe Carden from the land of the living.

Carden gave Ronan a lazy half-smile, but didn't speak. He didn't need to. Ronan saw Carden's right hand, held away from his side. His fingers splayed open except for the ring finger, which curled so the tip touched the exact center of his palm.

Every Vökumaðr knew that sign and what it meant.

Ronan felt his hackles rise, the muscles in his back tighten.

It was a threat, pure and blatant. If he wanted to—if provoked, or if he simply felt like amusing himself—Carden Sihtric could unleash the Beast. Ronan would dissolve into the background, and the Hoar Beast would come charging into downtown Buffalo. Using Governance, Carden had kept the Beast at bay in the Nor'Uaithne Valley. Whether he possessed the strength of will to command Ronan while he was still a man had yet to be tested— but Ronan sensed no fear or hesitation in Carden. Not like in the past.

Ronan needed to get Lynet far away from him. Now.

"You've made a new friend, I take it." Ronan held out his hand and waited expectantly for her to come. He'd spent these last few weeks gaining Lynet's trust, slowly rebuilding their relationship. Granted, it was nothing like the bittersweet love they'd shared while running as fugitives but, even so, it must count for more than an hour-long fling with this snake. "Are you going to introduce me?"

"Sure, of course," Lynet said. "Ronan, this is Carden Sihtric. He's an attorney here in Buffalo. A highly respected attorney, I've discovered." Ronan was relieved when she took his hand. It seemed a natural thing to do, and he gently pulled her to him while she continued to talk. "Carden helped me today at the courthouse."

"It was nothing," Carden said with a mocking smile.

"It was amazing," Lynet countered, turning to Ronan. "I was late and missed my court appearance. They threatened to fine me an unbelievable amount, and no one would listen. Then Carden"—Lynet smiled over her shoulder at him, and Ronan watched the hated man's eyes flicker in thought—"Carden rescued me. He took me to see the judge personally, and the two of them talked and got it all straightened out. I didn't have to pay a fine or anything. It was like magic."

"Really?" Ronan said, with a nod to his enemy. That was slick, playing the hero, gaining inner-circle familiarity in less than a day. While Ronan, fool that he was, had spent weeks moving into place, making friends with the Macarthurs; being patient. What he wouldn't give to wipe that smug look off Carden's face.

"How could I resist?" Carden asked. "No one refuses such a gift, appearing out of nowhere, alone, waiting to be scooped up. I thought it was my birthday. Imagine my surprise," Carden continued, "to discover hope once more within my grasp."

Ronan watched Lynet's brow furrow as she listened to the odd exchange. Knowing her questions would only delay their retreat, he tightened his hold on her hand and drew her slightly behind him. He was her shield, always.

"What does he mean? Hope?"

"Nothing to worry about, Lynet. Just two arrogant men posturing over a pretty girl." Ronan leveled a stare at Carden. "I'll see she gets home."

No matter his threat, Ronan knew Carden would not endanger Lynet. After all, *hope* could be crushed as easily as a life snuffed out. If they fought now, Lynet—hell, all three of them—could die.

Carden did not challenge him or try to stop them leaving. Instead, he draped his jacket over his shoulder and patted his shirt pocket. "I'll call you later," he said, then turned and headed down the steps. As he got to the sidewalk, Carden began to whistle a soft, haunting tune.

The notes hung in the air, even after he was gone.

"I recognize that song." Lynet frowned. "But I don't remember the words. Do you know it?"

For one awful moment, time stood still.

It was the *Kærásti Fórnsöngr*.

The implication of that tune came down on Ronan like a giant fist. *Carden intended to make her love him and take Lynet's magic for himself.*

Rarely did Ronan fight against the Nornir. It was never worth the effort. The hags twisted fate faster than a mortal man could counter. Their will was absolute . . . but not this time. Ronan would not stand idle while they destroyed his life—no, not just his life—with Lynet's magic, Carden could destroy so much more.

Every protective and possessive instinct flared inside Ronan's chest. Lynet belonged with him, not some arrogant, self-centered bastard bent on dominating good people on both sides of the Divide. He could not, would not allow it. Without thinking it through, Ronan grabbed a handful of Lynet's hair, and swallowed her startled gasp with his open mouth. She belonged to him, beside him, beneath him. In every way, Lynet was meant to be his companion, his lover, the mother of his sons. He poured every ounce of passion and frustration he felt into that one desperate kiss. His arm at her back held her up as she swayed, pressing her full against him. He listened, waiting for the dangerous song to swell, to take over their minds as it took over their hearts.

He heard only silence.

Ronan broke free of the kiss, his breath ragged against her cheek. Where was the song, the poisonous butterfly that had taunted him for months on end? He would sing it right here, right now, and end this.

It was gone.

He looked down into Lynet's face and saw tears. He frightened her. Hell, he frightened himself. Was he so jealous, so anxious to keep her from Carden, that he was prepared to do the unthinkable?

Slowly, he released her.

Lynet took a weak step back, her words a whisper. "I should go home."

"Sure." Ronan didn't trust himself to argue. "I'll follow you."

"You don't need to—"

"I'll follow you."

"You went off with a perfect stranger?" Maple came into the entryway, a place already filled to capacity with the rest of the family. "Someone you met at the courthouse?"

Lynet was tired of repeating herself. She'd already explained herself to Alder, who'd met her at the door. Ronan's physical presence at her side didn't help either. She couldn't get his kiss out of her mind. Her lips felt full and swollen, a potent reminder—as if she needed reminding—of the heat behind that kiss. The whole long drive back from the city, she relived that moment when he grabbed the hair at the back of her head and swallowed her breath. She was barely able to drive. One minute melting all over again, the next punching her fist on the steering wheel, frightened, offended, and angry with him all at once. What was he playing at? He'd made his intentions quite clear; he was not interested. But, when someone else came along, suddenly he was . . . what? Jealous?

"Yes," Lynet said. "I ran off with a stranger. We stole a car, robbed a bank, and had wild sex afterward. I'm probably pregnant. Now, can I go upstairs? I'm tired from my crazy criminal lifestyle."

She felt Ronan's posture stiffen and stepped away from him. "No, I'm not interested in more of the same with you either."

The room erupted with argument. Carden's name came up repeatedly, thanks to Ronan. The pitch grew until Lynet thought the neighbors might call the cops. She yanked off her sweater, slammed it on the peg, then threaded her way between them, heading for the stairs. She refused to answer any more questions.

"I am not done talking to you," Alder thundered.

"I'm sure you're not." Lynet didn't know where her bravado was coming from, but it felt exhilarating. "But I am certainly done talking to you. I'm a grown woman. I can take off with whomever I like. And it is honestly none of your damn business."

"How dare you talk to Alder like that?" Jól gasped. "After he's taken you in and kept you here under his roof. You ingrate. He should throw you out on your ear. Let you fend for yourself."

"Fine," Lynet snapped. "Obviously it's time I moved out. I've been thinking about it for a while, now. Thanks for helping me make up my mind." Lynet turned to storm up the stairs.

Treddian moved to bar her way. "You will apologize to Alder."

Lynet's anger boiled. Had they all lost their minds? "Move."

"Not until you—"

"MOVE!" Lynet's body flared a bright blue, the color tinting the air immediately around her, including poor Treddian, who wore an expression of absolute horror.

The room was silent.

Every molecule in Lynet's body felt alive, awake. It was empowering, exciting, as if she could control the world and no one could stop her. A shiver ran down her spine and she wondered if the sudden cold came from her.

"Ástin min," Ronan said softly behind her. "Be still. No one here is an enemy." He moved close, his arm warm as he reached around her to point to the gray figure standing in the corner of the room. "Except . . . him."

Lynet didn't know why she recognized the figure when everything else from her past was a blur, but know him she did. Knew his gray, unearthly body. Knew his purpose. His face. He was Death, a gatherer of men's souls, and her devotee.

His hollow cheeks stretched into a wide, toothy grin.

Lynet took a step back and bumped against Ronan; his hands came up to catch her, then stayed there, lending his strength.

"Have you . . . have you come for me?" Lynet asked.

The gray figure laughed. A silent laugh that curdled Lynet's insides. Then he spread his arms to indicate the room at large.

"He has no power here." Ronan's words warmed her cold cheek. "Only what you give him."

Lynet looked down at her glowing hands. She did not pretend to understand what was happening, but her gut told her that her anger was the cause of both the blue flames and the god's presence.

A screen door banged shut in the distance, and Lynet heard the clear ringing of Fig's voice. "Where is everybody?" In a blink, the boy entered the fray, looking around in interest. "Who are you?"

The gray figure slowly pointed to Fig.

"No!" Ronan and Lynet moved as one. Ronan scooped up the boy, his broad shoulders shielding Fig from that bony finger. Lynet sprang to face Death head on, so close she felt the ice of his breath. "Leave Fig alone. Leave them all alone. They are not for you."

The god of decay made a slow sweeping bow, then faded away.

The room remained as still as a tomb. No one spoke. Lynet held her hands in front of her and watched the blue ebb until it too was gone, the tantalizing tingle replaced with weak exhaustion.

"I'm going to my room," Lynet said finally. "I trust that isn't a problem." She didn't wait for anyone to answer, just pushed past Treddian and headed up the stairs.

Behind her, she heard Fig exclaim, "That was so cool."

Ashes and Salt

NEIRA STEPPED CAUTIOUSLY ONTO THE ROCK platform that made up the third level of the cavern. The south wall stretched high and wide in front of her. Like the carved stairs she'd just climbed, the wall's surface was unnaturally smooth—except for three huge overlapping circles in the shape of an inverted triangle, scorched deep in the stone.

The platform itself was quiet and empty. No Colm. No missing grooms. Just a dead end. *Damn.* All that pain and trouble for nothing.

She let herself feel frustrated and miserable for about two seconds before curiosity nudged her farther onto the platform. The diagram on the wall was enormous; Neira had to back up several steps and tilt her head to bring the entire thing into view.

The circles consisted of ancient symbols and letters compacted into tight formation, like sentences or phrases that went all the way around. Inside each circle was an image. One of fire, one a twisted horn, one a dead tree.

The circle at the bottom tip of the triangle, with its twisted horn, was familiar. Neira recognized several words from her study of the Fomorii. If this was a representation of Ogluidh, then the fire probably illustrated the heat of MórNathair. The dead tree was a common-enough symbol for Dao'theon, the land of the dead.

Where the circles overlapped, intricate, interlocking glyphs connected them all into one overall design. In fact, if the glyphs were actually part of the language, as she suspected, then it appeared this was a way to join four worlds into one. Norðrlönd with the three unearthly domains. It was fascinating, the way all Nos'kag magic was fascinating—and dangerous.

One thing was obvious: this was a portal. Through it, Eltanin could bridge the gap between Norðrlönd and—not only Ogluidh, but Dao'theon and MórNathair, as well.

Neira found it inconceivable. Why would he even want to? Weren't demons enough? In the short months he'd been king, Eltanin had summoned demons of all kinds. He'd used a host of little devils to incite the castle soldiers to slaughter the Vökumenn, and used another type of demon in his attack on the sea caves at Aros.

He had almost certainly used a demon's magic to create the spell protecting this cavern. Most Fomorii had a special power. The fat one Neira had faced in the woods had the ability to grossly magnify fear. A normal Fear spell reduced its victim to a sniveling mess, unwilling to take action, but the fear that monster oozed had literally paralyzed her. Neira bet the spell on the stairs included the fat demon's magic.

She noticed odd patterns on the floor directly in front of the wall. Were they part of the design? She went closer, covering her nose as she got a whiff of something rotten.

Neira froze.

They were not patterns at all; more the haphazard splatters and smears of a child's finger painting. Her heart lurched as the smell registered. Blood . . . and chunks of meat.

She covered her mouth to hold in the heaves of her stomach. There— where the floor met the wall—was a torn piece of Colm's embroidered tunic. Her belly churned. Unable to stop, Neira retched until she threw up.

Wiping her face with her sleeve, she stumbled to the back of the cavern, gulping in the stale sea air. Her limbs shook. She'd found them after all. Colm. The others. What was left of them.

Neira pulled up short, nearly stepping onto a small circle drawn on the floor. Four feet in diameter, it contained the same archaic writing as those on the wall. In fact, all three languages seemed incorporated into this one circle. Beside it sat a flat bowl filled with dark powder. Neira recognized the powder at once: salt from the earth, and the burnt ashes of sacrifice.

She stared at the circle of ash. There, within the circle, the summoner would stand, the salt and ash providing protection from the initial outburst of a furious demon.

And there—she glanced back to the wall—was where the gate opened up. Neira considered entering the circle to see if it would reveal its mysteries, then thought better of it. Nos'kag magic always came with a twist to catch the foolish. She preferred to not be foolish today.

So, how could she use this knowledge? Eltanin had opened a gate to the nether kingdoms, right here under the castle. It was clear, he fed live sacrifices—*her friends*—to the summoned creatures to appease them and make them easier to control.

He was an idiot.

Fomorii were too treacherous. One day they would turn on him. Surely Eltanin understood their all-consuming love of chaos. No matter their outward appearance or docility, their lust for ruin never waned. *They were miserable, and wished for all to be miserable like unto themselves.*

It was the first lesson any young apprentice learned about dealing with denizens of the lower worlds. It was a lesson Carden had drummed into her countless times, and for good reason.

Again, Neira's thoughts went to the friend and confidant of her youth. Had Carden ever learned to summon a demon? After returning from PenyCefn, he spoke of it often, but Carden was no fool. It was suicide to summon—without knowing how to send the creature back into the abyss. For all his strength of will, Carden could not maintain control indefinitely. He may have defeated a demon once, but Neira knew how much of that had been luck. She doubted he could do it again. No, if Carden summoned a demon without a way to send it back, it would not go well. Eventually he would grow tired, and the demon would kill him.

Behind the floor circle was an altar. Next to it, a pile of rubble. Cautiously, Neira disturbed the heap with the toe of her shoe. There were remains of small animals used for sacrifice, broken seashells, rock, and wood. Nothing important or of consequence.

She nudged a half-buried piece of driftwood and saw beneath it the smooth pink curve of a conch.

Her eyebrows lifted.

Neira looked around as if expecting someone to interrupt, or see her make this discovery. She knelt, and carefully dug out the perfect, whole conch shell. Eltanin was getting careless. Too sure of his invincibility, he had not bothered to destroy the shell—and the evidence it contained. She brushed away the dirt and held the conch to her ear.

Neira heard the rumble of the sea, and the quiet whispers of recorded history. It was too jumbled to make out without aid. Her fingers dipped in the first sign of the Speak spell—changing in mid-move to agitatedly brush a bit of dirt off her robe.

Tense moments passed as Neira waited for the collar to punish her.

No pinch of skin, no cutting off of her airways.

She sighed in relief. That had been close. Too close. She needed to get out of here before she made any more stupid mistakes.

Clutching the precious conch, Neira hurried to the stairs—then paused. Making up her mind, she raced back to the scorched wall. With her eyes fixed on the embroidered piece of fabric, and not the scattered bloody bits on the floor, Neira snatched up the last remaining evidence of dear, old Colm, and fled from the cavern.

Maple Macarthur walked through the garden at Laburnum House, holding her apron bunched up against her. It was evening, only an hour or so before the darkness would chase her indoors.

She stepped over the ruts left by the constant drip of piped spring water. The gardens didn't need irrigation, of course. The ground was blessed, and the rain in New York sufficient to keep the vegetation lush and thick. Still, the Macarthurs dared not take their good fortune for granted. Evil forces were at work in the world. Nothing was certain. The weather would not always be favorable. The soil could not always be rich.

Maple settled onto a stone bench under one of the ancient yews. Her back twinged, and she eased sideways until the spasm stopped. This body was old. By Outsider count, she was well over 200 years, though she had only been here for thirty-one Norðrlönd winters. Without the grace of the Mother, Maple would have died long ago. But, like all who found their way to this sacred spot of land, she had been given shelter and time to heal.

She opened her apron and sorted through the flowers she'd gathered—plain stems in one pile, thorns in another. When Lynet next left the house, she would need protection. Ysbail would find her this time. The girl had brought the god of decay into Maple's home. There was no hiding her anymore. Certainly not from Carden.

What a shock that had been. When Ronan told them *who* Lynet was dallying with, Maple thought Alder would burst his bark.

Yes, Lynet's stay at Laburnum House was over.

The plan had been for her to leave this night but, after the chaos of earlier, all agreed it might be best to give her time to cool off. In the morning, Maple would tell Lynet the truth and prepare her for her journey. From then on, it would be the Zerker's responsibility to keep the girl safe, to keep them all safe from her terrible power.

Maple chose a vine for the base of her garland and began weaving tufts of wildflowers into it. Lynet was precious, but things would be easier once the girl left. Carden was bound to follow her. Ysbail's probing would fade. The danger would pass. It would be quiet again. Perhaps quiet enough for Scartozzar to come home.

Scartozzar.

The boy was her pride, her joy—had been since the day she first crossed the Divide, her mind and body broken, her heart aching for the baby she'd left behind. Scartozzar was a small lad then, orphaned, and living with Alder here in this house. He'd latched onto her and called her Mother from the very start. The Outsider boy from Buffalo, who needed her as much as she needed him. Maple loved him, even when he frightened her—frightened them all with his obsession for magic.

"You can't use people like that."

"I didn't use her," Scartozzar said. "Drysi knew what she was getting into."

"But she trusted you." Maple could scarcely believe what she was hearing. Scartozzar was nineteen, a man. They knew this day would come—the day when he grew up and left them for good—but she never guessed it would be like this. "Drysi loved you, and you stole her magic."

"You can't steal from the Kærásti Fórnsöngr." Scartozzar continued to shove his belongings into a journey bag. "The magic was freely given."

"Don't play with words, boy," Alder's voice boomed. "You didn't love the girl. You knew it was one-sided, and yet you let her waste her gift on you."

Scartozzar turned to his foster father, his curly black hair falling over his brow. "Not wasted. I will use Drysi's magic far better than anyone else she will ever love. I will do great deeds with it. Strengthen borders. Help those who work the fields. Improve the roads. I will make the lives of Norðrlönd's people healthier, easier, better."

Maple sagged into a chair. "You did it on purpose, then."

"Drysi is a foolish girl. I did the world a favor redistributing her powers."

"She is the daughter of one of the chiefs of Prydr," Alder shot back, "and you are a non-magic Outsider."

"Not anymore," Scartozzar said shrewdly.

"You think giving yourself a fancy name and stealing someone's magic makes you a wizard? You don't even know how to use it. When her family gets hold of you, they'll tear you apart."

"Which is why I'm running, isn't it?" Scartozzar snapped. "I'll disappear, go to Eastern Europe. You need not worry about me again. Drysi has never crossed to the Outside; she won't think to look here."

"Her kin will." Maple stood. "There are few sanctuaries left, Son. You will be safer if you stay here where we can hide and protect you."

"And live my life a prisoner, like you do? No thanks. I deserve this magic—should have been born with it. I'll find some secluded spot, where I can practice and learn to use these powers." Scartozzar reached into his pocket, tossed something silver onto the dresser, then slung the journey bag over his shoulder.

"Please." Maple placed her hand on her son's stiff shoulder. "Wait. Let me talk to the Druce. Perhaps there is another way."

Maple braided the string of flowers in her hand. Scartozzar was headstrong, but he loved her. For her sake, he had met with Cian Druce, and even became one of the wise man's best pupils. But there was no changing him. Scartozzar would not give up his lust for magic.

It became his obsession.

Over the years, Maple averted her gaze many times, pretending not to notice when his powers suddenly increased. Still, Scartozzar was true to his word. Every spell, every drop of magic he took, he used in defense of Norðrlönd, to strengthen the seat of government, and improve the lives of the people. If he broke a few hearts along the way, Maple told herself it was for the greater good.

Now, if she believed the Watchman, Scartozzar was dead.

Killed by Eltanin.

Her hands shook as she fought back memories of her life before this one, before she escaped to the Outside. Maple feared Eltanin as she feared no one else. He must be defeated, dragged from the throne, and his body destroyed.

It would take courage and more strength than she possessed to accomplish such a thing. No, it was out of her hands. Others must see to Eltanin's demise. Her lot was to stay here, to keep Laburnum House hidden. To welcome any, like herself, who might need refuge when the battle for Caeraricin began.

Neira waited inside the tunnel door until she was sure no one lurked in the hallway. Once quiet, she slipped out and watched as the crack disappeared, the wall a smooth, uninterrupted surface once more.

She patted her robes, satisfied the conch and piece of Colm's tunic were safely hidden, then hurried to the library. Margaret would scold her for coming late to her duties, but Neira had a stop to make first. She dashed down the hall, then slowed her pace and walked nonchalantly into the common room.

None of the apprentices bothered to look up; they were too involved in their morning studies. Neira had a sudden impulse to smack them all on the head. They were a bunch of weak-willed cowards who'd abandoned their slain masters' teachings to kowtow to Eltanin. The few who resisted were locked at the top of the tower. Neira had more respect for them, though she doubted they would stay defiant for long.

Neira perused a row of books devoted to ancient botany, a topic suited to someone who worked in the kitchen. Once out of sight, she sped to the Animal section where she'd left the map, went straight to the table, and dug under the heavy books and parchments.

The map was gone.

Damn. How could she have been so careless? Who took it? Paldro? She would choke him. Hang that podge upside down over the tallest battlement until he gave it back.

Neira was pushing aside books and scrolls to make sure it hadn't slipped beneath the mess—when a high, sinister voice breathed into her hair. "Looking for something?"

Loptr snaked around her to perch on the table's edge, and get in her way.

Neira stiffened, her eyes wary. "Why else would I be in the library?"

"Oh, I don't know." He gave a half-grin, his thin mustache bristling on his pointed face. "Maybe you're looking for a quiet place to nap. After all, you didn't sleep in your bed last night."

Neira held her tongue. It was best to keep silent. Let him have his fun, and then escape.

"Now, where were you?" he wondered aloud. "Which of the castle staff walks lighter on his feet this morning?"

Neira's resolve weakened. "That's not your usual job, is it, Loptr? Checking up on me? But then, there aren't many backs left to stab, are there? I suppose snitching for Eltanin is just as good."

"You mean King Eltanin," he corrected, and got up from the table. "My work is hardly your concern, *sgalag.*" He said the word as a curse, but Neira didn't assign much value to titles—king, slave, or otherwise—so she didn't give him the reaction he sought.

Loptr lifted a book, glanced at the title, then tossed it aside. "What are you doing in the library? Aren't you usually cosseted in the kitchen this time of day, hiding behind the old crone?"

Neira did not answer. He had the map—that was obvious. Now he baited her. It was ill timed. She was sure she would need the map again, but a map was the same as a book. She'd read it. She could remember it, at least the parts she'd studied. The rest was lost, for even though her memory was extraordinary, there were simply too many conflicting, overlapping messages recorded on it for any one person to recall.

Neira gasped as Loptr's hand shot out and grabbed something caught in the tangles of her hair. He was rough and plucked out several strands with it. Neira jerked back, and pulled her silk hood protectively over her head. Would the missteps of this day never end?

"Shale," Loptr said, his expression one of triumph. "Now, would this be from the tunnel, or from the cavern itself?"

The footsteps last night! Loptr had followed her. Why hadn't he raised the alarm, or at the very least, hauled her limp body up to dump gleefully at Eltanin's feet? She'd been helpless. What stopped him? She recalled those frantic moments right before she passed out. The torch had sputtered, casting a long, distorted shadow onto the cavern ceiling. "I don't know." She couldn't help her mocking tone. "Maybe if you weren't such a coward, afraid of shadows, you'd have stuck around to find out."

Loptr seized a fistful of Neira's hair and hood, dragging her head back at a sharp angle. His own greasy hair slid from behind his ear and brushed her face. "You used an old map to find the dungeon cavern. You went down there last night," he accused, his fingers wrapping around her jaw and throat. "Only now do you return."

Neira was more mad than scared. "Be careful you don't leave any marks, Loptr. *King* Eltanin won't like it if you make bruises darker than his own."

Loptr released her with a shove, knocking her against one of the chairs. "The king doesn't care what I do with the castle slaves," he said, but the conviction had gone from his voice.

Neira scrambled away, knowing she should shut up, but succumbing helplessly to her own anger. "Don't fool yourself, Loptr; you're not special. Your master uses everyone, and when he's done with them, he feeds them to the denizens of Ogluidh. That place you were too afraid to go last night? One of these days you'll find yourself headed there—on a plate."

Loptr's eyes narrowed. "Oh, my position here is secure. I know too much. For instance, I know you freed the Watchman. I know the hag Margaret shields you by keeping you in the kitchens all day long. I know you come here to the library, always after the castle is asleep, looking for something. I know everything about you, *Gwyneira*."

Neira retreated until her back slammed against the bookshelf, the enchanted chains digging cruelly into her spine. *What* did he know? No one knew. Not Eltanin. Not even Carden. No one. Loptr was bluffing.

"A word from me is all it would take to flip your little world on end. Think on that, Neira. Think very hard. The next time I come up behind you, you may want to be more . . . accommodating." He left the thought hanging, and walked out.

Neira sagged against the shelf, her stomach rolling in revulsion. She would rather be thrown from the castle wall and dashed on the rocks than let him touch her—but how else could she keep him quiet?

Lynet sat in her chair by the window, watching Maple out in the garden, her brain abuzz with the absolute insanity of the day.

It seemed Eibby had gotten her wish after all.

Lynet had joined the circus.

First, Ronan wanted her, then he didn't, then—what do you know—he did. The red-haired man from her dreams turned out to be real flesh and blood—living and breathing right here in Buffalo. Next, she lost her temper, burned her bridges, and told the Macarthurs she was moving out, even though she had no idea where she would go. Oh, then she got really mad and turned nuclear, terrified her family, and in the process summoned the god of death who, in turn, tried to kill Fig. But it all worked out because, by some happy twist of fate, the Grim Reaper obeyed her when she made a fist and told him to go away.

Lynet started to laugh, but then didn't. It was too bizarre to be funny.

She got up and went to her handbag, to the stamped and dated traffic court documents that a clerk had dutifully removed from the city records as if they never existed. All at the behest of a man who for some reason called her *hope once more within his grasp.*

Ronan and Carden knew each other. So why the pretense of introductions, as if they'd never met? Then again—why not? Secrets were stock in trade around here, weren't they?

Lynet pulled the stapled business card from the top of the court pages and tapped it on her fingers. Ronan wasn't the only one who knew Carden. Her family had come unglued at the mere mention of his name. Seems her red-haired mystery man had some history. She'd bet anything she and Carden had a history, too. So, why not just say so in the first place? What kind of game did he play?

Lynet picked up her phone. Maybe she should ask him.

Answer to the Riddle

CARDEN SIHTRIC SAT ON THE EDGE OF HIS DESK. It was a huge, heavy, highly polished monster that had the whole big, bad executive thing going for it. Pity he had to leave it behind. He supposed once he was king he could have one especially made. Carden's mouth turned up on one end. Best to keep those kinds of thoughts to a minimum, at least for now. He had too many practical things to occupy him. Like how he was going to raise an army—and keep it secret.

He needed help, of course, and that meant going to Lann, his mother's birthplace, and possibly to King Trond in the Kyleglen Mountains. Father would be furious when he did not come straight home. There would be consequences—weren't there always? Carden was prepared to bear them as a necessary part of the deception.

He turned the page on his calendar and looked at a jotted address. There was an old, abandoned plaza in Alden—he would continue his search there. In fact, he would check it out tonight. The sooner he found a way across the Aragaidheal Divide, the better.

Especially now.

Carden still could not believe his luck in finding Lynet. Indeed, nothing could have been more of a shock. All this time, he'd assumed she reigned at his father's side, forever out of reach. The woman with the power to give eternal life to whomever she pleased.

It was the reason Carden had stayed in Buffalo: living in the shadow of his father-turned-god was not Carden's idea of living.

It never occurred to him that Scartozzar had sent Lynet to the Outside world at the same moment Carden went spiraling through the Divide. He would feel foolish for not suspecting, except his memories of that last battle in the caves of Aros were still too muddled. The more he focused on them, the more elusive they became. He did remember being clobbered in the back with some pretty powerful magic—strong enough to knock him into the Sphere with Lynet. He supposed he should be grateful he was still alive. A small snort accompanied that thought. Oh, he'd be sure to properly thank that fool Scartozzar for not killing him the next time he saw him.

Yet, to be fair, if he were the kind of man to acknowledge cunning in an enemy, he would have to give Scartozzar full marks for outwitting Eltanin. However sloppy his methods, the wizard had succeeded in keeping Lynet out of Eltanin's hands.

Carden pulled out his phone and looked for the most direct route from here to the Alden plaza.

Lynet wasn't the only surprise. Carden should have expected Ronan to appear out of nowhere, as per usual. However, he couldn't have anticipated the biggest surprise of all—Lynet and Ronan were no longer joined at the hip. That was a gift. The goddesses of fate had afforded him a priceless opportunity. All he had to do was take it. The gravity of it thrilled him in a way he hadn't felt in years, not since his sojourn into the bowels of PenyCefn.

The door opened, and Carden glanced up to see his father's latest henchman. The stag's steps were light and graceful, his russet hair curled neatly behind his ears. The Senteer had shown up without warning, two weeks ago, reconnecting Carden to the world on the other side of the Divide. Apparently, Father thought him dead all this time, which was why he had been left to fend for himself.

Carden knew better.

Ysbail, his father's *wicche*, had done some Divining recently and caught Carden unawares. In Caeraricin, Carden's ability to shield his mind was unmatched—and vitally necessary. Here, it hardly mattered. He'd gotten lazy, let his guard down, and that was all it took. Ysbail turned her eye his way and, in an instant, knew where he was and what he was up to.

Carden was shielded now. The *wicche* would not get a second chance to poke around his brain.

"What?" Carden asked in irritation, turning his attention back to the map on his phone.

Raknfeld dropped a thin stack of papers on his desk, "The Vökumaðr works in a metal factory. He makes his home near the woman."

Carden was impressed. That was quick. He'd sent the Senteer looking only a few hours ago with the information he'd gleaned from Lynet. "What about the family she lives with; have you found anything more?"

Raknfeld scanned the room as he spoke. "It's impossible to tell, really. The place is protected by powerful Earth magic."

"Let me guess: a garden?" Carden mocked. "Nothing a good backhoe couldn't fix. Make it a wasteland and we'll see what goes on in that house."

"A backhoe would attract far too much attention," the stag said. "You will never be the predator your father expects if you do not learn—"

"I'll never be anything my father expects. You may go. I'll be out late tonight. Do not come looking for me."

Raknfeld bowed his head slightly and backed out as gracefully as he'd entered. Carden's eyes narrowed. That grace annoyed him. On two legs, the Senteer should be off step and clumsy. Carden did not like it. Liked even less the idea of assassins running loose, spying on his every move. What were they up to? Surely, Raknfeld had told Eltanin about Lynet. So when would the stag double-cross him and go after her?

Carden needed to move fast.

In the past, the goal had been to snatch Lynet from Ronan and deliver her to his father. Times change. Goals change. Carden had proved to himself he did not need his father's name or influence. In fact, with Lynet's magic, Carden could do the unthinkable—replace his sire.

All he had to do was convince Lynet to share that awesome power with him. Charm and sensuality would be his weapons of choice this time around. It would be like drawing a skittish filly to the bridle. He would be elusive, tempting, promising the things she most desired. Eventually Lynet would take the bit, and he would have her.

It seemed simple enough.

But Carden never left things to chance. Controlling, governing, was what he did best. There was no reason not to use his magic to ensure success. With a turn of his hand, Carden began the first stage of a spell suited to his purpose. He would put the finishing layer on it the next time he saw her. The hours in between would give the magic sufficient time to mature.

The phone rang. Carden checked the time. Who would call this late? He swiped to answer. "Hello?"

A slow smile spread across his face.

The Nornir loved him.

Neira used her foot to pat down the freshly dug mound near the outer bailey wall. Most of the castle grounds were rocky and bare but, in a few places, like here behind the stables, sturdy grass grew in the soil. As a memorial, it wasn't much, but it gave Neira something symbolic to do to help ease her guilt. The last time she saw Colm, she'd been irritable and impatient. He was a good man; he'd deserved better, especially from his friends.

She heard Margaret approach. There was no mistaking that slow shuffle.

"What are you doing, child?" Margaret asked, as she came to stand beside Neira. "Did you bury something?"

Neira expected company. She'd caught a glimpse of Wilda earlier, and knew the girl would run straight to the kitchen to tattle. Neira hadn't slept in her bed last night, and now she was digging in the dirt. With little else to entertain the servants, her comings and goings provided gossip.

Neira wiped her hands on her robes and used her hood to brush some tears from her cheek. No point in lying. "I found Colm," she said. "What little was left. I thought he deserved a burial."

Margaret clutched her chest and wrapped a skinny arm protectively around Neira. "Dear girl, I told you not to go looking for him. You could have been killed."

"The demon was gone." Neira held stiff—then slowly slid her arms around Margaret. She'd been under the tutelage of men for so long, she'd forgotten what it felt like—the comfort of an older woman's embrace. Neira felt more tears burning the back of her throat. She hadn't had a proper hug since she said goodbye to her mother when she was barely nine.

They stood there for a while over the makeshift grave, recalling the times Colm helped them with their duties, or made them laugh with a bit of old man shenanigans. An inadequate farewell, but it was the best they could do.

Neira pulled away first. "Eltanin maintains a chamber in the cavern below the castle. He calls the demons from there." She paused. Margaret would not be pleased. "I disarmed a trap. Loptr followed me. By now, Eltanin knows I was down there."

Margaret sighed. "You will be the death of us all if you keep this up."

"If we continue to do nothing, eventually Eltanin will kill us all anyhow. One by one, he's feeding us to those monsters."

Margaret pointed her bony finger. "You will be next."

"No. He needs me. He won't kill me; not yet."

"So you say," Margaret muttered.

Neira took Margaret's hand. "Please don't be mad at me for trying to help Colm; I'm too tired and miserable to bear it. Besides, Eltanin will see to it I pay for my mistake; you don't have to."

"I don't wish to punish you, child," Margaret said. "I want to help you."

Neira paused, then reached into her pocket. "You could work a spell for me." She lifted out the conch. "It's simple enough. I can teach it to you."

Margaret peered suspiciously at the shell. "You want me to waste good magic on a seashell? Why?"

"Because I need cheering up," Neira said. "The spell will let me listen to the sea's secrets."

"I've never heard anything so silly."

"Which is why it's entertaining." Neira placed the conch in Margaret's palm. "Please do this for me."

"Very well," Margaret said, giving in. "Teach it to me."

Neira led Margaret to a place where she could write in the dirt and do a kind of charade to explain the spell. It wasn't easy but, in the end, she managed to convey all the intricate nuances without triggering the collar.

When the spell was complete, Margaret handed back the shell, but not without a warning. "Stay out of Eltanin's way. There will be repercussions for your snooping." Her aged voice grew gentle. "We need you, Neira. Don't squander your life. Promise me you will leave it alone."

Neira felt bad for lying, but what else could she do? Margaret didn't understand. Neira didn't want to die but, if she did, trying to stop Eltanin, it wouldn't be a misuse of her life.

She kissed Margaret's cheek, then hurried off to her room.

Once there, Neira secured the door with both the lock and a chair. If Wilda chose now to come knocking, she would simply have to wait. No doubt she'd be happy to believe Neira had a man in here with her.

Finally alone, she sat on the end of her cot and drew the conch shell from her pocket. Everything depended on the strength of Margaret's spell. She would get no second chance at this. Crossing herself for luck, Neira put the shell to her ear and listened.

At first, she heard only the rumble of the sea. Then, like the sound of people walking toward her down a long corridor, she heard voices—the mumbles grew louder until the conversation resounded with heartbreaking clarity. Tears stung her eyes as she heard Colm beg for his life, heard the screams of his tortured body, the loud slurp and crunch as the monster finished its play.

Neira stood, wanting to run, but there was nowhere to go. Her hatred grew until she wanted to tear down the castle walls and bring ruin on everything around her.

Eltanin's voice sounded from the shell. Neira listened in disbelief as he questioned the Fomorii. Did she hear right? Eltanin wanted the location of the Great Rift—and he intended to make a deal with Balor to find it.

Balor.

Eltanin could not demand an audience with Balor. If he was arrogant enough to disturb the dreaded god of the Fomorii, Balor wouldn't just punish Eltanin, he would exact every living soul in Caeraricin as penance.

It was madness.

Then, out of nowhere . . . she heard it.

The answer to the riddle.

The unknowable, unwritten phrases—to dismiss a demon. Neira held her breath to keep from missing even a syllable as Eltanin spoke.

Drogh Spyrryd, Ersooyl-jee!
Mac Imshee, Royd oo!
Mac Mollaght—Gow royd.
Iurinagh, Gow dty raad.
Niurinagh, Immee royd!
Immee gys Yn Jouyll.
Immee gys Niurin as Noid ny h-Anmey!

She needed to write the verses down, to replace the knowledge Eltanin had destroyed. If anything happened to her, not all would be lost. She would leave behind a record—the secret to defeating Eltanin's demons. In the basket by her bed were an inkwell and pieces of parchment for her studies. Neira rummaged through the papers, digging for the quill—jerking her hand back as the point stabbed her finger.

The conch slipped.

Neira scrambled to catch it, but the smooth pink shell flipped out of her grasp. It hit the floor and shattered. The last shrieks of the demon, as it was sucked into the abyss, rang around the room; then all went silent. Neira closed her eyes in disgust. That was that, then. Either people believed her, or they didn't. Since she had no proof.

Snatching the blasted quill, Neira wrote down every syllable of the incantation. Once dry, she studied the words, imprinting them forever in her memory, then folded the parchment and stuck it in her robes.

She needed to tell someone.

For the hundredth time since her capture, Neira wished for Scartozzar. He would know what to do. But Scartozzar was not here. He wasn't anywhere. Neira was alone—and possibly the only person, aside from Eltanin, who knew the usurper's mad plan.

Who could help? Who was powerful enough to help?

Isleen.

Yet again, Neira's life seemed held in the palm of the Annar's hand. If Isleen proved a traitor, Neira swore she would choke that snow-white seer with her bare hands.

She grabbed her cloak. Now, to escape the castle.

Beneath the Gate

N EIRA WHISPERED HER THANKS to Paldro, assuring him of extra goodies from the kitchen—knowing, even as she promised, that she might not get the chance to keep her word. Sneaking out of the castle was one thing. Sneaking back in and resuming her activities as if she'd never left was another. Still, what choice did she have? Once she delivered her message, she must return to this cheerless place to find the heartstone.

She waited while Paldro waddled around the bend, chanting to ward off the spells guarding this floor. He was a decent enough boy. Without his help, she wouldn't have made it this far into Ddewin Tower. Hopefully, no one would notice her missing. She hated to think of Paldro explaining himself to Eltanin, if anyone found out.

Once he was gone, Neira went straight to the room third from the left, across from the window facing GoðaBlót, and slipped inside.

Memories of another time washed over her. Silently—almost reverently—Neira locked the door, unwilling to disturb the magic that had once permeated this small space. It was simple, no more than an apprentice's room: a sturdy bed, a dresser and desk. The personal things that made it specific to an individual were gone; only the furnishings remained. Unless, of course, you knew what to look for.

Neira touched the table near the wall. Her finger traced the deep gouge cut by Carden's sword as he fell, knocking the table and everything on it to the floor. Bloodied and half-dead, he had been so full of triumph—and so afraid his father would find out he'd been to PenyCefn.

Neira sat on the edge of the bed, listening to the creaks and groans of the old wood. Carden said it was the noisiest bed in the castle, designed more for torture than for sleep. In the corner was the worn-out chair. Neira had practically lived in that chair while she nursed him back to life.

The wizard's son—the terror of Ddewin Tower—dependent upon the secret ministrations of a loyal, ten-year-old child who stole *lyfja* from Scartozzar's store.

So many secrets.

Neira got up and went to the heavy rolltop desk. She eased it away from the wall enough so she could reach her hand behind it and trigger the hidden switch in the stone wall.

She slid her fingers over the place where the trigger should be, frowning as she found only smooth stone. Her heartbeat quickened. What would she do if some stupid apprentice had uncovered the room's passageway and given the secret away to his master? She stretched until the edge of the desk bit into her shoulder. Where was it? Another inch, another fraction. . . .

Mad, Neira gave the desk a shove.

Oh. There it was.

A soft click echoed in the room. Cold air crept from under the bed and swirled around her ankles.

Neira eased the desk back into place and dropped to her knees beside the bed. There, beneath the headboard, one of the stones swung inward on magical hinges. Neira sidled under the bed. *Phew.* The odor coming from the passageway was stale. Neira shoved her cloak through first, then squeezed in the narrow doorway.

Halfway through—she got stuck.

Neira was not a *tiny* child anymore.

She turned onto her side, trying to work herself free. There seemed to be more room if she went at an angle. Neira struggled, gritting her teeth at the bite of the hated chains into her spine. It made no sense. Carden used to fit his broad shoulders through this doorway—why was *she* having trouble? Although, now that she thought about it, Carden had cursed a lot at the time. With an exasperated grunt, Neira continued to force and wiggle her way between the cold stones. If Carden could manage it, she certainly could— her hips were not *that* wide!

She inched, and squirmed, finally tumbling out onto the dusty landing of a hidden staircase. Neira lay there laughing. Now she knew why Carden was always such a grump whenever they snuck out this way. She felt bruised all over, and out of breath.

Neira sat up. She was near the top of a flight of enchanted steps that skipped entire floors on the way down. At the bottom was an underground tunnel stretching from Ddewin Tower, along the outer edge of the peninsula, all the way to the woods far beyond the city gate.

The door behind her squeaked and, on impulse, Neira wedged the cloak into the brick as it started to swing closed. She would miss its warmth in the forest, but she did not want to come back and find the door sealed by some aging Sentry spell that had forgotten how things worked. Normally, Sentry spells had excellent memories. They permitted reentrance only to those persons who left through their guarded exits. The doorway stayed closed to all others. This allowed the king's spies to come and go, as the spell would recognize them, no matter their disguise. Every few months, the Sentry was renewed, ensuring its memory stayed healthy.

This one hadn't been touched in years, and Neira was in no position to conjure a new one.

Satisfied her return trip was secure, Neira hurried down the enchanted stairs to the underground tunnel. It was two leagues from the main castle on the cliffs to the outer walls of the city. Miraculously, Carden's old Illumination spell still clung to life, providing a faint glow, so she didn't need to light a candle. The air was musty but breathable.

Neira remembered racing like mad along this tunnel as a child, trying to get back before Scartozzar discovered her missing. Her steps were similarly light now, her heart filled with the joy of freedom. The tunnel turned first right, then left, avoiding the well outside the stables, and the cellars beneath the granary. There were several bends along the route, although most of it was a straight path to the forest.

Neira ran nonstop for nearly twenty minutes, a good third of the way, before she noticed the chains on her back growing restless, heavier, dragging on the collar. Goaded, Neira put her head down, and kept running.

A half hour later, she stopped, gasping for air. Sweat dampened the hair at her temples and trickled between her breasts. She shouldn't be so winded. She was young, strong, and accustomed to running endless errands up and down the castle stairs.

Neira sank to the ground against the wall, unhappy with the truth. Her stamina was not in question—it was the blasted chains. Each step from the castle, each inch away from Eltanin, increased their weight. Her initial exuberance spent, she couldn't ignore it anymore. The weight was more than a simple burden. The chains intended to crush her if she went too far.

But how far was too far? If she got to the forest, Neira could cry for help. Surely a woodcutter or hunter would hear her. She need only deliver her message, then return to the castle before the chains got too leaden.

Neira knew it was a huge risk to keep going, but she could see no other choice. She had to get out, had to warn *someone*. Eltanin intended to summon the god of the Fomorii. Her pain was temporary; the doom brought by Balor would be without end.

Neira waited until she regained her breath, then stood. She shifted back and forth on her toes to shake away any stiffness, then tore off down the tunnel. The chains banged relentlessly against her bruised and aching back. Heavier and heavier they grew, but Neira refused to stop.

At last, the floor of the tunnel began to slope. The incline would take her under the city gate. Soon she would be outside Caeraricin's outer wall. It was little more than a furlong after that to the forest.

She tottered, her fingers wedged in the collar to keep it from dragging against her windpipe and cutting her throat.

"Keep going. Keep going," she schooled herself, even as her steps became those of a drunkard—one step back for each two forward.

Neira tucked her head down and used the momentum of the slope. Her reward was several fast, out-of-control hops that tripped her up.

She fell hard, skidding down the incline until the chains suddenly dug into the dirt and jerked her to a halt.

She found herself flat on her back, her head pointed toward the bottom of the incline. She lay with her arms and legs spread wide, held by the deadweight of the chains beneath her. Her silk robes bunched in a purple, blue and russet tangle around her waist, the front piece floating forward to cover her face.

In a panic, Neira shook her head and blew until the cloth slid away from her mouth and nose.

Fruitlessly, she struggled. She was weak from running, and the chains seemed bolted to the ground. Looking up, Neira realized she'd come to a stop directly under the wall of the city. It must be the boundary, the edge of maneuverability for the chains. On this side of the city wall, they were immovable. If she had been under them when they clamped down—they would have cut her to pieces.

Neira twisted her wrists, bent her knees, anything she could think of to be free of the invisible chains, but it was nothing more than a repeat of the things she'd been trying for weeks. The shackles were inescapable.

She stopped struggling.

The ground leeched her body heat. After a while, the chill seeped into her bones, numbing her arms and legs. She stared up at the roof of the tunnel and wondered if dirt would fall on her when the city gate closed for the night.

She was far beneath the earth. No one would hear her if she cried out. No one knew of this tunnel. She would lie here on her back like a stranded turtle until she starved to death, and her body rotted. She had failed. Eltanin would release Balor, and that dread demon would destroy the Northlands.

Neira did not fight the tears. Her mother, Scartozzar, Carden, Margaret— each of them had warned her that her bravado, her recklessness, would someday get her into trouble so deep even they could not get her out. That day had finally come, and not one of them was here to say *"I told you so."*

Raknfeld stepped through the gateway to Caeraricin. Each time he returned to his homeland, he vowed he would never leave. His word was in vain, of course; he did not have the luxury of choice. As soon as he delivered his message, Eltanin would send him back across the Divide to finish his task.

The gateway closed behind him with a soft swish. Raknfeld walked down the center of the great hall, his innate magic erasing the sound of his footsteps on the marble floor.

As usual, the king was not on his throne. Instead, Eltanin stood in front of one of the two elaborately framed *sgàthain* that hung on either side of the dais. Large magical mirrors, the *sgàthan* on the left wall revealed the land south of the sea inlet, while the one to the right showed all the land northward.

During King Urien's reign, Cian Druce trained the *sgàthain* to communicate with one another, and eventually, to speak to matching mirrors all across the realm. The system ensured the kingdom prospered. Through the *sgàthain,* the king could hold counsel with liege lords, or question merchants and sentinels. In this way, he was able to keep track of allies and threats, as well as surplus or shortage within the kingdom, which kept the economy strong.

Eltanin cared little for the country's economy.

"Not good enough," Eltanin snapped.

Such a tone could not bode well for whoever stood on the other side of that mirror. Raknfeld came closer, curious to see who it was.

Ysbail, the Red Wicche. The shock of flaming red hair that grew among her black tresses lay smooth and flat across her forehead like a sash, nearly hiding one eye. She looked agitated. The Senteer could not help smiling. The woman was friend to no one. It was a treat to see her at the receiving end of Eltanin's displeasure.

"He is too stubborn," Ysbail insisted. "Endless interrogation—and still he gives me nothing."

"I will not be thwarted by prophecy!"

"Of course not, my lord," the *wicche* purred. "We will find the answers. Surely others know where the weapons are hidden. What about the princess? Perhaps she would—"

Eltanin brushed aside her suggestion. "The girl's mind is broken. I have penetrated it many times—I'll get no more from her."

Raknfeld cleared his throat. As much as he enjoyed this, he had his own problems. The sooner he finished this job on the Outside, the sooner he could regain his true form and come home. He would press the king to let his herd snatch the *plaga norn* and be done.

Eltanin turned.

"Your Majesty." The stag bowed low. "Prince Carden intends to meet with the witch in a few hours."

"Good," said Eltanin.

"Master, is this wait necessary?" Raknfeld continued. "We can bring her to you immediately. A simple Ensnare spell—"

"Yes, but then I wouldn't know the mind and heart of my wayward son, would I?" Eltanin said. "Let him prove himself. Bring me word of his doings, but do not interfere. When Carden makes his move, grab her. Until then, continue as you have—I want to know everything he does."

"Yes, Sire." Raknfeld bowed again. He heard the whisper of the gateway opening behind him. Next time—he glanced at the windows high above the throne, to the cold Nordic sky—the next time he came, he would insist on freedom to run through the wet Northland grass and drink the fresh sea air.

"Do not fear, nimble stag," Eltanin said softly; "you will get your body back . . . when I am through with you."

Raknfeld wanted to believe it, but the word of a wizard meant nothing, of course. With graceful steps, he walked through the portal, to the hated concrete of the city.

Pain, sharp and quick, woke Neira, as something jabbed into her ribs. Her eyes flew open. Her silken robes had slid forward over her face again. She shook her head, trying to see who was there. Margaret? Paldro? She didn't care who found her. Someone had come. She was saved.

"My, my, what a pretty sight." The shock of hearing Loptr's weasel voice made her skin crawl.

He did not say any more, and Neira realized he was waiting for her to get up, to hurry and cover herself. Like her friends, Loptr was unaware of the chains. To him, it would look as if she were lying there, outstretched and half-exposed, with nothing holding her down but her own pigheadedness.

As much as she hated him, her only chance of survival depended on his goodwill. "I'm stuck," Neira said, desperately concocting a plan to gain his help, wishing she could see his face and gauge his reaction. "Something's poking in my back." She shifted her shoulders and groaned, as if injured. "Maybe you can dislodge it. Try pulling me toward the castle."

"Stuck?" Loptr crouched down near her head and pulled the silk away from her face. "On what?"

"I don't know." Neira wanted to turn away from his hot breath, but knew better. "I was exploring the tunnel, and got excited when I discovered it carried on past the gate. In my haste, I tripped. Something stabbed into me, and now I can't move."

Loptr reached underneath her, searching for whatever held her down. "I don't feel anything."

"Please." Neira coughed. "It hurts. Pull me back that way, toward the tower, and see if it will come out."

Loptr stepped between her legs, and Neira felt a moment of panic as he paused, a leering grin on his face. "You sure you're hurt?"

Neira held her tongue. She didn't dare provoke him. Not this time. She was helpless. He could easily force himself on her, and she would be powerless to stop him.

"It's bad," she whimpered.

Loptr shrugged, then bent down and grabbed her ankles. Neira felt a moment of hope as the wretched chains gave way enough for him to get his fingers tight around her, but it was in vain. He gave a hard tug. Nothing. Frowning, Loptr gripped one leg with both hands and threw his weight backward. Neira cried out as her ankle popped—but she did not move.

Loptr released her at once.

"What's going on here?" he demanded. "Where were you going? Why do you weigh so much?" Loptr drew his knife and walked around the tunnel, looking for a trap. "I should kill you and be done with it." He came back to tower over her. "What are you doing here?" He kicked her again, harder this time. "Answer me!"

Neira groaned, her side exploding with pain. She wanted to scream, to rant and bring down every curse she knew upon his head. But she couldn't. She would die without help. "Eltanin is looking for me," Neira said between harsh breaths. "If you go to him now, Loptr, you can say you caught me trying to escape. He'll reward you. But if I die, and he finds out you stood by and did nothing, he will feed you to his demons." She paused before adding, "He *will* find out, Loptr. What do you think is holding me in place? It is his will alone."

Loptr's face grew pale, and he glanced around as if expecting to see Eltanin watching him even now. "You are in so much trouble," he hissed, and drew his foot back as if to kick her again—then seemed to think better of it. With another curse, he sped up the tunnel.

Neira lay there, rehearsing excuses as she waited. Knowing, even as she did, that nothing she could say would satisfy Eltanin.

An hour or more passed before a portal crackled open beside her. The weight released at once, the shackles and chains returning to their normal, irksome bite. Neira got to her feet, jerked her robes back in place, and limped through the portal to the throne room.

Lost Soul

YNET WRAPPED HER SWEATER tight against the morning chill and tried to look nonchalant as she waited outside the back door of the diner. Her conversation with Carden Sihtric had been brief, but he'd agreed to meet her here first thing this morning. He hadn't seemed surprised or annoyed that she'd called. In fact, he'd been quite charming.

Lynet fussed with the pink bangle watch on her wrist, the only jewelry she'd remembered to put on. Sneaking out of the house this morning had her on edge. After yesterday's fracas, she didn't want to talk to any of them. At least not yet. First, she wanted some answers. Hopefully, Carden was the person to give them to her.

She glanced down the alley, then to the door behind her, wishing Carden would hurry. Last night it seemed a sensible place to meet up, since she could leave her car in the parking lot and the guys at the diner would keep an eye on it. This morning, she realized just how stupid an idea it was, since everybody wanted to know what she was up to, and *who* she was up to it with. Not to mention this was the first place Ronan would look for her, if he bothered to come looking. Her stomach fluttered with nervous tension and Lynet pressed her palm against her belly, willing herself to settle down. She wasn't doing anything wrong. She was an adult; she could meet up with anyone she liked. So what if her family had gone into a tizzy at the mere mention of Carden's name? Honestly, they acted like they were afraid of him.

A thrill of fear zinged beneath her skin, and Lynet rubbed her arms to get rid of the goosebumps. Should *she* be afraid of him?

A sporty, black BMW Roadster came down the alley and rolled to a stop in front of her. "Need a ride, miss?" Carden smiled up from beneath a pair of dark sunglasses, his smooth voice sliding over her like an intimate caress.

Lynet blinked and laughed. "Yes, I do." Her anxiety vanished in the face of Carden's devilish grin and hot car. Lynet loved to go fast, and the low-riding convertible looked like it could take hairpin turns at great speed. She went around to the passenger's side—then paused, not sure how to get in.

"You have to sit and scoot at the same time." Carden reached across, his shirtsleeves rolled up to his elbows, and opened the door for her. "You'll get used to it. Soon you'll love it so much you will never ride in anything else." He peered over the top of his sunglasses and winked.

Her dress rode clear up her thigh as she sank into the butter-soft leather seat. She laughed, tugged down her hem, then buckled the seatbelt. "Ready."

"Not yet." Carden pulled an elastic from his breast pocket—a mate for the one he wore in his own hair. "You'll need this."

Lynet agreed. "I rode on the back of Joey's motorcycle once, and it took me an hour to get all the knots out." She didn't mention that her hair at the time had been pitch black, straight, and baby fine.

Carden took a quick look over his shoulder and shot out into traffic.

"Nice car." Lynet grinned, as the g-force pushed her back into the seat. She quickly used the band to make a messy bun, then focused on him. She was here for a reason.

"You look pretty." Carden glanced away from the road. "You also look as determined as a bulldog. Should I be worried?"

"I don't think so." Lynet smiled. "I haven't bitten anyone lately."

Carden slowed down and flicked on the signal. "Not that I couldn't handle a bite or two." He made a turn into a fast-food joint and pulled up to the drive-through. "You like breakfast burritos?"

"Sure." She'd agree to almost anything, so long as he kept talking.

Carden ordered an assortment of breakfast items. "I hate sausage; do you want any?" he asked her.

"No, yuck." She shook her head.

"That would be a *yuck* to the sausage," he told the order screen, then turned back to her with a disarming smile. "Angola has some nice beachfront. I thought we might have something to eat, look at the lake and . . . talk."

Yes. Lynet knew she'd been right to call him.

Carden maneuvered the Roadster south on the I-90 toward Erie. The wind guard on the back allowed them to continue their conversation. He talked about weather, work, and world events. Lynet didn't mind. He had a pleasant voice, and she hoped he would be as open and free with his words once she started asking questions.

"The Macarthurs, they're relatives of yours?" he asked.

"Not really. Although they treat me like part of the family and not the lost soul I really am."

"You're not a lost soul, hon," Carden said, as he took the Angola exit. "They know well enough who you are, and why you're here."

"I take it that means *you* know who I am and why I'm here?"

"I certainly know why you're here with me." Carden turned on the radio. "I just haven't decided how much I'm willing to give you."

Lynet didn't know how to answer that. Did it mean he was going to start telling her the truth or not? She was so tired of the lies. Everyone she knew—aside from Eibby, who spilled her guts on a regular basis—was a barefaced liar. Ronan, her family, Carden. She needed to remember that the man beside her, no matter how charming, was just as bad as the rest.

They continued the last few miles without talking, the slow jazz on the radio filling the silence.

Finally, Carden pulled into a driveway and drove up the steep incline to one of the summerhouses edging Lake Erie. "Henry from the office owns this place." Carden flicked off the ignition and yanked up the emergency brake. "I don't have a key, but we can use the beachfront without worrying about being chased off." His roguish grin suggested he thought it would be more fun to be chased.

He opened the trunk and pulled out a blanket and six-pack of caffeinated soda to go with the sack of fast food.

"You had this planned, I see," Lynet said, as they walked past the house and down the path to the beach.

"Of course. How better to impress you?"

Lynet couldn't help feeling pleased as they walked onto the beach and found a spot where the sand was free of driftwood and lake debris. Carden shook out the blanket, and they both kicked off their shoes.

Lynet scrunched the sand into little hills with her feet. The simple act of playing with the sand helped relax her. The sun peeked in and out behind a few white clouds. The wind off the lake was mild. On the receiving end of the Great Lakes, Buffalo was notorious for having hot and cold days, one right after the other, at the oddest times of the year. They were lucky to have such a beautiful morning.

Carden suggested they eat before the food got any colder, and Lynet agreed, although she spent more time watching him than eating her burrito. Carden Sihtric was a good-looking man. High cheekbones, clean-shaven. The breeze lifted a stray strand of red hair and trailed it across his cheek, drawing her attention to his mouth. Not that she needed a prompt. Carden's bottom lip was full and naturally thrust out as if he were trying to prove himself. In contrast, his top lip was narrow. Thinner on one side, it gave his expression an almost perpetual sneer. The features combined in a look both sensual and stormy.

Lynet looked away. Honestly, she felt like cursing. He was too handsome, and she needed to concentrate.

Carden pointed to the speedboats on the lake, and said he'd like a turn driving one. Lynet agreed, although her patience with mundane conversation was growing thin. She wrapped up her half-eaten burrito, put it in the bag, then tidied up while he drained the last of his soda.

"Are we ready, then?" Lynet asked. "You didn't bring me all the way out here to look at boats."

"I brought you here because I thought the sand and the sun would please you. It used to." His voice lowered and he asked, "Why did you come, Lynet? Clear out here away from everyone, with a man you hardly know. What do you want from me?"

Something about the way he asked the question brought a heated flush to her cheeks, but Lynet did not hesitate. "I want answers. I want to know who I am, and why you pretended not to know me, and why my family freaked when Ronan mentioned your name. I want to know why I turn blue when I'm upset and how to stop it, because I think I could have hurt someone yesterday. And . . . and what do you mean, it *used to* please me?"

Carden chuckled. "Whoa. Slow down. I'll tell you what you want to know, but it will cost you."

"Cost me?" Lynet blinked. "How much?"

Carden pulled a quarter from his pocket. "Depends. Have you ever played Truth or Dare?"

"No. It's a child's game, isn't it?"

"Occasionally." Carden nodded. He tossed the coin into the air, caught it, and asked, "Heads or tails?"

Lynet had no idea where this was going. "Okay . . . I choose tails."

Carden opened his hand. "Heads. I win. I get to ask you a question, any question. You get to choose whether you will tell me the truth, or pay the penalty by taking the dare."

"What kind of dare?"

"Nothing too life-changing." Carden shrugged. "If you decide not to tell me the truth then you have to do whatever I say, like hop on one foot or bring me a shell from the beach. If you're worried"—he grinned—"you can always tell the truth."

"All right," Lynet decided. "I'll play—if it means I can ask you *anything* and you can't lie."

He smiled like a little boy with a secret. "Truth or dare. Tell me about the day you arrived here."

"I'll tell the truth, gladly." This was what she wanted. To talk about her life, about all the missing parts. "I woke up, two years ago, in the Macarthur home. I didn't know who I was, and I looked like . . . well, crap actually. I was all black and white and awful."

"Sounds like someone botched a Hide spell," Carden said. "Easy enough for Ronan to fix. In fact, he's probably the only one who could fix it."

Lynet's mouth dropped in shock, both at his ready discussion of magic, and his claim about Ronan. "Are you telling me *he* did this? That rotten, lying son-of-a-bitch. He pretended it came from a box. I'm gonna kill him."

Carden's brows shot up, and he reached across to cover her hand with his. "Yeah, let's not talk about killing anyone." He put the quarter in her palm. "Your turn to flip the coin. I'll take tails this time."

It was heads. "Oh, thank goodness." Lynet's voice nearly cracked. "Please. Who am I?"

Carden's voice grew serious. "It's okay, love," he said gently. "I won't disappoint you. Your name is Lynet. You were born in the valley of Lunedalr, on the outermost isle of Nairn, in the kingdom of Caeraricin. Your father was a miller, your mother the village seamstress. You lived with them—and three brothers, two of them younger than you—in a mill straddling the River Glerá. It was a simple, rustic life—until the day Ronan and the king's soldiers came to get you."

Lynet's hands shook. Was this true? Her *real* family. Mother. Father. It sounded lovely. She'd dreamt once of a towheaded boy splashing her in a river by a mill. Was he her brother? But why would soldiers come for her—and why would Ronan be with them? Who *was* he?

Carden watched the hope and uncertainty in her eyes, saw her linking ideas together, and making assumptions. For every piece of information he gave her, a hundred new questions sprang up. Before any of them could spill out, he took the quarter. "My turn to flip—heads or tails?"

"But wait." Lynet groaned. "I have questions. This is terrible. I need to know more. You're going to drive me nuts."

"Yes, I know." He winked devilishly. "Now, which is it?"

"Heads."

It was heads. "I win again!" Lynet said excitedly. "Where is Caeraricin, and how do I get there?"

Carden pointed to a place along the horizon. "There, where the earth touches the sky, is a veil. You need only to lift it."

"You're teasing me," she accused.

"Not this time," he said. "I can take you, Lynet. Not today, of course, but sometime soon. When you're ready."

"I'm ready now!"

Carden disagreed. "You only think you are. What about the Macarthurs? Your job? Would you just up and leave without telling anyone?"

"Sure I would." Lynet's shoulders dropped. "Okay, you're right. I couldn't do that to them. But you must know I'm dying to go there. I want to see my family, to try to remember the life I had before I came here."

"I know, love." Carden handed her the coin. "Don't worry. I *will* take you soon. Now, back to business. I get heads this time. It's been lucky for you, and I've a question I want to ask."

Lynet tossed, and won again. Her joy was like sunshine radiating out in every direction. He basked in the warm tingle of her power. Gods, she had no idea how strong her magic was.

"If I'm a miller's daughter," Lynet asked, "why did the king send soldiers to fetch me? Are you sure Ronan was with them? Why didn't he tell me? Who is he?"

As much as Carden wanted to continue basking in her light, he was not ready to answer those questions. "Nope. Sorry." He shook his head. "I'll have to take the dare, as it's cheating to ask more than one question."

"Nooooo," Lynet wailed. "Okay. Fine. Then I dare you to tell me the truth about something—anything."

"And you continue to cheat." Carden playfully flicked the end of her nose. "I am sure there are severe repercussions in the rulebook about this, but I'll give you what you asked for. I'll dare to tell you the truth about what I'm thinking . . . right this moment." His voice dropped to a whisper. "I'm thinking that, in this morning light, you are the single most beautiful woman I've ever seen. I'm thinking how much I want to crawl across this blanket and keep right on crawling, until I'm lying over you, looking down into your face." His eyes hooded as he leaned closer. "My thoughts don't stop there."

"Mr. Sihtric—"

Carden laid his finger against her lips. "Shhh, if you call me that again, I will take my quarter and go home and you won't learn another thing."

"Carden." Lynet wouldn't meet his gaze. "I think we should avoid any more of your personal thoughts."

Carden tucked a stray strand of her golden hair behind her ear. "I'm a healthy man, alone with a beautiful woman. What else could I think?" He stayed close, watching the unsteady rise and fall of her breasts, then slowly drew back, twirling the coin between his fingers. "Now, whose turn is it?"

"I've lost track," Lynet said. "I don't care. You can keep the coin. I trust you. I'll be heads; you take tails; whoever wins gets to ask the question."

She was so easy to manipulate—and he had used so little Governance on her. Time for his question. Carden flipped the coin. Obedient to his command, the coin landed as tails.

"How close are you and Ronan?" he asked. "Friends . . . or more?"

Lynet's cheeks flamed. "I take the dare."

Bound with a Kiss

YNET KNEW HER REFUSAL TO ANSWER was in itself an answer, but she didn't care. She was not prepared to discuss her feelings for Ronan. Especially when she had no idea herself how she really felt anymore. She'd been falling in love, but now. . . .

"A dare it is, then. Okay, I dare you to beat me in a race." Carden leapt up, pulling Lynet with him.

"What?" her voice squeaked. "Your legs are twice as long as mine!"

Carden led her toward the edge of the shore. "You chose the dare." He stopped and lifted a brow. "Unless, of course, you'd rather answer."

"No," Lynet said bluntly. "I'll race you. How far?"

Carden looked down the beach and pointed to a pile of driftwood half a mile away. "To there."

"And you expect me to beat you?" she asked.

"Nope, but I expect you to try." He released her hand and lined up beside her. "You ready?"

"No." Lynet laughed.

"Catch me." Carden winked, then took off like a shot.

Lynet followed, glad of the fresh breeze on her cheeks. She was light on her feet, but she could never keep up with him. As if to prove it, Carden turned around and ran backward. He ribbed and hooted outrageously, staying just out of reach. He was charming, funny, handsome, and interested in her. Lynet felt like the heroine in one of the many novels she'd read. Running along the beach, teased by a gorgeous, sexy man.

They got to the marker and Carden looped an arm around her waist, lifting her off the ground as he swung her around. "The pokey tortoise crawls across the finish line."

"I'm not *that* bad." Lynet's hands rested on his shoulders as he held her there, high against his chest. She stared down into his face. He had a small jagged scar beside his left eye, and fine lines of care around his mouth. Lynet wondered what his life had been like, and who he really was.

Slowly, he let her down. Her leg and hip slid along his side until her toes touched the sand. They stood there, the air around them quiet, intimate. Lynet felt her heart pounding.

"We better head back." Carden pointed to the choppy waves forming on the water. "Looks like the weather's changing." His words were a cold splash on her silly romantic thoughts. He took her hand and led her along the beach.

Lynet didn't resist. She didn't talk either. The sound of the waves and seagulls filled the silence.

Her thoughts were in a jumble. What was it about her that men found so unattractive? First Ronan acting like a yoyo. Now Carden. She sighed. Not that she expected anything. Not really. She barely knew Carden. Still, it would have been nice to get a normal kiss for once.

Carden heard the sigh, and guessed her thoughts. She was disappointed, confused. Good. It would make her all the more eager for his kiss—when the time came. When the spell he had fostered all night was ready.

"I left the quarter on the blanket," Carden said, as they walked. "So, I'll give you the toss. Ask your question. I promise to answer it. It's the last one for the day, so make it a good one."

Lynet stopped walking. "Can you do magic?"

Her voice was serious, direct, and Carden paused before answering. "Some. . . ."

"Show me."

She intrigued him with that simple, bold request. He needed to be more than intrigued though, if he intended to teach her magic. She would go wild with it at first, trying anything, and in most cases having the power to pull it off. Even with Governance, he would be lucky to keep her in check. The problem was, Lynet had a power above elementary magic. He could teach her everything from how to conjure fire to complex battle spells, and still not touch the surface of what she could do herself with a mere thought. He could spend all his effort teaching her to manage her ancient magic, and still die the first time she got frustrated or mad.

She could kill him without a word—but he didn't think she would.

Carden remembered quite clearly their battle in Sharsis. He'd felt her indecision—then the rip of his body being separated from his mind. *That had hurt.* She instantly brought him back to life and never killed him again, though she'd had plenty of opportunities. For whatever reason, Lynet considered him worth saving.

"All right." Carden nodded, looking around for ideas. He would show her something easy, something she could touch. "Stay there." He rolled up his trousers and waded out into the water.

The lake was green and cold, but he was intent on his errand and hardly noticed. Carden searched, until he saw a ledge about twenty feet farther out.

He waited. A shadow rippled near the bedrock, and Carden's hand shot out from his side. *"Diogelu amddiffyn. Tarian!"*

Under the surface of the water, a magical shield wrapped around the swimming shadow. Carden spread his fingers. Up from the lake whooshed a round ball of water, about a foot in diameter. Inside it swam a bass and a small goby. The ball came to him, resting on his open palm. Carden waded back to where Lynet stood on the shore.

"Here, take it."

She looked at him in alarm, and Carden chuckled. "It's okay. You can't break it, not with your hands. This shield can stop a four-pound war sword. The fish are quite safe."

Lynet took the ball in both hands. It was heavy, and felt alive, as if a low current of electricity held it together. The tingle flowed up her arms and down into her belly. A gentle blue glow spread over her skin—not the harsh glare like before, when she was angry; this was a soft, barely there blue. She felt the joy of the fish as they swam—no, it wasn't the fish. She felt the joy of the shield itself. It was alive.

She looked at Carden. "The shield is talking, maybe singing. It's happy."

"Of course it is," Carden said. "I created it, it's mine and, like everything I own, it is happy to serve me."

"You are truly conceited." Lynet laughed. "But it suits you." She poked her finger into the ball, testing its strength. It gave only a fraction, enough to keep it malleable, but no more. Curious, she flicked the shield with her fingers, to see if the water would ripple. It did not. The only movement inside the ball came from the fish. Her tapping did not affect them at all, though the sphere now shone with a soft white light.

"Unchallenged, a Shield spell is clear." Carden explained the change in the surface of the sphere. "Your enemies will not know if you are protected until they make their first move; only then will they see its color and know its strength. This is not true of animals, which have the ability to see shields before they are struck."

"Can I learn to do this?" Lynet turned the ball around in her hands.

"You can *relearn* it." Carden unrolled the legs of his trousers. "Muscle memory will help. Your fingers remember, even if your mind does not."

Your fingers remember. The idea she could do this—*had* done this in some other life—was like believing she could fly. It was impossible. Yet, the desire to spread her wings and attempt the impossible had been gnawing away inside of her for what seemed like forever.

"It will take time," Carden cautioned. "Raw magic has no master. Giving birth to a spell is giving reason and personality to the magic, in hopes that it will obey you. It doesn't always."

Lynet handed the ball to Carden. She wanted more than to play with someone else's magic. "Will you teach me?" She held her breath, waiting for his answer. If he taught her, she knew she could do *anything*.

"Perhaps," Carden said finally. He threw the ball out into the water. Before it plunged beneath the surface, he released the shield. The fish flipped, unharmed, back into the lake. "Magic is a tiresome subject at first. Lots of theory and ethics. You may prefer to learn from someone else. I've been told I'm a tyrant, not a teacher."

He could be a slavering three-eyed monster for all Lynet cared, so long as he taught her how to create that same tingling current of energy. "You've had a disgruntled student or two, I take it?"

"You have no idea." Carden chuckled as they continued to walk down the beach. "Young girls make terrible pupils. They want to know the answer to everything before the question is asked. No patience. Curiosity like a cat. No sense of self-preservation; just an insatiable need to get into trouble."

"Curiosity isn't a bad thing," Lynet said. The blue tint to her skin was fading, and it didn't bother her. She knew she would see it again, feel it again.

"Not always," he admitted. "It's why you're here now. You're curious."

They stopped in front of a line of sun-bleached clamshells caught in a ripple of sand. There were hundreds clumped together. Carden knelt down and turned a couple of them over.

"Zebra mussels," Lynet told him. "They've pretty much taken over the lake. It's awful, really."

Carden scooped up a handful. Each tiny mussel had been pried open and picked clean. "They seem happy about it." He pointed to a flock of gulls screeching and flapping on the shore up ahead as they competed for the chewy mollusks with an old man carrying a clam bucket.

Carden stood up, idly tossing away the handful of tiny would-be usurpers. "There's an order to the world, Lynet. Though some appear to be taking over, they're nothing more than fodder for those who are smarter and faster." Carden brushed the sand from his palm. "My advice—don't be the food."

"Ah, I'll remember that," Lynet said with a confused laugh, then added, "You know, the mussels from the bottom of the lake are toxic, from the pollution sediment. Eating them would make you sick."

"I'm used to poison." Carden smiled. "Come." He took her hand and led Lynet to their picnic spot.

The sun was high overhead; the breeze had picked up. "It's time we headed back to the city." Carden shook the sand from the blanket.

Lynet nodded, disappointed, but at the same time happier than she could ever remember being. Carden had answered her questions—even shown her magic. Magic she'd actually held in her hands. She couldn't stop thinking about it. She wanted to know everything, try everything.

They walked to the car.

Carden unlocked the door, then slipped his suit jacket around Lynet's shoulders. "Do you want to drive?" he asked.

Lynet's eyes widened in surprise. "Really? You'd let me drive your precious BMW? You do remember we met at the courthouse."

"I remember." Carden smiled. "The cops had you clocked at seventy-three miles per hour. I'm sure you can do better than that."

Ronan followed Lynet's reckless twists and turns. His anger at Carden, for letting her drive like an idiot, grew with each tire squeal. Not that he wasn't furious already.

Lynet had stolen out of the house early this morning, before he, or Maple, had a chance to explain. They should be across the Divide and into hiding by now, but instead, she'd gone gallivanting off—straight into Carden's waiting net.

Luckily, Ronan had been in the woods behind Laburnum House, scouting for Senteer, and saw her drive away. He'd tracked her to the edge of Lake Erie. Once there, he'd cast a Hide spell, taking on the form of an old man to get closer to them.

He'd been angry, intent on ripping into Carden, but then—he sensed Lynet's joy—the emotion so strong it knocked the air from his lungs. She was happy, deliriously happy.

An hour later, jealousy and self-reproach still twisted in Ronan's gut. This was his fault. Lynet had fallen prey to Carden because Ronan was a fool. He could have prevented this if he had controlled himself better, and not shoved her away. If he hadn't eaten the grizarbr. If he'd trusted her inner strength and told her everything—he could have armed her against Carden's lies.

Now it was too late. If he barged in, Lynet would not understand. She would hate him.

Ronan knew Carden's mind. He would not hurt Lynet, at least not yet. He wanted her Suthainn magic and, as far as Ronan knew, there was only one way to get it: the *Kærásti Fórnsöngr*.

But not even Carden could win Lynet's heart in a day. Ronan intended to take her across the Divide the second she got back to the Macarthurs' house. Carden wouldn't get another chance. Once in the wilds of Norðrlönd, Ronan would tell Lynet the truth, and clear up all of her misconceptions.

The black BMW shot through the light on the corner, skidded to a stop, then did a sloppy reverse and turned into the diner parking lot. Trailing a couple of cars behind, Ronan continued past the diner, then circled around. He came up the alley across from the diner and rolled into place behind a parked car, switched off the motor, and waited.

Carden held out his hand as Lynet returned the key fob to him with an exaggerated flourish.

"That was so amazing!" she laughed. "Thank you."

"Nothing will ever drive the same," Carden said with mock regret, as he slid his arm around her waist and led Lynet across the parking lot to her little yellow Neon. While she continued to talk, Carden took the handbag from her arm. He picked out her keys, unlocked the car door for her, then tossed both the bag and keys onto the seat.

Lynet tilted her head. "That's a bit cheeky, even for you."

"Not as cheeky as this." Carden stepped close enough to back her up against the car. Lynet's hands rested against his chest, but Carden wasn't bothered; she wouldn't stop him. He slid his fingers through her hair and drew her face to his. He could feel her trembling, waiting to be kissed. Carden let the moment stretch, appreciating the play of emotion on Lynet's perfect face. She was beautiful, desirable. He would have to make sure she didn't turn things around and enchant him. Annoyed with himself for considering such a thing possible, Carden bent his head and blew the final verse of his spell into her mouth before sealing it in with a kiss.

That man had to go. Ronan glanced up and down the street, looking for pedestrians or oncoming cars. He would not have chosen this place, but the time had definitely come. Ronan pulled the Annarian crystal from his pocket and opened the car door.

Damn. His fist bounced off the steering wheel. A dark, Nos'kag spell coiled around Lynet like a snake. She'd felt the Restore spell the other night, but Ronan doubted Lynet felt anything right now other than Carden's mouth all over her face.

The Beast roared, but Ronan forced the enraged creature to return to its slumber. Yes, Lynet was in danger, but it was too late to stop the spell; it needed to run its course. Carden must have been working on it for hours, waiting for the perfect moment to finish. Waiting for her to be so focused on something else, she would not feel the evil closing in around her.

Ronan slammed the car door shut again. All he could do now was be still—keep control of himself—no matter how badly he wanted to feel his claws rake a chunk out of that conniving bastard.

"I know you have questions," Carden whispered against Lynet's cheek. "But I'm not a textbook." He kissed her again, slow and deep, then pulled back, pleased with the sleepy, sexy droop of her eyelids. "I'm a man, Lynet. With an ego, and I'd prefer to imagine you enjoyed my company and weren't just plying me for information."

Her eyes widened in alarm. "Of course I like your company. I won't deny I want to know more. I want to know everything, but I'm not so shallow I forget you're a man, a person with feelings."

Carden's mouth curved slightly, and he dropped another kiss onto her lips before releasing her. "I'm glad. Now you'd better get on home before the posse comes after you."

Lynet blanched. "I'm sure Maple is worried sick. I took off without telling anyone where I was going. And, after yesterday's blow-up, well, they'll think the worst of me."

"You can't tell them the truth," Carden said. "It will only cause trouble. They don't trust me. We come from a different world, Lynet; a place far from here, where politics is brutal and magic is a way of life. There, you and I are enemies. It's all they see, all they want to see—your people and mine." He stroked her cheek. "We can change that. Together, you and I can be greater than any of them." His hand fell away. "But not today. Ronan will be looking for you. He's probably around here somewhere, right now. He follows you, you know."

Lynet looked behind her.

"Oh, you won't see him," Carden said. "Not unless he wants you to. His kind knows every Hide spell ever given to man." Carden stepped away from her. "Go on, now. Before he decides to show up like he did at the restaurant, spoiling for a fight."

211

"A fight? What, here in the street? Ronan's too sensible for that."

Carden swallowed back a laugh, his eyes scanning the surrounding buildings. *Well done, Zerker. She honestly has no idea* what *you are—pity I'll be the one explaining it all.* Carden lifted his hand as if to apologize for what he had to say. "There is a good deal about Ronan you do not remember. He can be violent and dangerous. Do not provoke him, especially if I'm not there to protect you."

Carden leaned over the car door as she got in. "Call me tomorrow," he said. "When you're alone and can talk."

Lynet paused. "I told them I was moving out. I was really mad."

"I'm sure you were, love. But now is not the time to give the Macarthurs grief. Go home; play along. Be a nice girl. It's better if they don't suspect."

He kissed her again to ensure the spell's strength, then watched as she pulled out and drove away.

Carden walked slowly back to his BMW. Ronan was here somewhere. Carden wondered if he would show himself now that Lynet was gone. Not that it mattered. Carden knew his Governance was strong enough to hold off the Beast—he'd proven that in the Nor'Uaithne valley. If they faced off again, Carden fully expected to win.

A car sped down the street after Lynet, and Carden smirked. "Run, Watchman," he said with deceptive softness. "Try to prevent the Binding from taking hold. Fool. It is not a magic *you* can control."

Assassin Blades

RONAN'S CAR SKIDDED TO A HALT in front of his apartment. He'd driven like a madman, barreling down the road parallel to Broadway, in an attempt to gain Briar Lea Road ahead of Lynet. He had gained them six—maybe seven—minutes, at most. Jumping out of the car, he dashed across the street, taking the green-painted porch steps two at a time, stopping only when his fist hit the door. Urgently he rapped against the wood.

Maple answered.

Born to lead in a crisis, Ronan did not ask for audience or permission, but went swiftly to work. "My lady, we need a countercharm. Sihtric has put a Bind spell on Lynet."

He turned, looking for the sprite. "Fig! Where are you?"

"Here, Ronan," the boy said as he popped up from nowhere.

"Listen carefully, Fig," Ronan said, kneeling down to the boy's level. "When Lynet pulls in, you must hold her outside for as long as you can. Dig your toes into the ground to slow her down—stop her outright if you can manage it. Collect every second you can from the air." He searched the boy's face, trying to gauge how much he understood. "We need more time than Lynet has; you must give it to us."

"I'll keep her suspended until you tell me it's safe." Fig nodded excitedly and zipped out the door.

"Suspended?" Jól said in disbelief. "Can he do that?"

Ronan had no time for explanations or theories. He only hoped his hunch was right, and Fig possessed the powers of his apparent ancestors. Although he did have the foresight to suggest, "Jól, get your baby out of the house and down the street, as far and as fast as you can go—unless you want him growing up before your eyes." Ronan didn't know for sure how much any of them would truly age, but it was best not to take a chance with the infant.

Ronan turned to Maple. "What do you need from me, from any of us, to prepare your spell?"

"I'll need Lynet's pillow," Maple told him, as she gathered vines and roots to augment her powers. "Oh, and any piece of jewelry you can find. I'll put magic on them too, so my countercharm will stay with her throughout the night—in case he attached a Renewal to the end of it."

"You can count on Carden to add all sorts of perversions to his magic," Ronan muttered, and took off up the stairs.

Up three flights, Ronan stepped into the pink-and-ivory chamber where Lynet slept. His senses swam with the scent of her—from the downy bed, to the perfume in the air, to the thrown-open closet filled with pastel dresses and worn, velvety sweaters.

The soldier in him recovered. He grabbed the pillow, snatched up a locket he knew she favored, and raced back down the stairs. He'd just handed the items to Maple when they heard the crunching sound of tires on gravel as Lynet pulled into the driveway.

It was up to Fig to buy them more time.

Jól fled out the back door, a bundled Eburos in her arms. Treddian shredded leaves and roots, releasing the power within their fibers. Alder stood over him, catching the wisps of magic in a glass jar. Already it swirled with the rich green of Earth magic.

"Could you use any of my magic?" Ronan offered.

Without a pause in her chant, Maple slid her hand inside Ronan's chest as if he were merely an illusion and not a solid man of flesh and blood. She plucked a single string from his fierce Vökumaðr heart and drew it out, adding its deep red to the swirl of white and green growing in her open palm.

Ronan staggered back. He had only ever given of his heartstring once before. He had been as unprepared then as he was now. Not that anything could truly prepare him for the cold ache of a foreign hand plunged inside his chest, grabbing at his beating heart. Or spare him the fleeting chill as Death hovered briefly, invisible, waiting for Maple to be careless, or greedy. Even without Lynet's presence, the last Vökumaðr was a prize to be collected by Death himself. Ronan shivered, grateful it was over, and that the physical invasion was not possible unless he, himself, made the offer.

Maple stood. Her chanting grew louder as Alder dumped the magic in his jar onto the spinning ball in Maple's hand.

"The sprite's doing something." Treddian moved to the window, holding the curtain to one side. "Lynet keeps flickering in and out. It's taken her this long to get her door open and climb out of the car."

That was still faster than Ronan liked. He put his hand on Treddian's shoulder. "I'll watch the door." Treddian nodded and returned to shredding.

The main ingredient in any serious spell was time. The more powerful the spell, the longer it took to prepare. It took hours, even days for the best spells to grow. Whatever Maple conjured needed to be potent enough to defeat a royal Bind spell.

Outside the house, time continued to crawl—inside, time shot ahead. Ronan reported Lynet's slow progress to the door, as it became a race to be ready before she opened it.

The different magics in Maple's palm swirled into a fine white glow. White magic got its name more for the color of the raw magic than for its intended use. Ronan knew quite a few deadly White spells, although the kill of White magic was always clean—unlike the agony or disease of Nos'kag.

Finally, the charm seemed ready, though it was not as bright as Ronan expected. Maple sprinkled a pinch of the liquid magic onto Lynet's pillow and a double pinch on the locket.

"Tred, take the pillow up and put it back in her bedroom."

"I could do that," Ronan offered.

"No, Zerker, I need you here. There wasn't enough time; my spell is weak. If Lynet runs, she will be able to shake it off. You must hold her until my spell drives out the Binding. She won't like it—by now, Carden's magic will have rooted. She will fight you."

Ronan nodded, glad for something physical to do.

"What if she goes all blue and kills him?" Treddian picked up the pillow.

"She won't," Ronan said. "Let's get on with it."

"Alder, tell Fig to let her in," Maple ordered, then looked to Ronan. "Be ready to grab her."

Time in the house slowed as Alder called to Fig from the door.

"You were up and out early," Alder said, as the timelines merged and Lynet came into focus.

"Oh, I know, Alder," Lynet apologized. "I took a drive out to the lake with a friend. I needed to clear my head."

Ronan stood back and waited until they were inside the house, then closed the door silently behind them.

"I am sorry. I promise not to—" Lynet's voice became a wail as she shielded her face from the bright light in Maple's hand and turned to flee.

Ronan sprang from the shadows, wrapped his arms around her waist from behind, and planted his feet wide.

Lynet became a spitting, scratching harpy. "Let go of me!"

Maple lifted the white spinning sphere high over her head and threw it into Lynet's middle. It exploded in brilliance, drenching Lynet—splashing onto Ronan's arms and shoulder—bathing both of them in Freedom.

Freedom.

Ronan could taste the spell on his tongue. It was the deepest desire of every Vökumaðr, to be free of royal control. But the spell was not for him.

Maple leaned heavily against the table. She could do no more.

Ronan held on tight as the magic flowed like a scorching liquid into Lynet's eyes and ears. It rushed up her nose, poured through her open, screaming mouth, filling her lungs and belly.

The black coils of Nos'kag Binding showed themselves, undulating up and down Lynet's body, jerking her one way, then another, as it tried to throw off Maple's magic.

Lynet was like a creature possessed. Her nails dug into Ronan's forearms, then swiped viciously behind her, catching his jaw and drawing blood. "Let me go!" she screamed, kicking and thrashing.

Ronan grunted as her heel kicked repeatedly against his shin. If she were an enemy, he would break her ribs and stop the fight at once, but she was his *ástmær*, his love. He would take whatever she gave and consider it worth the pain, so long as it helped her.

The screeching stopped. Her protests became tears. "Please, let me go, Ronan. You're hurting me. If you do not let me go, the spell will kill me."

Here was true danger. Black coils rolled up to cover Lynet's face. Ronan could literally feel the two magics battle. If the Freedom spell faltered, the Binding would strangle Lynet rather than release her.

What had Carden done? Nos'kag magic could not be trusted. Ronan was sure Carden did not want to kill Lynet yet, in his arrogance, the man had used dark magic to work his spell.

Deep inside him, the Beast awoke, its long howl bursting from Ronan's lips and echoing through the house. Ronan groaned—his will all that held back the raw animal power struggling to be free. The Beast could not save her from this. Only the man could help her now.

Lynet's struggles became weak, sluggish. Still Ronan held her, waiting anxiously for Maple to say the task was done. Lynet slumped against him, her head lolling; the pulse at her throat grew faint—and then stopped. The evil coils released their grip, falling away to form a shallow black pool that rippled and then dissolved. Ronan held her to him in stunned disbelief. Was she dead? His legs collapsed and he sank to the floor, still holding her. He pressed his lips to her temple, whispering her name. "... *stay.*"

"Do not despair." Maple got up and dropped a tiny silver-white spark onto Lynet's head. "I was prepared for this."

Lynet gasped once for air, but did not open her eyes.

Ronan brushed the hair from Lynet's face, willing her to wake, to live and breathe and stay with him. She stirred. The slightest movement, but it gave him hope, and he felt the Beast slowly retreat.

Maple fastened the locket around Lynet's neck and placed a simple spell on the latch to keep it secure. "You did not think I would let her die that easily, did you, Zerker? Take Lynet upstairs and put her to bed. I'll send up some *lyfja* tea to help her recover."

"Come closer." Eltanin's voice was quiet, thoughtful. He sat on his throne, an unusual place for the man who often paced the cold marble floor.

Neira stepped away from the portal and crossed to the dais. Behind her, the gateway whispered as it closed.

Loptr was nowhere in sight, but there was a stranger in the room. Tall, dressed in dark hues, he stood near the north *sgàthan*. Neira would have liked to give him more of her attention, but the situation was dangerous and she dared not take her eyes off the king.

She limped, her limbs cold and stiff from lying so long on the hard ground, her ankle swollen where Loptr had pulled it. Neira reached the spot where Eltanin usually bade her stand, and waited.

"Oh no, that will not do this time," Eltanin chided. "You have gone too far, little *sgalag*. There will be a penalty. Not a handful of noisome chains. No. This time the punishment must be . . . irreversible. Perhaps then you will come to understand your place in my kingdom."

Neira's stomach rolled as the finality of his words registered. Margaret had warned her of taking that step-too-far. She had honestly thought she was too valuable. Thought Eltanin would not kill her until he had his answers.

"Closer."

Neira fought back her panic and stepped up onto the dais.

"Kneel here." He pointed to a spot at his side where she would be in easy reach. Neira knelt, shuddering as he pulled back her hood.

Eltanin turned his attention to the man at the window, idly petting Neira while he spoke to his guest.

"Your search for the Watchman will take you to the Outside, Eigil," Eltanin said. "Is that a problem?"

The man turned from the mirror, and Neira marveled at his grace and unearthly beauty. Hope filled her breast. An Annar? Here? Had Isleen sent him? Did she know Eltanin planned to summon Balor?

He stepped into the light—and her hope withered.

He looked more like an assassin than a savior. His face was cold, expressionless. He wore a sleeveless, midnight blue robe over full black leathers. A thin belt of what appeared to be living stars cinched the robe at his waist. On his hips hung a pair of onyx-handled knives. His hair was as dark as his clothing. Neira thought he must wear a Shadow spell, for he was at once amazing to behold, while at the same time blending in, so that her mind kept thinking he had left the room.

What if he brought news of the dagger, Dwynai? What if Cian had given the dagger to the Annars for safekeeping, and this newcomer had stolen it and brought it to Eltanin?

"I cannot travel to the Outside. You know this; why do you ask?" Eigil's voice was pleasing, even if his words were not. "Do not think to play games with me, wizard. I could as easily slit your throat as that of your target."

"I can give you the means to cross the Divide," Eltanin said.

"Impossible."

"Tell me, Eigil, has it never bothered you that your people can create a gateway, but you cannot step through it?" Eltanin's hand in Neira's hair grew still. "I can give you this power—something no Annar before you has ever experienced. But it will cost you. I expect complete fealty from those who serve me. Will your pride allow such a thing? I wonder . . . in exchange for unequalled mobility . . . will you bow at my feet?"

If Neira had ever doubted Eltanin's power to summon Balor, all uncertainty evaporated in that moment. For, what mortal would dare expect an Annar to bow? Only one with supreme confidence in his abilities, who knew he was the greatest wizard in all of Norðrlönd.

She felt sick. He would become a god soon if no one stopped him. She glanced at Eigil and saw the same uneasy expression on his chiseled features. Eltanin was not bluffing. He could give the assassin freedom of movement— the coveted ability to cross the Aragaidheal Divide.

It was too tempting. Neira saw the light in Eigil's eyes as he considered Eltanin's offer. With an air of superiority, undimmed by his acquiescence, the assassin knelt at Eltanin's feet.

The king waited.

Minutes stretched. Neira shivered as she realized Eltanin's intent. He would not tolerate any pride or superiority above his own. Eltanin wanted Eigil to know what it meant to serve.

The mocking smile on Eigil's face faded.

"A token, then," Eltanin said, as he motioned for Eigil to rise, "of your willingness. I have a little problem I wish to see resolved."

Eltanin's fingers tightened in Neira's hair. Now it came—torture, possibly even death. Neira squeezed her eyes shut and prayed for the strength to get through this, for the ability to endure. She had so much to do. It could not be her time, not yet.

A shuffling sound at the far end of the hall interrupted them, and Neira opened her eyes. Margaret brought in the king's supper. She placed the tray on the buffet table, arranged the silver, and removed the dish covers. Neira frowned. Where was Wilda, or any of the others? Why was Margaret alone?

Loptr. Loptr must have bragged to the kitchen staff. Told them he caught Neira trying to escape. Margaret had come to her rescue; dear, sweet Margaret, who now risked her life for Neira's sake.

The old woman dropped a piece of silver to divert Eltanin's attention.

Neira cringed as Eltanin took the bait.

"Woman. Come here."

Margaret approached the throne, her back bowed, her crooked fingers curved tightly together. "Yes, Your Majesty?"

"Do you know this girl?" Eltanin gripped a handful of Neira's chestnut hair, tilting her head so Margaret could see her clearly.

Margaret did not look at Neira but nodded. "Yes, Sire. She is a slave, as I am. A hardworking girl who serves you well."

Eltanin pursed his lips, as if thinking. "Is she well liked?"

"Yes." Margaret shifted a bit in aging discomfort. "The girl does not shirk her duties, Sire. Your meals are all the more fine thanks to her efforts."

Neira balked at the lie. It was obvious Margaret was trying to save her, but Eltanin was not stupid. He would see through this.

Eltanin released Neira's hair and leaned forward on his throne, as if interested in Margaret's words. "Do *you* care for her, old woman?"

"Yes," Margaret said. "Of course I do."

"Good, good," Eltanin said. "Then you will not mind helping me teach her a much needed lesson."

Neira looked up at Eltanin's gaunt face in dawning horror. They had played right into his hands. He had known Margaret would come. Loptr was not here—because Eltanin had sent the weasel to the kitchens to stir her friends to action.

Margaret was in terrible danger.

Neira leapt to shield Margaret, but the wretched chains yanked her to the ground at Eltanin's feet. "Nooooo!" Neira cried, but her voice was drowned by Margaret's wail of confusion.

Eigil's twin blades flashed, slicing across Margaret's soft, protruding belly. The front of her apron gushed blood and fluids. Her insides spilled out onto the highly polished floor. The old woman fell onto her entrails, her thin arms jerking in agony, as her white eyes rolled back into her head.

Neira hid her face, unable to watch. Beside her the helpless whimpers and futile scratching of fingernails on the floor slowed, and mercifully ended.

Eltanin stood.

"You will not try to escape again," he said, his voice cold, stark. "In fact, you will henceforth serve my meals, so I may see your hate more often throughout the day. Now, get this mess cleaned up," he ordered, then motioned Eigil to follow him out of the throne room.

He left her there, shaking uncontrollably, with Margaret's blood splattered across her face and robes. Sobbing, unable to comprehend that her friend was gone, Neira looked at the pitiful heap that was Margaret. Grief overwhelmed her. This was her fault, her fault.

"No, Eigil, not yet," Eltanin's voice filtered through the fog in her screaming mind. "My son returns. He has a penchant for breaking things; that task is best left to him."

I Serve the King's Son

RONAN WALKED SILENTLY DOWN THE HALL toward Lynet's room, his pace slowing with each step. He held her nestled against him, her face pressed to the side of his neck, her breath warm and moist on his skin. It felt like years since he'd held her cradled in his arms like this. His chest ached with the memory.

He missed her.

He missed whispering with her in the night. Learning the way her mind worked, appreciating her strengths, while discovering the childhood fears that made her vulnerable. He even missed the days and nights of running, the hours spent huddled together without a fire, unable to let their guard down, listening for danger, even as they fought to ignore the ever present song that would spell their doom.

Ronan walked into the sweetly scented room. With his elbow, he flicked off the light, preferring the slant of the late-afternoon sun as it shone in through the curtains. He was loath to let her go for, once he did, she would belong to *them* again—to the Macarthurs, the Fates, the Æsir. He had held her when no one else could; taken the brunt of the vicious black Bind spell, and this, these few moments, were his *verðlaun*: his reward.

He went to the stuffed ivory chair by the window, where he often glimpsed her reading, and sat down. Lynet shifted in his arms, her voice a soft murmur as she burrowed closer against his chest.

Ronan brushed strands of golden hair from her face. Her eyelashes fluttered as she drifted deeper into sleep, her eyes moving restlessly beneath their delicate lids.

"Only good dreams, *ástin mín*," he whispered. "I am here *til vaka yfir þú*."

For all his noble ideas to save his father, to save Norðrlönd from Eltanin, Ronan knew that, if the Nornir offered it, he would abandon duty and spend his life in exile, if it meant he could stay with her.

An odd movement near the door caught his eye, and Ronan looked up.

"Mother Maple sent this for Lynet," Fig said softly, holding out the *lyfja* tea. He seemed uncomfortable. "She also said I should wait and bring you downstairs with me."

Ronan smiled and, joggling Lynet in his arms, stood. "It's okay, Fig, I'm coming." He carried Lynet to the bed and roused her enough to sip some tea. Gently, he pulled off her shoes and settled her under the covers. Then, on impulse, he wrapped her hair into a twist behind her, the way she used to do in the wild.

"Sleep well, *ástmær*. I won't be far." He kissed her brow.

"You're taking Lynet across the Divide, aren't you?" Fig asked, as they headed down the stairs.

"Yes." To what life or what future Ronan could not say but, yes, they were definitely returning to Norðrlönd.

"I trust you, Ronan," Fig said, in his melodic voice. "But not enough to let you travel alone. I will go with you."

Ronan shook his head. No. He had enough to deal with, getting Lynet safely to DuwaŴyr Mountain. The road would be perilous. They needed to travel light. He couldn't take on another responsibility—

Ronan released a heavy breath. His excuses sounded thin. The truth was, the boy was out of place here. Fig had no friends other than Lynet. He couldn't go to school or leave the property. Not to mention how dangerous his powers were. In a hive, puki learned to control their manipulation of time. Here, on his own, Fig was experimenting. That could not be good. Perhaps having the boy with them would be a blessing. It would certainly keep Ronan's mind off the *Kærásti Fórnsöngr*.

"All right," Ronan said. "If Maple will allow it, you can come with us." He looked around, but the sprite was already gone.

Neira rubbed the silk between her raw hands, dunking it feverishly in and out of the washtub. The thin threads frayed and separated, but she didn't care. She forced fatty lye into the fibers, trying to get out the horrid telltale signs of Margaret's death.

She mumbled as she worked, talking to herself, seeking some center ground where she could live and breathe and keep on going. It was her fault, all her fault. She should have found a better way to contact Isleen, or figured out how to escape Eltanin's chains. She should have placated Loptr, held her tongue and been more subservient. She should have confided in Margaret. At the very least, sent someone else into the forest.

Neira stopped scrubbing and laid her head on the edge of the washboard. *She* should be the one dead, not Margaret.

Tears blurred her vision, but Neira did not need sight to know the fresh blood on the silk was from her own bleeding hands. She dropped the ruined material into the tub, sobs shaking her chest.

Slowly, she slid to the floor and curled into a ball.

Eltanin would summon Balor, and their world would change forever. She had failed.

"How do you plan to take Lynet across the Divide?" Maple laid flowers in a row on the table, smoothing them with her fingers.

Ronan stood at the window, watching the woods behind the house. "I have a stoppiece." He reached under his shirt and pulled out a delicate hourglass hanging on a fragile chain of fine gold. "It was a gift from the Annars of DuwaŴyr Mountain."

Alder gave a low whistle. "How did you manage that? I'm surprised they didn't kill you."

Ronan smiled. "They tried. I convinced them my cause was just." He put the stoppiece back inside his shirt. Alder was right to be impressed. It had not been easy gaining entrance to their sacred halls, or soliciting their help.

Living high on the morning side of DuwaŴyr Mountain, the Annars were usually hard to find, preferring to avoid encounters with mortals. Ronan had gone only a short distance before the *arreyder* surrounded and disarmed him. It might have gone badly, but for Isleen. The Seer had stepped forward and allowed him entrance. Her good grace, however, was brief, and they had parted on uneasy terms.

"Cian helped, of course." Ronan turned back to the window. "He taught me what to say and do once I had their attention."

"Cian Druce?" Maple glanced up from her weaving.

"Yes," Ronan said. "Do you know him?"

"Well, everyone knows of Cian Druce," said Jól, as she poured what looked like juice, and smelled suspiciously like grizarbr, into a glass and offered it to him. "Few know him well, though. Maple does not like to admit—"

She was cut off by the matriarch's next question.

"When will you leave? I know you wanted to go tonight, but Lynet will not be ready to travel for a couple of days. That spell tried to kill her, rather than let her go." Maple shook her head. "Vicious. I'm not convinced the worst is over. My Freedom spell was not altogether strong. There may still be traces of the Binding inside her—festering, waiting to renew the assault."

"Nasty Nos'kag magic," Treddian agreed. "It knew what *you* are." He pointed to Ronan. "I didn't think you'd be able to hold the creature in—figured you'd kill us all."

Jól hushed him. "Don't say things like that. No one was in any real danger." She smiled up at Ronan and motioned him to drink.

"You were not here," Treddian said meaningfully. "I think we were all a bit scared by that howl."

Ronan swirled the drink around in the glass. Lynet's brush with death had shaken this little Northlander family. It would allay their fears if he took the drink. They assumed, as many did, that the leaf would distract him, so the Beast could not emerge. That belief was a myth. The grizarbr drug was potent, yes, but it had no effect on the Beast. If either he or Lynet were in danger, a simple plant extract could not prevent the transformation. If that were true, Eltanin would not have needed a traitor like Edan to help him murder the Vökumenn.

As much as Ronan wanted to reassure them, the time for inaction was past. Carden had made his move.

"It wasn't so scary," Fig piped up. "If Ronan had started to change, I would have suspended him until he was able to control himself."

Ronan tousled the boy's hair. "Good plan—wouldn't have worked—but good plan nonetheless."

"And why not?" Fig wanted to know.

"As fast as you are, Fig, you are still learning," Ronan said truthfully. "So, learn this: Time has no effect on the Beast. If I had lost control—Lynet would have died. The Beast does not distinguish friend from foe. He emerges in full *berserkr* form, ready for battle." Ronan glanced up at Maple. "My lady is the only one with the power to stop me, and she was already spent."

"Takes a strong will to quiet an enraged *berserkr*." Maple shook her head. "I doubt I would have had much influence over you either way. The only one controlling you, Watchman, was you."

Ronan lowered his head in humble acknowledgment. He knew well enough how little control the aristocracy actually had over the Vökumenn, although he would never say so in front of Maple. Nobles could summon the Beast easily enough, but there were few who could subdue the creature once it was unleashed.

Carden was one.

Ronan fingered the Annarian crystal in his pocket. He'd sacrificed a heartstring to possess it, and all for one purpose—to stop that redheaded bastard from ever using Governance on him again.

Ronan set the untouched glass aside.

"Lleth and I will watch the perimeter. As soon as Lynet wakes up enough to walk, we will leave." Ronan watched the Macarthurs' unhappy faces. "From now on, we can no longer pretend to play by the rules of this land. Carden Sihtric will come for Lynet. You must prepare to flee or fight."

"Lost, are we?"

Neira whirled around, the bolt of cloth in her hands tumbling to the floor. "Loptr. You startled me."

"I meant to," he assured her. "What are you doing here?"

Neira glared at him with all the hatred she felt. "What does it look like I'm doing?" She indicated the princess's sewing room, piled with material, threads, a loom and quilting stand.

"Stealing from the king." Loptr shrugged as he walked around her, leering at her breasts through the thin chemise.

Neira had given up, thrown her ruined robes into the fire, and come rushing to the upper level of the keep. She intended to make a tunic and apron with supplies the princess no longer needed. She wished now she had thought to grab something to cover herself with first. But she wasn't thinking clearly, hadn't been for hours. Not since she'd had to sew Margaret up in a shroud and drag her from the throne room.

Neira grabbed the bolt of cloth and rooted for thread. The sooner she gathered what she needed, the sooner she could flee.

"Let me guess," Loptr said, when she did not answer. "You're making another baggy wizard robe to hide behind. Would that be because your last one got covered in bile when that old crone got herself gutted?"

Neira gasped, her heart breaking, her mind screaming. She wanted to hurt him, to shut him up, to make him go away forever—

She snatched the shears from the table.

Loptr was quicker. Gripping her hand, he squeezed until her numbing fingers opened and the shears fell clanging to the floor. "You want me dead?" he asked, his face close to hers, eyes flashing with excitement. She felt the revolting heat of his desire pressing against her.

"Every slave in this castle wants you dead, you traitorous snake."

Loptr laughed. "I am no traitor. I serve the king."

In the hours since Margaret's death, there had been one thought, one flicker of hope to keep her from succumbing to despair. That hope fueled her words. "I serve the king's *son*."

Loptr released her. "What are you talking about?"

It was dangerous to bait him, but Neira was past caring.

"Carden is on his way home—did you not know? Your sojourn here is over, Loptr. Carden will brook no replacement. He will see you sent off, far from the castle, on some menial task. That is, if they bother to keep you at all. Once Carden is at his father's side, you will have no purpose."

God of the Fomorii

LYNET WALKED ALONG AN UNFAMILIAR PATH, *her feet shod in brown leather boots, her golden hair pulled into a loose braid. She stopped often to listen, her hand straying to a pouch she wore at her hip. She wished she had her weapon. A Shadow spell was not likely to help when there were so many.*

A sound from behind warned her to keep moving. There was no mistaking the snort and grunt of kobvald as they marched. Lynet quickened her pace and jogged deeper into the trees, searching for a suitable place to climb.

Kobvald were not the smartest of creatures. If she was quiet and quick, they would tramp right past her, and never know she hid in the leafy canopy overhead.

Lynet found a tree thick with foliage and leapt onto the lowest branch. As she climbed, the tree grew in height, and Lynet was amazed to discover the ground now far below. She looked out over the forest and saw someone in the distance running toward her. At first, she thought it was a man wearing a shaggy white coat, but then he dropped to all fours, and she realized it wasn't a man at all, but a creature, bulky in shape, similar to a bear, although its torso was tapered, not round.

It came closer. Lynet felt nervous. Was it dangerous? Should she run or stay hidden? Before she could decide, the bear-like creature stopped. From the grass in front of it rose an enormous snake. The bear roared and stretched to his full height, but the snake did not back down. Instead, its diamond-shaped head whipped, ready to strike.

A sharp blow to the tree nearly knocked Lynet from her perch. The kobvald had found her! She wrapped her arms and legs around the tree trunk and held on tight as it swayed and began to shrink, dropping her closer to the horde circling below. Lynet called to the bear, begging him to save her, but he was trapped, his body swathed in the unending coils of the snake. Lynet panicked as the tree continued to telescope down, until she was only a couple of feet above the drooling heads of the kobvald.

A mournful bellow rent the air.

In the strange world of dreams, Lynet saw through the trees. Saw the snake strike, its fangs sinking deep into the bear, filling him with poison. She felt the bear's strength fade, his heart flutter on the edge of life. Lynet heard her own sobs, heard the bear's sorrowful lowing—he could not come to her. He had failed, and was now called back to the gods who had sent him. His shaggy body melted away, and Lynet watched in awful understanding as the dying animal took on the face and form of a man. She screamed his name. . . .

"Shhh, it's all right, child." Maple pressed her cool palm to Lynet's forehead. "You're safe at home, in your own bed. All is well."

Lynet's eyes opened wide. "Ronan. Where is Ronan?"

"He's around somewhere," Maple said, and handed Lynet a glass. "Here, drink this. It will help. I imagine you have quite a headache."

Everyday life came sharply into focus and Lynet struggled to accept this waking reality—her room, her bed, the cloudy New York daylight, the rosebud clock on her nightstand. The tiny hands said 6:03. Was it morning or evening? Lynet pressed unsteady fingers to her temple as she took the drink. "Am I sick?" she asked in a thin voice.

"Yes, child. You've been asleep for two days. How do you feel?"

"I feel terrible." Lynet tried to sit up, but plopped weakly back onto her pillow. "My head hurts like there's an army marching through my brain, and my neck feels sunburned."

Maple sighed. "Not surprising. You've been very ill. You came home from the lake and collapsed. You've been sleeping ever since."

The lake. Lynet felt her cheeks grow warm. She'd gone with Carden Sihtric to the lake, then drove his car back to town. The blush deepened. He'd kissed her, and quite thoroughly.

"I called the diner and talked to them." Maple took the empty glass from Lynet and set it aside.

"Oh, Eibby is going to kill me. I need to get up and get to work."

"They'll get along fine," Maple said. "Aliysha was sorry to lose you. She said you're a good waitress, and she hopes you'll keep in touch."

Lynet gaped in disbelief.

"You didn't tell her I was *quitting*, did you?"

"Yes, I did." Maple smoothed the blanket, then looked into Lynet's stunned face. "It is time to go home, Lynet. Back to the life you left behind."

Lynet blinked, looking for any sign of jest. "Home," she said cautiously. "You know where my home is?"

"It is across the Aragaidheal Divide," Maple said. "Ronan knows the fastest way to get there. He will take you."

"To Lunedalr?"

Maple was surprised. "You remember your village?"

"No, I don't. Carden told me." Lynet struggled to sit up, her anger flaring. "Why is it I had to learn this from a total stranger, when my family and friends have obviously known all along? Why have you been lying to me?"

"Lynet, there are many things you cannot understa—"

"Try me," Lynet cut her off, her voice hoarse as she fought to contain the hot tears stinging her eyes. "I think you'll find I understand quite a bit."

"You have been in hiding," Maple said. "For your own protection and for the good of our world. It was not expedient for us to tell you anything that would cause you to become vulnerable or restless. We had to wait."

"'Restless'?" Lynet repeated incredulously. "Do you have any idea what I have been through these last two years? Not knowing who I am or why I'm here? Searching for answers, while you sat on a fat pile of them, doling information out only when it suited you?"

"Yes, I know how hard it's been," Maple said. "I have been here, watching over you every day of those selfsame years. I've protected you. Told you as much as I dared. There is danger out there, Lynet—right under your nose, but you don't recognize it."

"Carden," Lynet guessed.

"Yes. Carden Sihtric," Maple said flatly. "Imagine our surprise, our horror, after all these long months of keeping you safe, to find you'd run off with him in secret."

"But he's not dangerous!" Lynet blurted out. "Carden explained to me that in another place and time we would be enemies, but here we don't have to be. He wants us to be friends, and so do I."

Maple stood up and walked to the window. Lynet felt the distance between them grow. "The man is a liar. A smooth one, I'll grant, but as false and black as a soul can get." Maple turned to face Lynet. "He does not want to be *friends*. All Carden Sihtric wants is an easy catch."

"Catch? What are you talking about? He's been a perfect gentlem—"

"He is trying to win you, to gain your trust." Maple's voice rose. "Shake yourself from the spell he weaves, Lynet! Carden has one agenda—to snatch you away from us and take you to his murderous father."

"His *father*? Who's that? He never mentioned anything about his father."

"I'm sure he didn't." Maple came back to the bed. "Carden is too sly for that. But it doesn't change the fact that he intends to use you to gain his father's favor. And Eltanin, that black-hearted *cythraul*, will use you to subject all of Norðrlönd to his will, to rule unchallenged forever. You mean little else to either of them."

"Use me? How?"

"Your blue magic, Lynet." Maple was blunt. "It is unsafe and devastatingly powerful, and Eltanin wants it."

Maple lifted a brown leather journey pack from the chair beside Lynet's bed. "This is a proper Northlander bag. It is not a slaver's bag, but it is sturdy and easy to carry; you will find it serves your needs well enough on the trail. I'll send Fig up with some food. Once you have eaten, you can pack. I've laid out leathers for you." She pointed to a pair of trousers, a jacket, and a laced tunic hanging over the chair. "Alder is sharpening a sword. You will have no use for dresses on your journey, although you may want one for when you meet your betrothed."

Lynet was dumbfounded.

"Betrothed? You have got to be kidding me. Where is he? Who is he? Why haven't I met him?"

"Prince Edan Aricin does not run his own errands, girl. He has sent someone for you in his place—his royal Watchman, Ronan Loðungr."

Balor fingered the stitch of human gut holding his left eye closed and waited for the summons to finish. He was amused, curious. Oh, he knew of Eltanin Sihtric. The orchestrator of the Vökumaðr genocide had provided Balor with rousing entertainment—but that was in the past. Since then, the wizard had done nothing remarkable—killed a few slaves and tortured the heir into madness. Hardly a satisfying encore.

As the last lines of the chant sounded, Balor wondered again at the audacity of this tiny human to summon *him*, the almighty god of the Fomorii. He grinned, his yellow teeth jagged and broken. He was not, of course, the god of anything. There was only one fallen Son of the Morning, and that malevolent being seldom bothered with his minions. Still, Balor had for millennia enjoyed the benefits of myth and legend. Let the human world think him a god. It mattered not. He was the greatest of the Fomorii. That was all they needed to know.

The gateway crackled open, and Balor's voice boomed through, loud enough to judder the foundations of Caeraricin Castle. "Your door is too small," he bellowed as he bent down and reached in. His red hand swooped blindly, searching for the man who had summoned him. His thick fingers slammed into a barrier of magic, and Balor chuckled, glad the wizard had not disappointed him.

The gateway grew in size, until the entire wall of the cavern was one gigantic hole. It was a tight squeeze, but Balor cared little. He did not intend to pass completely through the gateway anyhow. To do so would give the human power over him. Unlike lesser demons in his kingdom, the god of the Fomorii knew the secret to keeping the balance.

"What do you want, little wizard?" Balor crouched halfway between worlds, his great horns scraping the roof of the cavern.

"Lord Balor." Eltanin gave a slight nod in deference to his guest. "Your wisdom in not putting up a struggle is appreciated. My time is valuable, as is yours; there is no point wasting it on resistance."

Balor snorted. "Why have you summoned me?"

"I intend to make myself ruler of the whole of Norðrlönd, starting with the Six Kingdoms—"

"—and you want my help." Balor's tone was bored. He had heard this speech countless times throughout the ages. He was as unimpressed now as he had been on those previous occasions.

"I hardly need your help for that." Eltanin brushed away Balor's assumption with a wave of his hand. "Giants, Annars—creatures of this world I can deal with. No, it is the tampering of gods that gives me pause."

The human's tone was flatly insolent, and Balor wondered if he should kill Eltanin now and be done with it.

"A recent *forspá* spoke of a rift in the Aragaidheal Divide," Eltanin continued. "Since the absorption of Norðrlönd into the Outside world would interfere with my plans, I intend to contain the rift and control it myself." Eltanin looked pointedly up at Balor. "I have summoned you to tell me where this Great Rift is."

Balor grinned, his broken yellow teeth glistening with spittle. Kleng had warned him of the wizard's preoccupation with finding a rift in the Divide. It was a useless quest. *There was no Great Rift.* Indeed, a rift of any size or duration would be of special interest to the god of the Fomorii. Balor had been trying to find a way back to the Outside world for centuries. Stoppieces and puki magic manipulated time currents long enough for mortals to slip through—but their portals were not substantial enough for the dense-bodied Fomorii who, upon entering, would break apart and dissolve.

A fixed door had once existed—before the Sòlasach closed it a thousand years ago. His followers tried daily to open Devil's Gate, but the Derwydd guarded it too well. There had been hope recently; Balor had sensed evil lurking near the Gate on the Outside, a great goddess of destruction, but she did not seem interested in Ogluidh, and only a few shadow wraiths had managed to glide through. Yes, a Great Rift would be most interesting.

"You think you can control the rift? By what means?" Balor asked.

"It is simple enough," Eltanin said, his tone that of a teacher instructing a dim-witted child. "To create a portal, one must tear the fabric of time. The minutes that normally occupy that space become displaced, pushed to the outer edge of the hole. The larger the hole, the more minutes accumulate around the border. I believe controlling the Great Rift is as simple as harnessing those excess minutes. This I can do."

Balor stared hard with his one good eye. Was it possible this arrogant popinjay had the ability to control raw time? Only the Sòlasach had ever been able to maintain a fixed portal. Was Eltanin as powerful as they were? If so, could he in fact . . . *create* a Great Rift?

"*How* would you harness them?" Balor pressed.

"That is not your concern," Eltanin said with growing impatience. "Now, where is the Rift? I grow tired of our exchange."

Balor's expression hardened. He had had his fill.

"FOOL!" The cavern walls shook with the thunder of Balor's voice. Shale and stone fell from the roof in chunks. "Your circle of ash and salt protects you from my crushing fist, but none can escape the devastation of my unveiled eye!"

Eltanin glanced at the demon's notorious eye. If the wizard was concerned, he did not show it. His back remained stiff, his head erect. But Balor could smell the sweet scent of fear in the air; it made him hungry.

"I have in my employ blacksmiths gifted in the darker arts," Eltanin said. "They fashion for me a metal ring, half the size of the doorway in which you so wisely squat. It will consist of five curved pieces supported upright on a stone base. Once you find the Great Rift, I will build the gate around it, stopping its expansion. Thus will I have total control of when—and for whom—the portal opens or closes. Is that sufficient information?"

"It is an interesting theory," Balor said, giving no indication of his inner glee, "but riddled with risk. If you attempt and fail, the Aragaidheal Divide will collapse. The barrier protecting this world will be gone. Norðrlönd and its people—including you, mortal—will crumble to dust."

"I know the risk."

Balor twisted the knotted stitch in his eyelid. "How will such a blunder affect my own domain? Do not misunderstand me; I would gladly help you destroy your world. However, I am not so inclined to let you ruin mine."

"My magic is not in question."

"Prove it," Balor challenged. "Reassure me my kingdom is safe. Prove you have the skill to back up your boast."

Eltanin's lips turned white with suppressed anger. "What would you consider proof?"

"Put your gate together, somewhere where I can watch you work. Into it put seven puki timepools—the oldest from each of the Six Kingdoms, and one from the Outside. If you can control the ensuing maelstrom, then I will be convinced of your ability to control the Great Rift of the *forspá*."

The wizard's eyes narrowed. "And how would you suggest I locate and retrieve these timepools? It is common knowledge that to venture too close to one is certain death."

Balor laughed, and the cavern shook. "Be not afraid. I do not wish you dead, not before I have seen with my own eye this braggart's feat you claim. I will provide you with a guide, and the means whereby you can gather the pools unharmed. When the last of the seven are imprisoned in your gateway—then will I show you your Great Rift."

Eltanin was silent, and Balor thought that perhaps his ploy had failed.

Finally, Eltanin nodded. "We have a deal. I will summon you when the gate is ready. *Drogh Spyrryd, Ersooyl-jee!*" He began the magic that would send Balor back to Ogluidh.

"Wait," Balor demanded. "In return for my trouble, I require a sacrifice."

"The castle is full of fodder," Eltanin said irritably. "Take your pick."

"I do not want your slaves."

Balor's plans could still be ruined—by the return of the Sòlasach, the ancients who first purged the land with their blinding Suthainn magic and locked the Fomorii and their kind in Ogluidh. A human had recently figured out how to communicate with them; that human was a threat.

"I want Cian Druce."

Broken Silver Chain

LYNET LAY FLAT ON HER BACK on the bed, watching a spider crawl across the ceiling. *Betrothed*. No wonder Ronan had pushed her away. She was engaged to a prince, and Ronan was the inconvenienced emissary sent to fetch her. The whole thing was ludicrous. Why would a prince want to marry her? She was a common miller's daughter. She couldn't even spin straw into gold . . . could she?

Lynet twisted her hair into a loose braid, uncertain which she felt more: anger or fear. She supposed she felt furious. No one was going to tell her who to marry. On the other hand, betrothed to a prince might not be so bad. If she married him, would she become a princess? If so, could she *command* someone to teach her magic? Would she finally be in control of her own life?

Prince Edan Aricin. He sounded stuffy. Was he nice? Would he treat her well? What if he was mean and ugly and beat her?

Lynet sat up. Yes, fear was definitely the dominant emotion. Not that she'd put up with it if he did beat her. She was pretty sure turning blue would cause the same misgivings in a prince as it had in Treddian and the others.

She massaged her forehead. Her head still throbbed.

The air in the room rippled, a sure sign Fig was nearby, probably skulking outside the bedroom door.

"Come in," Lynet called.

In an instant, the boy stood next to the bed, a tray piled with food balanced precariously in his small, trembling arms.

"Hungry?" Fig asked breathlessly.

Lynet scrambled to take the tray. The aroma of hot cinnamon pancakes nearly made her swoon. Buttered squash, scrambled eggs, boiled red potatoes, and thick, crispy bacon filled the plates. "There is too much food here for one person. You'll have to help me," Lynet said, glad for his company and the break from her miserable musings.

Fig grinned. His impish face lit up as he pulled a second set of silverware from his pocket and leapt up onto the bed to sit across from her.

They dove into the mound of food. Lynet was starving. She gobbled eggs and bacon, washing it down with a glass of cold milk.

"I'm glad you're eating," Fig said through a mouthful of potatoes. "I was afraid you weren't going to wake up."

"I guess I was pretty sick." Lynet dipped her fork, stuffed with pancake, into a side bowl of strawberries and cream.

Fig stopped eating. "You weren't sick, Lynet," he said with a frown. "You almost died."

Lynet stopped eating as well. "What are you talking about?"

"He put a spell on you, the *jöfurr*. When Mother Maple tried to take it off—I think the spell wanted to kill you. If Ronan hadn't held you, I don't know what would have happened, but I'm sure it would have been awful."

Lynet slouched back against her pillow as memories crowded in. She remembered Carden's kiss, and the drive home. She remembered feeling so sluggish it seemed to take forever to get in the door. She remembered talking to Alder, apologizing—

Lynet's eyes grew wide. She remembered Maple, towering and fearsome in front of her, a swirling ball of white suspended in her outstretched hand. Lynet gasped and dropped her fork. She remembered the pain as magic poured in through her eyes to blind her; into her ears so she couldn't hear; into her mouth to suffocate her. And through it all—Ronan had held her— forced her to endure the torture of Maple's wretched spell. Lynet didn't know anything about a *jöfurr*, but she remembered with absolute certainty being attacked by her own family.

She wasn't hungry anymore.

"Are you done eating?" Fig asked, as Lynet pushed away the tray and slid from the bed.

His melodic voice intruded on her thoughts. Fig. She loved Fig, but who was he . . . really? Who were these people she had spent the last two years with? She trusted them, believed they loved her—but what if they didn't? What if the Macarthurs had some ulterior motive? They'd certainly lied to her. What if they were lying about the prince and taking her home?

Lynet closed her eyes against the fantastical rush of questions brewing like a storm in her head.

"Lynet?" Fig jumped from the bed, landing light on his feet beside her.

"I'm not hungry," Lynet said. "I am tired, though. I . . . think I need more sleep."

"You don't look so good," Fig said gently. "I'll take the tray. Maybe you'll feel like eating after you've had a nap."

She nodded, but didn't say any more, and Fig soon disappeared.

Lynet felt sick. After two long years of silence, suddenly they were rushing her off into the unknown. Why? Why was it so important she leave today, now, without time for explanation?

Carden.

They were afraid of Carden—afraid of her friendship with him.

Lynet rubbed her neck—*ouch*. Why did her skin hurt so much? She went to the vanity mirror. Her lips were chapped and red as with a fever. Was it from Maple's attack? She examined her throat and found odd, reddish scorch marks under her chin. Was it a rash? She lifted her locket out of the way. Thin welts streaked her neck beneath the chain.

Was it an allergic reaction? She'd had this locket a long time; ever since she'd found it lodged behind the dresser when she first came here. It had never turned her skin red before. She reached behind her to unfasten it, but the latch seemed stuck.

Lynet turned the necklace around and tried again, but her fingernails couldn't get hold of the clasp. When had she put the locket on, anyhow? She couldn't remember wearing it. In fact—her movements became frantic—she distinctly remembered racing out of the house the other day without any jewelry on except her pink watch. Panicked, Lynet grabbed the chain with both hands and yanked it apart. The locket flew across the room.

The pain in her head melted away. Lynet gripped the edge of the vanity, and thought she might throw up what little food she'd eaten.

What just happened?

Lynet looked suspiciously at the broken silver chain. Something was wrong with the necklace, something evil. Her eyes widened—someone had placed a charm or spell on it. Not only that, they had deliberately fastened it around her neck while she slept, and jinxed it so it would not come off.

Someone in this house.

She was not safe here. She had to get out.

Carden. Carden would know what to do.

Lynet grabbed the journey pack and filled it with clothes. She took a fistful of underwear and some toiletries and stuffed them in too, then dropped the bag on the chair. There; it looked like she was obeying Maple's orders.

Next, she checked the hall. At least they hadn't posted a guard. Lynet shut the door, dug her phone from her purse, and quickly dialed.

"Carden?" she whispered when he answered. "I need help."

"Where are you, love? What's happened?"

"I'm at the Macarthurs. I think I'm in danger. Maple says I am going home, but I don't know if I can believe her. I'm frightened, Carden. They did something awful to me. I've been asleep ever since we went to the lake."

"Can you leave the house?" Carden asked.

"I don't think so; not without a distraction."

"Oh, I can provide a distraction." Carden's confidence reassured her. "Be ready. After dark, when you hear the commotion, slip out and look for the BMW. The keys will be in it. Drive to the empty shopping plaza in Alden. Park behind the old McDonald's. I'll meet you there. Until then, be yourself. Don't let on you're running away."

Raknfeld stood before the crackling gateway. His message was brief, so there was no need to step through the Divide. He waited for Eltanin's attention. The king seemed agitated. He was in a small, dark room that the hart did not recognize. Books and parchment were spread out with purpose on a table in front of him. A seething sphere of dark magic hovered inches above one of the open scrolls. Eltanin glanced his way, and Raknfeld spoke: "Your son makes his move."

"Bring them both to me, now," Eltanin said. "I am too close to my goal to allow my son even an inch of leeway in this." The wizard paused, his molten eyes shining. "Once you have the witch—kill everyone who knows her. Start with those in the house. Burn it. I want all knowledge of Lynet of Nairn erased from the Outside world."

"Isn't it dangerous to do something so conspicuous?" Raknfeld asked, shocked by Eltanin's demand. "If my herd is seen, it could damage the Divide—"

"Burn it down!" Eltanin cut him off. "Kill them all, or you will remain a two-leg forever."

Downstairs, the Macarthurs fussed over Lynet, giving her advice and saying their goodbyes. Alder presented her with a short sword, which involved a bit of ceremony. Lynet accepted it awkwardly and promised to keep the sword safe until Ronan had time to teach her to use it.

Auntie Jól fussed the most, pushing more food on her than a person could possibly eat. In fact, everyone was sweet and kind, and Lynet grew confused.

She loved them. She wanted to believe they loved her too. But how could she—knowing what they had done to her?

At last, they shooed her upstairs to bed to get some added rest. Ronan would arrive soon.

Once alone, Lynet changed into a pair of worn jeans, a sweater, and tennis shoes. Then she began to pace. She checked the journey pack repeatedly, adding anything she thought might be useful. She didn't know where she would end up, or what she might need. In a moment of sentimentality, she even threw in the short sword. She didn't want to hurt Alder's feelings by leaving it behind, although she had no such fancies about the leathers, which she hid in the bottom of her closet.

Twice Lynet tested the weight of the bag, amazed that it could hold so much and still be light to carry. Nice.

Sifting through the food Auntie Jól had prepared, Lynet packed away as much as she thought would travel well, and ate some of the rest. Now that the locket was gone, Lynet felt stronger by the minute. Luckily, no one had noticed it was missing.

She watched the sky deepen into night. Soon, Carden would create his diversion. This was a quiet street, in a suburb far from the city. They were practically in the country. It wouldn't take much to have the whole neighborhood in an uproar.

Lynet peered out across the street, to the blue-gray building where Ronan lived. His apartment lights were out. That was strange. They were supposed to be leaving soon. Where was he?

He follows you, you know. Carden's warning echoed in her mind.

Startled, Lynet drew back from the window. Ronan could ruin everything. He would not be as easily fooled as the rest of the family. Lynet wondered if she should go downstairs to try to find out where he was. A glance at the clock told her there was no time. She needed to be ready. Carden would not let her down. Any moment now, she would hear a ruckus. She must not miss her opportunity.

Balor watched Eltanin levitate the last piece of the ring and fit it into place. "Well done." The demon laughed, the sound echoing in the sea cavern under the castle. "It is small, but it might work."

"Size is irrelevant," Eltanin said coolly. "It will work. Now, where are the seven timepools? You promised a guide and a safe means to collect them."

"In time," Balor said. "As an act of good faith, I will reveal the location of the first timepool myself. The rest will follow only after I have my prize."

"I will need more than Kleng," Eltanin told the demon god. "Cian Druce has powerful allies. My own forces prepare for war. If you want the Druce, you will have to provide additional support."

Balor agreed. "I will send you Baobh. As for the oldest timepool in Caeraricin, you will find it north of here, in the Nótt Forest." Balor drew in the dirt on the cavern floor. "It is beyond the *scaaghey loghan*—here." He placed a big X on the crudely drawn map. "You will need this." Balor opened his clawed fist and dropped something the size of a round loaf of bread onto the ground. "Inch that into the pool, and it will be yours to control."

The red giant shifted his shoulders. The space between worlds felt cramped. He was impatient to return to his own domain, where he could stand properly, stretch his muscles, and swat annoying fools like the one standing in front of him.

"When I summon you again, bring Kleng and this Baobh with you. That is"—Eltanin paused—"if you think two Fomorii are enough to wrest Cian Druce from his place on DuwaŴyr Mountain."

Balor threw back his horned head and boomed with laughter. "You have yet to meet my lovely Baobh. She is worth ten of Kleng. Do not fret, little human. They will be enough—more than enough."

Arrows and Flame

WORKING IN THE DARK, Ronan stuffed the last of his things into a slaver's bag. Maple had handed him the bag last night, already packed with several seasons' worth of herbs, roots and pollens from the matriarch's garden. Ronan was to deliver the bag to Cian Druce, who would find the contents of great worth. Ronan did not doubt it. Earth magic from the Outside was highly sought after as a potent enhancement to complicated spells.

Plants grew differently here, especially in areas with rich soil and plenty of rain, like Buffalo. They were thicker, greener, bursting with the life-giving ingredients strong magic needed. Norðrlönd's brief, cool summers did not produce the same rich harvest.

Maple Macarthur had been squirreling away her dried goods for years. The bag was nearly full, though like all slaver's bags, it somehow stretched to hold that little bit more: weapons, change of clothing, food, his leather jacket, plus a couple of books Ronan knew Cian would find interesting.

Ronan glanced out the window, keeping an eye on the Macarthurs' house as he tightened the laces on the bag. He hoped Cian had room enough in his hut for all the barrels, bundles, bales, and jars—so Ronan could keep the slaver's bag for himself. Such bags were rare and amazingly useful. He could cram an armory of weapons into the thing and never feel more than the weight of the bag on his shoulders. Besides, if he had it, that was one less trick in the hands of those scum slavers who made a living using the bags to transport and peddle human flesh.

Lleth trotted in from the kitchen, the click of his toenails echoing in the empty room. Ronan had meant to clip those nails, but he supposed the wilds of Norðrlönd would file them down soon enough.

Ronan walked through the rooms of the apartment one last time, then tossed the key onto the kitchen table. The Outside had been good to him.

He'd enjoyed the hours spent in honest labor. In another life, he would choose this—a home in a quiet neighborhood with Lynet—and be content.

He knotted his belt and made sure his knife fit securely at the small of his back. He'd packed the longsword in the bag. Ronan figured he looked menacing enough in his dark pants, inky shirt, and black leather jerkin—without adding a longsword into the mix. He'd worked a Shadow spell into the cloth and leather, enhancing his ability to disappear when necessary.

The sharp sound of shattered glass broke the quiet.

Drawing his knife, Ronan melted into the shadows. On silent footsteps, he crept to the window and peered out. Firelight flickered, casting an orange glow onto the scene below. The house across the street burned. In the road, he saw Senteer.

They had come for Lynet.

Three of them leapt over the hedges that bordered the Macarthurs' front lawn. Flaming arrows sprang from their bows as they circled. The two that remained sent a barrage of arrows toward the house, breaking windows, speeding their deadly shafts deep into the lower-floor rooms.

Ronan sheathed his knife and pulled his longsword from the slaver's bag.

"Come, Lleth," he said to the pacing wolfhound, as he fastened the belted scabbard around his waist. "The hunt is on."

Lynet heard the sound of breaking glass and jumped from her bed. She switched off the light and looked out the window. A fire burned in the yard below—the diversion she'd been waiting for.

She scooped up the journey pack and slipped out into the hall. Whatever Carden was doing needed to last long enough for her to sneak out of the house. She paused at the third-floor landing and heard Maple calling out orders below.

"Fig, go get Lynet. Tred, take your wife and son and try to get out of here. They're going to burn the place down around us."

More glass shattered, and Auntie Jól screamed. "Senteer! They'll pick us off as we try to leave."

Lynet couldn't make sense of it. Senteer? The fear in Auntie Jól's voice was unnecessary. It was a diversion, nothing more; they were not in any real danger. Lynet felt the wrinkle of air that announced Fig's coming. She pressed back against the wall, watching as he zipped past her and into the bedroom. He sped from it a moment later, shouting to the others. "She's gone!"

Ronan and Lleth moved silently, sliding in and out of the flickering orange-and-black patterns created by the fire and smoke. When they were level with the two archers, Ronan gave the signal and Lleth leapt first.

The hound went straight for the kill, ripping out the throat of the closest Senteer. Ronan sprang to face the second, swinging his longsword in a wide arc. The startled Senteer rose up on powerful hind legs to strike at Ronan with his hooves—but it was too late. The longsword sliced through ribcage and lungs, catching on splintered bone. The stag crumpled to the ground, his rich red blood spilling onto the pavement.

Ronan yanked the sword free and looked around. He could see both *cornioggath* dead on the lawn several feet away, riddled with arrows.

There was no time to hide the bodies. All around them, neighbors were spilling out onto the street. He heard voices shouting to call the fire department. Ronan hoped in the confusion no one noticed that the deer lying dead on the side of the road were half-human, or that the Macarthurs' housecats had become monsters.

It was unlike the Senteer to do anything this blatant. Even Carden would not take such a risk. Ronan could think of only one person with such contempt for consequences—Eltanin had ordered this attack.

Ronan cursed the many delays that had made this possible. Especially those created by Maple. He should have used the Oath to disobey her demands, as Cian had counseled long ago. Now it was too late. All Ronan could do was grab Lynet and run.

"She's gone!" Fig yelled, as he sprinted down the stairs. "I found the locket on the floor. Lynet is unprotected."

Lynet peered over the banister.

Below her, Alder bellowed in outrage, his tirade interrupted by the splintering of the back door as it was kicked open. Ronan stood in the doorway, his silhouette briefly outlined by flames. "Where is Lynet?" he demanded as he slammed the door against a new barrage of arrows.

"Gone." Fig tossed the locket to Ronan. "I found this on the floor."

243

"I can feel her," Ronan said. "She is still in the house."

Lynet felt blindsided. How could he know that? Hitching the journey pack over her shoulder, she ran down the hall toward the south stairs.

"Out! Out, before the place burns to the ground," Alder cried.

"No!" Ronan shouted over him. "Senteer hide in the trees out back. You would not make it across the grounds alive." Ronan reached inside his shirt and pulled out the stoppiece. "Gather everyone together; we will cross the Aragaidheal Divide from here."

Jól's voice cracked. "And leave our home?"

"Your home is lost." Part of the ceiling crashed to the floor, accentuating his words. "Hurry. I will get Lynet."

Outside, Gitta drew back her bow. Her forearms bulged as she aimed again. The flames and falling debris kept getting in the way. She sidestepped closer, vying for a better angle. The order was to kill everyone in the house, except the witch. Raknfeld had warned them to be cautious, but their usual stealth was pointless this time. She caught a glimpse of movement and, with a snap, released the arrow.

Gitta cursed, as a piece of falling ceiling knocked the shaft from its course. No one had escaped the house. Her instincts told her the family sought another way out—a portal perhaps. She looked to Stian; his frustration mirrored her own. The house would burn to the ground, but there would be no evidence of the Macarthurs' deaths to give to King Eltanin. Already, humans gathered out front, and she heard sirens in the distance.

Caution would not get this job done. The heat and flames blocked most of the view from the street. Besides, they would be back later to kill these people. King Eltanin wanted all knowledge of the witch erased. Boldly, Gitta pranced out onto the lawn, away from the cover of the hedge and trees. Someone had to take charge. Raknfeld was off in search of the *jöfurr*. It was the perfect time to step into his place.

"Stian. Clunainach!" she called to the males at her flank. "Take those windows." She pointed to the left and right. "There is only one way to be sure the humans die." Gitta nocked another arrow and cantered toward the house, knowing a hard hit would assure them success. A glance over her shoulder confirmed her kin followed her lead. Satisfied, she approached the window. Her heart leapt in excitement as she picked out a target and drew the heavy bow. She would make the first kill.

The smoke was thick. Ronan dashed up the stairs, covering his nose and mouth with his sleeve. At the third-floor landing, he reached out again for Lynet. She was running; he sensed her desperation and fear. The Bind spell was not dead after all.

Without the protection of the locket, Lynet would soon lose her ability to distinguish between her own thoughts and Carden's. In the end she would see the world through Carden's eyes, accepting his beliefs and values as her own. That must never happen.

Ronan turned south, coughing as he ran. His Vökumaðr body could fight the damage to his lungs, but it could not supply him with oxygen.

He got to the south stairs, swung over the railing, and dropped halfway down the next flight. He was to the second floor when he felt her leave the house completely. *Damn! Again, too late.* Was he doomed to forever be one step behind? Always too late to save her?

Jól's screams split the air. Someone was hurt.

By the time Ronan got to them, Treddian was bleeding heavily, his lower left side torn open, bone and gristle exposed at his hip. Acid ate away his flesh. Fat and skin melted, dripping onto the floor. His face was white and contorted in pain; only Alder's strong arms kept him upright. To live, he needed a healer. Ronan yanked the stoppiece from around his neck and handed it to Maple.

"Use it. Find the Cú. They can save him."

"Aren't you coming? Where is Lynet?"

"Gone," Ronan answered. "Don't worry—I'll find her."

"How will you cross the Divide without your stoppiece?" Maple huddled her family close. The fire raged. They had to leave now, or all of them would die in this inferno.

"I can take him," Fig piped.

All eyes turned to the youth.

"You can do this?" Maple asked sternly.

Fig nodded.

"Go then. Take the boy."

Ronan and Fig started toward the side door.

"Wait!" Maple dug into her bag and pulled out a glass jar. Inside it swirled a brightly glowing spell. "Here—I have had two full days to prepare this. Find Lynet. Use it on her. She will throw off his magic, and Carden will never again have power over her mind."

Ronan sprinted back and grabbed the jar.

Beams from the second floor crashed through the ceiling, exploding in a spray of sparks and flame.

"Go!" Ronan shouted, then raced to catch up with Fig. He paused, just inside the door, to watch as the Macarthurs stepped through the Aragaidheal Divide to safety.

The Beast

RONAN SHOVED FIG OUT OF THE WAY as Senteer arrows flew through the open door. "Most of the arrows come from the trees on the right," Ronan shouted over the roar of the flames. "When we go outside, you must use your powers to stay between moments so they cannot hit you. Do you understand?"

"I'll be all right," Fig yelled, his voice barely audible over the din. "I can slip between them—I've done it twice already."

They raced out into a storm of whizzing arrows. Ronan dodged them as best he could, but still caught two, before diving into the bushes at the edge of the garden.

Ronan ground his teeth and, using a fistful of grass to protect his hand, snapped off the corrosive arrowhead at the back of his thigh. The wound made a soft sucking sound as he pulled the shaft out the front. Blood squirted and flowed onto the grass. Ronan held still, trying to catch his breath. Already the acid ate into his flesh, leaving stringy strips of muscle and cloth.

Sweating, Ronan broke the fletching from the second arrow, the tip still inside him. The only way to get it out was to force it the rest of the way through. His arms shook as he pushed the shaft deeper into his lower ribs, and out through the other side. He crouched, gasping in agony. His Vökumaðr body could stanch the flow of blood—but it could not spare him the pain. Panting, he called to Fig, "Here," and handed him the glass jar. "Go to my apartment." His words grew thick and harsh. "The door is open."

"I won't leave y—" Fig started to say, but Ronan cut him off.

"Listen to me," Ronan said sharply. "It's too late, Fig. I cannot stop it this time." He trembled. "You must *run*."

A growl filled Ronan's throat as he ripped off his boots and weapons, throwing them to the ground. His shoulders and arms bunched with massive bulk, tearing his clothes even as he struggled to get them off.

"Go inside and lock the door." Ronan's voice grew harder to understand. "Do not come out for any reason."

He tried to say more, but the words became an unintelligible roar as Ronan's mouth elongated into a jagged-toothed muzzle. He turned and crashed through the trees, taking the Beast away from Fig while he still had some sense of self left.

Fig picked up Ronan's hunting knife, wielding it like a pirate as he blinked in and out of sight. Flitting across the yard, he zipped between arrows and onlookers, weaving through the crowd of neighbors and police, and finally skipping across the road.

The door to the apartment was wide open. Lleth lay on the floor in the kitchen, whining and licking at an arrow sticking out of his hind leg.

Fig locked the door, put aside the knife and glass jar, then hurried to Lleth. The arrow had speared the muscle, but there was no sign of acid—only smoky, char-blackened fur. Relieved, Fig patted Lleth, then ran to the window. Fire engulfed Laburnum House; the repeated volley of flaming arrows had ensured a quick burn. People in the street below moved farther away to avoid the heat. Teams of firefighters took up positions, streaming jets of water onto the house, but the best they could hope for was containment.

Fig stood on a chair, trying to get a glimpse of the trees at the back of the house. A battle raged there, one he was disappointed he could not see—a *berserkr* of Caeraricin shredding through his enemies.

Gitta yelled for Stian to move forward on her left as they targeted the back porch. Two humans had already escaped the house; she'd sent scouts to bring them down, and others to dispose of the bodies of her comrades out on the road. She felt confident in her leadership. They would get this done, clean up the mess, and preserve the Divide.

The door in front of her had the least amount of smoke pouring from it. If the humans ran, she expected them to come out this way. Gitta motioned again for Stian to come up beside her.

Precious seconds passed.

Stian did not come.

Angry he would choose *now* to question her authority, Gitta turned—her furious expression melting into one of horror.

A monster towered over her. Thirteen feet tall, its bulk filled her vision, blocking out everything but the open-eyed stare of Stian as he hung limp and lifeless from the creature's claws. Gitta ducked as her comrade's body hurtled past into the flames of the collapsing house.

She raised her bow, prancing out around the porch, giving herself room to maneuver. Clunainach and Maoltuile cantered around from behind, firing arrows at the Beast's head and chest. Many stuck in the monster's hide; others tangled uselessly in the shaggy mane.

With an impossibly wide swipe, the Beast caught Maoltuile, lifting him up off the ground. The old bull's legs flailed as he struggled to break free. Gitta abandoned her bow and drew her sword, charging in to attack the creature's exposed belly. She got in one good strike, but had to retreat.

The Beast swung Maoltuile like a club, knocking away Clunainach, and then IwonaRae, a young doe who came forward to help.

Maoltuile cried out in pain as his body twisted in the air. Gitta heard the loud snap of his spine as the human half was broken and then ripped from his graying flank. Grief made her reckless. Wildly, Gitta attacked, slicing at the Beast's legs, his abdomen, hacking at any part she could get to. Too late, she realized Maoltuile was gone, thrown aside, no longer the center of the creature's attention.

Gitta felt no pain, just the odd rush of air leaving her lungs. She watched, perplexed, as the house turned upside down. Her heartbeat sounded so loud in her ears, she could no longer hear the crackle of the fire.

Clunainach looked up at her. She saw his face contort with emotion, his quiver empty, his bow useless at his side. She wanted to yell, to tell him to throw his sword into the creature's belly, to use this opportunity to bring the Beast down—but words could not get past the weird angle of her neck as it snapped. Clunainach disappeared in a bright flash of light that seemed to come from behind her ey—

Maple Macarthur studied the tangle of trees around them. They were too far south. She had hoped they would emerge at the foot of DuwaŴyr Mountain, close to the Druce, but they were nowhere near it.

"We need directions." Maple turned to her family. "Ask. Hurry."

Alder nodded. Still supporting Treddian, he leaned his head back and opened his mouth wide, the sound issuing from his throat no longer human—more the rustle of Spring as it floated through the woods, coaxing to the surface each growing thing it touched. "Oh, Father Forest, hear the weary cries of your children. We are injured and far from home. Tell us the way to life, and succor."

The trees stirred, slowly, as if awakened from a deep sleep, their golden leaves quivering without wind. Whispers formed in the topmost branches, then dropped like rain in answer:

> *two leagues*
> *to the east*
> *the shepherds' flocks*
> *find water*
> *rest*
> *two leagues to the east*
> *blue dogmen wait*
> *two leagues*
> *to the east*

They headed east.

Maple watched as her husband struggled to keep Treddian on his feet. With each step, Treddian grew weaker. His lips were as pale as his face, his eyes closed, his feet dragging and nearly useless.

Jól's face was scorched from the heat that had blasted them as they escaped across the Divide. Alder had ugly burns all along his left side. Maple knew he kept his pain to himself. He paused often to cough, and she saw flecks of blood caught in his beard.

They were not going to make it.

Even at a decent pace, it would take two hours to reach the Cú. Treddian would be dead before they got there and, the longer it took them, the worse the others would get.

Maple turned abruptly and called them to a halt. Expectant faces lifted. She knew they thought she'd spotted the shepherds' tents.

"Tred," Maple said firmly, throwing off the rustic tone she'd used on the Outside. Her voice was strong and regal, meant to cut through the cloud of suffering in Treddian's head. He needed to stay coherent. "You will not make it if we keep going."

Jól sobbed, but Maple ignored her. "You must root, or you will die."

"No!" Jól wailed. "He will miss Eburos growing up."

"One child." Maple steeled her heart against Jól's tears. Maple knew what she asked; knew the anguish of separation from those she loved. "One child," she repeated, "is all he will miss. If he does not root, he will die, and there will be no more children."

Alder helped Treddian off the path. Maple was grateful for his silent acceptance. It was no small thing. Once the Derwydd rooted, it would be a lifetime before Treddian regained his sense of humanity and came back to them—but there was no other choice. Alder half-led, half-dragged Treddian to a clearing where the sun found its way through the overhanging boughs.

"You'll do well here," Alder said. "The soil is rich. Time will pass quickly." Alder paused to cough. "You root and heal yourself. Jól will be waiting when you wake up."

Jól handed the baby to Maple and threw her arms around her husband, her tears mingled with kisses.

Maple patted the squirming Eburos, giving the couple a moment of privacy that must last them an age. She turned back when she heard the sound of earth crumbling. Treddian's feet grappled into the ground; his arms stretched weakly toward the sky. Maple hoped he had the strength to do this.

Slowly, his body grew thick and brown, his features disappearing beneath a cover of heavy bark. His exposed hip filled with pale green layers of new wood. His fingers spread out, elongating to become thick, waving branches.

They watched, anxiously waiting for the leaves that would give him strength and life. Knowing, if he did not finish—if he did not produce foliage—he would not survive. Time passed, but there were no buds, no tiny shoots; nothing to catch the sun.

Jól threw herself against the trunk. "Don't stop!" she cried. "A few leaves, Tred. A few . . . even one."

The moments stretched, but there was no change. Maple sighed and went to her weeping sister-in-law. "Here," she said gently, "take the boy. He needs you." There was nothing they could do. The damage had been too great. Treddian would not live.

Alder stroked his hand over Treddian's bark. "Needs a push is all," he said thoughtfully. He looked to Maple. "There are too few of us. I cannot let him die. There must be more children."

Maple did not understand.

Alder's eyes spoke of love and regret. "You have been a good wife. I will love you until the sun no longer rises." Then, before Maple could protest or interfere, Alder wrapped his big arms around Treddian and fused into the newly rooted tree. His body grew thick with bark. His life force pushed through the stymied veins, bursting through with an abundance of leaves, buds and blossoms.

Maple stared in shock at the wide, lumpy tree.

Alder was gone.

Gone.

Maple's voice broke. "His feet did not root."

"He grafted himself." Jól gave a helpless shrug. "You never know if a graft will take or not. Alder is the wisest of us, Maple. He must have thought a graft the best way to ensure Treddian survives. Only time will prove the wisdom, or folly, of my brother's choice."

Time. Maple did not have many years left. She would not live to see whether either of them ever woke up.

Numb. She did the only thing she could do: she turned away from the grove and walked east, toward the Cú.

Behind her, Jól trudged along, carrying a fussing Eburos.

Maple did not hear the baby's crying, too wrapped in her own plight. She was back in Caeraricin, alone, without Alder to protect her, the runaway wife of Eltanin Sihtric.

Loptr opened the canvas sack, his nose curling at the unpleasant sight and smell. It looked to him like a ten-pound fingernail, yellow and hard with many ragged layers. He swore he saw dried skin and blood along the edge.

"What do you want me to do with this, my king?" Loptr continued to kneel at Eltanin's throne.

"Take it into the Nótt Forest. Near the puki caves, you will find a timepool. A rather large one, so I am told. You must be careful . . . it will kill you if you get too close." Eltanin smiled, and Loptr grew uneasy. "Drop that into the timepool. Then, gather up the pool and bring it to me."

"Gather it up?" Loptr stood in alarm. "Gather a timepool? But you yourself just said it would kill me." Eltanin's eyes narrowed, and Loptr immediately bowed his head. "Forgive me, master. I am confused. I wish only to serve you."

"Then trust me," Eltanin said. "Throw the demon part into the pool. Wait . . . then reach out your hand and gather it all up."

Loptr's stomach twisted at the thought of touching a puki timepool, of watching his limbs shrivel and age into dust before his dying eyes.

"As you wish, my king."

Twenty minutes later, Loptr was still furious, incredulous. He rode his horse hard, slapping the reins angrily around the animal's neck. In his head, he heard Neira's vicious taunt, telling him Eltanin would soon send him from the castle on a fool's errand. His mind reeled with the enormity of Eltanin's request. He slapped the reins again, driving his mount through the forest.

Neira's violet eyes swam in front of him. If he survived this, he would reward himself with her body. He had tolerated the girl's scorn long enough. Whether she welcomed him or not, he would slake his lust. Then they would see how brave and defiant she was, with her virtue despoiled and her will mercilessly crushed beneath him.

The thought spurred him on. Loptr beat the horse, anxious to get this errand done, and his hunger filled.

From her Chair of Dreams, Isleen watched Loptr's anger grow. This would not do. Isleen had been slow to act the first time Loptr's anger turned into backstabbing treachery. She had underestimated the harm one hate-filled soul could cause.

She would not make the same mistake again.

The Seer left her chair and walked out into the open air. The Derwydd had returned—the trees would talk again. Isleen had to word her message carefully. Loptr must be stopped. Luckily, there was one mortal who owed her strict allegiance. One who was grateful for her 'interfering' in his life. His special talents would be just the thing to give Loptr pause.

It was an hour before Fig heard the clang of the rickety handrail and the sound of faltering, bare footsteps outside Ronan's apartment.

Laburnum House was nearly level to the ground. The little yellow Neon had exploded into a flaming ball of molten metal not long after the first fire truck arrived. The mood in the street below was subdued. Paramedics and firefighters kept the area clear as the final, skeletal pieces of the house swayed and threatened to tumble.

"Fig . . . let me in," Ronan called wearily.

Fig hurried to open the door and stood back as Ronan lurched into the room. Gashes, punctures, and distorted patches of charred, black skin covered the Watchman's naked body. Blood was everywhere, both his and the rich red gore of the slain Senteer.

Ronan dumped his boots and sword on the floor, stumbled to a chair, and collapsed. At some point, the transition to human form had to get easier. Jolts of pain rattled his nervous system as multiple wounds struggled to clot, repair, and knit themselves together.

Sitting didn't help. He pushed up and limped to the shower, leaving a slippery trail of blood on the floor. He felt his organs fighting for priority over badly severed muscles. He needed to rinse off, to see the worst of the damage, so he could focus the healing.

Ronan fumbled for water and soap, holding back the cry that gurgled in his throat as the spray hit his lacerated skin. Not for the first time, he told himself he should be grateful to the gods for the ability to heal at all. He just wished they had made it easier to endure.

He stood still as the pulsing water washed away blood and flushed out his wounds. He had taken quiversful of arrows, most at short range. The Beast's dense mane had protected his throat and the vital parts of his chest; still, two had gotten through. He was lucky to be alive. It never ceased to amaze Ronan how the Beast could beat the odds. He supposed he had the Nornir hags to thank for that.

Ronan placed a palm over the gouge in his abdomen and focused his mind on slowing the internal bleeding and rejecting the acid burning deep inside the wound. Fluid and melted flesh bubbled out through the opening and between his fingers. Ronan choked, swallowing mouthfuls of shower water as he tried to keep from sobbing out loud.

At least the battle had not been all one-sided. Ronan had dealt his enemy a huge blow. Only one of the score of archers had escaped. The Beast had plowed through them like a Hrím Giant amidst a clan of tiny Grót. His only regret was the damage to the Divide. More than one Outsider had witnessed the Beast's rage and, even though Ronan had dragged as many Senteer bodies as he could find into the fire, forensic teams would recover bones and clues from the wreckage tomorrow. What they would make of it, and the horned cats still on the front lawn, he couldn't begin to guess.

Ronan stepped from the shower, his body burning with the prickly needles of repair. He would live, but the next couple of hours would be hell.

Hobbling out to the living room, he found Fig lying beside Lleth, stroking his wiry fur. The hound's hindquarter was dressed in a tight bandage. The supplies Fig had dug from the slaver's bag were strewn on the table. Ronan picked up a roll of gauze to wrap the wounds on his arms and legs. They would be the last to heal, while the more vital parts of his body repaired first. He tied up a run of gashes in his thigh where one of the Senteer had hacked at him with her sword. Working past the pain, Ronan pushed the flesh together, forcing the edges to meet. With a pull of his teeth, he tied the gauze tight, then gingerly tested his weight on that leg.

His body was beaten, his heart heavy with defeat. The house was gone, the Macarthurs uprooted, and Lynet missing.

He fell into the cushioned living room chair and closed his eyes.

As his body healed, Ronan dozed in and out of a shallow sleep. Images of Lynet filled his dreams. Longingly, he reached out for her. He thought he would give almost anything to hear her laugh, or feel the gentle touch of her hand. He knew it was useless. She was gone. Still, he searched.

A golden thread.

A clear note.

Ronan's eyes flicked open in surprise.

"She's still here." Ronan rummaged through the slaver's bag for a clean change of clothes. "Lynet's in trouble. She's fighting, resisting the Binding on her own." He tugged on his boots, ignoring the pain as he prepared once more for battle.

"Stay," Ronan quieted the hound, as Lleth struggled to get up and follow him. "Not this time. I'll be back."

"Lynet is fighting the spell?" Fig asked in awe. "Without magic?"

Ronan strapped on his knife and shoved the glowing glass jar Maple had given him into his jacket pocket.

"She has the imprint of the Sòlasach," Ronan said, as he limped out the door. "That means more than just some fancy line in a prophecy."

Stalemate

YNET SAT INSIDE THE BLACK BMW at the end of the street, watching in horror as the last of the smoldering timbers crashed to the ground. Laburnum House was gone. Firefighters shot streaming jets of water onto the smoking embers, but it hardly mattered. No. What mattered was the empty red-and-white ambulance parked still and quiet in the street. Two Lancaster paramedics stood nearby. Watching, but with nothing to do. No one to save.

Lynet wiped her face with her sleeve, but fresh tears kept trickling down. Her family was dead.

Not family. They were tricksters. The Bind spell had a voice.

It had revealed itself shortly after Lynet fled the house. Confident in her obedience, the spell abandoned mere suggestion, and instead plied its evil as a reasoning argument in her head.

They lied to you, tried to kill you. It is better now that they are gone. You are free to do as you please.

Lynet covered her ears and screamed as loudly as she could, trying to drive the foul voice away. She felt the spell retreat, as it had twice before, but it was not gone. It would slink away during her outbursts, only to swell again as she grew tired.

"Yes, they lied!" she shouted fiercely. "To protect me." She realized that now—now that it was too late to apologize, too late to stop the fire.

The moment she weakened, the spell resumed its poison.

You were abducted, betrayed, attacked, lied to. Now you are free. Free to learn the truth about who you are. Free to return to the life that is rightfully yours.

Lynet screamed again, but the sound trailed off to a low, heartbroken wail. Rocking, weeping, she cried out, until the hated voice became a muted undertone in the background.

It was a stalemate.

Stunned by the house on fire, by the loss of her family, Lynet was not as easily seduced as she had been earlier. Even so, she was no closer to opening the door and running away. For all her resistance, the spell still held her. Her fingers strayed often to the keys dangling in the ignition.

Weary, Lynet did not know how much longer she could hold on. Her throat was raw. She was tired—soon she would be too tired to fight. Desperate, she turned away from the charred remains of her home, searching for a way to stay focused. She looked past the firefighters and the empty ambulance, past the people who stood around talking and shaking their heads. She searched until her eyes found the blue-gray building with the iron stairs.

The lights were on in Ronan's apartment He was finally home. Where had he been all this time? He could have saved them.

The more Lynet repeated it, the more convinced she became. Ronan could have saved them. Deep inside, she knew this. An image, like a picture in a storybook, took shape in her mind: Ronan, his teeth bared, splattered with blood, a sword clenched tightly in both fists.

He could save her now.

As if conjured from her thoughts, Ronan appeared, racing across the lawn toward her. Joy bubbled up into a sob of relief. Ronan was coming for her.

From inside her head, the Bind spell's voice boomed. *Flee, before the* hamhlepa *catches you!* In one final push, the spell crushed her will and took control. *Flee! Flee now!*

Powerless to resist, Lynet flipped on the ignition. The sports engine revved. Without another glance at Ronan, she shifted into first gear and pulled out, heading east to Alden.

Ronan changed direction in mid stride, running to the rusted-out Malibu, intent on following her to the ends of the Earth. He eased his nearly healed body into the driver's seat and started up the cold engine.

The passenger door jerked open, wide enough for Fig to squeeze through.

"I was watching from the window." Fig pointed to the apartment where Lleth still waited, nose pressed against the glass. The boy climbed up onto the seat and buckled up. "Think we can catch her?"

"We can try," Ronan said, as he floored the gas pedal. The tires spun and squealed, as they skidded off down the street in pursuit.

Loptr stood beside his lathered horse, pounding his fist on the mare's flank to calm its skittish dance. It was no use. Loptr himself was so disoriented he thought he might puke.

The timepool undulated in front of him, stretching and contracting—distorting the ground, the very air. Trees leaned this way and that, their branches grown lopsided in an effort to avoid the deadly swirl. The ground was smooth, the rocks long since eroded into sand. No creatures scampered nearby. Loptr had seen for himself what happened to any animal unfortunate enough to get too close. A bird, zipping by overhead, had aged and plummeted—decayed to feathers and bone before it even hit the ground.

To avoid the puki caves, Loptr had ridden north, then doubled back through the forest. Puki were devils in disguise. Should they discover him here, they would use him for sport. The timepool was no less dangerous. It was not alive. Not like magic. It had no awareness of itself or others. It had neither malice nor compassion. It simply killed you.

Loptr yanked the canvas bag off his saddle horn. The demonic fingernail weighed as much as a rock. It wouldn't fly very far if he flung it. His magic had better work here, or this was a wasted trip. He refused to get any closer.

Loptr upended the sack and dropped the fingernail onto the ground. With a shove of his hand, he used a Push spell to send the nail skidding and rolling into the timepool. It was probably a wasted trip, anyway. How was a fingernail supposed to—

The timepool froze, suspended in mid-stretch.

Loptr blinked. Doubting what his own eyes could see, he edged closer.

Like everything that came in contact with the pool, the fingernail had instantly broken down. Only, instead of dissolving into nothing, the dense demon particles mixed with the individual moments of displaced time. The resulting concoction looked like grains of sand suspended in the air.

Dare he touch it?

Loptr balled up the canvas bag and threw it at the pool. It made a shallow imprint in the grains and dropped unmolested to the ground. He peered closer. The area where the bag hit seemed compacted. Loptr stripped off his jerkin and flung it against the unmoving timepool. Again, the granules scrunched, and the jerkin dropped, unharmed.

Loptr extended his hand—then snatched it back. He swore, if Eltanin had tricked him, Loptr would fight his way up from the Netherworld to gain revenge. Hesitantly he grazed his fingertips over the edge of the pool. He felt the grains of time and demon cells shift beneath his touch.

Loptr gave a short harsh laugh He was still alive. Still young. He eased his hand inside and crunched a handful of grains together, squeezing out the air. They stayed packed together in a neat ball.

He squeezed again, adding more of the sand-like particles to the first.

It took Loptr over an hour to gather it all together, pushing and forcing the grains into a tighter and tighter space. What had started out as an active timepool, the size of two stable stalls, was now no bigger than a knapsack. Loptr wrapped a blanket around it and tied the bundle securely to his saddle.

How long would the strange mixture hold? He jiggled the bundle. What if the canter of his horse dislodged the demon particles and they jostled to the bottom? Would he suddenly find himself sitting on top of an active timepool? He wished he had a portal, and wondered why Eltanin hadn't given him one. It was as if Eltanin wanted him to fail, wanted the timepool to swallow him.

Loptr swung up onto his horse. If this was a portent of what life would be like once Carden returned to the castle, Loptr would be a fool to stick around.

But where would he go? He had no real skills. As a distant cousin of the old king, Loptr grew up leeching off the goodwill of his kin. He'd spent his life in the shadow of his goody cousins, the heirs to the throne. Loptr was good at staying in the background, avoiding work. Though he had come forward occasionally to tag along as companion to Prince Maxwell—if the conditions were right—as in, the task sounded interesting, no danger was involved, and a suitable reward seemed likely.

Even Loptr's daydreams reflected his lack of ambition; in them, the royal family died in a terrible war, and he became high king, his every whim catered to, no matter how obscene, and any real work was delegated to committees and underlings. Ironic. The royal family was dead, or dying, and he was still no closer to having his whims fulfilled.

His only talent was sneaking. A worthwhile habit, as it had saved his life. Skulking around the castle, snooping into others' business, Loptr had heard Eltanin plotting with his *wicche*. Sensing an opportunity, Loptr deftly placed himself in a position to offer aid. Switching sides was easy. The royal family never considered him a threat. Maxwell had even taken a blow for him that fateful day on the west gate. The fool hadn't realized it was Loptr who'd knifed Torin, and lifted the castle portcullis. Pity Maxwell fell—he was the only relative Loptr actually liked.

Still, things had turned out well. Eltanin was generous, and Loptr enjoyed a measure of power and authority previously unknown to him.

Carden would take it all away.

The way Loptr saw it, he had a couple of choices. He could run. He could retreat and become a nobody again—or, he could try to outfox the fox.

It was dangerous. Carden was his father's son—ruthless and unforgiving. Still, he had to have a weakness. All men had weaknesses. Loptr would simply have to find Carden's.

It was that—or stab him in the back.

Raw Magic

CARDEN WATCHED FOR HEADLIGHTS in the distance. The night wind blew his unbound hair as he waited on the roof of the abandoned McDonald's. Ames, the department chain retailer that used to dominate this strip mall, had gone out of business years before, taking most of the town's economy with it. As businesses folded, or left, the plaza became little more than a meeting place for rowdy adolescents and drunken loiterers.

The lot was empty now, the pavement broken from multiple winters without repair. Tufts of weeds grew out of the many heaves and cracks in the parking lot. The paint on the building peeled in flaky white strips. By its nature, the place attracted vandals and hoodlums.

Carden's mouth twisted. A rather fitting description for the puki who had moved in. Inherently mischievous, puki thrived in dark places. Living in caves throughout Norðrlönd, they would sneak into villages at night to curdle milk or tangle yarn. Here, on the Outside, they preferred boarded-up buildings, where their antics tricked the locals into believing them haunted. Carden snorted. The ghosts of men were far less troublesome. He would not bother with the sprites at all, if there were any other way to get Lynet across the Divide to Lann without his father's knowledge.

Carden had been looking for them ever since Raknfeld first arrived. The puki offered alternative passage back to Norðrlönd, bypassing the Senteer, whom he did not trust. It was irksome really, because he used to have an escape to his homeland—a black swan chain Trilla had given him in his youth. Although he seldom used it, Carden had appreciated the ever-present back door. Somehow, he'd lost it on his trip here to Buffalo. Another thing to thank Scartozzar for the next time he saw that weasel.

The headlights he waited for finally appeared in the distance. Carden climbed down the oddly pristine ladder at the rear of the McDonald's. It was one of the mysteries of the puki: some things decayed rapidly with unnatural age, while others stayed fresh and new past their appointed time.

In his youth, Carden once asked his father why he didn't use puki to give himself immortality.

Fool. Puki magic exists outside of time. What good would it avail me to live forever—if the world around me moved at a different speed, always out of reach?

They were words Carden remembered with interest. After all, they described a rather intriguing form of torture: to be suspended outside of time, watching helplessly, as the world moved merrily on without you.

Carden strode past a large duffle bag lying in the center of the parking lot. A patch of wildflowers grew near the road—he could use those. He bent down and tore the flowers and stems off near the roots, cleverly twisting the strands into a delicate garland for Lynet's hair.

Earth magic carried a simple, yet effective, power that needed no spell enhancement. By virtue of the life within it, Earth magic hid the presence of children, delicate-minded youth, or honest fools from the searching fingers of divination. Lynet was no child but, with her memories gone, she was unspoiled enough that the garland should be sufficient to shield her from Ysbail. Eltanin's *wicche* was always searching. Lynet would be vulnerable the second she set foot across the Divide. Carden would not lose his prize again.

He looked around for something to boost the magic and spotted lupine among the weeds—a tall, succulent plant, it reminded Carden of the poisonous bracken that grew in his mother's homeland. The fat stem would be perfect. He pinched off a piece, braiding it through the weave of garland. The plant's juice stuck to his fingers, and he felt the tickle of Earth magic absorb into his skin.

Too bad he wasn't conjuring right now; it would have extra kick.

Maybe he should have used Earth magic in his Bind spell. He certainly hadn't expected the Macarthurs to thwart it. Who the hell was in that house, anyhow? Probably some idiot from Mynyddgarðr. That poor excuse for a kingdom was one of the first things Carden planned to gut when he started his modernizations.

Fortunately, he'd had the foresight to entwine a lesser spell into the tail of the Binding—a Renewal charm. Lurking secretly in the back of the mind, it could rekindle a vanquished spell. The effort had served him well, it seemed; still, it annoyed him the charm had been necessary at all.

As soon as they were safely on the other side of the Divide, Carden would force a second Bind spell on Lynet, ensuring no further interference. Let the Vökumaðr try to release her then. Once complete, Lynet would be Carden's acolyte, believing everything he said, obeying without question. Carden could even send her after the Watchman, if he wished.

What would Ronan do if the woman he'd sworn to protect attacked him? He wouldn't be able to defend himself or strike back. What *could* he do?

Turn tail and run.

Amusement rumbled in Carden's chest. That would be funny.

The chuckle was short-lived. Shame really. He didn't laugh often enough. He used to laugh more.

A pair of wide, violet eyes, and a youthful smile brimming with mischief, popped into his mind. Yes, he remembered laughter—the deep, satisfying kind that filled the empty places inside him. If he wasn't careful, Carden would become his father—cold and unfeeling. Where would be the joy in that? If he were king of the world, and had the disposition of a snake, even unlimited power might grow dull.

Headlights reflected off the department store glass as his Roadster pulled into the parking lot. The lights dimmed but didn't go off, shining into the vacant store, revealing an untidy row of empty shelves and a sagging poster announcing the final days of a long-forgotten sale.

The car turned off. The lights went out.

Carden continued tying the garland. She'd taken her time to get here. Perhaps the Bind spell was too badly damaged, in which case he might have to conjure right here and now to get her to obey a little quicker. He would wait and see.

The car door opened straightaway, and he smirked with satisfaction. Good, the spell was still strong. His satisfaction evaporated a moment later as the door slammed shut and the ignition started up.

Almost immediately, the engine turned off again.

Carden's eyebrows rose.

She was fighting. How unexpected.

Doubt pricked at him. He had misjudged her. Carden prided himself on being able to accurately gauge his opponent. He had anticipated Ronan causing some kind of trouble. Lynet, however—Lynet was the unknown.

Well, he used to know her. After months of chasing her, he'd come to understand her hot temper and sharp intellect; he'd felt for himself the horror of her power and, likewise, her indecision. Up until this moment, Carden thought he knew how far he could push her. Her memory loss, however, had reshuffled the deck.

The car started up again.

Carden let out a curse and marched across the parking lot. A mental tap to her mind would knock her out. He could deal with her issues on the other side of the Divide.

The Roadster lurched forward, the tires screeched—then shuddered to a stop. The motor stopped and Lynet scrambled out, a journey pack clutched tightly in her arms. Her hair was loose and wild around her shoulders, her eyes bright. She looked ready to bolt.

"Lynet," Carden called, his voice smooth as silk. "Come here, love. What did they do to you?"

Lynet responded to that silken voice. She ran to him, throwing herself against his chest. "They attacked me," Lynet said in a rush. "Mother Maple attacked me with magic, and Ronan—Ronan held me while she did it."

"Shhh, it's all right. You're here now. No one can hurt you." Carden smoothed his palm over her back as he digested this bit of news. So, it was the Macarthur matriarch who'd helped Ronan defeat the royal Bind spell. Interesting. Her disguise was well done. He hadn't guessed; neither had the Senteer. It was not unheard-of, of course; nobles frequently went into hiding to escape the backstabbing of court life. Still, Carden wondered which royal house Maple was from and how she was involved with Scartozzar.

Lynet pushed away from him. "She's dead. Maple is dead."

Carden frowned. Had Lynet been doing this all day, yo-yoing between submission and rebellion?

"They're all dead." Lynet's voice rose. "The house burned to the ground. It's gone. They're all gone."

Then he understood.

Raknfeld had betrayed him. They were not safe here.

Carden scanned the area—but too late.

Tires squealed as an unexpected vehicle skidded into the parking lot. The headlights blinded him as they glared first straight on, then reflected off the storefront glass.

Carden grabbed Lynet and shoved her behind him. His right hand shot out, away from his body, as he conjured. With exacting control, Carden held the spell tight in his fist, forced it to grow from spellbirth to full maturity in seconds—stripping it of its natural will—until the spell became a thunderous blast of angry power.

The rusted-out Malibu rolled to a stop. The door swung open, and Ronan stepped out of the car.

The Watchman had come to reclaim his own.

Carden was unimpressed. He let the blast go. It plowed into the ground directly in front of the Malibu, gouging a deep furrow of destruction. Chunks of concrete shattered the windshield and ripped off the driver's door. Carden saw Ronan's head whip back as the debris hit him.

It was a momentary respite. Carden needed a gateway to Norðrlönd opened—now—before the Vökumaðr had time to recover.

His lungs swelled with authority as he raised his hands and called aloud, "*Thig thugamsa. Tha e'n tràth!*"

From every dark and brooding space in the abandoned site came small, almond-eyed creatures. Their wings buzzed like a thousand dragonflies. Their long, pointed feet dangled above the ground as they flew in a swarm to encircle the *jöfurr* who summoned them. Green, gold, brown, and blue—they hung like fictional fairies, awaiting his command.

"*Tha mise ullamh. Theid sinn dachaidh.*" Carden ordered the puki to prepare him a way home.

Swooping and darting, the chaotic mass took shape as first one, then two, then hundreds played Follow the Leader. They flew in a clockwise direction, their blurring bodies forming a circular doorway.

"What are those things?" Lynet swiped at one as it fluttered in front of her. Carden had feared Ronan's arrival would strengthen her resistance to the damaged spell, but Lynet didn't remember puki so, for the moment, they were an effective distraction.

"Nasty little buggers, so don't touch." Carden put the garland on her head and laced two golden locks through the weave to hold it secure. His movements were fast—then slooooow—as time began to shift and slip around them.

Threads in the fabric of time snapped and gave way. Pockets of unfilled space pooled to the center, creating an opening for them to pass through. Half of the creatures split off to circle in the opposite direction, their small bodies navigating at increasingly faster speeds. Fragile dragonfly wings slashed against one another, tiny pieces breaking off to spin in the air. The largest of the puki, those refraining from the frenzy, floated lower to the ground, ready to dig their feet into the cracked asphalt.

Carden felt alive with anticipation. Soon the males would dig their pointed toes into the ground, and the gateway would crackle open. He had been gone a long time. Soon he would be home. Soon he—

"What the—?" Carden cried out in pain as a crossbow bolt tore through his sleeve and bloodied his arm. He whirled around.

Raknfeld moved in on his left, calmly reloading the crossbow.

To the right, Ronan pulled free of the car.

A cluster of puki females broke formation—chattering and flying across the parking lot toward him. The Watchman was not alone. A boy stood beside him. His body was twice the height of the largest puki, but his features spoke clearly enough—he was one of them.

Carden was incredulous. Could this child stop the doorway from opening?

Beside him, Lynet clutched her head, her eyes starting to clear.

Raknfeld was mere feet away, raising the crossbow.

Carden's face contorted in fury. He would not be stopped. Not now. Not this close to victory. With no time to conjure, Carden dipped his head and, with clenched fists, ripped pure, undisciplined magic from his chest.

With his left hand, he shot a writhing black ball at Raknfeld.

With his right, he flung a second at the deserting puki.

Uncontrolled by any spell, the raw magic seized the Senteer, lifting him off the ground. The crossbow skittered across the parking lot as Nos'kag magic tangled all around Raknfeld like a thin wire, then pulled tight to pop off limbs and burst organs.

The female puki dropped in agony, curling and thrashing like insects, as the second ball of magic mercilessly smothered and squeezed, cracking wings, breaking bones, crushing tiny lungs.

Butchery complete, the two black balls of Nos'kag magic turned from their dying victims . . . to their creator.

There was a reason why no one used raw magic as a weapon.

Without pause, they attacked Carden from both sides.

Carden watched them come, too angry to be afraid. The seething Nos'kag spheres hurtled toward him—then froze—suspended in the air, inches from his face. Carden's body trembled as he held them in place and struggled to conjure even a simple spell.

Sweat broke out above his lip. Finally, a spark ignited in his palm, and Carden took deep satisfaction in using the faithless magic as fuel. The flame blazed up, consuming the black balls, the intense heat dripping onto the pavement in molten gobbets. Unable to hold them any longer, Carden hurled the fireballs toward the wrecked Malibu.

The car exploded, metal and rubber heaving into the air. The force of the blast hit Ronan in the back as he ran, knocking the Watchman to the ground. Fiery pieces rained down to litter the parking lot. The strange boy was nowhere to be seen.

Carden stood pitilessly over the dying Senteer. "Did you think me less deadly than my father?" he spat, then turned his anger on the remaining time porters, daring them to disobey. "*Fritheil orm-sa!*"

The terrified puki flew at frenzied speeds. The males pointed their toes, grinding them into the earth.

The air thundered.

The plaza windows shook.

Time tore.

Slanted sunshine split the darkness as a blast of Nordic air rushed through the rift. Carden's nostrils flared as he drank in the chill scent of home. He grabbed the duffle and slung it over his shoulder. Then, pushing Lynet ahead of him, Carden stepped across the Divide.

Ronan stumbled to his feet, his body bleeding in a dozen places from flying glass and car metal. Wiping blood from his eyes, he pulled the glass jar Maple had given him from his pocket and dumped the Freedom spell onto his palm.

He had one chance.

Gripping the sphere, Ronan flung it toward Lynet's disappearing back. He cried to the Æsir for aid—and watched in grateful wonder as the orb stayed its course, travelling true through the shimmering gateway.

With a brilliant splash, the spell struck Lynet between the shoulder blades, knocking her to her knees on the hard tundra. The flash was blinding. The puki shrieked and scattered in all directions.

The doorway to the Northlands collapsed.

The parking lot went dark and eerily quiet, but for the fading whimpers of the dying puki females.

Ronan turned from the empty spot where Lynet had disappeared, and limped to Fig, who stood guard over the crumpled puki. Wearily, Ronan knelt beside them, pulling a piece of car metal from his upper arm.

One after another, the puki wings ceased their frail beating, and lay flat.

"Can you slow them down?" Ronan asked. "Keep them alive; give them time to recover?"

"I'll try." Fig nodded.

Ronan lifted a pale green maid and held her as gently as he could. He had tried once before to share his Vökumaðr healing with another. He'd failed. Far from home, and without the aid of the Cú, Edan had nearly died.

This creature, however, was not a full grown warrior.

Ronan was in agony, his exhausted body healing as fast as it could. It was foolish to try to save her when his own life was in jeopardy—but he was Vökumaðr, born to sacrifice in the service of others.

Besides, she was so small.

Ronan pulled open his shirt and held her close against him; her stiff wings tickled the hairs on his chest. Silently, Ronan asked the restorative properties inside him to accept this small creature as an extension of himself, just another broken piece that needed mending.

The knitting of his abused body slowed. Trickles of blood began to leak anew. Nerve endings stopped their growth. All attention turned to the dangerous, nearly fatal wound throbbing near his heart. Healing slid along the muscles of his chest, searching for the wound, but not finding it.

"A little farther," Ronan begged.

To his relief, curing red threads stretched up through his skin to wrap around the pale green maid. A warm glow of life enveloped her. Tiny lungs expanded; broken bits grew together. The female's pulse fluttered with renewed strength. Her quivering wings unfolded, stretching to their fullest.

Her almond eyes popped open.

"Aaaaaaaaaaaa!" she shrieked.

Shooting up, the puki zipped back and forth in front of him.

"It's okay." Ronan tried to calm her, his tone soft and gentle, worried she was not sufficiently healed. "I won't hurt you."

She flew closer, hovering as she studied him.

Ronan held still, allowing her to take her time. She was a pretty thing, fully five inches tall and slender as a reed. Every bit of her colored the palest green, from her bare feet to those huge, inquisitive eyes. A multitude of waving antennae moved and flowed around her head in long green strands that resembled hair. The filmy dress she wore seemed a part of her green skin.

She examined the calluses on his palm, then flew up to his neck and sniffed. "Vökumaðr," she said, as if she had solved an important puzzle. Her voice, like the happy splash of water drops on crystal, was as small as she was.

"Yes, I am Vökumaðr."

The puki glanced behind Ronan, her happy expression fading to one of disbelief and alarm. She screamed and flew out around him. Growing more and more frantic, the pale green maid darted from one body to the next, weeping for her sisters lying still and broken on the cement.

"I could not keep them." Fig blamed himself. Tears dripped down his pointed chin. "They were so fleeting. I tried with all my might, but they slipped away anyhow."

Ronan wrapped his arm around Fig's shaking shoulders. It was not an easy thing to bear—the utter helplessness of watching someone die, when even the greatest of efforts cannot stop it.

Without warning, the pale green puki flew at them—shouting, diving at their faces, driving them away from the fallen. They scrambled back, giving her room. Fig was horrified she had turned on them, but Ronan motioned for him to stay quiet.

"She is grieving. Wait."

The tiny female flew in wide circles around her dead sisters; a sound like the wailing of the wind issued from her thin, green lips. Others left the shadows to join her. Their voices rose in a haunting, cheerless song. They flew as they sang, the circle growing, their speed increasing until they were once more a shimmering, multicolored swirl.

Ronan and Fig watched in morbid fascination as everything inside the circle aged. The fallen bodies bloated, then caved in. The skin fell, peeling away from the fragile, birdlike bones. The bones became bleached and brittle, then crumbled to dust, scattering on the breeze.

The song ended.

The puki gathered around the pale green female. They chattered wildly, waving their arms and shaking their heads. Ronan felt uneasy with their reaction. Had the blood that saved her, *his blood*, tainted her in their eyes? His mouth formed a grim line. He would be angry if they rejected her because she was alive by him. Alive was better than dead. It should not matter who, or what, had done the saving.

They continued to chatter in agitation, glaring at Ronan and Fig. Two breaking off from the rest to dive and dart at Ronan.

Fig didn't like it. "Can they hurt you?"

"While I am a man, yes."

As the Hoar Beast, Ronan could not move nor be moved through time. Like the Annars on their mountain, the gods had appointed some to live each moment in the here and now. While he was the Beast, neither the pale green maid nor her clan could touch him. Only as a man was he subject to the ticking of the clock and the revolutions of the Earth.

In the end, it seemed they accepted her back into the fold. Members of the hive tugged on her arms, calling for her to go with them. Ronan waited for her to disappear into the shadows with the rest of her clan.

She did not.

Once the others had gone, she came forward, hovering in front of Ronan.

"I am Nissa," she said.

"I am called Ronan. This is Fig."

"Fig is one of us." Nissa smiled shyly at the boy, then turned to Ronan. "You will follow the *jöfurr* across the Divide?"

"Yes."

"Then I will come with you."

Ronan did not argue. It did no good to argue with obvious revenge. This tiny creature would fly off, with or without him, to avenge her sisters. It did not matter that she would come no closer to hurting Carden than a hummingbird could harm the sea. To survive long enough to calm down and recognize the futility of her quest, she had best travel with them. Ronan could keep her safe and out of trouble until then.

Once it was quiet again, a wheezing sound from the other side of the parking lot caught Ronan's attention. He drew his knife and walked warily closer. Close enough for his Vökumaðr senses to see through the transforming magic. This was no human.

"Shoes . . . no shoes." Raknfeld spit blood through his torn mouth and nodded to legs no longer connected to the rest of him.

Ronan put his knife away. There was no danger here—only sadness. Senteer were like any other race struggling for survival in the harsh Northlands. Ronan often fought them, but he did not hate them.

He knelt beside what was left of a once-proud leader and asked, "What do you want me to do?"

Raknfeld stretched the stump of his arm—but the effort was all he had. The stag died, pointing to the shoes still clinging to his unnatural human feet.

Ronan stood up. There was no time to hide this. His father would have been furious with him for leaving such a wake of destruction, but there was nothing he could do.

"We must move." He looked at Nissa. "I don't suppose your kin would like to come out and help us on our journey?"

"They obey the *jöfurr*," she admitted. "We were told to stop you if you tried to follow."

"It doesn't matter," Fig said. "We don't need them. I know how to get across the Divide. Let's go back to the house."

Ronan frowned. "There is no house."

"It doesn't matter," Fig repeated, a wide grin on his upturned face. "I know a secret."

Across the Divide

WHITE MAGIC FLOWED OVER LYNET, washing her body. It rushed up her nose, poured down her throat, flushed through muscle and bone, cleansing her with brilliant, purifying fire. "What . . . is happening to me?" Lynet clung to Carden as he helped her to her feet. Her teeth were chattering from the harsh tundra wind. The muddled babbling of a million whispers rang in her ears.

The expression on Carden's face spoke plainly that, whatever it was, he was not happy. "The Watchman's parting shot," he said flatly. "Don't fight it. There's nothing we can do about it now." Carden pulled her close, wrapping her in his arms, as they waited for the spell to run its course.

The magic faded, absorbing into her skin, leaving Lynet with the odd sensation of being refined, clean, and whole.

"But . . . but what was it?" she managed between still-chattering teeth. When he didn't answer, Lynet looked up, surprised to see a frown of indecision on his face. "Carden?"

Carden released her and dropped the duffle bag.

"You'll figure it out," he said dryly, as he knelt and dug into the bag. He pulled out two hooded sheepskin coats and tossed one to her. "Put that on," Carden said, as he shrugged into the other. "The wind will take your life faster than any spell."

Lynet burrowed gratefully into the thick wool. She pulled the hood up, blocking out the worst of the wind, and realized she could still hear whispering. She turned all around, looking for the source, but there was no one there. "What are those voices?"

"The dead, maybe; no one knows." Carden continued to dig through the duffle. "You only hear them when you're close to a rift, like the one we just came through. They can't hurt you. They're just sounds. They'll go away in a couple minutes."

"Why couldn't I hear them before, when we were in the plaza?"

"Because they are only in the Northlands, not the Outside. Even here, sometimes the voices are so faint it is only a rustle."

Lynet brushed away small stones sticking in her hands. Her palms were bruised and stinging. Her knees, too, hurt from landing on the frozen ground. After the fog of the last couple of hours, the pain was sharp and bracing. It quickened her mind—a mind steadily filling with questions.

Why was she here?

Why had she left her family when they were under attack?

Why had she felt, just a moment ago, that pleasing Carden was so important, when clearly it was not important at all? The safety of her family was important.

Carden tossed her a scarf and gloves.

Lynet held them idle in her cold hands, her disjointed thoughts coming together at alarming speed. She'd been running. There were flames, smashing glass, fire trucks—and an *empty* ambulance.

Her family was dead.

Her family was dead because Carden Sihtric had orchestrated a terrifying *diversion* to get her to run away with him.

Carden shoved a pair of thick leather gloves into his pocket and stood. "We need to—"

Lynet slapped his face.

Hard.

The sound echoed clear and sharp in the wind.

Before she could retreat, Carden snatched her wrist, twisting her arm painfully around behind her back. His face lowered to hers. "Do that again and I will kill you."

"No, you won't," Lynet shot back, her heart racing with fear and anger. "You need me for something. You went to an awful lot of trouble to get me here." She watched his mouth pull into a snarl so tight she saw pink gum above his teeth. For one terrible moment, Lynet wondered if she had gone too far, if he would kill her and damn the consequences.

"You'll wish you were dead." Carden released her, then picked up the duffle bag and started off. "Let's go. I want to be well away from here by nightfall. We have to get out of the wind."

"You killed my family." Lynet did not budge.

"I doubt it. They are Scartozzar's kin, and that weasel could slip out of anything. Now move, before I come back there and drag you by the hair." Carden kept walking and did not look back.

Lynet trembled with the choices in front of her. She could run and try to escape, or pick up a rock and attack him from behind.

Or . . . or go with him, and find out what he meant by *I doubt it.*

Hope won out. Hope the Macarthurs were somehow still alive.

Lynet ran to catch up. Carden turned briefly, his smirk confident. That expression made her furious. He had known she would come. After all, where was she to go? They were miles from anywhere; the sun was setting and the winds were glacial. There was no way Lynet could survive out here alone, and they both knew it.

Her fists balled. Two years of frustration boiled inside of her, fanned by this unwanted dependence on a man she barely knew. It was enough. *Enough!*

Like a phoenix rising through cinnamon-myrrh ashes, Lynet was done with the past. She was through waiting for memories that might never come. It didn't matter who she *had been.* This was who she was *now.* She refused to be held captive by a past she did not know. She certainly wasn't about to let Carden dictate her future.

"Don't touch that garland," Carden snapped over his shoulder, as if he felt her eyes boring into his back. "Not unless you want an army of kobvald swooping down on top of us. Whether you like it or not, you need me. Get me killed, and your fate will be immeasurably worse than it is now."

Lynet reached up to find the twist of grass and wildflowers in her hair, sorely tempted to tear the thing off and fling it at him. But she had learned from Maple that plants held protective properties. Kobvald would come if she removed the garland. Something about that seemed familiar. Either way, it sounded bad, and she was in enough trouble without courting more.

Lynet trudged angrily behind him.

What was she doing here? What had possessed her to go gallivanting off with a stranger? What did she know about him? Nothing—except he was an arrogant, sleazy, smooth-talking lawyer. What had she been thinking?

He put a spell on you, the jöfurr. *When Mother Maple tried to take it off—I think the spell wanted to kill you.* Fig's words held meaning now.

"What is a *jöfurr*?" Lynet asked coldly.

Carden did not answer.

"Is it you? Is it a name? A title? Is it your father?"

He stopped.

"*Öðlingr, æðeling, jöfurr.* Take your pick," he said with self-aggrandizing conceit. "Prince. Noble. Chief. *Me.*" His mouth lifted on one side. "So you better get used to taking orders."

"Order all you want," Lynet snapped. "I'm not your slave, or your servant, or your anything."

His lack of reply told her exactly what she hoped: Carden had put some kind of spell on her—to make her submissive and blind to his motives—and the white scalding light had released her from it.

A white light—like the one Maple had thrown at her. Fig was right. Maple hadn't meant to hurt her; she'd been trying to protect her from Carden. It was so obvious now. If only she'd understood, she wouldn't have run away. There wouldn't have been a *distraction*, or fire. This was all her fault. She was such an idiot.

There had to be a way to fix this.

Carden believed the Macarthurs were alive. Lynet would hound him every moment of his life until he told her more, until he gave her what she needed to find them.

She brushed frozen tears from her cheeks as she marched after him. Carden wanted her. Fine. She would stay this course and follow him. But he was a fool if he thought it would be solely on his terms.

Lynet wanted answers, and this time she would get them.

All of them.

The air in the deserted parking lot crackled. A Nordic breeze stirred the grass and weeds. Eigil stepped through a portal to the Outside world. He stood, embracing the moment. No Annar before him had ever crossed the Aragaidheal Divide. Not one of them had ever heard the haunting whispers, or escaped the confines of Norðrlönd. He, Eigil of Dŷ Ddinod, was the first.

His elation withered to disappointment.

The Outside was hardly impressive.

The street was dark, the buildings empty. He sensed puki ripples—and the stench of death—but no sign of the Watchman.

Eigil walked across the pitted landscape. His footsteps were light as he sidestepped pieces of concrete and twisted chunks of metal. There were traces of time manipulation everywhere.

He found the remains of a dead man. Eigil knelt and studied the wounds. This was not the work of the Hoar Beast. It was Nos'kag magic. Eltanin's son had been here. A wildflower lay nearby. Eigil picked it up and rolled it in his fingers. The stem was bruised. Bent—no, braided. A divination circlet.

Wings fluttered in the shadows.

Eigil stood. "Come out," he ordered.

Hesitantly, two puki flew toward him.

"What has happened here?" he asked, knowing he would receive an answer. The lesser races feared the Annars. They always did what he told them to do. Those few who resisted—were not afforded a second chance.

"The *jöfurr* bade us fashion him a doorway," the puki answered. "He has crossed to Norðrlönd, near the lakes of Lann."

"Was he alone?"

"No. A maiden of great power was with him."

"What of the Watchman?" Eigil asked.

"The Watchman was here." The puki nodded. "But, he is gone. He took two of us with him."

"Did you aid him?"

The puki exchanged nervous glances. "No. We were commanded not to." One pointed to the road. "The Watchman returned the way he came."

Interesting. Eltanin's son had crossed the Divide, taking with him the woman from Isleen's so-called prophecy. Instead of bringing her to Caeraricin, as Eltanin expected, he'd gone to Lann.

Eigil tossed the wildflower to the ground. Carden was hiding her, but from whom—the Watchman or his father? Not that it mattered what Eltanin's son did. Eigil was interested only in the Watchman.

Where would he go? He would follow the woman's trail, which meant the Watchman needed to find a way across the Divide.

"Are there any other hives nearby?" Eigil asked the puki. "Any Northlanders, or hidden gates?"

"There are only the Derwydd." Again, the puki pointed the direction the Watchman took. "We do not go there."

Eigil looked around him. This was not his mess. Still, it was not the assassin's habit to leave clues or witnesses. He twisted a ring on his finger, and the doorway Eltanin had made for him opened. Eigil pulled a glass vial of volcanic fire from his pocket and casually tossed it behind him, then stepped through the portal.

The vial smashed against the pavement.

The portal closed.

All evidence—the plaza, the parking lot, the puki—went up in flames.

Return to Norðrlönd

VERYTHING AT THE MACARTHURS HAD BURNED. Everything except the lilac bushes in the northwest corner and two of the yew trees. The fire trucks were gone; the neighbors had all returned to their homes. Tire tracks and heavy boots had left deep ruts in the front lawn filled with pools of blackened water.

Ronan and Lleth picked their way across the debris.

Ronan could not imagine how Fig intended to bridge the gap across the Divide, but the boy was part puki. If there was a way across, Fig would find it, or figure it out.

"Oooo!" Nissa giggled as she and Fig paused near the lilacs. "I feel magic—not just Derwydd magic." Her giggle turned to a gasp of amazement. "I feel the Oldest!"

"Yes," laughed Fig. "I discovered her last summer. She lives in the lilacs. The magic here is strong, very strong. I found, if I dig my toes in deep, the Divide opens for a split second, and I can cross."

"Wait, wait, wait," Ronan said as he joined them. "You mean to say you've crossed the Divide? Does Maple know this?"

Fig blushed. "Well . . . no. I was afraid she would tell me to stop."

"Yes, and she would have been right to do so," Ronan said. "There are many dangers in the Northlands, Fig. If you found yourself in trouble, we could not help you. Think. Is it wise for a man to walk into danger without a friend to keep his back?"

Ronan examined the boy's face. The reprimand had been clear, yet his tone was that of an ally, not a chiding guardian. Ronan knew the hearts of men. A student learned more readily when he felt his teacher respected him. Ronan had great respect for the boy. Fig was clever, loyal, and good-hearted. A man could ask for no better qualities in a companion.

Fig smiled up at Ronan. "I have friends now."

"Yes, you do." Ronan placed his hand on the boy's shoulder. "I'm wondering, though; if the Divide opens for only a second, how are Lleth and I to get through? We are not so quick as you."

Fig's large eyes grew even larger. It appeared he hadn't thought of that when he offered to take Ronan across the Divide.

"Okay." Ronan turned to Nissa. "Can you help him hold it open?"

"I am but one." Nissa shook her head. "Three are needed to open a proper crossing door."

Fig jumped up and shouted. "The Oldest will help us!"

"Who?" Ronan asked.

"The Oldest. She is outcast." Nissa flew around Ronan's head. "She was sent away from the hive."

"Sent away for what?"

"She has thoughts of her own," said Nissa, scandalized. "She does not think as the group!"

"She thinks as you do, then," Ronan suggested.

"No!" the sprite protested. "Nissa thinks as . . . the group," she ended with a confused frown, then flew away.

Ronan knew she would not go far. Nissa had a mission.

"You better stand back," Fig said uncertainly. "I'm not sure how the Oldest will take to strangers." He knelt down and looked up through the branches of the largest lilac bush. "Hello," he called quietly.

There was no answer.

"I have brought friends who need your help. Please come out."

The lilac rustled gently. A soft light glowed from a spot close to the center.

Lleth circled around Ronan's legs, sniffing the air. As a sighthound, any movement in the bush was, to him, fair game. His instinct was to flush it out, chase it down, and kill it. Ronan signaled Lleth to back off and sit. Fig and Nissa would not be happy if he coursed their friend.

The glow intensified as an exquisitely fragile puki came floating silently through the leaves. So different from Nissa's rapid buzz, the Oldest fluttered waiflike until her dainty feet tiptoed onto Fig's open palm. Wise eyes regarded Fig, then turned thoughtfully to appraise Ronan and Lleth.

I know you, she said, in a voice that whispered in his mind like the gentle fall of rain. She floated to Ronan. *You are Vökumaðr.*

Ronan nodded, grateful she had not sniffed him first before saying so.

The sanctuary is gone. The ancient puki pointed to the broken husk of Laburnum House. *It will regrow.*

Ronan was not surprised. To him it seemed the house, with its endless porches, nooks and crannies, grew every day. He did not doubt that somehow it would come back.

Those who survive will return, the Oldest said as if to comfort him. *The human girl will not. Her destiny binds her to the northern sun. She will not be free—not until the evil has passed and her task is done.* The fairylike creature studied Ronan. *It is your lot, Guardian, to follow her?*

"It is," Ronan said quietly.

I will help you.

Ronan was relieved.

Ten minutes later, he wasn't so sure. The Oldest and Nissa flew in opposite circles. Fig dug his toes into the earth. The Divide tore open. Only, instead of a wide-flung doorway, the opening was small and low to the ground. He would have to crawl through.

Ronan supposed he should be grateful there was a doorway at all. Without Nissa, it would have been impossible. It amazed Ronan how closely related *fate* was to *choice* and *action*. If he had not acted and tried to save Nissa, he would be trapped here.

Down on one knee, Ronan saw the deeply slanted Nordic sunlight. Lleth sniffed at the hole in the Divide. His round eyes looked up at Ronan.

"I know it's small, but it's the only way." Ronan was sympathetic. The wolfhound was as big as a man; it would be a tight squeeze for both of them. "Go on. I'll be righ—"

Ronan spun around.

His eyes narrowed, trying to see through the darkness. Something felt wrong. They needed to hurry.

Ronan pointed Lleth's nose toward the doorway and gave a mighty shove. The hound growled in surprise and backed up, but Ronan pushed his shoulder hard against the dog's haunches. Lleth sidled awkwardly on his wounded leg, digging in his paws—then his nose twitched. Wet nostrils flared as he caught a scent. The Nordic breeze carried an interesting odor, and the hound scrambled through the portal to the other side.

Ronan got down on his belly and pushed the slaver's bag through the small opening. "Fig, as soon as I'm across, I want you and Nissa to—"

Ronan rolled sharply to the right. Twin onyx-handled blades stabbed deep into the earth where he had just been. "Hide!" Ronan shouted to Fig as he sprang to his feet, knife drawn. His eyes scanned the ruined garden.

Movement in the dark.

Ronan knew the trickery of Shadow spells. He could not trust his eyes. If his mind said the attacker was to his left, then the true danger was *there*—he hurled his hunting knife.

Chunk.

The sound of pain, and the lightest of footsteps. Who was after him? Those were not Senteer weapons.

Ronan looked for Fig, but the boy and puki were gone. They'd disappeared into that in between place where their kind could vanish.

Now, where was his enemy?

Ronan snatched up the twin blades. He was Vökumaðr. Uncovering deceptions in the dark was his birthright. He ran toward the charred remains of the house and stopped at the pile of fallen beams that had once been part of Maple's kitchen. Ronan paused, listening—

A small, midnight-blue dart stuck in the burnt wood near his face. Ronan twisted as he dove for cover, flinging one of the blades behind him.

Chunk.

This time he smelled blood.

The Watchman reached out, searching for his enemies. How many were there? Where were they hiding? He sensed one hostile life-thread. Only one—and that one remained confident, even with his wounds.

Who was after him?

For centuries without number, the Reveal spell had served the Vökumenn. It exposed secrets, brought invisible objects to light, and dissolved the counterfeits of thieves and assassins. Silently, Ronan called the spell to life. Soon, he would know his attacker.

Movement in the dark.

Ronan jumped up and hurled the spell—at the same moment, a dart stabbed his shoulder.

Instantly his arm started to go numb. Ronan yanked out the dart and flung it aside. He didn't need to smell it to recognize the fatal clutch of Auðn scorpion venom. *Who was after him?* Scorpion venom was the weapon of giants, not common assassins.

Ronan fell to the ground as the poison attacked his system—killing cells, paralyzing muscles, deadening nerves. His sword arm sagged, useless. His body, already exhausted from repeated healing, struggled to slow the poison and expel it through his skin.

With astonishing swiftness, the venom spread across his chest. Gasping for breath, Ronan forced his lungs to suck in air and push it out again. Draw in air. Push it out. In. Out.

His heart fluttered, and missed.

Mother Earth. What creature had produced this potent a poison? Desperately, Ronan struggled to stay alive, to keep his organs functioning. A squeeze of his heart to pump his blood, an intake of air, a squeeze of his heart, a release of air, a squeeze of his heart.

The Beast rammed against Ronan, demanding to be set free.

Ronan's body shook with the effort it took to hold the creature in check. The Beast would not stay still to heal, would not keep his heart beating, his lungs gulping for air. The Beast would rush to attack, and they would both die. Sweat beaded on Ronan's face. He refused to die. Refused. It was more than mere survival instinct. He would not leave this world and let that redheaded, arrogant bastard have Lynet. By now, she would be free of Carden's puppetry, but not him. In that volatile environment, any rebellion on her part could spell death for entire villages. No, he had to survive. He had to get to her, help her control her magic, stop the killing.

Ronan threw back his head and roared—using the last of his strength to push, purge, force the poison to the surface. The vile black venom bubbled and hissed, burning his chest and shoulder as it broke through his skin.

Free of the destroying toxin, Ronan's heart grew stronger. The rush of blood grew to a healthy thud in his ears. His lungs relaxed, the paralysis melting away as he drew in deep, starving breaths. He ripped a piece of his torn and bloody shirt, wiping the bubbling venom from his skin so it wouldn't seep back in.

He still did not have use of his sword arm, but he would live.

Ronan raised a shield. He did not like to use shields in battle; they interfered with his inherent abilities. Vökumenn depended on parry for defense, skill with a sword, and spells to disguise. Those tactics would not work this time. He was too weak to fight.

Ronan heard the whispered shift of ash. The assassin would think him dead, the roar his final death throe. And why not? The poison on that dart had been enough to fell a dragon.

Ronan gripped the remaining blade with his left hand, and waited.

Another whisper of footstep—so light Ronan doubted his hearing.

What magic did this fiend possess that he could walk so silently on crumbling char? Was it a wizard? Had Ysbail found a way to imbue her servants with talents far beyond their normal skills? Had the Kynneeyn Gorrym learned even darker magic?

Ronan wished in that moment for the strength of his father. Jarl Bernhard would not let fear distract him while an enemy stalked. He would be calm, focused—waiting for the opportunity to strike.

Ronan cleared his head of questions.

He could feel the enemy—only feet away.

Another step.

Closer.

Ronan's arm swung wide, and behind, to slice at his opponent's hamstring. The onyx-handled blade was sharp. The knife cut deep, and caught on bone. Ronan let go, and scrambled to his feet. His sword arm hung limp. He had no weapons left.

Ronan faced his enemy.

The Reveal spell had done its work.

His adversary swayed before Ronan in his true form. He was tall and elegant. His wounds bled freely; his face was beautiful in spite of his pain.

Ronan was dumbstruck.

What did the gods mean by this?

For surely gods were involved.

How else could an Annar be here, on this side of the Divide? And what in bloody hell had he done so wrong that they would send an *assassin* after him? He was the last. Didn't that count for anything?

Deep inside Ronan a vital thread broke. He'd lived his entire life in service to the Æsir. Based his moral compass on their wishes.

No more.

He was through serving them.

They could find another lapdog to prod and beat.

He was Vökumaðr—and, from now on, that meant he was a law unto himself—a force for whatever *he* thought was right.

The Annar smiled. His lithe body fell to the earth, but he seemed not to care. He held something in his hand, something small that Ronan could not see. The smile widened.

Ronan backed up, heading for Fig and Nissa.

A portal crackled open beside the Annar.

Ronan ran. "Open the gate!" he cried, "Open the gate!"

Nissa and the Oldest flew in wild circles. Fig dug his toes into the ground.

The doorway ripped open.

"Follow me!" Ronan shouted as he dove through. Whispers echoed around him. Ronan rolled to his feet on the other side of the Aragaidheal Divide. He yanked his sword from the slaver's bag, holding it awkwardly in his left hand.

Nissa and Fig appeared as the passageway collapsed.

"Where is the Oldest?" Ronan demanded.

"She would not come," Fig said helplessly. "There was no time to argue. Everything was on fire!"

Ronan turned around, scanning their surroundings, waiting for some sign the Annar had followed. After a while, he lowered his sword. They were alone. Wherever the Annar had gone, it wasn't here.

Ronan drew in a deep breath. Cold Nordic air filled his lungs. He studied the mossy hillside, the angle of the sun, and the mountains in the distance. They were south, in the middle of nowhere, at the farthest edge of the vast kingdom of Caeraricin.

Close enough.

He was home.

Eltanin held the puki timepool in his hands. Curious, that something so deadly could be so easily manipulated. Displaced moments suspended in Fomorii biology. It was ingenious. Not that he would ever say so aloud. Praise was dangerous. It engendered confidence—a poor trait in a servant. And, as far as Eltanin was concerned, Balor was a servant. Everyone in this wretched land was, or soon would be, his servant.

Eltanin levitated the pool and sent it to the center of the large metal ring. Using a common Pull spell, he extracted the demon particles, letting them drop to the ground. Instantly, the timepool came to life, the raw moments swirling, expanding—but they were held in check, imprisoned by the boundaries of the ring.

"Well done," Balor chuckled. "But there was never any question you could contain *one* of the timepools. It will not be so easy to subdue all seven of them together."

Eltanin did not bother to defend himself. His patience with this demon, who only pretended to be a god, waxed thin. He would not be drawn into needless debate. "I have done as we agreed," Eltanin said succinctly. "You will now provide a guide, additional Fomorii parts, and this Baobh, who you claim is sufficient to deliver Cian Druce."

Balor smiled, his horned head nodding in amusement. "You will soon find my claim justified, little wizard." Balor reached into the abyss behind him and ushered Baobh across into the mortal world.

Eltanin's eyes narrowed, prepared for a trick.

The demoness stretched. Thin, leathery skin unwrapped from around her, flicking into bat-like wings. They arched sharply above her shoulders, hanging in folds that connected to the sides of her shapely legs. She stepped toward Eltanin, her hips swaying with invitation. She was wickedly beautiful, with hair the color of coal. Baobh smiled. Her fangs gleamed white against the blood red of her lips.

"Balor has commanded me to serve you," she purred.

"Good," Eltanin said coolly. "Go to the foot of DuwaŴyr Mountain. There you will find the wise man, with a guard of *arreyder* protecting him. Isleen has seen your coming. They will be prepared for you."

"Oh, I doubt they are prepared for me." Baobh sounded amused.

Balor laughed. "Baobh appears to each man in the form closest to his own heart. A faithful husband will see his wife; a thief will see the object of his designs; a priest, his god. They will not attack, until it is too late."

Baobh studied Eltanin's circle, then walked seductively around it as she spoke. "You cannot pretend you do not like what you see," she told him. "This is what you have created in your mind. What you think a demoness sent to serve you should look like."

Behind her, Kleng heaved his fat body across the abyss.

"We will kill the *arreyder* and return with the Druce." Baobh flicked a distasteful glance at Kleng as he came to stand beside her. "Then I shall be your personal guide to the five remaining timepools in Norðrlönd."

"You will guide my servants," Eltanin corrected. Balor's tactics were crude. Did the demon think him foolish enough to fall for Baobh's seductions? Ridiculous. Balor was plotting—had been from the beginning. Eltanin could guess his intent—the demon wanted more worlds to devour. His desires would render him careless. Eltanin had only to wait, and the greatest of the Fomorii would be his slave.

Eltanin looked at Baobh, noting her impatience. The demoness held only mild interest for him. His mind was set on immortality. Soon he would have the almighty power of the Sòlasach. But first, he must find the stealing dagger. If anyone knew its whereabouts, it was Scartozzar's apprentice.

"When you have returned with your master's prize," Eltanin addressed the waiting pair, "I have a task for you to perform; a young mind that needs to be . . . opened."

"Whatever my Lord Eltanin requires." Baobh bowed her head.

With a flap of her leathery wings, the demoness swept into the air and flew down the crooked tunnel leading to the sea. Kleng plunged into the cavern lake and plodded after.

Eltanin watched them go, two more pawns moving into place on the board. The game was nearly won.

Soon, Balor would lead him to the Great Rift. Baobh would break the girl and retrieve the dagger, Dwynai. Eigil would kill the last Vökumaðr.

Best of all, his wayward son would gift him with the *plaga norn*.

Even now, Eltanin's mercenaries marched south, to join with the forces of Llanerc. Before winter closed Tochail Pass, they would attack Mynyddgarðr. The fortress would topple, and Eltanin would control the only outlet to the sea. With its supply route blocked, nearby Lann would have no choice but to surrender. Eltanin would sweep across the remaining kingdoms like a storm; and with the witch's blue magic, he would subjugate all of Norðrlönd. Every knee would bend, and he would finally . . . finally have the army he needed to march north to his icy fatherland and repay those who had rejected him and forced him from his home. Soon, Eltanin's power would be greater than even the almighty *Lifetaker*.

Who then could stop him?

Ronan strapped his longsword to his back. He was home. He felt the change in his heartrate—his internal rhythm slowing as it adjusted to the lingering pace of the Northlands. He hadn't realized how much he had attuned to the Outside world. Lynet, too, would at last be in her element. Perhaps now time would be gentler to his *ástin mín*.

Ronan did a quick scan of the area, then closed his eyes and called on his Vökumaðr tracking skills. The magic within him leapt to do his bidding, his abilities strong and vibrant on this side of the Divide. Swiftly, the notes and colors of Norðrlönd came into focus: newly hatched minnows quivered in a nearby stream; flowers and trees sang their hurried songs of summer growth; not too far away, an immense creature awoke and stirred.

Nowhere was Lynet's golden thread.

She was too far away. Like when he first crossed the Divide into the Outside world, Ronan felt only a faint *pull* in her direction. North. It confirmed Ronan's suspicions. When Lynet fell to her knees on the other side of the portal, Ronan had seen no trees in the landscape. She and Carden were in the tundra region above Lann.

Ronan released the tracking and pulled his bow out of the bag. Not a longbow, like those he used in battle or on the training field. This one was short, light, and practical for swift travel. Ronan checked it for cracks, hooked the string, and fastened the quiver at his hip. Automatically, he patted the small of his back, then remembered—the hunting knife was not there.

It would be missed.

Here in Norðrlönd, Ronan was a wanted man. The people had loved King Urien, and the price on Ronan's head was high. Not only bounty hunters, but farmers, merchants, and shipbuilders alike would gladly take a swing at the king's reputed killer.

Ronan would deal with them as they came. He was home. No more pretending to be someone else. Here, he was Vökumaðr. Soldier. Guardian. Hunter. Yes, he had many enemies, but he also had allies. Allies he would soon need to call upon.

An idea had been forming in his head. If the kingdoms of Norðrlönd remained separate, Eltanin would pick them off one by one. No single power could defeat Caeraricin. Even without the Vökumenn, Caeraricin retained the largest army in the Six Kingdoms, to which Eltanin had added Kynneeyn Gorrym. Without cooperation between the remaining kingdoms, there would be no stopping him.

Once Lynet was safe, Ronan would sit with the rulers of the north, and rally them together if he could. He was not his father, but he would try to inspire them to battle and great deeds. It would be no easy task, faced with mistrust, ancient squabbles, and a clutch of border disputes. Ronan did not know which of the ruling families had gone over to Eltanin. He was not foolish enough to think all had resisted; after all, Edan had joined—Ronan stopped himself—time would prove Edan's innocence or guilt. For now, Ronan's task was to find Lynet. Then, before he returned to Caeraricin castle to free his father and kin, Ronan would raise a rebellion against Eltanin.

Ronan called to Nissa and Fig. There was a faded footpath farther down the hill; they would follow it until they were clear of the woods. He glanced around, looking for Lleth.

Where had the hound gone?

Unconquered

NEIRA STOOD ON THE EASTERN battlement, overlooking the sea. The wind blew her chestnut hair, wrapping it around her face until she was blind to everything but her heartache. Eltanin had struck a bargain with Balor. The whole castle knew it. The sound of the demon's laughter shook the foundations each time he appeared in the caverns far below.

Neira brushed back her hair and continued staring out to sea. She'd come up here to clear her head—and to hide from Loptr. He searched for her even now, rampaging through the castle. It was not like Loptr to be so bold. He liked to sneak, to catch her unawares.

A shadow passed over the sun, and Neira turned. Behind her, a hideous, black-winged creature flew off to the west.

The first of the Fomorii was loose.

It had all become so big—too big for her to do anything about. The world she knew was ending. Eltanin had enlisted Balor, and now demons roamed unfettered, unchecked. She felt helpless, alone. An apprentice with no magic. She couldn't save the world. She couldn't even save her friends.

Neira shivered and wrapped her arms around her shoulders. Twice, Rán had called to her, offering her solace in the depths of the sea. Neira had considered it. It would take so little to climb over the battlement wall and drop into the foam far below.

But, even in her despair, Neira understood duty. She had a duty to her family and to her people; they had risked too much for her to quit now. She had a duty to Caeraricin, to find the heartstone and make it flesh. Moreover, she had a duty to her friends, to take Margaret's place and focus Eltanin's attention on herself, instead of them.

Neira had no idea how she was to accomplish any of it. She was drained of energy and almost past caring. Everything she tried came to naught.

The wind died.

It was enough of a change that it wrested Neira from her thoughts. She looked around. Behind her, the castle banners still flapped madly in the wind. Below, the waves continued to froth and churn. She turned completely around in a circle, searching for the source of the calm.

Snowflakes began to fall. Neira caught some on her hand; they were cold, and real, not magic.

She wished she could use magic, right this minute, to conjure a shield. Some villainy was afoot, and she was completely unprotected. The snow fell more heavily, bringing its own harsh, icy wind—the wind of winter.

She looked up in time to see something small, but solid, bearing down on her from above. With a yelp, Neira jumped out of the way. The sound of metal on stone rang through the air as the object hit the floor and rolled.

The snowflakes thinned, then stopped.

The object came to rest against the battlement wall. Neira walked cautiously toward it. It was a piece of cloth stuffed through a gold ring. Her heartbeat quickened as she snatched it up. She recognized this ring, with its falcon emblem. She knew the elaborate embroidery on the cloth. It was part of her master's sleeve. Neira yanked the material free and unrolled it. Scrawled in a script she knew well were the words:

Be brave. Rescue the heir. I am coming.

Neira sniffed the cloth. Campfire. It smelled like campfire smoke. The words were written in charcoal, not ink. He was out in the wild. Somewhere where the winter snows still fell.

He was alive.

Scartozzar was alive!

Neira was no longer alone.

ABOUT THE AUTHOR

Deborah lives in Kent, in South East England with her husband, Lawrence, and the occasional stray puki. When she isn't writing, or strolling through the town market, Deborah can be found online enjoying a good chat. You can join in the conversation:

Twitter: @DeborahJDean (or) www.twitter.com/DeborahJDean
Blog: www.deborahjdean.com
Facebook: www.facebook.com/Nordrlond

If you want to learn more about Norðrlönd, check out Eibby's Sketchbook. Use what you find there wisely, as the minx has posted all sorts of details that threaten the Aragaidheal Divide.

Eibby's Sketchbook: www.nordrlond.com (or) www.Norðrlönd.com

Look for more books in the series: WITCH'S RUN and WIZARD'S STAND.

www.ingramcontent.com/pod-product-compliance
Lightning Source LLC
Chambersburg PA
CBHW070600260626
47161CB00002B/659